I0739419

Camille

A NOVEL BY
M.A. HENDERSON

Camille
By M.A. Henderson

This is a work of fiction. All characters, character names, institutions, organizations and events portrayed in this novel are fictional, derived from the author's imagination or employed fictitiously. Any semblance to real persons, living or dead, is coincidental and unintentional.

Published by Killer Bs, Richland, WA, 99352.

www.ninefruitbooks.com

Library of Congress Catalog Number 2017903130
ISBN: 978-0-9987195-0-4 (trade paperback)
eBook ISBN: 978-0-9987195-1-1

Cover photography © Nick Lippold

Cover design © Spark Design & Communication
Chapter artwork © Spark Design & Communication
and Tessa Bunton.

Chapter nineteen artwork derived with permission from
Tamara Gooch Photography (www.tamaragoochphoto.com)

Printed in the United States of America.

Pam – what an amazing
adventure we are on together!

PART

1

"The mind and the heart are
no good at steering the cart.
What they need is someone with
a strong hand at the reins…"

Mama

CHAPTER

1

WHO AM I TO ME

Being stubborn's a hundred times wrong, but being at peace is forever times right.

Get yourself right, Child!

She repeated to herself that thing Mama would say to correct a bad attitude. Though she had not kept count, her instances of stubbornness that morning had likely exceeded the limit. At least Mama's words helped her tolerate each hand extended, each warm welcome offered, and the many y'alls uttered. Personally, she loathed the contraction, having purged her speech of it years ago. Yet she always smiled back politely, as that was what Mama would want her to do.

Having completed the two and a half hour bus trip from Carlton, she next took a taxi from the station to the campus of Garland State University. In actuality, the whole journey had only been a slight geographical change in a modestly-sized Southern state, but one amounting to a light-year displacement for a girl who had not set foot out of her hometown in six years.

Her taxi stopped on a looped driveway near a cluster of dorms. Scarcely had she finished paying the fare before becoming swarmed by three enthusiastic females tasked with greeting new arrivals on the first day of the rest of their lives – their first day as college freshmen.

Man – these girls are well trained!

Having identified her as one worthy of extra greeting, they were on her like gnats. She, not at all comfortable in social settings like this one, checked that her hoodie was properly situated. The gnats observed the gesture and moved in closer.

Of course, she *always* wore a hoodie in public. The hood must be situated with its brim at the brow, but not blocking sight, as it was important that she see without being seen 'seeing.' As to hearing, she could perceive conversations surprisingly well despite the covering, though some seemed to think it limited her recognition of what was said behind her back. She was asked for the name of her dorm, and with her response of 'Switson,' a greeter's arm extended toward a nearby building. While gathering her belongings deposited on the curb by the driver, the whispered evaluations began.

"Lordie me – wearing a hoodie in all this heat!"

"I know! That girl needs serious help!"

"Y'all look – she's totin' a duffel bag!"

"Strange as all get out!"

She heard plenty of such things beneath the hoodie, yet never cared whether anyone thought her strange. Stepping on to the walkway toward Switson Hall, she did her usual thing of reasoning away such hurts.

'Strange' is a point of reference thing. It's kind of like sitting on a beam of light and seeing time stand still. In reality, you may be moving at the speed of light in someone else's frame of reference, but you're standing still in your own… and they're the ones moving away at light speed. Maybe I'm normal, and they're strange!

She smiled to herself at having reached this conclusion, for even physics made more sense to her than people. Of course, she considered her best quality… and conversely her chief weakness… to be imagination. Hers often functioned like a mental game of hopscotch – one thought jumping to another, carrying her along an unpredictable pathway. The ensuing thought – the next hop – was that this perspective was the very reason why Mama had placed her on a bus bound for Garland – because she did not understand people.

And the reason I don't understand people is…

All hopscotch patterns chalked upon the sidewalks of her mind inevitably led back to the same ending – a most painful moment in the past. She quit this particular game to concentrate instead on the series of events that had brought her to this campus.

There had been no wounds, nor any sign of tumult or destruction. In fact, to the casual observer, the disagreement hardly amounted to anything approximating a battle... or a skirmish... or any other descriptor drawn from mankind's extensive experience at making war. Yet to her and Mama, the subject of college had constituted a nearly yearlong conflict... unseen simply because no one was in their lives. In high school, she kept to herself and had no friends. When the two of them did venture out together, it was for employment. In that, they were always unified in purpose – get the job done. Outside of work, no one in town came near them, so no one witnessed the struggle that comprised most of her senior year. Yet war had been waged, culminating that summer... and she had lost.

She spent a considerable portion of that bus trip searching for a historical analogy to her situation, partly because she was still fuming at Mama, but mostly in order to avoid dwelling on the uneasiness facing her at the other end. Finally settling on a familiar epic contest, the combatants were introduced in her mind the way a title fight was announced at ringside.

In this corner, the underdog, the noble General Robert E. Lee, embodiment of the true South, both faithful and dutiful.

In her imagination, she became Lee... who was still revered by many Southerners.

And in the other, the Accursed. The man whose name is rarely spoken of favorably in Mississippi. That cigar-smoking, vile-mouthed, whiskey-drinking, son of the North – Grant!

Historically, Mississippians had their reasons for hating Grant, the obvious being that he had defeated Lee. Yet earlier in the war, Grant had severed the South's only artery of hope – the great river – with his victory at Vicksburg.

That battle cleaved the South in half two different ways. The eastern confederacy got cut off from its western states, as was all river traffic moving north and south.

Unfortunately for her, the mental analogy had completely broken down. Although quite frustrated with Mama, she knew full well that her mother never smoked, never swore, and definitely never drank. The link to Grant also failed because Mama was pure Southern, whereas she… who nonetheless loved the South… still strove to diminish its influences in her thought, speech and mannerisms. She knew Mama yearned for her daughter to be a true belle, though long ago had abandoned that hope. It had been many years since she last wore a dress or makeup. Instead of embracing afternoon tea, canning preserves or learning needlepoint, she spent most of her teenage years with her nose stuck in a book.

"Mama, I'm just a 'read-neck,' not a 'red-neck.'"

This rebuff most often got flung out by her while peering over the spine of some book that had captured her fancy. She would then spell out 'r-e-A-d-n-e-c-k' to ensure Mama understood the homonym, even though it had been repeated many times in their home.

As the bus progressed toward Garland, she still stuck with the historical comparison despite its obvious inconsistencies. She did not venture to look out the window for fear of seeing Carlton disappearing and Garland appearing, nor did she take pleasure in studying the occupants of the bus. Either activity would normally have engaged her imagination for the entire journey. Instead, resting chin upon palms and elbows on knees, she stared singularly into the back of the seat before her, desperately attempting to equate her brand of misery with that of General Lee's.

Lincoln had selected Grant, his most competent commander, to lead the Army of the Potomac after his successes in Mississippi and Tennessee. The goal: destroy Lee's Army of Northern Virginia. Grant was the first opponent Lee encountered who put him completely on the defensive. Like Lee facing Grant, she had dug her heels in against Mama's onslaught. But Mama, as with Grant in the Wilderness Campaign, kept forcing the opponent off guard. 'Move to the left, move to the left,' was Grant's motto, as his army pushed Lee's from northern Virginia to Petersburg, south of the state capital. That summer, Mama began relentlessly shifting her out of the fortified positions of her mind.

"I'm not nearly smart enough for college."

"Sweetie, you're just about the brightest thing that ever came out of Carlton."

"No one there's going to accept me."

"Nonsense! You're a beautiful young woman. No one cares where you came from."

"It'll cost too much."

"Gracious me! I've already told you! The scholarship's covering everything."

"But you need me here."

"I don't need help from any child! I'm a true woman of the South!"

The two armies, Grant's and Lee's, dug into defensive positions at Petersburg, initiating the world's first, greatest and… to a Southerner… most ill-fated display of trench warfare. Mama had been unable to find a way around her 'I will not go!'… which was sort of like Lee's entrenchment. So the two of them then settled down to a summer of siege that exhibited little in the way of interaction outside of occasional sniping.

Grant's forces dug a massive tunnel under Lee's fortifications.

Which was very devious of him!

In the same way, Mama tried undermining her defenses by entertaining a college alumnus of Garland State University – a pudgy old lady who obviously had attended long ago.

Like… before I was even born!

Grant detonated explosives in the tunnel in order to tear up the Confederate lines, except his army then hastily rushed into the resulting void in disarray and got mowed down by the enemy. It was an utter fiasco for the North. Likewise, Mama's clever attempt failed because she had donned a hoodie… something not normally worn in the house… and sat inanimate in the parlor with the two women. The visit was short-lived and ineffectual.

I certainly got her with that one!

Yet Mama, like Grant, had the advantage of time. Time had been running out for her. Not just to the day when the bus left for Garland, but also the time spreading out past that day, to the weeks… and months… and years beyond. That time did not exist for her. In fact, it had already run past her ability to imagine. She could see no future beyond the summer… and Mama knew it.

The day came when Grant sensed Lee's breaking point. Lee fled westward… and she escaped to the imagined safety of her own room. Grant sent cavalry ahead to destroy rail lines, occupy key escape routes, and cut off supplies. Mama confiscated the things she enjoyed most – her books. Though he never made it, Lee had intended to march over the Appalachians to join the remnant of the Confederate Army of Tennessee… yet she had no place to go and no one to join.

Inevitably, their Appomattox courthouse was the small kitchen table where all family business was conducted. Placing hands on her cheeks and looking squarely into her eyes, Mama offered terms.

"Camellia, I know you don't want to go, but the time's come. Trust me. I've been here for you all along. You know I love you more than life."

Lee signed Grant's settlement of unconditional surrender on April 9th, 1865, whereas she set off for college on the morning of August 23rd, 2002, being unable to refuse her mother's love.

And I guess that's why I'm stuck here…

She was born on March 20th, 1984, the only child of Evalyn Mae Larson, of Carlton, Mississippi.

As a child, she had sometimes said such silly things out loud whenever she was by herself… mostly to dispel her loneliness. She would imagine some future historian commissioned to pen the biography of that great Southern warrior – Camille Larson. In her mind, she would picture ceremonies in which bridges, schools and stadiums were rededicated in her honor. Maybe even the town of Carlton would be renamed 'Camille'… though she knew that name would never be accepted. Besides, it was self-evident – she did not possess the spirit or will to be great. But such imaginings, made alive through her books, were her distraction from heavier lines of thinking. Books brought life and hope to her. In fact, they redefined her, for she had altered her name because of something she read in a book. Her daddy, expecting a boy, had the name 'James Jay Larson' all but inked in on the birth certificate when out popped a girl. Shocked by the disappointment, Mama said he relegated the naming to her, insisting only that 'Jay' be kept as the middle name. Somehow, he had hoped that the baby girl might develop… on the inside at least… the toughness of a blue jay. Mama had always hated the birds, as they ate the fruit off her fig tree and generally behaved like bullies. She chose 'Camellia,' her favorite flower, desiring her child to be delicate and lovely on the outside.

She was fairly certain that neither parent got their wish.

Growing up, the middle name turned out to be fine enough for a girl, despite the occasional confusion it caused for substitute teachers.

"What's the 'J' stand for?"

"Jay."

"Yes, what's it stand for?"

"Jay."

"Don't you dare sass me, child!"

By second grade, the nickname 'jay bird' had been bestowed upon her by her friends. This would later morph into 'jail bird.'

Best not dwell on those times.

Yet, it was the first name that most irritated her on transitioning from child into teenager. In grade school, she vaguely remembered herself as a carefree daydreamer who frequently doodled her name into ornate patterns. Her classwork was adorned with flowers and trees… or buzzing bees… or rays of light from a big bright sun. 'Camellia' was a perfect fit.

Unfortunately, that name lost its appeal somewhere along in middle school, and was changed for one reason and only one reason… though she offered many other excuses for abandoning what Mama held dear. For example, she would complain that her birth name was so pompous because it possessed three syllables. Disdain for the pronunciation, 'kuh-**meel**-yuh,' was shown by repeating the 'yuh' sound over and over again… just to irritate her mother. The name, she told Mama, must be shortened… though not to one syllable. That would be too hick for her.

Not Cam! Might as well be Bud.

Instead, she liked the thought of two syllables. Not so short that the saying of it was over too soon, but not so long that it got tripped over on the way out. Obviously, 'Camel' would not do. She remembered giggling at the thought.

Will that be one lump or two?

She discovered her new name in the summer before seventh grade, not long after Daddy had left them, and not long after they had closed themselves off from the world. Not owning a television (…*actually, Mama had destroyed Daddy's*…), her mother would borrow books from the town library in an effort to distract and stimulate her. A wide variety of titles were selected from over the millennia in which mankind had recorded their stories. One particular piece of ancient literature, *The Aeneid*, held special meaning for her. In this poetic work, written in the first century B.C., Virgil described the heroic deeds of 'Camilla,'

'a warrior dame; unbred to spinning, in the loom unskill'd.'

This sounded like the perfect un-Southern woman. Camilla, the orphan queen of the Volscians, had a mythical upbringing and chose war over domestication. She was instantly captivated by Virgil's descriptions of her as both beautiful and deadly. Most of all though, it was that this woman chose a path of courage.

'sustain'd the toil of arms, the danger sought'

Hers was a heroic existence, ultimately leading to disaster.

'greatly to dare, to conquer or to die'

But also to an everlasting remembrance.

'but after ages shall thy praise record'

In Virgil's tale, Camilla achieved great deeds of valor, but was cheated by an early death. At twelve, this was exactly the person she longed to be – tragically heroic, and hopefully one day revered. The similarity between the warrior's name and her birth name was the needed confirmation. Yet it did not seem fit to take for herself the exact name of that noble queen, so she had adopted a variation as a tribute. She chose the French derivation of the Latin 'Camilla,' as it replaced the ending 'a' with an 'e.' The French, however, pronounced 'Camille' as 'kuh-mee,' which sounded incomplete to her. She opted for the British pronunciation – 'kuh-meel.' The new name was the perfect phonetic shortening of Camellia, accomplished simply by removing the 'yuh' sound.

From then on, she would be known as Camille, the mythical Roman warrior queen. Flowers and trees became armor and shield, bees gave way to arrows and spears, and sunbeams got replaced by lightning bolts. She entered middle school demanding to be called by the new name and would not respond to anything else. So many teachers had refused to accept the change, calling it utter nonsense. But she would not budge, being fully fixed upon the woman who had valiantly fought and tragically died.

Mama suffered her name change for a while in hopes that it would be outgrown, but the tacit acceptance became her victory. The name stuck. As she went into her teens, the adaptation suited her more and more. There was meaning, safety and comfort in this new identity. She would never go back to Camellia. She knew she could never be a flower again.

CHAPTER

2

CHECKED IN AND CHECKED OUT

"Go to college, Camellia. Learn what seeing and hearing really means."

That was the last thing Mama said before putting her on a bus bound for Garland.

She stood for a moment outside her new home, Switson Hall, surveying the campus for the first time… seeing and hearing what she could. As to sight, she had to admit that Garland possessed much beauty. Red brick buildings fronted with tall white columns framed lawns brimming with well-tended gardens and hedges. Moss-covered trees lined walkways alive with color, energy and enthusiasm, as fifteen thousand souls moved onto a campus eager for activity after a summer of solitude. While observing all the movement, a thought came to her of time-lapsed photography. She really enjoyed those accelerated videos of plants growing… or the moon rising… or cars forming rays of light at night on a highway. For a moment, she imagined what the campus might look like if this day got replayed at many times the normal speed.

In truth, the concentrated human activity was a blur to her at any rate. The lobby of Switson Hall was jam-packed, totally overloading her senses. The cackle of arriving coeds was nearly as intense as the suffocating amalgamation of their perfumes. Moving through, she accidently bumped into a man carrying a laundry basket loaded with linens, and the contact instantly caused her to recoil. She was not afraid of others, as if possessing *anthropophobia* – a condition she once looked up in search of an explanation for her antisocial ways. Instead, her case was *misanthropy* – she simply did not like people.

Yet even the most extroverted sort would have agreed that this dorm lobby was in chaos – something akin to stirring up a fire ant nest with a stick. Parents and students swarmed throughout. She noted streams of heavily laden adults flowing in with baggage, while their female offspring bobbed alongside merrily. For a moment, she tried to read the expressions on display, imagining that both parent and child had anticipated this day for months… maybe even years. On one extreme, some parents likely embraced the chance to rid the house of an annoyance, whereas on the other, it was the dreaded moment of separation from their little girl. As for her, she never had much of a family life – it was only Mama and her. Their goodbyes occurred hours ago at a bus's door.

What kind of a daughter does that make me?

Perhaps there's a third category – the rejects.

Shaking off the thought, she returned to the study of her surroundings. The lobby was decorated with streamers and bows in a blur of purple and silver – Garland's colors. Over a check-in counter hung a huge welcome sign bearing the phrase 'Go Warriors' along with the profile of a Roman helmet. Why this small detail about Garland had gone unnoticed all summer, she could not say, but the image instantly became a small sign of encouragement.

Maybe this place won't be so bad after all.

Joining the check-in line, her eyes continued to pan the lobby. There were clusters of couches displaying durable feminine weaves.

No matching throw pillows?! Don't girls love those things?

Maybe the accessories had been casualties of late-night pillow fights, or just wore out faster from years of so many 'have-a-good-cry' moments. She then noticed the alcove seats, big enough for two, yet perfect for one to stretch out in. The accompanying bay windows afforded excellent views of the grounds. She could envision love-struck girls sitting there searching the approaches to the dorm for the man of their dreams… but she had a different purpose in mind, desiring to occupy one with a good book on some stormy weekend.

A significant portion of the lobby traffic was flowing through an opening on the far left of the counter. She caught a glimpse of what lay beyond – a confluence of hallways with a stairwell leading to floors above and below. In contrast to the stream of parents moving through this door into the interior, she noticed others depositing their daughter's belongings in the lobby. There, they administered kisses and hugs, then promptly departed. The two tactics exhibited – shared labor versus dump and run – might correlate with how challenging it had been to sever the parent-child relationship. It occurred to her then that the first week of college might be difficult for some freshmen not accustomed to being away from home. Not her. She did not want to be here, but was determined not to shed a single tear due to homesickness.

The procession along the queue was slow. Before her was a family of five: two parents, two young children and a coed. She, having no siblings, kept her distance, feeling inadequate around such families. The coed, full of insights regarding the dorm, was rapidly conveying details to her parents... who outwardly displayed delight that the college transition was going so smoothly. The mother, as mothers often do, noticed her alone, and decided to get a leg up on her daughter's social life. Though an introduction was mediated by that woman, she would not remember the girl's name after that moment. In fact, she never saw her again.

The instructions to new arrivals were repeated several times while waiting her turn. She happened to learn that the defining feature of the lobby was a door leading into the inner regions of the dorm. This barrier selectively allowed one sex... with their magnetic swipe cards... to flow freely back and forth, while strictly prohibiting passage of the other. Under no circumstances were males allowed beyond 'the door.' She knew that not all female dorms on campus were like this. Some maintained relaxed standards and some were actually coed. Switson Hall was offered to parents as a safe haven for their daughters, which fit well with Mama's way of thinking.

Civilizations arose and advanced by overcoming barriers. That was the beauty of science, which in her mind was one of the few redeeming attributes of mankind. Knowledge opened doors. Ironically though, civilizations fell for the very same reason. Enemies found ways around barriers to steal resources and technologies, undermine populations, and capture cities. So she doubted seriously whether this rather heavy-looking door was all that effective at keeping guys out of the dorm.

Now getting closer, she noted that the counter was bordered on both sides by bulletin boards already jam-packed with fliers, announcements, and calls to 'get involved.' She then got her first good look at the woman behind the counter who had repeatedly introduced herself as Mrs. Riley, a graduate of Garland and the dorm mother. She was a pleasant enough looking woman, having invested effort into dressing fashionably, styling her gray hair, and applying makeup. Glancing about at the many 'done-up' girls, she visualized impatient fathers sitting in fully loaded cars, honking their horns while their daughters lingered inside primping for their first appearance on campus. Mama always said that beauty was an essential attribute of the Southern woman.

"Beauty takes time, Camellia!"

To her, the phrase should be 'takes too much time.'

The check-in process was being handled efficiently by this Mrs. Riley, who seemed to appraise each waiting girl before they reached the counter. She quickly went through a mental exercise undertaken countless times before.

What does she see when she sees me?

This self-imposed activity often got her through the awkwardness of being in public, becoming yet another invaluable 'frame of reference' game to her.

So… this dorm mother would have noted that she was about five foot six in bare feet… which at the moment filled anklet socks and plain white tennis shoes. As to her frame, she was rather thin, though still with an athletic sort of appearance… despite having never been involved in sports. She currently wore a pair of cut-off blue jeans terminated just above knee level. Two strands of a braided belt poked out from beneath an untucked tee-shirt, itself partially covered over by a very-much faded crimson hoodie. The hood bunched her blond hair up all about her neck. She like it that way.

There was nothing particularly special about this hoodie. In fact, she owned dozens of them. Some were heavy for winter weather, and some light for sultry summer days. But rain or shine, hot or cold, she always wore a hoodie in public… and always with the hood up. The current article was of the 'zip-up' variety, it being too warm out for a pullover. The zipper was slid up by a few inches, a practice developed the hard way. Unzipped, cruel kids at school could sneak up behind and pull the hoodie right off.

Her hands were presently tucked into the pockets of the hoodie, contributing to the appearance of sagged shoulders. This was not from poor posture, as her heavy backpack necessitated a bit of a slouch. Her only other luggage, a large canvas duffel bag, was packed with as much clothing as it could hold. Mrs. Riley would probably also notice that she was not wearing makeup, nor had she styled her hair. Here was a girl unconcerned with appearances. A loner... which potentially signaled a troubled girl... and troubled girls tended to attract trouble. In her defense, the concepts of beauty, breeding and likeability were very much foreign to her.

Mrs. Riley would also notice that cosmetics were not the only thing missing – there were no parents.

A waif thrown up onto the shores of Switson Hall.

OK... enough of that!

Too often, she was inclined toward over-analyzing the presumed thoughts of others... a tendency often criticized by Mama. ("Until you can climb up into someone's head, Camellia, don't you dare go imagining what's happening in there!")

As the dorm mother finished with the family of five, she briefly turned about before approaching the counter... just to see what was behind her as through Mrs. Riley's eyes. The action was misinterpreted.

"Yes, dear, you're next. Step forward – don't be shy. Your name please?"

"Camille Larson."

Mrs. Riley scanned a clipboard.

"I have a 'Camellia J. Larson.' Is that you?"

"Yes, ma'am."

"We have you sharing a room. Here's your packet containing all the information you need to know about the dorm. Your room key and access card are inside. There's also a lanyard if you find it a convenient way to carry your card. Miss Avery here..." She motioned to a greeter who approached from the side. "...will escort you to your room. I expect a bright girl such as yourself has already heard me go through the introductions several times over while waiting in line. Am I correct?"

"Yes, ma'am."

"Of course I am. I can always spot the intelligent ones. Now off you go."

"Thank you, ma'am."

The kind words caught her by surprise. Quickly hoisting up her duffel and moving in behind this Miss Avery, she was disappointed with herself for having thought the worst.

Yet again, Mama was right.

CHAPTER

3

THE ROOMIE AND THE HOODIE

She followed Miss Avery through 'the door,' ascended stairs, and turned down a long hallway, all the while lagging a good way behind so as not to bump her guide with the duffel bag. On such occasions when she found herself in an unfamiliar setting, she would engage in a mental exercise of tracking the compass points. The practice came about because she read somewhere that certain aquatic mammals exhibited innate directional skills, as if their brains were attune to Earth's magnetic poles. The method she employed was to maintain a bearing on north, which required knowing that direction before entering a building.

Heading north; right turn, north now at nine o'clock; another right, north at six.

She treated this as a game, though her hidden motive was to always know the way out. As to her 'internal magnet,' it almost always pointed to Mama. The displeasure she had experienced on the bus ride had already faded, being replaced by a desire to have her mother there. She was not sure why Mama had chosen to stay home. 'I'm not up to it,' was all she would say.

"There's a coin-operated laundry in the basement, as well as some vending machines… and every floor has a common area." Miss Avery pointed back the way they had come while pivoting her head between her and the rooms they passed. "Your hall resident will probably come by today to meet you. You'll want to get settled in, then get started decorating your door. It's a perfect way to tell girls on the hall something about yourself."

In moving past many such exhibits, she gained a feel for door 'adornment,' which ranged from overly girlie to fairly meager. One such example was currently being covered in gift-wrap paper – a shiny silver background with cascading purple hearts on the foreground. Aside from names, all doors seemed to have one thing in common – a small whiteboard on which one could leave or receive a message. She seriously doubted she would ever use one.

"Your room's up here on the left."

An open door, Miss Avery explained, was a sign of the occupants' availability to socialize. The door to her new room was ajar, and already decorated with colorful ribbons and the calligraphed name of 'Amber Bruinen.' Miss Avery performed the introductions, concluding her responsibilities with enthusiastic parting words for the freshman.

"Welcome to Garland! I just know you'll simply love living in Switson Hall."

A brief hug, and Miss Avery was gone.

Her first impression of Amber, a sophomore from Gulfport, was not so flattering. Her new roommate, dressed in a lily-patterned kimono, was a tsunami of makeup. There was 'stuff' all around her eyes, with lashes perked up and cheeks powdered over, and a mouth so thickly painted that it reminded her of the red ring marking a target's bull's-eye. On top, Amber's auburn hair was piled up and secured in place with what looked like chopsticks. A sparkly substance had been lacquered on as a finishing touch, its effect strangely resembling fine dew glistening on a spider's web. Yet it was the perfume that most affected her – an intensely citrus-honey smell.

Gawk! I'm drowning in sweetness!

Awkwardly extending a hand to accept Amber's, she immediately felt uneasy, having never shared a room before.

"So good to have you as a roommate! You have perfect timing – I just came back from a sorority mixer. Now... this side of the room is yours." Amber extended an arm to the left... so she took note of that side's vacant desk, bed, dresser and closet.

"Is someone helping you bring up your things?"

"Nope, this is all I have."

She gestured toward the duffel on the floor, with the backpack sitting astride it. Amber was clearly scrutinizing those things, apparently working through a significant inconsistency. '*How can a girl carry everything she needs in that?*' The progression of thought was apparent. '*Where are the dresses, shoes, and accessories? Where's the makeup?*'... which slowly transitioned into '*Poor soul!*'... followed by a dispirited '*Why me?!*' All this she gathered from a series of facial expressions: astonishment marked by raised brows, pity by a briefly cocked head, and mild irritation in a poorly concealed scowl.

Here I go again – reading too much into someone!

But then a final stage of Amber's countenance materialized as a complimentary reflection of the Southern woman. A weak, yet sincere smile forced its way onto the girl's face, which she imagined was accompanied by the thought: '*Let's make the most of it – there's work here to be done.*'

Amber next pointed out other aspects of their room, most important the shared bathroom located through a door concealed by the inwardly opened room door. She closed the latter to open the former, which revealed a space with a toilet, a shower, two sinks, and cabinetry. At the opposite end was another door.

"We share with two others. I've not met them yet."

"Did you live in Switson last year?"

"No. I was in a different dorm."

Amber then abruptly changed the subject with a somewhat unnatural display of eagerness. "Hey, what do you think?! I know someone who can sneak us into a bar in town – up for exploring?"

She just had to look away before answering. "No thanks. I'm… not really into that sort of thing."

Returning her attention to the room, she scanned over both halves. Amber's was well-decorated and monogrammed with 'ALB' on just about every free-standing object… although that trio did have to compete with the Greek letters of a sorority. The mirror, in particular, caught her eye. It was adorned by a kaleidoscope of random items – cards, notes, motivational sayings, drawings, and mementos – all wedged together around its border, which left only a small section in the center for reflections. Amidst these items were many photos of Amber posing with other Garland students. Suddenly, she was seriously perplexed. Surely a sophomore, and a sorority member, should have plenty of friends from which to select a roommate… rather than having one assigned to her. The question of 'why' surfaced, but she quickly put it down to her ignorance of college ways.

"What's the 'L' stand for?"

She immediately regretted asking.

"Lisa. What's yours?"

"Jay."

"What's that stand for?"

She just mumbled out J-A-Y.

"Oh."

Awkwardness aside, she promptly deemed the space as livable and got to work unpacking. Though her possessions would not come close to filling the allotted storage, Mama would ship boxes of clothes, books and anything else she might need. As Amber watched, she extracted hoodie after hoodie from the duffel bag.

"You sure have a lot of those." This was delivered with a tone of astonishment that any Southern girl should devote so much of her wardrobe to such a crude and limiting form of apparel.

"Yep." Though Amber could not possibly understand, she was proud of her hoodies… each and every one.

While unpacking, she became aware of girls moving along the hall. Some were politely greeting neighbors, whereas others were 'kickin' up a ruckus,' as Mama would say. She ignored the activity, focusing instead on making her half of the room 'hers.' Yet all of a sudden, the hall noises died down… and then Mrs. Riley appeared with an upperclassman, stopping first at the room across the hall. Amber took the opportunity to seat herself pleasantly at her desk.

Turning next into their room, Cameron Stokes was introduced as the hall resident. This girl was a senior, a member of the women's lacrosse team, and a physical education major. Speaking with evident authority… much as a coach might in instructing her team… the hall resident detailed her expectations, building off the dorm's general policies of no boys, no drugs, no alcohol, no smoking, no weapons, no vandalism, and no 'borrowing' without permission. Cameron's addition to the list was a general quiet time after 9 PM on those nights before class days.

Very unexpectedly, she found herself being drawn to this senior despite the lack of commonality between them. Cameron was tall, strong and athletic, as well as a born leader, whereas she was none of those things. And Cameron was black, which in the South constituted a significant cultural distinction. Yet most fascinating to her was an instant association to Virgil's warrior queen.

This is not a woman to be underestimated!

Imagination took momentary control of her, as she envisioned the resident moving up and down the hallway in lacrosse gear, forcing miscreants to hit the floor and 'give her ten.'

A voice abruptly interrupted this vision.

"Any questions…? None? Good! My room's across from the main stairwell."

Cameron gave her a brief and piercing glance before moving on to the next room. Only then did Amber eased back in her chair.

"Whew! I heard she's really strict… She has a room all to herself. It's got its own bathroom and two windows. You know… they put it across from the stairs so the RA can keep track of who's coming and going."

She replied more to herself than to her new roommate.

"I like her."

After unpacking, she turned to the envelope given to her at check-in, the contents of which included the items mentioned by Mrs. Riley, along with a campus map and pamphlets about the university. She selected one and began reading.

Garland State University was a liberal arts college founded in 1888. It was named after Colonel Buford T. Garland, who was killed on September 17th, 1862, at the Battle of Sharpsburg (…*it's called the Battle of Antietam in the North…*) when the Mississippi regiment he commanded became part of the slaughter dubbed 'the bloody lane.' He had owned a large plantation on the current site of the University. His only heir, a daughter named Clara, died at the age of nineteen during a rubella outbreak that moved through most of the country in 1872. The state then took ownership of the plantation, which had fallen into neglect, chartering a university on the site in honor of the Confederate colonel. The early planners started with a cluster of three buildings around which the campus slowly expanded and modernized. The town of Garland had not existed prior to the University, but became incorporated in the 1920s.

Most parents assumed a small college town meant fewer big city temptations. Garland State University was depicted as a desert isle of learning in the bucolic sea of Mississippi, presiding as a sanctuary in which Southern gentlemen and ladies could entrust their precious offspring. She knew that a majority of students would spend their four years here comfortably isolated within that academic bubble. Yet even here, members of either gender could… if so inclined… get into whatever variety of trouble they so desired, just as on any other college campus in America.

Later that afternoon, she received her first exposure to the cleverness of college guys. The room's door had been left open when Amber departed to visit friends in another dorm. She froze on glancing up from her desk to see three males pass down the hall. Before she could relax, a fourth appeared at her door, smiling and summoning back his friends. She quickly inspected herself – the hoodie was in place. The leader knocked, then asked if they could come in. Her hasty response of 'why?' got delivered from a temporary deficiency of speech… and she was immediately disappointed with herself that it had been taken as coyness.

"To get to know you, of course." His remark was accompanied by smirks and promptings from the other three.

Despite preferring to remain seated, she nonetheless rose and moved to the door… actions apparently interpreted as an encouraging sign. The ringleader took a step into her room.

"No thank you."

Then she just closed the door on them. An unmistakable 'bitch' penetrated the plywood barrier. She just shrugged off the insult, for it was far from the first time such a thing had been hurled her way.

On returning to the desk, her initial thought was relief. Had Amber been present, all four would likely have been invited in. She next wondered whether the breach of rules should be reported. It would be so captivating to witness Cameron wage war on those guys just as Camilla had done in Virgil's poetry. Yet her cautious side warned that running to the resident on the first evening might be seen as a sign of weakness. So instead, she directed all thought toward pondering over a simple question – why had they congregated at *her* door? Back in Carlton, plenty of boys had taunted her unceasingly, though most simply avoided her. Not one had ever treated her as either a prospect or a friend.

CHAPTER

4

PLAN THE PLAN

The uneasiness brought about by those intruders eventually subsided, permitting her to focus on drafting a weekly schedule. Mama's oft repeated adage came to mind. 'A good plan makes sure nothing changes.' This was usually followed by an addendum.

"Get it?"

Sometimes she would feint confusion just for the fun of it.

"Get what?"

Mama would then explain, as on every prior instance, that a person had nothing without a plan, but a plan changed nothing into something. Her mama was a 'lean, mean plannin' machine,' having transformed her into one too. For the last two years of high school, she had been in charge of their combined schedules that included school, chores, church and employment. As the reality of college was now fully upon her, there was no longer a reluctance to plan for it. Seated at her desk, she extracted pen, paper, highlighters and ruler from a drawer. Amber… having materialized shortly after the boys passed through the hall… detected the activity and came to lean over her shoulder.

"What're you doing?"

"Laying out my schedule. It'll only be a temporary one. I'll make it final after the first week of class is over."

Being watched, she meticulously went about tracing out eight vertical lines on a sheet of paper, with the seven resulting divisions headed by days of the week. Horizontal lines delineated rows designated with times, progressing from 6 AM to 10 PM. She then labelled the first row of seven boxes as 'wake' and the last as 'sleep,' the former highlighted in yellow (sunrise) and the latter in purple (dusk). Aware that Amber was still peering over, she looked up to see a face covered with consternation.

"Girl, nobody wakes up before seven… and I can guarantee you nobody goes to bed before eleven… especially on weekends. Glad this is just a temp."

Amber turned back to her own affairs… which mostly involved arranging items in a small suitcase propped open on her desk. She craned her head over to see.

Makeup.

After consulting her class schedule, she reserved time slots for breakfast, lunch and supper. These were colored green. Mama frequently emphasized the importance of three meals a day, fearing that her daughter might otherwise waste away. A food plan had been negotiated as part of the scholarship, with a magnetic swipe card providing access to various on-campus dining options. She smiled to herself on recalling the disdainful look upon Mama's face after seeing that card arrive in the mail. It might grant her daughter access to regular meals, but that piece of plastic could never substitute for a mother's love, skillfully lavished out by the plate-full.

The next step was to fill in the times for her courses. The class schedule had been planned out by Mama that summer in a running monologue that she was compelled to hear… being confined to the kitchen table through it all. At first, Mama had displayed a glaring lack of logic in her suggestions, proposing upper level courses clearly beyond a freshman ("How about Quantum Mechanics? That sounds interesting!")… or ones she knew would be despised ("What about this introductory course in agriculture? That could be useful in your future."). She remembered almost taking the bait before recognizing this as yet another example of Mama's cunning. The strategy… which almost worked… was to get her involved. Instead, she gave Mama only silence. Ultimately, Mama selected courses based on recommendations for an undeclared major – three credits of English,

World History, Chemistry and Calculus, and one each for Chemistry Lab and a recreational elective. Fourteen was an acceptable load for an incoming freshman.

Mama's determined efforts to draw her in had also included commentary on a variety of topics purposely selected to elicit a response. For example, she voiced frustration over the term 'credit.' ("Don't they think students earn their marks? Credit means owing someone something... and that means debt... doesn't it?") She had remained silent. Mama then feigned irritation that college freshmen could not be kept busy with classes each and every hour of the weekday. ("Camellia... I'm worried you'll fall into idleness.") Again, she stayed quiet. Mama next proposed staggering the courses – humanities on Monday, Wednesday and Friday, and the sciences on Tuesday and Thursday. ("That way, you won't get confused if your courses are sorted properly.") Mama had finally gotten to her. She could not keep from laughing, imagining her mother organizing a class curriculum in the same way she did laundry.

Of all her courses, it was the recreational elective that was most debated over. ("I expect you'd be as excited as all get out to be taking swimming...") She could not remember having ever been in a concrete pool, though she had often swum in Carlton's small portion of the Tombigbee waterway on many mother-daughter Sunday afternoon picnics. ("...but you need something safer – like karate or fencing.") Mama did not have to say it – the thought of her daughter in a bathing suit around boys was more perilous than dodging kicks or sword play.

After reading the class requirements and making certain that equipment was provided, Mama settled on racquetball. ("That sounds challenging and fun.") At the time, she could not have cared less, but now... seated in her new dorm room... a feeling of uneasiness swept over her. She had foolishly missed out on a very special opportunity – to plan courses with Mama... who had never attended college.

I'm so stupid! I can't believe I shut her out. Next term, I promise, things'll be different!

Having inked in course titles, she began color-coding the various boxes. Studying, personal reading and letter writing would be added later. Part of her scholarship package included a work-study program, to be defined during an evaluation on Tuesday. This was the only reason why every hour of every day had not yet been accounted for.

To her, combining work and school was a way of life simply because they could not have survived otherwise. Many employers in Carlton did not object to having her work alongside Mama, as the two of them maintained a reputation of dependability. While Mama kept eyes and ears alert for better paying work, those new opportunities for Mama meant potential hand-me-down jobs for her. She had bussed tables, cleaned bathrooms, performed clerical tasks, stocked shelves, gathered trash, delivered papers, mended garments, and collected spent shells at a gun range. One of her favorite town jobs was 'seasonal decorator,' which was nothing more than hanging banners and placards for every conceivable event or holiday. The only work she absolutely refused was anything involving animals... especially dogs.

While taping the temporary schedule on the wall above her desk, she became aware again of noises outside the room. It took her only a few hours in the dorm to realize that status on the hall was based primarily on how frequently your room got visited. From her vantage point, she could tell that the girls across the hall were going to be popular. For her part, she had no plans for visiting anyone, and would only file away two names in memory – that of her roommate and the hall resident.

If Amber had thought the temporary schedule to be presumptive, the girl surely became convinced of its veracity when she retired at 10 PM on a Friday night, and then woke the next morning at six. Her alarm elicited only a weak moan from Amber. She showered, but did not blow dry her hair... actually never had... before quietly dressing and departing the room. She only had two days to prepare. This one would be spent exploring the campus and locating her classrooms, then mapping out the best routes that connected these to her dorm, dining facilities and the library. Popular gatherings such as the student union, the football stadium, fraternity and sorority houses, and off-campus hang-outs were of no interest to her.

As school supplies had already been gathered from discount stores in Carlton, she lacked only her textbooks. College bookstore prices were outrageous, even for used items, so she devised a less-than scrupulous means of obtaining what was required. Though the library had these books, availability throughout the semester could not be counted on. Fortunately, her scholarship granted her nearly unlimited access to photocopiers. While the majority of the student body was embroiled in the festivities of the first home football game, she secluded herself in the library duplicating textbooks.

She spent the last day before officially becoming a college student the way she felt every Sunday should be spent. Although not keen on attending a strange church… especially without Mama here… she nevertheless had promised to be faithful about Sunday services. ("Go every week, Camellia. Preferably Baptist… maybe Methodist… but definitely not Pentecostal. And don't bother ever speaking to me again if you go Presbyterian!") She knew Southern church services to be one part announcements, one part music, one part sermon, and many parts socializing. Some were so friendly that the preacher had visitors stand up and introduce themselves. To her, that was not unlike the school yard gag where a 'kick me' sign got taped on her back… except in church the sign would read 'greet me.' No way was she putting herself through that! So she came up with an alternative that obeyed the spirit of Mama's request… if off a bit on the letter. She went to the University's one-room chapel. No preacher, no congregation and no service – just her by herself with benches, stained glass, and a large cross on the wall.

The remainder of that first Sunday was occupied with reading a book on the naval history of Britain. She had noticed it abandoned on a table while exploring the library the day before. Returning to the dorm after lunch, she positioned herself comfortably in one of the lobby alcoves and read about the demise of the Spanish Armada in 1588. Philip the second, king of Spain, intended to invade England and depose Queen Elizabeth… partly because of religion, but mostly from a fear of England's growing continental influence. His armies, however, never landed on the British Isles. A combination of Sir Francis Drake's naval forces, some poor decisions, and a violent North Sea storm claimed much of the Armada, with the remainder returning to Spain in disgrace. It was the turning point in the balance of world-wide naval dominance toward the British… a supremacy that would last more than 350 years.

She casually perused the remainder of the book, stopping at various places to enjoy historical accounts, snippets regarding naval maneuvers, and intricate diagrams of warships. A notion was forming in her head that History might provide her with both a major… and a meaning.

CHAPTER

5

FIRSTS

Her first dining hall experience at Garland would likely be the best all term. Seasoned chicken, flaky crescent rolls, fruit, salad and vegetables… all fresh and all served up by energetic staff. The excellence was likely due to the large number of parents still roaming the campus to experience… or re-experience… college life. On that opening weekend, the University put its best foot forward for their visitors. In the coming days, she fully expected the food quality to regress toward the reputed level of cafeteria cuisine.

Her first college class would be Honors History at 9 AM. Having finished breakfast by seven, she faced a long interval with nothing to study, no notes to re-copy, and no errands to run. Inactivity drove her to the library's newspaper room where current periodicals were displayed. Though disappointed not to find *The Carlton Courier*, it being too insignificant for a university library, she instead flipped through the day's edition of *The New York Times* – the first copy she ever laid eyes on! For New Yorkers, she imagined it to be just a normal part of their daily routine. Yet for her, it was an exhilarating experience to hold in one issue what would otherwise comprise a year's worth of happenings in Carlton.

Entering Cunningham Hall for History, she made her way through corridors packed with students waiting for other classes. This building had been barren two days previous when she mapped out routes. The change did not suit her. It was impossible to avoid being bumped into, and the noise level was comparable to standing beneath a waterfall. She drew up into a corner outside her room to wait until the previous class had spilled out… then she and her new classmates pushed their way in to stake out seats. She secured a third row position on the far edge, affording her some measure of privacy. With a tiny air of self-satisfaction, she decided to make this 'her place in history'… at least for the remainder of the semester.

By far, this was the most modern classroom she had ever seen. It ran upward in terraces, each occupied by a long counter spanning the width. Stations positioned along were equipped with electrical outlets, internet connections and swivel seats. The room's walls bore intermittently spaced sound-absorbing panels, and though there were no windows, ample fluorescent fixtures brightly lit the space. She noted an overhead projector aimed at a large screen up front, next to which were overlapping whiteboards that could be slid up and down in layers. A digital clock displayed '9:00' without an accompanying bell to announce the start of class.

Guess we're expected to manage time without reminders.

Shifting attention to the students, she noted that several were plugging in personal laptops. Her experience thus far with the electronic age had been limited to high school computer lab, which taught only the basics of word processing and spread sheets. Giggling to herself, she imagined pulling out a popcorn popper and setting it up in plain sight. The humor, however, quickly wore off with an odd observation – no one was greeting their neighbor. There were no 'hellos,' or 'where y'all from?' or 'what courses y'all taking?' In fact, many appeared skittish and aloof. Though she would never have engaged in such small talk, it nonetheless was unnerving to see an entire class exhibiting the exact same behaviors as her.

At that moment, the collective attention of the class responded to a noise behind and above. Swiveling in her chair, she observed a young man emerge through a door at the top terrace. Descending steps on her side, he positioned himself quietly in a front corner. This could not be the professor, but clearly not a student either. Presently, another man – this one crowned with gray hair – came through the same door, also descending on her side. He was the iconic portrayal of a professor, from his scruffy beard to a sweater vest beneath his much-worn elbow-padded blazer. He transferred the bundle to the young man, who immediately began distributing pages. Her copy revealed the stack to be the course syllabus, with goals and expectations, key dates, office hours and a list of resources available for supplemental study. She was already perusing the latter when the professor stepped up to the lectern, adjusted his wire-rimmed glasses, and then cleared his throat.

"Welcome to Freshman Honors History. I am Prof. Dunsmore."

It was a true measure of the seriousness of college that nobody snickered at this name. At her high school, 'Dunsmore' would have elicited many whispered variants ('Dumb-smore,' 'Dunce-more,' and 'Dunsmore-or-less') complete with accompanying chuckles. The professor's tone, though, carried with it a singular note of self-importance conveying an obvious pride in his scholarly position. No one would dare make light of that.

"I have taught Honors History at Garland for over 25 years. You should know – being an honors student is a privilege. While standard sections of this course are taught to hundreds at a time, you are afforded more individualized attention. However, this comes with higher expectations. I will cover much more material and in greater depth. I test rigorously, grade strictly, and offer no extra credit… as the syllabus clearly indicates. You will find your other Honors courses to be equally challenging, so I will state this quite plainly – you must maintain a B+ average overall to continue in Honors classes. It is sad to say that many of you will enter your sophomore year on the outside of this program."

Now she understood the mood of the class. This was a competitive environment – winners moved up and losers moved out… and the professor was not here to help.

"The last page of the syllabus that my teaching assistant has passed through the class is…" He had been flipping through his copy, but abruptly stopped. "Excuse me. Allow me to introduce Mr. Reynolds, who is currently in his second year of our graduate program." The young man briefly nodded to the class, then the professor continued on. "As I was saying…"

With the room returning its focus to the professor, hers remained on the TA… even though it was rare for her to ignore an authority figure as they spoke. Like most Southern women well-versed in manners, Mama would not have tolerated her daughter showing disrespect toward an adult. Such behaviors earned an all-expense-paid trip to a 'whuppin.' Yet she did not think Mama would have regarded this situation in that way, as there was something intriguing about this TA.

He appeared to be in his mid-twenties. Coming off the wall where he had been leaning, this Mr. Reynolds waved to the class and remained standing there as Prof. Dunsmore gestured toward him again… though she missed the context. Looking now at the professor, she detected an unmistakable sense of ownership over this TA.

"The service of individuals such as Mr. Reynolds is a privilege granted to professors of Honors classes. He will be assisting me in many aspects of your education."

She was sure that meant doing the arduous chores of grading and tutoring. As confirmation, the professor was now referring to weekly help sessions to be led by *his* TA. Mr. Reynolds, the academic servant, did not appear bothered in the least.

She could not say whether the young man was handsome or not, considering herself unskilled in such appraisals. Still, he was not uncomely standing there in blue jeans, a V-neck shirt and loafers. Shy of six feet with an average build, his light-brown hair seemed well-groomed. Yet it was his demeanor that caught her eye, as he stood at attention while the professor continued.

To her, he seemed to portray the look of a person managing something of a compartmentalized mind. At least one part was focused on the current responsibility… which included making himself available for the professor's utility and the class's scrutiny. Other parts of him seemed elsewhere, as suggested by periodic glances in the direction of the floor or ceiling. His, though, was not a 'far away' look, as he was all there, paying close attention to his boss. While regarding him, a peculiar notion came over her that he did not seem to belong in this time… or any particular time. Maybe it was her imagination playing with the concept… and the acronym… of a TA for a history course, but she had the distinct impression that he would be content anywhere in time. His was a 'Time Away' look.

Prof. Dunsmore was now reading verbatim from a paragraph on the consequences of academic misconduct. Venturing to look about, she found that most of the class were staring at their computer screens.

She returned her attention to the TA, who had just begun an oddly systematic study of the class. Starting in front, his consideration moved from person to person along the row. It could not be to count heads, as his eyes lingered much too long on each student. The professor continued to pour through the syllabus, stopping from time to time to offer an anecdotal reference to an event that had inspired a particular clause, or to relate an experience not directly pertinent to the material. The TA was forgotten, though she kept her eyes on him, endeavoring to work out what he was doing. In the process, she smiled to herself.

The student studying the teacher studying the students.

From her vantage point, there appeared to be no bias compelling the TA to dwell on any one person, or dissatisfaction quickly shifting him past another. He seemed pleased to give each, male or female, their appropriate due. So absorbed in this activity, she was caught off guard as he progressed from the second row up to the third. She found herself suddenly staring directly into his eyes… and him into hers. The hoodie, she hoped, was doing its job of concealment, for the heat of her blushed face had completely filled it. Despite the awkwardness, she willed her eyes not to look away… to stay on his for as long as he chose – which was *much* longer than for any of the previous students. Surprisingly, her initial rigid determination subtly transformed into something more relaxed, as she found him neither menacing or intimidating. To her, he seemed to be offering something of himself – some small bit of support to counterbalance the professor's stern words.

He eventually moved on to the next person, and she relaxed. Looking down at the counter, she was suddenly displeased with herself for having not anticipated her turn. Equally, she was completely befuddled within, wishing to have looked away but glad for having not done so. Regardless, it would be unwise… and a bit rude… to continue a study of him as he finished his progression through the class. One thing was certain – his peripheral vision might detect her. Another measure of those eyes would be too much.

The professor was now pointing upward to the top terrace and telling the class not to use the upper doorway, except in an emergency, as it was only for professors and staff. He then concluded by referring once more to the last page of the syllabus, which was an acknowledgement to be signed. Instructions were given to pass these along, with her becoming the collection point for the third row. Mr. Reynolds moved from row one to row two, and then to hers. He offered a pleasant 'thank you' as she transferred the pile into his outstretched hand… then he moved out of sight up the terraces, presumably exiting above as the professor dismissed the class.

On Mondays, her schedule provided an hour break before the one credit recreational class at 11 AM. Though there was ample time to cross campus for Racquetball, she hastily gathered her possessions and departed, wanting to be out of that classroom as quickly as possible. Having exited the building, she nonetheless carried along with her an unsettled feeling… one never experienced before.

CHAPTER

6

WORK STUDY

She had successfully made it through the first two days of classes, yet still felt uneasy about the entirety of college as one aspect remained undefined. She departed the dorm heading to the appointment that would determine her work-study position. Her mind, held captive by the dread of uncertainty, sought escape within imagination.

At 3 PM, the height of afternoon classes, every walkway was alive with motion. To her, the campus seemed a living thing, and she latched onto a notion of fifteen thousand blood cells coursing along arteries and veins... always moving in and out of the brick-inlaid central concourse – the heart of student activity on campus. Stopping on the dorm's walkway, she explored the analogy, consciously relying upon it to cover over her apprehensions.

Students leave classes with knowledge like blood cells depart the lungs with life-sustaining oxygen. So... if the concourse is the heart and the classrooms are the lungs, which buildings best fit with the other organs?

To her, the library must be the brain of campus, though administrators would probably say the office of the university president merited that distinction. The cafeterias were obviously the digestive system, and the athletic grounds had to be the body's extremities – the arms and legs. She, fully immersed, began turning about in a circle to take in as much as could be seen… until her eyes fell upon Switson Hall. Being suddenly mindful of herself, she sighed deeply and moved on.

I'm probably living in the gall bladder.

A unique aspect of her scholarship… as specified by the University's granting board… was a personalized work-study program. Months before, Mama had read aloud about this from the award announcement, being convinced that her daughter's love of work could be used to erase an aversion for going away to college. The work-study position was pitched by the university… and Mama… as an exciting opportunity for obtaining invaluable career experience. In exchange, students would render back to the University service in the form of labor… for nominal compensation. Mama had paraded a pamphlet about containing images of energetic students working alongside their esteemed mentors. There was a photo of a smiling student in front of a computer, along with a professor leaning over his shoulder pointing at the monitor. To her, it would have been better had the man not been pointing, as the message was painfully clear: 'Look – you made a mistake.' In another, a student and professor, both wearing lab coats and safety goggles, were peering intensely into a flask containing a purple solution. Both displayed euphoric expressions conveying the sense of a major discovery. Yet from her perspective, it looked as if they had simply synthesized grape Kool-Aid.

Mama had been most intent on one photo. ("Camellia, you should get this job.") That image showed a beautiful young woman with blond hair streaming down about her shoulders. Where the strands left off, the heads of a cluster of elementary children picked up. They were all gathered close about… not as in a group pose, but something resembling a hug… with each child bearing an expression of adoration. In response, the young woman's countenance conveyed deep satisfaction and gratitude at having enriched so many lives. She had not been sure whether Mama's real message was 'you'd be great as a teacher' or 'get rid of the hoodie and let your hair flow down.' Irrespective, she had just grunted.

I'd rather pickle frogs in the biology department!

In actuality, it was the brochure's reference to a professional assessment preceding placement that most bothered her. To her credit, Mama had sensed it. ("That's just some kind of… what's it called… aptitude test. You've nothing to worry about. Why, they'll take one look at you and see the brightest future!") Of course, she had thought otherwise.

Right! One look at me, and they'll decide they just found their next great grease trap monkey.

Being both skinny and flexible, she had been ideal for that job while working at Fergie's Diner in Carlton.

Perfect for getting up under that nasty fryer and slopping out all that golden-brown goo!

The recollection made her shudder. A few summers back, she had reached up underneath to unscrew the trap cap when a rat ran down her arm like it was the mooring line connecting a freighter to its wharf. Her resulting screams were so loud and long that Mr. Ferguson thought a fire had broken out in his kitchen. Yet Old Joe the cook just busted a gut laughing… and then spent a week reenacting every detail of her fit.

Having the cardiovascular imagery abandon her, she was once again forced to confront the question that persisted from the summer.

What if I'm no good at anything?

This insecurity, combined with the discomfort of being alone, had caused her to fall asleep the previous night dwelling not on the experiences of her first day in college, but on the potential outcome of the evaluation. Her restless thoughts gave way to disturbing dreams.

A panel of experts proclaimed that they had never encountered a case like hers. Here was a person ill-suited for any position. She was referred to the psychology department – not for work-study, but for clinical study. She became a test case that earned an up-and-coming professor a tenured position… and big government grants… and guest appearances on morning talk shows. There were images of her being strapped to a metal chair with electrodes taped all over her body, naked except for a thin hoodie pulled down as modestly as possible over her hips. The same lab-coated, Kool-Aid inventing scientists in Mama's brochure were leaning over with clipboards, feverishly capturing every moan emitted with every electrical shock imposed. She woke abruptly in a sweat to a darkened room, a soundly sleeping roommate, and a clock lazily moving past 4:25 AM.

She entered the work-study office in a state of high anxiety. No analogies presented themselves to comfort her, so she sought distraction in a purposeful accounting of the room's layout.

A desk and twelve chairs in a three by four pattern.

Half the space was occupied by students chatting over pages of prospective job descriptions. She ignored them and timidly approached the desk of Mr. Tzichinski, a balding man neatly dressed in suit and bow tie.

Hopefully a proper pronunciation of his name won't be part of this.

"Hello, sir. I'm Camille Larson. I'm here for a work-study evaluation."

Mr. Tzichinski returned the greeting, then searched for her name in an open ledger before him.

"Camellia J. Larson of Carlton, Mississippi… freshman… major 'undeclared' – is that you?"

"Yes, sir."

He handed over a computer scan sheet along with a list of questions and a pencil, pointing her to an adjacent door.

"Answer these to the best of your ability. The directions are self-explanatory. Take your time, and feel free to ask about anything not making sense."

She thanked the man, then moved into a small meeting room… yet immediately froze just inside the doorframe on discovering the space to be occupied. Two students, male and female, briefly looked up from their questionnaires… though the guy did a painfully obvious double-take upon seeing her. His eyes then tracked her as she took a seat at the table as far away from him as possible.

The evaluation consisted of fifty questions in which occupations were to be rated on a five point scale from 'I could never see myself doing this' to 'I have aspired to do this all my life.' Pretty simple. The questions, she was relieved to discover, had been fashioned in such a way that students could express vocational preferences without reference to experience or skill level.

After only a few minutes, her concentration was broken by the guy.

"What do you think about the one on horses? Does Garland have a vet program?"

Her response to that question ('I could never see myself doing this') was already recorded, it being the fourth on the list. After a moment, the girl replied.

"I don't know, but I like horses. How about you?"

She did not look up, attempting instead to give off an indifferent air. The small room suddenly became overly warm, as she felt four eyes irradiating her with their attention. To respond was out of the question. She instead reached up with her free hand, grasped the hoodie's draw strings, and began to nonchalantly twirl them about a finger. This action, intended to convey a distracted mind, was actually undertaken with the purpose of slightly collapsing the hood over her face so as not to be seen.

Fortunately, the remainder of her evaluation progressed without further interruption. The two eventually departed, being replaced by three girls... none of whom paid her any notice as they set about registering their preferences.

Three quarters of the way through the list, she encountered a question regarding working in a bookstore. Because she wished nothing more than to be around books, she filled in the bubble corresponding to 'I have aspired to do this all my life.' When finally finished, she left the evaluation room displeased with herself for all that unnecessary angst.

When am I ever going to learn?! Always so much energy wasted on imagining the worst!

The prior occupants of the entry area were gone, replaced by the guy and girl from the evaluation room. They were busy pouring over pages of work-study options, though the guy stopped to eye her as before. She ignored him and handed over the scan sheet, which was promptly fed into a reader. After a short delay, a printer started to spit out page after page – eighteen by her count.

"Here are available work-study positions compatible with your preferences. Select the most interesting ones, and we'll use those to find the best position for you. Any questions?"

"Yes, sir. What if I select one that turns out... different than what I thought it would be?"

"You'll have two weeks to make a final decision. Your preferences are stored in this computer, so if you change your mind it'll be easy to regenerate a list of remaining positions."

She now faced a completely new problem – too many possibilities. Leafing through the pages, she noted that many were clerical, whereas a few involved lab work or being outdoors. She laughed to herself at how disappointed Mama would be that none read: 'attractive, self-confident, hoodie-less young woman needed for idolization by the next generation of Mississippians.'

Yet in the pile was the ideal position for her involving work around the very things she enjoyed most. She separated out that option, relegating the remainders to future work-study students. Mr. Tzichinski examined her selection, clicked some computer keys, and the job was done. The printer then spat out three copies of the same page – one for her file at the scholarship board, one for the work-study supervisor, and one for her. A date and time – Thursday at 4 PM – were displayed at the top, below which were the supervisor's name and location on campus.

She was still standing there, not knowing whether anything was lacking, when Mr. Tzichinski looked up.

"Do you understand where you're to go and when?"

"Yes, sir."

"Then you're done. Have a fine day."

She left the work-study office with a spring in her step. She was going to be a librarian's assistant – a dream job for someone who loved books. Despite her fears, the evaluation was a total success… and there had been no electrodes.

CHAPTER

7

PREDATORS AND PREY

.It being Friday afternoon, the grounds were packed with students basking in the radiance of college freedom. Enthusiasm was high, energy boundless, and time stretched on to infinity. Though August was at an end, Southerners knew that September would not cool off simply because the equinox was near at hand. The weather would effectively remain warm well into October, as the season was not revealed by the calendar, but in the combined effects of temperature and humidity. For most students, the splendor of this first weekend of the fall semester could not possibly be wasted on school.

She was moving along the main walkway of campus, sweating beneath her cream-colored hoodie. Having left her last class of the day – English – she was heading through the concourse on her way to the library. Clubs and associations of all kinds routinely set up booths here to inform the passerby of their activities. She got approached by numerous students handing out fliers, some distributed as advertisements and some as protests. Though the intrusions were unwelcome, the causes fascinated her. She had heard of 'Save the Whales' and 'Save the Planet,' but had no idea there were so many other things in need of saving. The inner city, the farmer, trees, animals, women, veterans, minorities, handicaps, countries, children, and souls… even the air and water needed saving.

She stopped briefly to watch an R&B dance routine being performed as a club's recruitment effort. Walking on, she passed small clusters gathered about guitar players, and circles of boys kicking around soccer balls and those little bean-filled bags. Blankets and towels staked out prime locations affording the dual benefits of comfort and exposure – of seeing and being seen.

The booths and displays eventually gave way… on the left to a three story building she had not yet been in, and on the right to a low brick wall. Beyond this lay a wide lawn spreading out toward the cluster of dorms that included Switson Hall. Students were scattered across this green expanse, sunbathing or playing. The air was filled with flying things – footballs and Frisbees. Other students were sitting along the wall, reading, conversing or just relaxing.

Some distance ahead, about a dozen guys occupied this wall for a distinct and obvious purpose – to eye the sunbathers on the lawn. Either by chance or strategic design, this group had chosen the prime location. As the afternoon waned, the shadows cast by the dorms on the opposite side slowly shrank the sunlit portion of the lawn, forcing the sunbathers to periodically shift their positions – directly toward these males. She immediately thought of lions waiting at a Serengeti waterhole, knowing that the prey would soon come their way. Just then, a skimpily clad female at the edge of a shadow got up and moved her blanket some twenty feet closer to where the lions lay in wait. All eyes diverted in her direction.

The newly formed shadowy territories were not wasted. Footballers and 'Frisbee-ers' moved in. These males adopted a different tactic with regard to the females. Objects were being *accidentally* thrown into the midst of the sunbathers, resulting in screams and giggles. The lions on the wall appeared displeased with the 'cheetahs' prowling amongst their prey. Smiling to herself, she imagined the scene in that moment when the sunlit lawn shrank to nothing, and the antelope were trapped between the two groups of predators. She, however, would be situated comfortably in the library, rewriting her notes.

Without warning, one of the pride suddenly sprang off the wall directly at her.

"Hey, beautiful! I know you. Aren't you in what's-his-face's intro-course."

He moved alongside as she walked, contorting himself about at the waist in an effort to capture her eyes around the hood's edge. Though she had much experience in dealing with taunts, the eagerness in this young lion's face was altogether different. It scared her. He was too close, and that proximity prevented her from converting clever thought into clever word. So she was left only with simply speeding up her walk, wishing very much for him to go away. After many silent strides, he reproached her in a last-ditch effort.

"Don't be rude, I'm just trying to… oh, forget it!"

She finally left him in her wake, though it took the remainder of the way to quiet her racing heart. She was so disappointed with herself for having not handled that situation better.

You know… an experienced female like Cameron would have told him to drop dead!

But what really bothered her was being considered prey. The lions and cheetahs stalked the sunbathers for obvious reasons.

They had virtually nothing on! But why target me? Surely he could see that my hoodie meant 'leave me alone!'

Just inside the library doors, she stopped to consider the building from a different perspective. Later in the semester, when prey would be driven indoors from lack of sunshine and threat of storms (weather or exams), the library would become the new watering hole. Where would the best hunting be? This was not purely an imaginative question, for she, feeling as vulnerable as a young gazelle, was in search of safety. Surely the lions and cheetahs would not exert much effort – they would prowl the lower levels. The upper floors should be more secure.

Making her way up three flights of stairs, she headed to a secluded section. A cluster of desks lined a windowed wall affording a panorama of the trees bordering that side of the library. She sat down at the most private spot and extracted class material from her backpack, focusing initially on the syllabus for Racquetball. It had only been the first week, but she felt confident that this class was going to be easy. There were two skill tests, one midsemester and one at the end. The only written exam was next month.

She took out the calendar that Mama had given her as a going-away present. It was beautifully made, opening side-to-side rather than top-to-bottom, making it more like a book and less like a wall hanging. For each month, the right side was the calendar and the left provided space for detailing tasks. She opened to September and began recording class information.

Certain dates were already specified as a feature of the calendar. The 2nd was Labor Day, the 21st a full moon, and the 23rd the first day of autumn. There was also a brief list of important historical events for the month. She noted that Francis Scott Key penned the words for the Star-Spangled Banner on the night of the 13th to 14th in 1814 while being held onboard the British warship HMS Tonnant anchored in Baltimore harbor. Also, Nazi Germany started WWII in Europe by invading Poland on September 1st, 1939… which reminded her of having read William Shirer's *The Rise and Fall of the Third Reich* when she was only fifteen. That book had overwhelmed her with mankind's immense potential for evil. Turning her eyes to another list, that of September birthdays, she noted William Faulkner, born September 25th, 1897 – in Mississippi, of course! She was suddenly ashamed for having skipped over the confusing parts in *The Sound and the Fury.*

After finishing the task of entering important class dates for the fall semester, she stowed all the syllabi in a back flap for future reference. Closing the calendar, she took a moment to enjoy its cover. The front, along with the back, was decorated in her namesake flower – the camellia. The images were not photographs, but in watercolor print style… sort of like something Monet might have painted.

She liked Mama's gift very much.

Suddenly, homesickness threatened to overwhelm her. She wondered what Mama was doing in that house with only the company of the ghost of Daddy… and now of her Camellia. A surge of regret flowed over her – for having left Mama all alone, for experiencing things Mama could not share in, and for arguing so much about going to college in the first place. With renewed determination to make her mother proud, she suppressed tears from her eyes and sadness from her heart, then proceeded to stow the calendar in her backpack. Stopping with it midway in, an unexpected thought came to her. She quickly opened the month of March. There on the 20th was a hand-written note filling the space allotted for that day.

'Happy 19th Birthday! I love you, Sweetie!'

She feasted on the message, intended for many months from now, and the tears began to flow. She had thought herself so strong and so independent, but had barely made it a week.

After regaining her composure, she commenced the intended task of rewriting that day's class notes. The calendar, though, was not put away, but instead propped up against the hutch and held opened to the month of March. The view provided by a small box was far better than anything the outside trees could provide.

It was dark when she exited the library. The campus grounds were not deserted, though the antelope, the lion pride, the cheetahs, and all the other participants of the afternoon safari were gone... being replaced by students with destinations on their minds. She took a secondary pathway leading to Switson. There was ample lighting such that she felt quite safe on this short walk to her dorm. Mama had made her promise to never be out past 9 PM, to only use routes scouted out in the daytime, and to make sure there were no obvious hiding places for 'boogiemen.' That was Mama's word for true predators.

Entering at five minutes shy of nine, she was not surprised to find the lobby overrun with students of both genders. Switson Hall maintained a nightly lobby curfew of 9 PM for males, though females were free to come and go as they pleased. Many guys were only just now collecting their girls from the dorm, while others were returning their dates... or just loitering about to enjoy the high density of feminine presence. Mrs. Riley roamed around doing her best to disperse the crowd, but like flocks of birds disturbed by a passerby, the student clusters would scatter as she approached, only to re-form after she had passed through. It also seemed to her that sunset had blurred the distinction between predator and prey. Many of the guys were making efforts to leave, though the girls were dissuading them, either covertly by starting fresh conversations or overtly with blatant acts of affection.

In passing through a flock in flux, someone suddenly grabbed her sleeve. Amber, in the process of reconstituting a group, found her presence to be useful.

"Camille, come over here... I want you to meet some of my friends."

Several introductions were then provided to demonstrate Amber's connections.

"This is Willie Jenkins, from Talladega, Alabama. Yes, Camille...

the race car place." No such question had been on her mind. "His daddy went to Garland and his daddy's daddy before him… Right, Willie?"

She glanced from Amber to Willie, who had jumped up from his seat like some jack-in-the-box anxious to shake her hand. She, however, maintained hers within the pockets of the hoodie, as her opinion of him had been forged by his choice to remain rooted on a couch during Mrs. Riley's recent dispersal effort. While nodding her head at each of Amber's friends, she kept track of Willie in the fringe of her vision as he edged closer.

Not another one! I've gotta get out of here!

So she abruptly excused herself and headed for 'the door.' Yet Willie, exhibiting superior dexterity and speed, arrived ahead of her.

"Amber says you're from Carlton. Do you know Judge Evans in Tylerville? That's just north of you in Comberton County. He's my uncle on my mother's side. Maybe you've heard of him – he's actually quite famous. He's the first to…"

"No, sorry."

She reached around him to swipe the magnetic access card that would unlock 'the door' and provide escape from this Willie.

Perhaps this persistent male adhered to a notion that compliments were the key to a young woman's heart, for he next flung out an offering.

"You know… you have really beautiful hair."

She instinctively stepped backward, even though forward through 'the door' was safety.

"What?!"

"It's really nice… the little I can see of it. It would be so much nicer without that hood…"

Leaning toward her, he most definitely expected her to respond by lowering her hood. Though accustomed to creeps being cruel, she was far less prepared for them being creepy.

"Excuse me please!"

And contrary to the norms of Southern decorum that would have her wait for compliance, she forcefully pushed past him. Stomping up a flight of stairs to her floor, the challenges of her life as the weaker sex were manifest once again. Though this Willie had not touched her, she nonetheless felt violated by his proximity… and equally insulted by his presumption of familiarity. She wanted to scream and curse out loud… though the sight of Cameron's door brought immediate restraint.

I'm so going to need help dealing with these college guys!

And as if adding variables in an equation: 'guys' + 'help' = 'Cameron,' she knew what to do. There was just something about the senior that conveyed trustworthiness. So after a brief hesitation, she knocked.

"Come in."

In entering, she did not venture far beyond the doorframe. There were two windows, as Amber had proclaimed, though the space was not that much larger than the standard dorm room. Aside from lacrosse gear piled in one corner and a ten-speed propped against a dresser, it could have belonged to any girl. Just as with Amber's mirror, Cameron's was rimmed with photos of teammates, friends and what looked to be family members.

The senior was lounging on the bed reading the campus newspaper.

"Hello. I'm Camille... in room..."

"Yeah, I know. Said hi to you about a dozen times already. What's up?"

She froze, as it was now abundantly clear that Cameron protected her privacy.

"I'm sorry to bother you... I was hoping..."

She could not keep from stalling again... so Cameron imposed a 'spit it out' look on her.

"I just... wanted to get your advice on something. Actually... about guys."

The senior instantly relaxed... even smiled... before discarding the newspaper and nodding toward the desk chair with a sort of 'at ease' gesture.

"Sorry, I thought you were here to complain about your roommate."

"Why would I do that? Amber's fine."

"Never mind. It's just part of being an RA. There's always someone who wants me to fix their problems. So... let's start over. How can I help you?"

Despite her initial boldness in asking, she was now struggling with how best to describe her 'problem' without going into detail. Diverting her eyes toward the lacrosse equipment, she spoke haltingly in order to check each word before it came out.

"I come from... a small town... and a pretty... guarded childhood. I never... associated with boys in high school. They... pretty much ignored me."

She turned now to Cameron, though still with less confidence than hoped for.

"I don't want to go into why. That's not important. I just ignored them too. My problem is that since coming here, boys have been... pestering me."

"Pestering you?! What do you mean?"

The confused look on Cameron's face just added to her discomfort. The thought suddenly occurred to her that a normal person... with normal social experiences... would not be in need of such help.

"I've had several situations where they've tried to... get close to me."

She had almost whispered the last four words, but they might as well have been shot from a cannon considering their impact on Cameron, who instantly fell back on the bed howling with laughter. Startled, and even more embarrassed, all she could do was sit rigid in the desk chair, waiting to discover the source of humor. After a short while, the senior made a determined effort toward control... though the remnants of chuckles only slowly faded.

"I'm sorry." Yet more giggles bubbled up as she silently mouthed out her four words. "No, really, I'm sorry. I mean it. That was just plain rude of me... but I couldn't help it. I'm not making fun of you. I just... certainly didn't see that coming! Girl... all I've got to say is, you're doubly ignorant, aren't you?" Before adding more, Cameron shifted with purpose to the edge of her bed and deepened her voice. "First of all, there ain't a girl on the hall who wouldn't kill for your looks."

"My looks?"

"Yeah. I don't know what you're used to back in... wherever..."

"Carlton."

"...but here, lots of girls are looking for husbands... and those perspective husbands are looking for beauty."

"What's that got to do with me?"

"You can't be serious?! One look at you the other day and I could tell the impact you'd have on guys. You've got such a pretty face... for a white girl... and a stunning figure for any kind of girl. There's not an ounce of flab on you. And on top of all that, your baby blond hair and those blue eyes... they're literally guy magnets. Not at all surprised you've been hit on. I'm sure there're lots of guys who'll want to get to know you, and get closer – real close."

She was in shellshock. The last thing in the world she wanted was to attract attention… and getting 'real close' was just plain nauseating. This talk with Cameron was not helping… only triggering a greater agitation in her… so much so that she suddenly felt herself shaking.

"Don't freak out! You should be complimented. Most girls probably envy you for your looks. Actually… it's not the guys you should be worrying about – it's the girls. Like I said, you're serious competition."

"I don't want to be competition… or a magnet… or anything like that! I just want to be left alone!"

"Most guys'll respect that… though there are plenty of creeps and morons out there."

"Then what do I do?!"

"You're just gonna have to get used to being beautiful. Even that hoodie can't hide it. My advice… be yourself. If this is who you are, then be that. Figure out how you wanna handle the attention and stick to it. Don't let anyone make you be something you don't want to be. But you know… even that's not enough."

"Meaning… what?"

"You need to understand who you really are – on the inside – and protect that. Know what I'm saying?"

"I think so. Thanks, Cameron. I really appreciate it."

As she rose to leave, the senior extended a hand to delay her.

"Mind if I ask you something?"

"Not at all."

"I don't mean to pry… I'm just curious. Why do you wear those hoodies all the time?"

From ingrained habit, she fixed upon Cameron her most impenetrable stare – a look that somehow made the senior lean away from her.

"It's a long story. Maybe some other time."

"Yeah… maybe some other time."

That conversation gave her much to consider. Entering her room, she found Amber seated glaring at the doorway, waiting for her to return. Her arms were folded tightly across her chest in the internationally recognized sign of female ire. Amber then stood and moved to within a foot of her before speaking.

"How can you possibly justify being so rude to my friends! I'm going out of my way to help you make something of yourself by introducing you to important people, and you embarrass me! That's the thanks I get?!"

Amber's voice quickly rose to a level such that the neighbors could surely hear. The door across the way opened, and a head poked through. All too well, she knew from being the brunt of much abuse in Carlton that certain people flocked to spectacle and strife, feeding off the disharmony in others. Being the focus of bottom feeders was nothing new to her.

"What're you talking about?! That idiot from Talladega?"

"Yes, Willie! And he's not an idiot! He comes from a very affluent family with considerable influence at this school. And where do you come from?! Nowhere!"

That word was punctuated by Amber's head thrusting forward so as to touch at the heart of who she was not – somebody of importance.

She could not bear this. Trembling, she turned away to her own desk, purposely staring at the schedule on the wall as Amber continued to rant on. Everything within was compelling her to flee the room. To run even farther. To leave Garland altogether. No college was worth this. To be forced among people who did not understand… and did not care to. She wanted to be with Mama at the kitchen table where it was safe.

Then, the thought of Mama became the thing that made the difference.

Amber had finished venting. In the resulting silence, she heard the door across the hall close. So she moved to shut theirs before facing her roommate. Mama's many examples of calm throughout her turbulent youth led to the gesture. She lowered the hood off her head before speaking. The significance was not lost on Amber, who noticeably relaxed her arms.

"I'm sorry I embarrassed you."

"Humph!"

"No, seriously… it wasn't my intension. Please believe me. I would never do anything to hurt you. But… he made me really uncomfortable. He blocked my way out of the lobby and asked me to take off my hoodie." Amber's brow rose a bit at this… before being pulled back down into her imposed scowl. She took the inadvertent facial response as progress. "Some may view his attention as a compliment, but not me. What he did was rude and very personal to me. I don't want to be around anyone like that." More 'humph,' but with much less conviction. "Amber… please… I don't want you to better me. I just want to be good roommates… and good friends. So please don't take this wrong, but I'd appreciate it if you didn't try introducing me to boys. Can you… please promise me that?"

Amber finally allowed her arms to fall, nodding in the process.

"I don't understand you at all. Sure… we've only known each other for a week, but I can truly say you're one of the loveliest girls here. And you insist on keeping it all hidden under a hoodie! Camille… I just know if you'd only show yourself off, you'd have more friends than you'd know what to do with. Why… the best boys at Garland would flock…"

"That's exactly why I wear a hoodie every day!" Though she had interrupted decisively, her voice now wavered. "I'm… just… not ready for boys."

"Why not?"

It was an impossible question to answer, one fit only for a shrug of the shoulders and an awkward severing of eye contact. After an uncomfortable moment, she moved to the bathroom on pretense. Now alone, she pulled the hood back onto her head, purposely avoiding the sight of herself in the mirror, then leaned over a sink and silently began to cry.

CHAPTER

8

BOXES

By far, separation from Mama was the worst part of college. Being deprived of her mother's support gnawed at her in unexpected ways – as if a void in her life could produce so much more discomfort than the presence of any outward affliction. As they could not afford phone service, mail was her only means of communicating. So she compensated with neatly written letters full of thought and feeling… hoping that the act of detailing every aspect of college life could somehow also dull her own pain.

Sitting at her desk, she was struggling with how best to describe to Mama the University's organizational structure… something she only recently learned for herself. But how to put it in a way that Mama, who had no concept of college, might find interesting? After much thinking, she settled on the imagery of a tree. Problem was, there were two ways of doing this. The regents and the president were the apex, so in one model, these would be the very top of the tree – the part bathed in sunlight. The lower branches, large and small… along with the trunk… were the faculty and staff who did the day-to-day things that kept the tree growing. Her model stopped there, as she was not sure what to do with the remainder of the tree. The student body as the roots did not make sense to her, as she felt that they were not part of the University at all. They were the customers… like the creatures on the forest floor living off of the tree.

No model of a university's structure that placed 'her Camellia' at the bottom, like a grub, would resonate with Mama. Of course, she was not so naïve as to believe that the mother's world revolved around the daughter… but there were times when Mama would say something absurd to that effect. ("Sweetie, you're the cream of the crop, the crowning achievement of Southern graces, and the very embodiment of all my hopes and dreams.") So she chose instead a tree model where the students were the leaves. Incoming freshmen were the green buds of spring. As their college careers progressed, the leaves would grow by soaking up the sun's energy and the tree's nutrients, broadening in experience and knowledge… thus providing evidence of the tree's vitality. The whole tree was there to support the leaves. Conceptually, this model was not anywhere consistent with how she felt about herself, but it should provide Mama with some imagery of hope.

She clung to a single inescapable truth – that there was one person on this planet who cared about her, and that person would do whatever it took to keep her off the path of despair. So it was important to her that Mama believe those efforts bore fruit. This alone was sufficient reason to fill every letter with optimism. Always focus on the positive. The food was great, the weather was great, the people were great. Everything was great. She would make sure Mama believed her daughter to be a happy and healthy leaf.

She *was* thankful. Thankful for a mother who loved her, for opportunities presented, and needs met. She was thankful, but lonely. There was no one with whom she felt close… from whom she could draw strength. Though of little conciliation, she intuitively knew that others here were in this same condition. In fact, many of the girls on the hall likely came from broken homes. They carried in themselves evidence of that brokenness, patched back together only by necessity. But she saw the cracks, apparent in their cynicism, hedonism, excessive competitiveness, and so terribly undisciplined lifestyles. Most were hiding their loneliness just as she was… only with different coverings.

And then there were the damaged ones with secrets needing to be survived. Cosmetics, jewelry and fashion did not fully conceal them, just as no hoodie could truly cover her. She knew what it was like to be one of those girls… and sometimes could recognize them because she knew herself, suspecting that they also knew her. Those girls were too painful to consider, because it meant considering the reality of herself.

Nobody wants to think about us.

With the letter to Mama completed, she headed down to the dorm's mailroom, it being located on the ground floor. In route, she passed a cleaning lady finishing with the lobby restroom. Looking back, she reproached herself for having not included that part of the university in her tree model. This woman, like the other custodians, cafeteria workers, grounds keepers and general laborers, did the jobs no one else wanted to do. They were at the bottom. To designate them as the roots might seem appropriate, but to do so glossed over how they were treated. They were the dirt.

This cleaning woman's outward distinction was in being black, which so often delineated the 'have' and 'have not' categories of the South. In actuality, it was being poor that placed her at the bottom. The poor cooked and cleaned, and did the things 'sensible' people were not meant to do. She understood, for she and Mama had done those jobs in Carlton for years.

But she also knew she was looking at that woman upside down. Some of the happiest and wisest people she knew of were at the bottom… like Old Joe at Fergie's Diner. He could sure make her laugh. To him, the hoodie was her small way of 'being black'… and he had often teased that there was still hope for her to go all the way. Old Joe had exposed her to Motown. He would say that his music possessed real soul – the kind that reached deep inside to touch the truest part of a person's being. Her favorites… because they happened to be his favorites… were the well-dressed, fast-moving, harmonizing groups like The Chi-Lites, The Spinners, and The Four Tops. She thought they displayed 'felt life' in every song… and it was so hilarious when Old Joe tried to imitate their moves over a greasy kitchen floor. He cooked other people's food, but she knew they had nothing on him.

Old Joe had died of a heart attack during the winter of her junior year in high school. She spent a week crying, and refused to ever work at the diner again. He was only fifty eight – not nearly old enough to have earned his nickname. Maybe he smoked too much, and drank too much… or maybe it was all the fat he inhaled six days a week. She often wondered, had he been granted access to the cultural and financial means bent toward proper healthcare, would Old Joe still be alive?

Mama took her to the funeral. There were hundreds of mourners, both black and white. The two groups paid their respects to Joe's family, but did not mix. It had always been an enigma to her that the most racially segregated place in the South was church. During the eulogy, she lowered the covering on her only black hoodie as a tribute to him, being ashamed that it was the best she could do.

Returning from her contemplations of Old Joe and the unnamed cleaning lady, she entered the mailroom hoping for a package to brighten her mood. Mama's preferred method was small boxes, typically of different sizes… anything she could get her hands on. One parcel had utilized an empty cereal box… the variety Mama ate when neither of them was in the mood to fry an egg. Most every box usually contained only a short note… as Mama was not an accomplished writer… along with one centerpiece item surrounded by odds and ends filling up the space. In her first week at Garland, an ill-timed summer downpour trapped her for twenty minutes under an awning in a no-man's land between class and dorm. After waiting for the sky to drain, she dispatched a letter to Mama requesting an umbrella. The next box from home contained a small retractable model, cushioned in an assortment of items seemingly collected at random – pencils, socks, Band Aids, a tube of antiseptic cream, and various feminine hygiene products. The note simply said 'Stay dry, Camellia! I love you, Mama.'

It was supremely ironic to her that a simple item such as an umbrella could so accurately reflect a student's persona on campus. Many varieties proclaimed allegiance to Garland State University with colors of purple and silver… along with silly cartoon images of the school mascot. Some models were sturdy, made to withstand just about anything Mother Nature could unleash, whereas others would be lucky to survive the first serious storm. Rich fraternity boys carried wide golfing umbrellas flaunting the names of their exclusive country clubs, while rich sorority girls seemed to have as many ornately patterned ones as they did shoes. On rainy days, she would sometimes stand before her closet and voice out a mocking imitation toward Amber: "Now which umbrella do y'all think best matches this blouse? Oh, not the jade paisley! Miss 'So-and-So' used the exact same one just yesterday. Remind me to donate it to Goodwill." They would then fall apart laughing while prancing about the room for a bit… before finally heading out into the rain.

A slip of paper in her mailbox indicated that a package waited for her behind the counter. While the attendant… a female work-study like herself… retrieved the item, she contemplated the one thing Mama never included in her boxes – food. It was not because Mama had a low opinion of her prowess in the kitchen. Like most Southerners, she swore by her mother's cooking, and would fight to the death any insult laid against it. Boxes and boxes of cookies, cakes, snacks… anything she wanted… would freely be sent if it were not for one thing – roaches! Mama was both terrified and enraged by those insects. To her, they were living proof that God was still judging the South. As a child, she remembered her mother reading in Sunday school about Moses and the plagues on Egypt, and how Mama replaced 'locust' with 'roaches.' She spent years in the mistaken belief that those insects were a sign of Biblical judgment… at least until, as a teenager, she read through the entire book without finding one reference to a roach.

Mama would never risk sending her daughter a box containing anything that might attract those creatures. Maybe she envisioned a package merrily being opened only to have the world's evils stream out in roach-form – the Southern version of Pandora's box. So sending packages was one area in which Mama was quite extravagant. Tape was not a resource to be skimped on. Every seam and every corner was layered over. Then the box was covered in brown paper from a grocery bag, addressed, and coated with even more transparent tape. No roach could ever find its way into a Mama-packed box.

The excessive taping effort was unnecessary, though it greatly amused her. Being at college had presented plenty of opportunities for 'quality time' with roaches. The two most common on the Garland campus were the American cockroach, which was big, black and could fly, and the smaller brown German cockroach. The big ones were not too much trouble as they *mostly* stayed outside… though that variety did display a kamikaze tendency for running directly at a person. If, while crossing campus, she happened to hear a random 'girly' scream (uttered by either gender), it was a good bet that it resulted from an American cockroach encounter. However, the German variety was far worse. They lived indoors.

The first tips she received for dorm life were: lock your door, hoard toilet paper, never loan clothes, and always have a handy assortment of roach killing tools. Her hall maintained a healthy barter system, with commonly traded items being 'roach-inators': swatters, traps, sprays and poisons. And there was always that one true warrior who was called upon to fumble around under furniture… or root through a darkened closet… or explore a vanity cabinet, all to rescue a damsel in distress. On the hall, that person was her… though it was not what she had envisioned in selecting the persona of the Roman Warrior Queen. She was not an especially brave person, having her own share of little phobias (*Yikes – spiders and clowns! Ick!*), but roaches were no big deal. She actually took pleasure in hunting them down and exterminating them.

Sad to say, she had bad news for Mama – roaches did not need her cooking to survive. They could live off of anything! She was once awoken in the middle of the night to the sound of munching, only to find a huge roach feasting on a dried corsage from one of Amber's sorority events. She did not wake her roommate… nor did she attempt to kill the roach. Addressing it directly, she whispered out a message.

"A man's got to do what a man's got to do, so bon appetite. But if I see you in the morning, you're dead."

When she awoke, the insect was gone… as was a sizeable portion of Amber's memento.

The mailroom attendant came back with the package from Mama. The only way into a Mama-packed box was with a blade, and she owned just the thing – a multi-purpose Swiss Army knife. It was one of her few prized possessions – Mama's present on her 14th birthday. She immediately brandished this and started attacking the wrapping. In the process, she noticed the most unpleasant expression smeared across the attendant's face, who was so visibly appalled by the savagery with which she slashed and hacked.

Southern women were supposed to exhibit 'grace' at all times, but that word had always rankled her… for she considered it the most abused descriptor in the history of the South. It was meant to convey a core value instilled by proper breeding… that is, the attitudes and behaviors outwardly manifested in the lady-like traits of sweetness, hospitality, refinement, etiquette, and respect, all flowing from inward disciplines of humility, sympathy, patience, and – above all – self-control. A Southern woman without grace was nothing more than a hick. Yet she knew of many a Southern woman who portrayed this trait outwardly without any trace of it being present on the inside.

It was clear to the mailroom attendant that here stood a graceless sort. She did not care. Had not cared for years. It was not the hoodie or the social stigma she carried about Carlton that had fostered this mentality. It was her way of coping. A well-timed, wide-bore yawn was a very valuable tool… especially if accompanied by sound effects. She maintained other useful displays of gracelessness: slouching, hands-in-pockets, mumbling, avoiding eye contact, and grumpiness… though not 'pouting,' which could easily be pulled off in a very cute Southern-belle sort of way. As a teenager, she experimented with many graceless tendencies, selecting those that procured for her the social separation she desired without actually leading to any serious character deficiencies. This attitude was her box, fully taped over, protecting her from those she considered incapable of showing true grace.

She, with knife in hand, was in the process of sending the mailroom attendant a subtle message: 'I want you to not want me as a friend.' She did not have to resort to wearing camo, going barefoot, or getting a revolting tattoo. She knew how to keep Southern belles away.

Now, if I can only figure out how to do the same thing with the guys!

CHAPTER

9

I DO NOT KNOW

The demands of college soon shifted loneliness into a back corner of her mind. Keeping up with coursework became the imperative. Chemistry and Calculus were the most intense, as every period the professors filled multiple whiteboards in rapid-fire progression through their material. Her Chemistry Lab was tiring, though strangely reminiscent of cooking with Mama. ("Follow the recipe, Camellia… and everything'll turn out right.") There had been challenging quizzes in all of her classes, though the one in History on the Fertile Crescent was so easy. This was the most well-trampled region on the earth, but also equally well trod upon in every world history book she had ever opened. In particular, she remembered Mama having once brought home a colorful account of the pharaohs' fruitless attempts at immortality through the building of pyramids. The only aspect of the History quiz that actually unnerved her was the 'very nicely done' penned beneath her perfect score.

Of all her courses, Honors English was the most unusual. With only a dozen students, it met in a standard classroom rather than a large lecture hall. The instructor, Ms. Kelley, was her favorite. Ms. Kelley arranged the desks in a circle so the class could face each other. A typical session started with a brief description of a literary technique, such as analogy, simile or motif, followed by Ms. Kelley leading a discussion on a random topic. The subject was allowed to bounce about, but if the class lapsed into silence, then the student nearest Ms. Kelley got poked.

"What do you think, Miss Larson? Are women's fashions becoming too similar to those of men's?"

"I only wear what feels comfortable." Which she knew to be true and untrue at the same time.

A classmate then just had to pipe up.

"Is that why you always wear hoodies?"

"I wear hoodies because it is my personal choice to wear hoodies."

As such conversations progressed, Ms. Kelley would set a timer. When it went off, no matter what was being discussed, everyone stopped, took out their journals, and began writing on that topic employing the literary subject of the day. It was Ms. Kelley's way of promoting new thought while also forcing the class to write intelligently about a wide variety of subjects.

She delighted in this approach. It did not matter what the topic was – it was stimulating Ms. Kelley's way. Journals were collected on Fridays, then returned on Mondays. Ms. Kelley did not grade the entries. Instead, she made corrections and pointed out flaws in concept development. Grades would come in the latter part of the semester, she said, but for now it was important to get a feel for the class's writing.

On one occasion, the timer went off during a discussion of a popular TV show, and she was the only person who knew nothing of it. Ms. Kelley instructed her to write about how it felt being left out of something that everyone else had experienced. This was easy, as she had lived it for years. She wrote six journal pages about the things people missed out on because they were absorbed with television.

In that essay, she described sunsets reflecting off the river's wind-rippled surface, the little echoing sounds of insects at night, the struggles of a plant growing up within the crack of a sidewalk, and playing 'pick-up-sticks' with fallen pine needles. She wrote about timing the period between lightning and thunder to see how far off a strike was, about chasing leaves riding the rapids of a rain-drenched gutter along First Street, and about exploring the complexities of erosion patterns cut into red-clay hillsides. She had once followed a bumble bee all over Carlton just to see how far off it would take her... but ended up instead sitting on the curb outside of Fergie's Diner counting passing cars – with those going left as 'plus one' and those going right as 'minus one' – just to see how random the road traffic really was. But mostly, she wrote about listening to stories from Mama's youth. Her journal came back the following Monday with a single word scrawled across the top of that essay – 'refreshing.'

The eighth meeting of this class ended up posing the first truly challenging moment for her at college. The timer sounded while a female classmate was discussing love and marriage. Instructions were given for them to write about the love in their parent's relationship, their personal aspirations for love, or love in general. The class got right to it, with some males besting the females at depositing text. She, however, was stymied. Her essay could not possibly be about her parents – there was no love there to describe. But she also had no idea of what to write on her own behalf. She could not see herself as being suitable relationship material for anyone, irrespective of what Mama… or Amber… or Cameron, might say to the contrary. And she certainly was not going to explain why.

One by one, classmates found something to focus on while she sat transfixed upon a blank page. To mask her inactivity, she leaned forward, allowing the hoodie to fall about her face. Though pencil touched paper, completing a circuit from the mind to the journal, no thoughts flowed and no meaningful words were produced. In the end, she managed only a single line, complete as a sentence and more revealing than intended.

'I do not know.'

When the period ended, she quickly handed over her journal and fled before being noticed by Ms. Kelley. Somehow… she just knew that she was about to spend her loneliest weekend at Garland, for it deeply disturbed her that she could not formulate a single opinion on such a simple concept as love. True… it carried with it much personal baggage… especially in relation to her parents. Yet try as she might, it was just not possible to envision what it would be like to love someone… *other than Mama, of course*… and the thought of declaring such feelings was equally incomprehensible. It was difficult enough understanding love as a thought piece – a mental puzzle to be sorted, assembled, examined, and then stowed back away. Come Monday, she was absolutely certain that her journal would return with the essay marked 'incomplete'… though a more accurate judgment would be 'failed.'

Late summers in the South can go from sunny to stormy with little forewarning. This was hurricane season. Every Gulf coast resident from Brownsville to Key West had their eyes peeled on the news for any report of an Atlantic low pressure center. Hurricanes were not a subject to be joked about, especially to those who had lived through one. She happened to share her name with the most powerful and deadly storm to have hit the state in recorded history. Hurricane 'Camille' was category five when it slammed into Mississippi just before midnight on August 17th, 1969. It flattened the entire coastline up to a quarter mile inland, picking it clean of all trees and structures, before moving on to damage or destroy nearly everything from the coast to the heart of the state and beyond. Over 130 people had died in Mississippi alone, with the death toll exceeding 250 before the storm found its way out into the Atlantic four days later. Many believe 'Camille' to be the very reason why Mississippi was regarded as the most backward state in the South.

That hurricane obviously occurred long before the person 'Camellia Jay Larson' was born... even before her daddy had moved to the state. Most people her age did not associate the name 'Camille' with the storm, but folks Mama's age did. To Mama, as a teenager in high school, the three days of August 17th to 19th in 1969 were the most terrifying of her life. The approach of the storm, the landfall, and the subsequent flooding were a continuous nightmare of wind and rain. Mama said the term 'wind' did not do justice to it at all. By some estimates, sustained speeds of 200 mph were reached prior to landfall, followed by endless hours of roaring noise and projectiles flying about at deadly speeds. Pebbles became bullets, twigs were spears, and nothing, but nothing, could be nailed down well enough. Mama said even rain drops moved so fast they could hurt. The very air was made of water.

Most people Mama knew suffered great loss. Her family had survived, but lost that year's plantings... lost their fruit stand, their orchard and their entire house. The storm was long gone in a week, though its effects lasted decades in the lives of its survivors. Hurricane Camille destroyed so many dreams, yet it also made Mississippians incredibly resilient. According to Mama, there was no one in this country tougher than a person who had survived Hurricane Camille... which was probably why her name change had offended Mama so deeply.

That hurricane had nothing to do with why she changed her name – something her mother never quite accepted. To Mama, it was her daughter's way of getting even with Mississippi for betraying Daddy… with Carlton for how it had treated her family… but mostly with Daddy for what he had done.

This fall of 2002 was exhibiting a few tropical storms and weak hurricanes that only made minor impacts on the Gulf coast. Tropical storm Hannah approached the panhandle of Florida on Saturday, September 14th. That was the weekend of her post-essay gloom… a somberness compounded by the grief of a nation pausing to reflect on the anniversary of the 9-11 terrorist attacks.

She spent her first stormy Saturday afternoon at Garland sprawled out in one of the dorm's lobby alcoves. Rain splattered the windows and wind tossed tree limbs about, but there was no enjoyment in it for her. Not the way she had envisioned on that first day. This day, she sat with her head against the glass watching drops flow down, being replaced by more drops in an endless procession of fluid sadness. She did not contribute tears – only emptiness. The rain, in its soft, irregular wind-swept voice, was unable to provide any better answers to the question of love than her 'I do not know.'

The following week, Hurricane Isidore would pound the Yucatan. Though it would initially make Mississippians nervous as it turned northward, it weakened to a tropical storm before approaching the Louisiana coast on the 26th. The next week, Hurricane Lili would hit Louisiana on October 2nd as a category four storm. Fortunately, landfall rapidly degraded it, with far less damage occurring than expected. Mississippians were silently thankful for the state of Louisiana during hurricane season. It was like having a big brother who took punches for you.

Yet life along the Gulf coast always moved on. More hurricanes were sure to come, but the South could withstand the worst thrown at it.

On her own for the first time, she was being confronted with her own personal storms regarding who she was and where she was going in life… and equally weighty, to what extent the past complicated her finding answers. And like rain to the landscape, this introspection was moisture to her mind and heart. As raindrops continued to pelt her alcove window, a new thought came… one she was immediately ashamed of for having taken so long to see. Though she honestly knew little about the hurricane prior to the name change, that was not what Mama must have believed. To Mama, adoption of the name 'Camille' was a way of getting back at her personally… for surely Mama must have felt in her heart that she was responsible for Daddy's actions.

It's true… Mama should have known. She should have anticipated the dangers. There were things she could have done to protect me.

Yet she no longer held those things against Mama. They had both suffered far too much together. But it should have mattered to her what Mama thought. She had repeatedly asserted to Mama that the new name represented a new start… yet not for her mother. To Mama, it was a daily reminder of that terrible hurricane of 69, which… after doing decades worth of damage to Mississippi… was somehow reborn in 96 to do decades of damage to her most precious Camellia. 'Camille' was a brand of shame upon Mama – a terribly apt judgment for having failed to protect the flower from the storm.

Her next English class was Monday afternoon. She did not know it at that time, but it was the turning point in her life. As the journals were handed back, she sat reluctant to receive hers, believing that within lay the first failing mark of her brief college experience. She opened the cover, found the page, and the message brought her instant relief. Ms. Kelley, in her typically thoughtful hand, wrote only a single line. Below the 'I do not know,' was penned 'Camille, that is why we learn.' It suddenly seemed as if one had crossed out the other. That doubt and despair were no match for hope and perseverance. Here was a reason to push on… to plan… to overcome… and it was so 'Mama,' as if the journal had been driven to Carlton for grading.

Tears swelled in her eyes as she glanced toward Ms. Kelley… who was still in the process of returning journals. A barely perceptible smile was the 'you are welcome' response from the instructor to the tearful student's inaudible 'thank you, so very much.'

CHAPTER
10

I'LL BE THERE

Lying in bed that night while contemplating Ms. Kelley's encouragement to learn about love, she was struggling to develop a plan. Of course, it was preposterous to presume that Garland State University offered a course on the subject... or that reference material in the library would be of any practical use. So she began to boil the problem down and get at its essence. It all started with boys.

This is going to be much more difficult than I imagined.

Still, the raindrops-coursing-down-a-window-pane mood was long gone. Her mind was in gear, and the engine was revving... But where to go?

Don't scientists study specimens in order to learn?

And since she very much wanted to be no more than a scientist on the subject of love, then a specimen was needed. Yet the sudden thought of studying Willie Jenkins from Talladega made her gag.

The weeks since coming to Garland had reinforced her earlier supposition that guys were... as Cameron had put it... either creeps or morons... or both. She would have liked to write Mama and say that a new species of male had been discovered – a third category that was wonderful. But it would take a miracle to find such a person here, and she was not a believer in miracles. In her experience, guys were only really interested in three things: sports, sex and alcohol… and not necessarily in that order.

Of course, her mother had tried to prepare her for the alcohol aspect of college life. That summer, Mama had played out an illustration that started with her placing an orange on the kitchen table.

"See that? Looks pretty good, doesn't it? Nice and shiny, with perfect color and texture. But Camellia, when it comes to fruit, there's just no telling what's inside based on the peel. Now, when it's gone completely bad, everybody knows it. There's mold on the outside… with insects and a smell rising to high heaven. But when it's fresh off the tree – like this one here – you can't know by looking at it. Some's full of juice with no sweetness, some's dry and fibrous, and some's got so many seeds there's absolutely no joy in the eating. Camellia, you stare as hard as you please but you'll never know the taste on the inside… even with those good seeing eyes of yours."

Mama paused then to give her the chance of boring a visual tap hole in the side of the orange and imagining herself sucking out its essence.

"Problem is – people are just like that orange. You can't see what's in a person's heart… no matter how hard you try… or no matter how smart you are… or even how much they tell you what's there. Even you don't fully know what's in there… unless it's opened by very skillful hands."

With an arm outstretched across the table, Mama pointed directly at her chest… but then scooped up the orange and began slowly removing the peel. Somehow, she had known that her daughter being captivated by the process would help bring back the words later.

"The thing I'm trying to tell you is this – people are good at hiding what's on the inside. Hiding it from others and hiding it from themselves. But drinking… it has a way of ripping the peeling right off a person. In so doing… it doesn't just reveal what's on the inside – it damages it. The drunk just can't peel right… that's the sad part. Once the peel gets ripped off, you see them for who they really are. Drinking reveals the bitter, the vile, the vulgar, the angry, the violent, the sad, the foolish, the… ahh… I'm sure there's more to that list… but you get the idea."

Mama momentarily halted the peeling activity in order to extend a hand over to her forearm.

"Camellia… I know this is difficult for you to hear… and I know you know it more than most. Drink makes a person lose control."

She patted gently a few times, then returned to her task.

"Thank the Lord for the peel. Imagine the world we'd be in without it."

Off came the final piece, revealing the fully exposed fruit. She then sensed that Mama, in examining the bare orange, was wrestling with a small bit of regret in completing the job… almost as if her illustration might somehow be spoiled by the fruit's sourness. Nevertheless, Mama isolated a single wedge and slid it into her mouth.

She was immensely relieved to see a smile widen on Mama's face.

"Mmm, mmm – gooder'n grits! Sweet and smooth and perfect… just like you, Camellia."

They both laughed… but she did not miss that Mama's hand came to her mouth in removing a seed or two. She must have blanched at that sight… having momentarily contemplated what hardness might reside within her own heart and the unbearable thought of being peeled to find out… for Mama responded instantly.

"Let's renew our pact from years ago, you and me, not to ever talk about your daddy unless we're sitting right here at this table. The rest of life will be free of him, but in this place… we can be open and honest about him. Agreed?"

"Yes, Mama. Agreed."

Still lying in her dorm bed reflecting on Mama's story of the peeling, She had finally reached a decision regarding Ms. Kelley's admonition to learn. She was surely not looking for love… and definitely not a relationship! In fact, it was a bit repugnant to think about how girls on the hall categorized guys in terms of 'husband material.' But she was lonely, and one thing she never had was a guy her own age as a friend.

What's it like to get to know a guy who's worth getting to know? How do I see on the inside well enough to choose? And what risks do I have to take in finding out?

It was certainly going to be a challenge finding a worthy male.

This is a 'Willie's world,' but where are the true men?

After nearly four weeks, dozens of letters there and many boxes back, she finally heard directly from Mama. It was ridiculous in this era of telecommunications that her mother refused to own a cell phone. She had had enough. So she purchased two small pre-paid models, and requested in a letter that Mama call one of the numbers. It was a Tuesday afternoon when her phone rang just before Chemistry Lab. She answered hoping for Mama, and received her wish.

"Hello, Sweetie… I just got your letter today."

"That's great, Mama. Guess what – I'm coming…"

"Case you're wondering, I'm calling on Mr. Ferguson's office phone. He's such a dear. We're having a good ol' time reminiscing and talking about all sorts of things. Like when…"

"I'm sorry, Mama, but I need to make this quick… or I'm going to be late for class. I'm coming home this weekend. I've got it all arranged. I know a girl who'll give me a ride both ways. I'll be there…"

"That's wonderful! You've made a new friend!"

She did not bother to explain that she had pulled a tab off a bulletin board posting. The driver, an upperclassman in her dorm, was expecting gas money for the distance there and back.

"Umm… I just wanted you to call me so you could see how easy it is to chat on the phone. I love you, Mama! See you this Friday around suppertime."

"I love you too, Sweetie."

The week dragged on. Nothing mattered compared to catching that ride to Mama.

CHAPTER

11

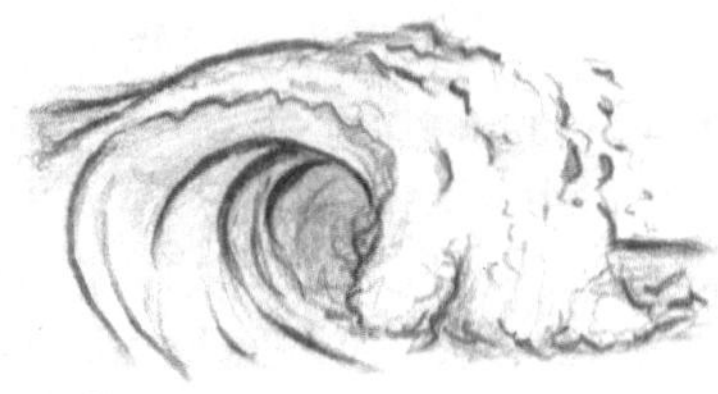

COUNTRY MEMORY LANE

As per plan, she was to be waiting in the dorm lobby at 3 PM. Her driver, a Brandi Spencer, had made it clear that if she was not there on time, then she would be left behind. Finishing with classes at two, she had an hour to cross campus, collect her belongings, and get down to the lobby. She was there with twenty minutes to spare. The time moved up to three, and no Brandi. At fifteen after, she was convinced she had misunderstood… and her ride was gone. But at half past, Brandi came through 'the door' carrying an overnight bag in one hand and pulling a roller with the other... whereas she had only a backpack. No apology was offered, only a 'let's go' delivered in a brusque tone akin to 'don't make me wait.' So without delay, she followed in behind to the dorm parking lot.

"Just don't stand there – get in!"

Her vehicle was one of those mega utility trucks with extra cabin space behind the driver. This, she learned later, was not Brandi's, but her daddy's.

"Buckle up..." She already had. "...and don't touch stuff."

Hardly another word was spoken after that, as she was quite certain that her driver desired nothing from her in the way of conversation. Her seat was set too high, but she resisted an urge to make adjustments for fear of being snapped at. The radio was tuned to a hip-hop station and they took off. The next two and a half hours, she was sure, were going to be so very uncomfortable.

With her head pressed against the passenger side window, she began to watch the South roll by as they moved out of Garland and into open country. This sort of drive might be considered as boring by most, but to her it was like sitting on the beach watching a wave approach, crash onto the shore, and then flow back out… to be repeated over and over again. She had been to the Gulf several times as a child. In her memory, it was a place of power and simplicity… mesmerizing in its repetitiveness. Each wave was unique, though also the same as countless others before and after it. Driving along small state or county roads in the deep South had that same feel. Imagination began to crystallize, pushing Brandi out of her thoughts.

With the ocean, if you're quick enough, you can catch a glimpse of the calm between the waves.

It was, in her mind, like a snapshot of what the sea might look like without weather or the gravitational influences of moon and sun. In the Southern countryside, she likened that glimpse of calm to the miles and miles of pine forests, so vast that they seemed to run on forever. She envisioned 'tree-top' sailors navigating a sea of green, straining to see beyond the horizon with a longing to know where the forests ran out and 'land' might be spotted.

Yet just as it was not possible for the sea to avoid the wind or the pull of heavenly bodies, she knew that it was not possible for the countryside to escape the influence of man. Oceans of pines were interrupted by large tracks of farmland tilled for corn, soybean or cotton. It was late September, and the corn was now being harvested. Regions stood pristine while others were being shredded to yield their crop. In her mind, that harvesting machinery was not unlike trawlers raking their dragnets through schools of fish. In contrast, the cotton fields lay forlorn with only speckles of white remaining from their glorious form of summer. Those struck her as great barren stretches of sea bottom, seemingly devoid of life. Other fields were occupied by herds of cattle, which brought thoughts of whales. A line of bramble cutting through one such pasture marked the path of a hidden drainage ditch, like a current moving through the deep. In this were multitudes of birds flittering in and out of thickets, not unlike small fish darting amongst coral.

Her gaze then momentarily rose above the fields – to cumulonimbus clouds towering on the horizon. The farmer and the sailor were at the mercy of nature's fickle tendencies, so both needed to be alert for storms.

The ocean and the Southern countryside might teem with life, yet both were also strewn with the wreckage of lives long since extinguished. Tumbled down shacks, derelict barns, and overgrown fields all too frequently told a story of hard times, bad luck and poor decisions… like hidden reefs that had claimed the lives of many a seafarer. They passed a lone chimney rising up from a tangle of kudzu, all that remained of a regal Southern manor destroyed by a careless moment with fire. Though the house was gone, the brickwork stood as a sad reminder… like the mast of a once great ship protruding above the surf, the hull lying in ruin beneath.

Of course, there were many functioning farms, but their yards were often scattered with rusted-out vehicles. Like ships that could no longer hold out the sea, they had been pulled up onto the shore to await Nature's most powerful force – decay – to remove them from memory. She wondered if, in a small way, those derelicts were allowed to remain… to be prominently displayed… because they represented something. That someone had come, had a dream, and pursued it with all their vigor… but were now gone. The ruins echoed their voices over time. 'We were here, we existed, we were the South – remember us!'

She would have liked to believe it possible, but knew that no one really cared.

Now the wave was forming… building momentum to make its distinctive approach to shore. No doubt her driver had made note of road signs foretelling the approach to 'this-ville' or 'that-junction'… though she personally had seen other indications. The forests were more sparse and fields more prevalent. The regularity of farmsteads had also increased. Some of these where actually not farms at all – just country folk who liked their privacy, yet still wanted to live near town. Like vessels meant for short voyages, they could sample the open sea without straying far from port.

Then, as a hint of white foam, came the first indication of a breaker forming. A welcome sign appeared, built of red brick and accessorized with flowers. A tall tower prominently displayed the town's name, doing double duty in supplying water pressure and an identity. Next was a large church set back on a wide lawn, it bearing an electronic sign that proclaimed 'First Baptist.' There was a new car dealership, its balloons bobbing above each vehicle like so many multicolored jelly fish. A modern gas station complex offered fuel and food in a hurry... which contrasted sharply in her mind to the lonely atolls that were the single pump stations out in the 'sticks.'

She then saw a sign proclaiming allegiance to the high school football team. Distant stadium lights warming up in the late afternoon foretold of a home game that night. Like a lighthouse's strobe, their glare was a warning of dangers lying ahead for the visiting team.

The wave was still building as they passed along parallel lines of colonial mansions and antebellum-style homes. Some had seen better days, but many were being restored to the glories of Southern ages long past. Ornate iron fences, wide porches, tall columns and cobblestone walkways lined with pruned rose bushes and azaleas – all brought back thoughts of lemonade... and gentle breezes... and cicadas chirping high up in the pines... with nothing to do other than rock on swings and thank the Lord for the South.

A grass-filled meridian formed with the appearance of the first mansion, providing a graceful separation from the oncoming traffic. Though this space belonged to no one, someone had invested considerable effort in its upkeep and beautification. There were flower beds... and benches... and walkways cutting across that connected heaven-on-the-right with heaven-on-the-left.

The wave was almost at its peak. And then there it was – town square, the crowning glory of the South. This was the very center of the community, where festivals and holidays were commemorated. She knew that somewhere a committee would soon be meeting to discuss the Christmas decoration theme for that year.

Traffic slowed considerably as the road wrapped about the square. She hazarded a glance over at her driver, who was clearly put out at being denied a straight shot through this nothing in the middle of nowhere.

"What the hell are you looking at?!"

"Sorry... nothing."

Momentarily lost in her embarrassment, she missed out on seeing some of the shops and diners that rimmed this town center. But in turning back to her window, she barely noticed in time the war memorials situated about City Hall... like cannons guarding the deck of a fleet's flagship.

They had reached the other side, and she sensed that her driver was already searching for the open sea... but they were not there. Not yet. The wave... so beautiful... so powerful... so majestic, came crashing down on the shore just as Brandi's truck lumbered over three sets of parallel railroad tracks. The scenery instantly changed. The beach was now strewn with debris washed up by the wave. There was driftwood, dead sea life, broken shells, dislodged seaweed, and the discards from generations of sailors. They cruised past an abandoned and boarded up textile mill, once the economic heart of the town. Tracks running up to this mill were rusted over from decades of disuse. Marooned box cars got anchored where they had been left when the mill closed down. Their surfaces, like those of the surrounding buildings, were covered with so much graffiti that the company's name, once prominently stenciled for all to see, was now completely obscured. It was as if barnacles, growing in layer upon layer, had coated over this abandoned and decaying pier.

Of course, everybody knew that rail lines bifurcated nearly every Southern town. Houses on this side of the tracks were small, cheaply built and poorly maintained – not the kind of neighborhood the driver wanted to be in, so the truck got sped up to 10 mph over the limit. Her driver saw the worst, but she found the best even here. As the wave receded, it also washed clean the shore. Tidal pools teemed with life, able to exist... even content to do so... with nominal connections to the greater sea. People on front porches were fanning themselves and talking with neighbors, as children played on bikes or threw basketballs into portable hoops. There were also many small shops doing brisk business, like secluded taverns in ports of call. Though their shabby parking lots were filled with junkers... nothing compared to the size and power of this truck she rode in... out there were fine old gentlemen in vintage Cadillacs and classic pickups true to the name. As Hemingway might have put it – tiny fishing boats with their 'old salts of the sea.'

They then passed a small church, so different from the mega-church on the other side of town. It looked about ready to fall apart and equally in bad need of a paint job, yet was doing its best to offer what it had to anyone sailing by. Its parking lot was half-gravel and half-grass... an unpleasant-looking rock-strewn beach... but it was packed with cars on this Friday afternoon. Maybe a football prayer-and-pep rally.

The speed limit increased and the landscape began to open up. They passed several antique shops, rich in Southern essence. She was reminded once more of the tidal pools, and how much fun they would be to explore. One last diner with its signage a battleground between Coke and Pepsi… and then the Southern countryside. The open seas! The wave had receded back to where it began, and she was so looking forward to the whole cycle starting all over again.

"Where to?"

The approach to Carlton brought her out of her musings and into the anticipation of seeing Mama. She gave directions… and as they pulled in front of her house, Brandi made no effort to hide her disdain.

"You've got to be kidding me! *This*… is where you live?!"

Having paid up front, not another word was offered. She got out and watched as the truck did a quick U-turn… then Brandi was gone.

Just moments before, she had been set to dash inside, but Brandi's disparaging comment now held her hostage at curbside, forcing her to reconsider her childhood home from an unwelcomed perspective.

The yard was overgrown – a neglect very much unlike Mama. Four warped wooden steps ran up to a porch. She suddenly remembered flying up and down those as a small child to show Mama treasures of nature she had found in the yard. Many an evening had been spent there waiting for Daddy to come home from the sawmill. Their porch spanned the width of the house in typical Southern style, with a post-and-rail network defining its borders. She recalled that it once had been outfitted with swings and rocking chairs, and its beams and pillars adorned by streamers, chimes, hanging plants and the flag.

All now was barren.

The front porch is the 'hug' on any Southern home… or so said Mama… but a long time had passed since this porch last properly hugged anyone.

She lifted her eyes to the second floor windows that were Mama's and a spare room. The view brought back a long ago memory – of coming home from grade school and seeing the curtains gently streaming outward as a breeze flowed through. Their flapping motion was the house greeting her, foretelling of Mama's hugs… and questions about the school day… and a plate of freshly baked cookies on the kitchen table. Those windows were now closed off. Her eyes went to the siding. It had not been repainted in her recollection, though Mama said Daddy once took on the whole house by himself, finishing it in a week. She lowered her head and decided that remembering was a foolish way to start this visit.

She recognized the light eking through the front windows as emanating from the kitchen in the back. Moving around the house along the red dirt driveway, she purposely averted her eyes from seeing into the backyard. Climbing the rear steps, she experienced an unexpected moment of pause.

Does one knock before entering a childhood home that's been left for another life?

She was spared the quandary by Mama, who just then swung open the back door. Mama must have been waiting, knowing that she would soon come through as promised. There they hugged – mother in and daughter out. The symbolism was not lost on her. But then she was promptly dragged over the threshold and the door closed behind. It was Mama and 'Camellia' all over again, as the hoodie was discarded onto the counter. On and on, they just laughed and cried together.

"Oh, Mama… I've missed you so much! I can't believe it's been four weeks since seeing you. Never thought I'd make it a day!"

"My little girl's all grown up. I'm so proud of you and your accomplishments. It just busts me up inside – in a good way, mind you. Come, sit. You need feeding up, I can see that, nothing to eat but cafeteria food."

Mama plopped her down and set a plate of store-bought cookies before her. She thought that a bit odd.

Not homemade?

As a matter of fact, Mama knew she was arriving at suppertime, yet nothing was on the stove.

"That oughta hold you. Shall I make fried chicken with all the fixins?"

That was Southern food code for corn bread, collard greens, mashed potatoes, and to top it off – peach pie. Frying was as Southern as sautéing was French. Not that the latter would ever get excited about the former… or vice versa, for that matter. By most non-Southern standards, take away fried chicken and nothing much of value would be left over in the region's cuisine. Yet to Southerners, just about anything that trots, waddles, flies, swims, or grows in the ground can be battered and fried to a golden state of ecstasy. She had never tried it, but once heard about a restaurant in New Orleans that had perfected fried ice cream. Still… to her, anything cooked by Mama meant home… and at last, she was home.

"Mama… that's way too much effort!"

"Nonsense, Child. Done the same and more every day of your life."

Instead, they made BLT sandwiches and lemonade. Just as on countless evenings before, they sat at the kitchen table together for hours nibbling on their meals, giggling at their jokes, and sharing their hearts.

In the midst of a lull, she sprang up from the table to her backpack.

"Mama, I have a present for you. It's a cell phone."

"Well, I declare! Look at that little thing. That's a phone?"

"Yes, Mama… and it's pretty simple to use. Let me show you."

She then meticulously demonstrated its basic features, as well as how to do the recharging. She next stressed the importance of Mama having it with her at all times, knowing how to make that happen.

"Sometimes I just need to hear your voice. I miss you so terribly."

When Mama smiled back, she knew she had her. So, she programmed each phone number into the other and then suggested that they try them out right there at the kitchen table.

"Why're we calling if we're in the same room?"

"It's a test, Mama."

When that did not work so well, she tried again by moving into the parlor with Mama staying at the table.

"I can still hear two of you, Child. This is confusing."

So… she would go upstairs to her bedroom instead.

Ascending the steps, she did not expect the flood of memories that came washing over her on entering her childhood room. She was fussing with the cell phone while pushing open the door and flicking on the light. The scene instantly brought back a life only recently forgotten. Though it was merely four weeks since last being here, what she saw was not the past summer, but that miserable one of 1996. She was instantly back there again… not to relive it, yet compelled to see it being lived out in memory. Her no longer being a part of it, yet it reclaiming a part of her. Scanning the entirety without entering, she noted that a significant portion of the contents had been displaced to college. The little desk was barren, and the bookshelves bore large gaps where her favorite volumes had once resided. She knew that the drawers were mostly empty, as was the closet. It was as if the good things from her childhood had vanished right before her eyes, leaving only the parts she did not want… those not worthy of being carried off into the future. She had to sleep here tonight, but did not welcome the thought. This room was haunted.

The phone in her hand suddenly began chirping, pulling her back to the present.

"Mama? Can you hear me? I'm in my room – I'm coming back to you now."

They spent the next day together, mostly in the kitchen and mostly at the table. She tried all day to bring their conversation around to 1996… yet without actually talking about 1996. It was tricky, and she never really succeeded. She wanted to make sure Mama knew that she did not blame her for Daddy, but such a thing could not just be blurted out. Mama was a tough woman… toughened by hurricanes and hard Southern living… as well as having to be both a mother and father to a tragically damaged daughter. From both of their vantage points, Mama had done a good job. So certainly there was no reason in Mama's mind for digging it all up and doing the job all over again just to see if something had been left undone. She had her daughter's future to consider, not the past, and was better positioned in their relationship to steer the conversation in a direction of her own choosing.

"What do you want to be?"

It was a boomerang Mama kept throwing out. No matter how many times it was pitched and dodged, the opportunity to ask this question always came back to Mama.

"For the umpteenth time, Mama… I don't know what I want to be! I've only just begun! I know loads of freshmen at Garland who've not yet declared their major."

That, unfortunately, was Mama's opportunity to open a second line of questioning.

"Well then, if we can't talk about *what* you like, tell me about *who* you like. Tell me about these friends you've made, and if there are any nice boys."

Truly, she would rather talk about careers than this! How could she say 'I have no friends, and all the guys are either creeps or morons, or both.' She suddenly remembered an instance as a child in vacation Bible school where she had fabricated a falsehood for her own amusement. Taking two different verses, the front half of one and the back half of another, she reassembled the fragments into a believable sounding new one. It was probably a terrible sin, as she happily passed it off on a volunteer. The whole place was thrown into an uproar as adults debated the legitimacy of 'Camellia's verse.'

'A *lie is an abomination to the Lord, but a very ready help in time of need.*'

So she chose to answer Mama's 'who' question with just such an abomination. But first, she needed to rise from the kitchen table. It was strictly forbidden to provide anything other than the truth while seated there. Moving to the sink as if to get a glass of water, she replied most matter-of-factly.

"Mama, I have loads of friends on my hall and in my classes. I can't possibly go through them all."

This seemed to satisfy her mother... which *really* worried her. Mama knew the trick of leaving the table – it had been attempted on almost a daily basis throughout her teenage years. But now she had not been called on it. Mama was acting strange... as if some item had just been checked off a mental list as a job well done, with her moving on to the next.

"And what about the boys? Is there anyone special who you're... interested in?"

On this topic, she could not lie. Whatever was going on in Mama's head, anything but the absolute truth would be challenged. Her eyes shot over to the hoodie, lying on the counter where it had been left. Fighting back the impulse to retrieve it... to put it on and cover herself... she instead sat back down at the table. Lowering her eyes to her lap, she spoke slowly and quietly, giving Mama an honest answer.

"You know my feelings on that subject. We've talked about it so many times... right here at this table. I can't go there again."

Her mother could be as tough as nails, but also as soft as thrice-spun cotton. She felt all of that softness as Mama reached across to gently stroke her hair.

"Don't worry, Child. You'll find him."

CHAPTER

12

SPECIMEN SELECTION

Brandi arranged the pick-up for Sunday morning at 9 AM. Though she had wished to stay longer, it was not open for debate. ("It's either then or get yourself another ride.") At 8:50, she was packed and seated with Mama in the front parlor, hoodie in place. Brandi was right on time... and now driving a brand new Mazda Miata convertible. Mama and she kissed and hugged, repeatedly saying goodbye, though she did not linger. She could imagine Brandi laying on the horn... or just speeding off. Either would be difficult to explain to Mama.

Upon entering the car, the first utterance from the driver was a demand for more money.

"I need another five, 'cause this baby goes through gas much faster than Daddy's truck."

Fairly certain this to be a lie, she nonetheless handed over the money... well out of view in case Mama was still watching. A change instantly came over Brandi – she was now the life of the party.

"Let's burn rubber, girl! Hang on!"

She threw the car into gear, and did a much less graceful U-turn before peeling out down the road.

The atmosphere of the return trip was as different as the vehicles employed. Aside from it being impossible to have a nostalgic perspective on the Southern countryside while cruising in a sports car, she found Brandi to be excessively talkative, sharing a wealth of information on topics she could not care less about. The driver detailed her favorite bars, how to recover quickly from a hangover, which sororities slept with which fraternities, and the cost of each new item of clothing being brought back to school. She had only returned with a few extra toiletries, a towel, some spare coat hangers, and a book on Roman architecture.

Having depleted her reservoir of useless insight, Brandi eventually settled on a country music station. With the volume cranked up, the driver began screaming out the words to a song, leaving her to wonder why hip hop had been chosen for the truck and country for the sports car.

After a few choruses, Brandi compelled her to join in, but she did not know any of the lyrics.

"Girl! What rock have you been hiding under all your life?!"

It was a throw away question – one she did not attempt to answer. The rock, she knew, was an exceedingly heavy one indeed.

Back into the college routine on Monday, her thoughts returned to Ms. Kelley's admonition and the identification of a male worthy of knowing. She had not bothered to explain the specimen plan to Mama, who would not have understood… and definitely not approved. Mama was Southern, and Southern women did not study men… at least not in ways resembling science. That week, she spent a few moments before and after each class evaluating the available stock of males. Although she could not formulate for herself exactly what she was looking for, it soon became straightforward to make exclusions.

The Racquetball boys were the first to fall off her prospective friend list. She was really beginning to enjoy this game, having quickly grasped the relationship between angles and trajectories, and how spin and speed could be used to accomplish her objectives. Z-shots were a favorite, and she was becoming quite good at kills. Most of all, she was discovering herself to be athletic. At first, guys in the class were drawn to this, but her competitive spirit arose and became relentless. She mercilessly beat the weaker males whenever she could, while doing her best to provoke the more capable ones… just to see how they would respond. She saw anger, frustration and excuses.

Lord, can they ever make excuses!

No prospects stood out in her Honors classes. Most of those males were consumed with their status relative to their classmates. She did not begrudge them for the competition – it was no different than in Racquetball – but she despised the arrogance that permeated the program. When a guy bragged about his intelligence, achievements, possessions, exploits or conquests… or if he ever spoke about drinking… she crossed him off the list. Similarly, the shallow, the dull-witted, the self-absorbed, the vulgar and the unfeeling were all eliminated.

The challenge of finding a male 'worthy of knowing' in one of her classes was becoming so untenable that she had to contemplate the unappealing prospect of extracurricular activities. She had overheard a fellow Honors classmate talking about the many opportunities available for freshmen to get involved. So… she took an initial step in that direction by asking this girl for help. Wednesday morning was the first exam in History, so Charity had agreed to assist her afterward in exploring possibilities at the student union.

The exam was simple enough, covering the time period from the dawn of civilization… which she joked to herself had not yet risen in Mississippi… through to the iron age. Prof. Dunsmore had reluctantly agreed to exclude from the exam all material pertaining to the iron age itself, owing largely to the insistence of a very vocal minority of fraternity types who had something that week called 'trials.'

Mr. Reynolds administered the examination. There were a few dozen multiple choice questions, nearly as many fill-in the blanks, and three full-page essays – all straightforward enough to anyone who had studied. After cruising through the choices and the blanks, she hit the first essay with a mental 'whoa.'

'Describe at least one theory for the rise of iron in the context of the end of the bronze age, giving examples of how iron usage reshaped the ancient world.'

Obviously, she was not concerned for herself. Having studied ahead, she knew that the rise of iron and the fall of bronze was due, in part, to new discoveries of the former and a scarcity of tin, a critical ingredient in ancient bronze. Iron came to prominence over 4000 years ago in the regions now known as Europe, the Middle East and China. Some believed man's first exposure was from meteorites, whereas others thought iron might first have been discovered in the ashes of fires built over iron-bearing minerals. Its initial usage was in ornaments, then tools. Iron weaponry, which came later, was far superior to that of bronze, resulting in a sort of ancient arms race in regions like the Fertile Crescent. Civilizations with access to iron slowly exerted control over the previously dominant ones limited to bronze.

As she was composing this information into an essay, other classmates were reaching the same point. A three part harmony of rebellion was rising, constituted from indignation, frustration and apprehension. While Prof. Dunsmore sat comfortably in his office, Mr. Reynolds had no idea what was about to come over him. She was starting in on the last essay when two students approached the podium. The class's less-courageous… though nonetheless equally concerned… stopped what they were doing to listen, fully expecting Mr. Reynolds to address them all and exclude the first essay from consideration. Instead, he shook his head and asked these forerunners of malcontent to retake their seats.

She completed the final essay and scanned over the entire exam. Double-checking was in her nature. She then descended the terraces, depositing her completed exam on the lectern where indicated by Mr. Reynolds. First done and first out the door, she was anxious to escape the brewing storm… but had not gone three paces into the hall before recalling plans to explore the student union with Charity. In a moment of inner conflict between conscience and the instinct for flight, the former won out by virtue of the memory of Mama's words. ("The good person swears to their own hurt and does not change their word.") So… she slouched down to the hallway floor and waited.

At first, only a trickle of students emerged. Those prepared for the iron age essay connected with her by rolling their eyes before fleeing. The trickle turned into a stream, the members of which no longer made eye contact with her, but either fumed off alone or congregated with other disgruntled students to plot. The stream then abruptly ceased as the exam time expired… even though over half of the class remained inside.

One of the hallway conspirators went to the door, opening it without entering. She, from her vantage point on the floor, could easily see past this doorkeeper into the front podium area. At least a dozen students had encircled Mr. Reynolds, peppering him with objections, accusations and corroborating testimony regarding the iron age essay. She had not caught sight of him until one person moved off to compare facts with another. There he was, standing in the center of hostility, patiently listening and calmly responding. The onslaught had not diminished one iota in the time since the door was opened, but neither had the control of Mr. Reynolds.

The mob eventually dispersed in order to make room for the next class, which had piled up in the hallway. She heard many voices of exasperation from those exiting, with one student speaking directly to the doorkeeper.

"Reynolds says he'll talk to Dumb-ass about that essay. He wants to see if it can be a bonus question, but I told him that's bullshit. Everyone knows Dumb-ass doesn't do extra credit."

The indignant blended with the wronged in the hall, and they all moved on. Charity passed by without even bothering to search for her. As the next class entered, she caught a glimpse of Mr. Reynolds ascending the terraces to safe havens above. Smiling wide under the hoodie, she spoke in a voice heard only by herself.

"I see you."

Mr. Reynolds did not yet know it, but she had found her specimen.

CHAPTER
13

STUDY QUESTIONS

She now had a plan... and Camille Jay Larson with a plan was a force to be reckoned with.

Back at the dorm that evening, she removed the schedule from the wall and commenced construction of an updated version. The time slot between 7 to 9 PM on Thursday evenings would be rededicated to the History study session, with library work-study moved to another evening. She felt equal parts excited and foolish in making this new weekly contract with herself. Using neatly printed block letters, she inked in 'History study session,' and was about to add 'with Mr. Reynolds' when a more prudent part of her objected to the inclusion of the subject's name. Mama had told her plenty of stories about families that allowed their children to become overly fond of their farm animals. ("Best way to turn dinner into a pet is to give it a name.") So referring to him in such a familiar way felt too close for her. At the same time, another side of her insisted on naming him properly.

He shouldn't be called a specimen – that's disrespectful.

So simply thinking of him as 'Mr. Reynolds' would have to do.

Repeating the previous shadings on the new schedule, she stopped in considering what color to make the study session. Of the assortment, only two markers were not currently being employed. Obviously, shading in anything with black would make it impossible to read the words written beneath. Looking at the remaining highlighter in her hand, she stuck out her tongue in a mock gagging gesture, rolling her eyes for only her own benefit, and then resigned herself to the providential forces that had prevented her from purchasing a greater variety of colors. The History study session would have to be highlighted in pink.

With a new schedule prominently displayed above her desk, she set about refining her plan for studying Mr. Reynolds. In assessing the risks of learning about friendship with a worthy male, her greatest concern was not her feelings but the fear of giving off the wrong impression. Mr. Reynolds was a graduate student – an entirely different caste compared to a lowly freshman. He was the last person to have any real interest in her. He would be safe.

So… she would focus first on some experiment to confirm Mr. Reynolds as a guy worth knowing. What she witnessed after the exam was promising, but she still wanted to personally put him to the test.

Now, how to go about it?

She amused herself for a moment with the thought of writing out a step-by-step procedure, complete with hypothesis, data entry and analysis… followed by conclusion… just as was done each week in Chemistry Lab. That approach, though, felt off. Instead, this would be a social science experiment, where a controlled stimulus was applied to a subject and the researcher recorded the response. Testing him in that way, she admitted to herself, was likely a poor pathway to friendship… but hopefully a much safer one.

So how would someone worthy of friendship respond to being bested?

As per her experience in Racquetball, she decided to challenge Mr. Reynolds at his own game and observe his reaction. A solid three step approach should do it.

Step one: attend the study session, discover the areas of history that interest him, and then research those to a depth unusual for a freshman.
Step two: display the knowledge in a manner that challenges him.

She stopped here in considering how best to do step two, knowing that extensive library research might be required of her. However, the mental hopscotch game took over and led her on an indulgent pathway of fanciful prospects. She pictured herself moving through a hidden doorway in the librarian's break room, where she descended spiraling stone steps into deep, dark catacombs beneath. Another hidden door revealed a rock-walled chamber piled with scrolls containing ancient knowledge about the Carthaginians... or the Han dynasty... or Magellan's voyages. Whatever he was into. She would then prepare a flawless technical paper enlightening the world. Her work would receive rave reviews among the prominent scholars of the time, and the University president would personally thank her for bringing so much honor to Garland. Then, she envisioned herself entering Mr. Reynolds' study session, slapping down a reprint of her work, and watching him squirm.

Without realizing it, she had jumped up to act out the 'slap down.' Catching sight of herself in the mirror above the desk, her first thought was surprise at having acted silly. So she closed her eyes in embarrassment, yet on reopening them found that the glass had disregarded her childish display in order to get at something deeper. It had a question.

Could he, being a man, find anything of interest in you, who was little more than a girl?

Surely Mr. Reynolds, as a TA, had been around many attractive and interesting females. Why should she stand out to him? The reflection then drew her in to hear its glassy surface ask other questions – ones she had never considered before.

The oval staring back at her... could this actually be a nice face? Cameron and Amber seemed to think it pretty, but she was not so sure. So she leaned in closer to examine the blue eyes. Were they the proper shade and shape, and were they spaced appropriately? Her appraisal shifted to the complexion, which Mama said was flawless. That was a plus. Yet there were a few faint freckles on the nose and cheeks. Were freckles acceptable? The nose, for its part, seemed to be appropriately proportioned. That had to be good. The lips were a bit thin, but the mouth and teeth bore no significant irregularities. What about the hair clumped up in the hoodie and flowing out on the sides, it being forced down onto the neck and collar bone – was that good or bad? She lowered the hood and studied again. Parted in the middle without bangs, the strands now extended well below her shoulders. Cameron had called it 'a baby's blond'... ice cold and creamy. Maybe... though she had always preferred the less accurate term 'flaxen.' The senior said guys were drawn to this shade, though she could not understand why.

Looking into the mirror, she found it asking questions for which there were no answers. Questions from a perspective entirely foreign to her previous way of thinking. Questions that revolved around what Mr. Reynolds might think of her. Before this examination could progress toward other features – her figure, bearing, and mannerisms – an intensely rational side of her awoke.

Camille – you're being an ass of a girl! What do you care what anyone thinks of you?!

She fell back onto the desk chair, shifting her gaze from the mirror to the new schedule taped below. There was a sudden mad impulse to rip it off the wall and replace it with the previous one... but that lay in the trash, torn in many pieces.

That's odd... I don't remember doing that.

Another part of her was deeply satisfied that the old schedule was gone, that the bridge was burned, and there was nowhere to go except forward.

No problem! This is just a class project, and I can handle any project thrown my way.

With bolstered confidence and reassured indifference, she rose from the desk and headed for the bathroom to ready herself for bed... completely forgetting about step three.

She woke up in the morning immediately aware of this being a Thursday... the first day of her new schedule... which meant attending Mr. Reynolds' study session that very evening. Having not yet even rolled out of bed, she was already experiencing an intense battle with nerves boiling up within.

There are innumerable ways this could go wrong! What if I'm the only one to show up? What if I say something stupid? Or worse, what if I freeze up?

Only her will, as a heavy pot lid, kept the inner turmoil under control so she could go through the motions of getting ready for the day. Yet her mind and heart still remained in conflict, alternating between opponent and proponent of attending the study session. Most often, though, her thoughts and feelings were in a state of confusion.

This is so childish! The experiment will be harmless. He's only going to be discussing the outcome of the exam with me, so what's the big deal?

She abruptly halted her walk across campus to her first class of the day in order to shake the silliness out of her head. Her inadvertent pronoun selection – 'me' rather than 'us' – was too much a sign of the conflict within.

The morning rolled slowly into afternoon… and then evening was upon her. She had already gotten approval for moving her work-study time from Thursdays to Tuesdays. But if not, would she have been relieved or disappointed?

Honestly… I'm getting super tired of all these questions without answers!

CHAPTER

14

ON A WALK

The entire day had been an insignificant blur compared to the nervousness she felt in heading over to Mr. Reynolds' study session.

To make matters worse, it was raining… the doing of Hurricane Isidore off the Louisiana coast. But really… she had no space left in her brain for pondering on meteorological mysteries. In fact, she was not herself at all. She had failed to take notes in class for the first time since arriving at Garland, dwelling instead on an imaginary battleground of thought and emotion involving a three part version of Virgil's Camilla. Two parts – her mind and heart – clashed, while the will wavered in rendering judgment.

This is a specimen… not a guy!

No, Mr. Reynolds is a person!

Well, yes… he is… though not really.

Yet it was the feet, insensitive to the struggles above, that… in obeying a plan conceived the night before… brought her to Cunningham Hall. Arriving a few minutes early, she found the History lecture room dark and the door locked.

Do I wait? Do I have the wrong classroom? Or the wrong time?

In a sudden panic supplemented by the day's tension, she turned about in a dash for her dorm… then recalled that the class syllabus was instead lodged in the back flap of her calendar. Whipping the backpack off her shoulder, she spilt its contents in a frantic search. The absurdity of the situation came home, enabling her to calmly collect her belongings… and wits… before retrieving the syllabus. That paper indicated the help session was in a different wing. After putting the backpack in order, she adopted a metered pace that delivered her to the right location only a few minutes late.

The sounds of a large gathering greeted her as she approached the designated classroom. Coming to a stop at the door, she tried to gauge the turnout before entering, but was startled by a classmate who suddenly appeared out of her periphery. As he swept the door open to enter ahead of her, she caught sight of Mr. Reynolds sitting at a front table facing toward some assembled students. It was not too late to change her mind, as he had not yet become aware of her presence. But in the brief time it took for the door to swing back on its hinges, she decided. Quickly thrusting her hand into the shrinking gap, she pulled open the door and entered.

Nearly the entire class was there. Clear to her now, the huge turnout was because of the exam. Already, it would appear that groups had formed, one of which was comprised of the most vocal students in the class… these seeming eager to get started on Mr. Reynolds. Those, she supposed, had done poorly on more than just the iron age essay. Another cluster, one in which Charity resided, appeared more smug than outraged. Those had probably done fine on the essay, but were likely there in hopes of obtaining some leverage for the future. A third, congregating behind these two, displayed the most timidity. Sitting quietly, they hung back in being drawn to the drama about to unfold, yet not confident of how best to benefit from it. These individuals, she thought, would be the first to sense which way the breeze blew.

It was only after several classmates looked her way that she realized she was still standing just inside the door. Quickly moving to the very back, she joined a fourth, much smaller fraction of the class – those who, like her, had studied all the material, handled the iron age essay with ease, and were not part of the uproar following the exam. They had positioned themselves behind as observers, not personally caring how the proceeding concluded, only desiring to see the spectacle unfold. This fourth group received her with nods, recognizing her as one of their own… though none knew her ulterior motive for being there.

Mr. Reynolds represented the lone member of a fifth group – the besieged authorities. She had noticed him register her entry into the room… and he even seemed to follow her progression to the back. A bit of indulgent flattery enticed her into imagining that he had been waiting for her.

In preparing to address the gathering, she noted how he first moved in front of the table, an action she supposed was intended to diffuse tension.

"It's nice to see so many attend this study session. As the exam's not yet been graded, there's little value in going over it at this time. Let's begin with a discussion of the iron age."

He should have realized that this subject accounted for the large turnout. A lit torch had just been tossed into a Chinese fireworks factory. The first two groups – the 'angry' and the 'manipulative' – exploded, bombarding him with accusations of injustice and incompetence. Several of the 'followers' pitched in words of support, while her group simply observed. She, however, was singularly interested in Mr. Reynolds, who was displaying the very same self-disciplined demeanor exhibited after the exam. The onslaught did not seem to faze him, even though his voice required heightening to be heard.

"I'm sorry… Prof. Dunsmore wants the exams graded first."

This message should have been sufficient to re-establish order, assuming a reasonable class. But reason resided only in the back row.

"I can't comment on… Yeah, sure, when the time comes you should… No, that's not right… You have to make an appointment first… We can't just… Enough! I'm not going to say anything else on the subject!"

He moved back around the table and opened his copy of the text to read about the iron age, though she was certain no one was listening. Through it all, she marveled that he showed no anger and gave no ground. His calm manner was eroding away the rebellion. Several of the 'followers' left the study session, accompanied by her entire group. They had seen enough, and had better things to do with their time. She, however, stayed to silently root for him, having disregarded the role of a social scientist. Soon, nearly the entire angry group stormed out… with several manipulators trailing in behind. Only Charity and a few persisted, perhaps thinking that their odds would improve once the weaker of the herd had been thinned out. Yet Mr. Reynolds still did not budge.

Finally, with only two students remaining, Charity stood up. After a penetrating look back at her, Charity then exited the classroom. With only fifteen minutes of the two hour study session transpired, she found herself completely alone with Mr. Reynolds.

"Well, Miss Larson… it would seem that you're the only one left with unanswered questions. So now's your chance… how can I help you?"

Before she knew what she was saying… before any rational part of her could intervene… a soft voice arose from an unknown source with an unexpected request.

"Will you walk me to my dorm?"

Mr. Reynolds was utterly taken aback. He looked up at the clock, gathered himself, yet still struggled to form a response. Though shocked by her own bluntness, she was equally pleased with how a simple question… though highly unorthodox… had accomplished what two dozen angry and manipulative students had failed to do – totally unnerve him!

"Umm… I can't leave. There's still an hour and forty five minutes left in the study session."

"So you think more students will be showing up for history help?"

She watched him glance away, swallow, then turn to the clock again as if to secure its assistance. He came back to her slightly quicker than before.

"OK… you've got a point. I doubt anyone else'll be showing up. But I'm supposed to stay here until the time's over."

"I understand."

It was clear that he expected her to leave, but she instead opened her backpack and got to work reconstructing notes for that day's lectures. He was watching, she was sure, waiting for some change in her behavior.

"Do you have a history question?"

"Nope."

She still did not look up, remaining focused on moving a pencil across a page… even though she invested little true concentration in the effort. The idiocy of the situation must be dawning on him – her in the back row with her head down intent on other classwork, and him absurdly standing in front with nothing to do. This may not be the social science experiment she had originally conceived, but nonetheless was turning out just as well.

"Then what're you doing?"

"Working on Chemistry."

"But this is a History help session."

"I know that."

"Then why are you still here?"

Now she looked up to make her meaning clear. "Because the only way I'm getting you to walk me is if I wait here for the next…" She glanced up at the clock. "…one hundred and two minutes. So I just thought I should be doing something constructive in the meantime."

She went back to Chemistry, knowing that to peek once more was to risk succumbing to laughter. It did not take more than thirty seconds before he caved in.

"OK, you win. Yes – I'd be happy to escort you to your dorm."

I can't believe that actually worked!

The adrenaline of success pulsed through her bloodstream, making it a fight to maintain a placid bearing. After gathering her belongings, she moved to the front, positioning herself a few feet away. The effect on him was surprising. He bumbled about with his notes, picking them up and then putting them back down again, as he tried to work out the order in which those things should be stowed. At one point, he retrieved his umbrella from the floor and shoved it into his backpack… only to realize that it was still needed. He finally decided to scoop up the entire contents of the table and cram the lot into his bag. So controlled… so unflappable under the onslaught of an entire class… he was a complete muddle gathering himself together for walking a freshman to her dorm. She thought it cute.

Whoa! You did not just think that about a guy! Pull yourself together!

"Ready to go?"

"Yep."

Though she delivered her response nimbly, she suddenly realized a significant complication to her bluntness. They moved to the doorway where Mr. Reynolds turned out the room lights. The momentary darkness seemed to accentuate her predicament. The walk – the very thing so serendipitously orchestrated – was something for which she had no plan.

How far away from him should I be?

No clarity came as they moved into the lighted hall.

And how fast should I go?

The echo of a closing door followed them down the empty hallway.

Obviously not so fast that he thinks I want the walk over quickly... but not so slow that he gets the wrong impression.

Her reasoning was of no practical use as a more pressing issue suddenly came forth.

Oh no! What do we talk about?

Panic once more churned within as the only sounds she could muster were those of her footsteps. To her great relief, he made the first conversational offering.

"Why is it that students never come to study sessions before an exam but always show up after? And for the wrong reasons."

The irony was not lost on her. The reason for her presence... though private... had not been so noble either. Unable to control herself, she uttered a faint grown... and quickly tried covering it up with a false chuckle. Fortunately, he smiled... so she relaxed a bit. They emerged from Cunningham Hall and opened their umbrellas. She was immediately thankful for the rain. Its pattering sound calmed her, while the two overhead canopies provided a natural spacing between them, removing a degree of awkwardness from this, her first-ever escort by a young man.

She quickly showed her approval of his conversational offering by continuing the theme.

"Maybe it's just human nature... thinking you know enough beforehand, and then afterward coming to argue about the deficiency."

"Seems to me that students should take advantage of every opportunity to excel... just like you do."

She thought this a bit presumptive, but was equally surprised by the modicum of pleasure found in him suddenly talking about her.

"How do you know that?"

"I grade your papers. I know an excellent student when I see one."

She flushed at the compliment, hoping the hoodie was doing its job as a shield.

"Oh... yeah. Thanks."

"So, tell me... why did you come tonight? It couldn't be to argue about the exam. I shouldn't say this, but I've already seen everyone's iron age essay. You did quite well."

"Really?" She was not sure how to answer beyond that... until Ms. Kelley's encouragement in her journal reminded her that she was there to learn. "I guess I was just curious to see how the class responded and… how it was handled."

Ugh – I so botched that! Now he's going to think I'm all… cold and critical!

"You mean by me. Well then… how'd I do?"

She turned to offer him a view of her face before replying. "Alright. Fantastic, actually. Better than I'd have done. I don't like whiners or complainers… or manipulators." She could not keep her voice from falling a degree with the last word, as she… in reality… had manipulated him into this walk. "And I don't like people being cruel." She was not thinking of the study session, but of how the class had encircled him after the exam.

"That back there was nothing. They were just testing the boundaries. Happens all the time."

All the time? What's that supposed to mean? Like now… with me too?!

Fortunately, she remembered then the first step in the plan conceived in her dorm room the night before – to learn about him.

"So… umm… what's it like being a graduate student?"

By way of a smile, he seemed pleased with this question.

"In many ways, it's like being an undergraduate in that I also take courses… although I do write a thesis. I have to come up with a new topic for that. My first one was deemed…" An unfortunate interruption ensued as they steered around opposite sides of a large puddle. "… unacceptable. That's normal. Coming to an agreement with one's supervisor can be a long and torturous process, full of give and take. We'll get there."

"Is Prof. Dunsmore… challenging to work with?"

"No. He's fine. But he's not my thesis advisor. I was just assigned to him as a TA. Prof. Simpson's my supervisor. Her expertise is in native American and colonial studies. I'm interested in the latter… but not so much in the former… which is where she wants me to focus."

He then proceeded to describe these topics in the context of his interests and those of his supervisor… and she found every word to be fascinating. To soon, she looked up to see that their walk was almost over.

"That's my dorm just ahead."

As they drew near, he abruptly halted on the walkway, perhaps deciding from some ingrained TA code of ethics not to escort her up the steps and onto the porch.

"It was nice chatting with you, Miss Larson."

"I enjoyed it too. And thanks for walking me to my dorm."

As she turned her back to him, he softly added something surprising. It was not clear if he intended the words to be heard. Maybe it was yet another example of people not realizing what could be perceived under the hoodie.

"My pleasure."

Smiling to herself, she ascended the dorm steps. There was the temptation to look back… to see if he was still there watching her all the way to the door. The urge was replaced by the actions of lowering her umbrella and shaking out the rain in as lady-like a manner as possible. Nothing could be allowed to tarnish the ending to her first intelligent interaction with a male.

Perfect!

CHAPTER
15

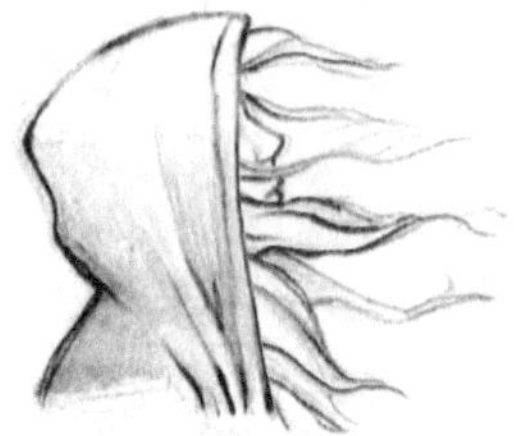

HOODED

Human nature interprets the passage of time within the context of the events occupying it. A car drive to a favorite destination is perceived differently from that of the return trip. Similarly, while a deadline might seem to approach rapidly, monotony over the identical time span can be absolutely interminable. Anticipation and dread work the mind's timepiece at rates unlike those of day-to-day happenings. For her, the routine of the week seemed to drag her back and forth through the clock, so intense were both her desire and apprehension in returning to a Thursday evening.

Ironically, the moment arrived for the next History study session with her showing up five minutes late. She had been delayed in the library looking up anatomical terms for an English essay comparing a butterfly's emergence from its cocoon to a college student's ultimate graduation. Having hurried across campus, she entered both pleased and relieved to find Mr. Reynolds still there – and alone.

"Hello, Miss Larson. Have you come to discuss the Peloponnesian War... or are you already an expert on the subject? Or perhaps you wish to work on chemistry instead?"

"I'm not an expert... of course... but I do think I've got it fairly well covered. And I've already finished my chemistry. I was just...

passing by on the way back from the library and thought I'd check in on your session."

A quick cartographic assessment in her mind revealed the obvious – Cunningham Hall was nowhere near 'on the way' from the library. She made a mental note to kick herself later, though Mr. Reynolds showed no awareness of the inconsistency.

At this second study session, she was in no hurry to be escorted, purposing to take full advantage of the opportunity for getting to know him better. She sat down in a front row desk as they chatted casually. He asked about her courses, and she took pleasure in providing answers. They then transitioned into a discussion on Alexander the Great, and she could not restrain herself from criticizing the course's Euro-centric curriculum. Throughout, their conversation was spirited and mutually enjoyable.

After nearly two hours, he casually glanced up at the clock.

"I think we're done here. No one's coming... other than you, of course. Not that I was expecting... I mean, I'm glad you... came." She just smiled back pleasantly while he tripped through the words. "You're probably one of the few student still not angry at Prof. Dunsmore for refusing to remove the iron age question from that exam. Oh well. So... can I offer you my company on the remainder of your walk?"

What a relief – I didn't have to ask.

"That would be most kind of you."

As they rose to leave the classroom, she took over the conversation... as per her plan.

"So what do you like about studying history?"

He smiled warmly before responding... which encouraged her greatly as to the worth of the question.

"I guess you could say that history teaches me about me. I know – that sounds a bit egocentric... and I don't mean it to be. It's just... I think the greatest challenge a person faces is understanding themselves... and for some reason I can do that better in the pages of a history book."

They had just reached the lobby of Cunningham Hall, so she purposed to wait until they were outside before contributing something of her own experiences from reading literature. As he pulled open a door, she thought nothing of it... only that he intended to move on through ahead of her. Instead, he came to a stop with his back restraining the door, clearly inviting her to pass through first. They, in almost colliding, came face to face there... and she hesitated as her lungs held in breath for fear that lips might dare form words with that air.

Oh my! Such green eyes! They're... so alive!

Quickly moving on, she took a slight lead in order to contemplate the discovery... but also hide its effect upon her. So she offered a routine question as a distraction.

"What do you mean?"

He then began to talk about something he had read... something about the East India Company... which she knew to be an extension of the British Empire that had colonized parts of Southeast Asia over three hundred years ago. But she was actually having difficulty paying attention. He was saying something about how the ruling caste of India had made a mistake. They had not expelled the Company, but instead embraced it. Within a hundred years, the British had complete control of India and all its resources. He then said something about not letting things get a foothold in his life... but she could not shake free from those wonderful eyes.

"Oh."

It was all she could think to say.

"I'm not implying that historians, by nature, are as curious about themselves as they are about history. There're plenty drawn by a feeling of superiority that comes from studying other people's mistakes... and some like to reinterpret the past so they can reinterpret themselves in the process."

They then halted under a lamppost, allowing a group of students to pass before them on an intersecting walkway. The resulting delay presented her with another opportunity to face him directly. So she studied how the smooth skin of his face nicely framed those eyes... and how tuffs of his light brown hair danced about on his forehead in the breeze. Though the students were long gone, he still stood there... which supremely delighted her.

"I like to think that a true historian has no agenda, which is to say they're not really a historian at all... just someone trying to find themselves in the past. You know... I guess it's an odd way of thinking... but I find myself to be hidden in the present but scattered openly throughout the past. This'll sound crazy, but when I read a history text... I imagine myself gathering up pieces of me... so I can know myself better."

"That's not crazy – that's... deep."

Gah! I must sound like such an idiot!

To cover her embarrassment, she turned to reinitiate the walk, striving to craft a question that both sounded clever *and* gave her an opportunity to recover.

"So... when in time are you searching for pieces of yourself?"

He immediately turned toward her, adopting a bit of a sideways canter.

"That's a well-phrased question with double meaning! Everyone should 'take time' to 'search time' for themselves! I mean... to find themselves."

He returned to a normal gait, but in so doing inadvertently brushed up against her. She registered the contact without displeasure.

They walked on for several paces before he continued.

"I've got some... family issues to sort through... as I suppose most people do. That's on top of the usual 'what does it all mean' and 'where's it all going'? You know... the kinds of questions everybody faces. I guess the best answer I can give is that I don't know... but I'm learning."

Wow! He's on the same mission as me!

At that exact moment, she happened to stumble over an uneven seam between two sidewalk slabs. His hands were instantly on her arm, steadying her until she could regain balance.

"Are you OK?"

"Yeah, thanks. I just... sort of... tripped a bit there. I'm fine."

But she was not in the least. His touch just further muddled her insides.

"You know, I'm sort of like you in that I'm a 'freshman' in graduate school... though technically this is my second year. I got off to a bit of a slow start, so the department's giving me more time to find my topic. By the way... have you decided on a major?"

"No... but how'd you know I was undecided?"

"Every student on a class role is designated by their year in school and their major. You're listed as an undeclared freshman."

Since stumbling, she had been concentrating fully on her footing, but in glancing up, came to realize that their walk was almost over. Perhaps he noticed too, for he decided to change the subject.

"So... I've... been wondering about something. Though I've seen plenty of students on campus wearing hoodies, I think you're the only person I've noticed who always wears one… and always with the hood up."

He hesitated, and she waited in disappointment for the question that would most definitely come – one asked of her many times before.

"Now maybe you only wear them when we're… together. Maybe in all other circles of your college experience you go… hoodie-less."

At least this was new. There had been many introductions leading up to the question, but never one with the word 'together.' It momentarily threw her off.

"You know… I'm a firm believer in the separation of church and state… that is, between student and TA. I'm the state, by the way…" She noted the awkward effort, and credited him with the sensitivity it implied. "…so I probably shouldn't be asking…"

After a further pause… perhaps in which he considered the point of no return… the question was posed.

"Why do you wear a hood all the time?"

They were near enough to her dorm, so she delayed in replying. The walk, originally envisioned as an examination of him, turned out to test her instead. A strong desire for self-protection warned against anything beyond the trivial, yet somehow she sensed this particular response would be a deciding factor in more than just a silly social science experiment on friendship. It represented real opportunity… and potential cost. So she decided to lower the shield a degree, and reciprocate with a measure of transparency. It would only be a very small amount, but infinitely greater than ever provided before. Choosing words carefully, she spoke only after they had reached the dorm walkway.

"It's very difficult for me to explain. It's about my father."

With a hardened decisiveness born of much pain, she immediately turned up the walkway, climbed the steps, and entered her dorm.

CHAPTER

16

BUCK

Vernon James Larson met Evalyn Mae Campbell during his first year as a firefighter in Prescott County, Mississippi. 'Buck' grew up in the Smokey Mountains of western Virginia, receiving his nickname from killing a deer at the age of seven. She knew little about his upbringing, as he had exited her life early on. She remembered only that he had been recruited by the Army Corps of Engineers in the 70's to be a part of work teams managing forests along the Tennessee-Tombigbee river project. The government was pouring money into Mississippi, with hearty souls drawn to the outdoors and good pay flocking from all corners of the South.

Work eventually dried up on the project after a few years into Daddy's time in Mississippi, as did the forests – from drought. He found temporary employment fighting wildfires, and met Mama as she volunteered serving food and water to fire crews. Mama was raised just north of Hattiesburg where her parents had owned a fairly prosperous produce stand for as long as Mama could remember. Growing up a jack-of-all-trades, Mama helped manage the business, tended gardens, repaired equipment, and did marketing to local grocers. She was capable and independent, yet fully reared in the Southern graces.

They married on New Year's Day in 1978.

Mama once said that she had been attracted to the man's muscles and the way he could make folks laugh with his imitations. She had no memory of the imitations, but vividly remembered the muscles. Her earliest recollection of him was when he taught her how to swim. Mama said they would picnic along the river project, and afterward Daddy would throw his terrified little girl into the water time after time… each progressively a bit farther… making her four year old self fight the way back using both the river's surface and its bottom. She remembered sitting in the back seat of the family car returning from one such outing listening to an intense… almost violent… argument regarding the proper way to raise a daughter.

A year after marrying, Daddy took a job at a sawmill and moved his young bride to Carlton, Mississippi. Daddy loved wood… maybe even more than anything he ever loved. He loved its strength, the feel of its textures, and how it smelled while being cut. He was truly content only when opportunity placed him near lumber or trees. A hard worker, he climbed rapidly in job status and pay at the mill. Starting out as a sorter, he moved into plant cleanup, then made a significant jump to an assistant shift foreman, followed by an equally impressive transition into labor relations.

Mama became pregnant in 1983. A new way of following the progress of the unborn – the ultrasound – had entered their small county hospital, and the Larsons… like so many first-time parents… were mesmerized by the images provided of their child within the womb. 'Definitely a boy,' proclaimed the technician, as body part after body part was pointed out to the young couple. For the following day and onward, Daddy announced confidently to anyone who would listen that he was soon to be the father of the next Larson man. Grand plans were already being conceived that involved hunting, fishing and woodworking. The boy would be 'Buck's buddy,' raised exactly as he had been – to be daring, adventurous and rugged.

This baby was born healthy on the first day of spring in 1984… but as a girl. Daddy took the news hard, withdrawing early on from the routine aspects of parenting, never intending to bond with the 'mistake.' Or so she gathered years later on overhearing Mama summarize the father-daughter relationship over the phone to a distant relative. She was never sure… and did not want the certainty of knowing… whether Mama had meant the technician's mistake or hers for being a daughter rather than a son. She grew up with an intense affinity for her mother, and a persistent insecurity at having not turned out the way her father wanted.

Still… times were good, and Daddy was making plenty of money in his new leadership position at the mill. The family purchased a small two story house one street over from the select neighborhood that constituted the prominent people in town. The house came cheaply due to fire damage from the previous owners. Daddy labored evenings, weekends and holidays, eventually restoring the house to a habitable state. It was paid off in record time because he had negotiated a favorable deal with the bank, which was delighted to rid itself of the property. Folks in town would point to Daddy and say the South needed more men like him – industrious, capable and self-sufficient.

Yet the technology of cutting wood was rapidly changing, and the Carlton plant was lagging behind. It soon became more profitable for foresters to ship uncut pine to markets overseas rather than have harvests processed locally. Throughout the South, mills were reducing production or shutting down altogether. Surviving owners were making wild promises to workers… but also pushing them, hoping to keep their mills operating for one more month, one more week, or just one more day. Daddy also got caught up in the promises, although not in receiving them. He was tasked with delivering those promises for the owners.

The inevitable came when she was eight. Employees arrived one morning to find a 'closed' sign draped across the mill's iron gates, now chained shut. There were town meetings in which accusations were widely distributed, with Daddy receiving an inordinate share of blame for convincing folks to stick it out. Some even accused him of stealing from the company in order to pay off his house. Fights erupted, and Daddy spent two weeks in county jail for shattering a man's knee with an axe handle. Mama said he was never the same after that.

Daddy's reputation in town got so severely tarnished that local employers were averse to hiring him. He initially did odd jobs, then tried to scrape out a living making furniture. He even built a shed behind their house for woodworking. This structure was, in fact, much larger than a typical shed, being about the size of a one-car garage. He even plumbed in a toilet and sink. The family just called it 'the shed.' Once finished, Daddy threw himself into woodworking. Yet all his enterprises amounted to little as he lacked the skill of a craftsman, being not much more than a hobbyist. Before the year was out, Daddy had lost his heart for wood.

By the time she was ten, Daddy had become a full-blown alcoholic, frequently escaping into the shed to drink… and then sleep it off there on a cot. He still lived in the house… that is, until he started beating her. Mama kicked him out after that, threatening to end his life if he ever laid a hand on her daughter again.

She could not recall much in the way of interaction with him during that time, only that Daddy took Mama seriously and started living in the shed. For nearly two years, he refrained from touching her.

She remembered answering the front door once during that time to find the town sheriff there. Although Mama sent her away, she lingered just out of sight in order to listen. The sheriff was making inquiries about Daddy's activities, and the word 'dealing' was clearly uttered. She knew Daddy to be clever, cautious, and highly successful in his new line of work. He was never caught for any illegality… though she was tried, convicted and punished daily in the courts of fifth and sixth grade. Because of him, she lost all her friends. No one would come to her house, and she was never invited to others. There were birthday parties and sleepovers before Daddy's fall, but none after. Mama became her best and only childhood companion.

Looking back, she was certain that Mama caught it equally bad. Her status in town went from sky-high to dirt-deep in a matter of two years. In order to survive, Mama was forced to work multiple 'undesirable' jobs because she would have nothing to do with her husband's drug money.

She was pretty sure that Daddy never paid special attention to anything during that time… except maybe the dog. One day in the spring of her fifth grade year, Daddy came home with a dog. It was not a pet. It had no name – just 'the dog.' This animal, being huge, ugly and mean, had only one purpose – to keep people away. It was chained up outside the shed when Daddy was around, but accompanied him as his guard while he conducted business. The day it showed up, the dog allowed her to approach, perhaps to better smell her. Thinking this a new family member, she nearly lost fingers for her gullibility. Daddy came storming out of the shed cursing, frightening her more than the dog had.

On those occasions when Daddy was out, she had free access to the backyard... but never approached the shed. When he was home, whether sober or not, she remained indoors. An unspoken understanding had arisen within this small family – the two inhabitants of the house would have nothing to do with the two in the shed... and vice versa.

CHAPTER

17

INTO THE SHED

On her 12th birthday, Mama gave her an ivory-white dress. It was layered, with thin, nearly transparent lace over a satin lining, and a sash about the waist that tied in a bow at the back. An accompanying petticoat made the knee-length skirt poof out. On first opening the box, she knew instantly why Mama had chosen that dress. The lace possessed an intricate pattern of delicate flowers not unlike the camellia in appearance. It was the prettiest thing she had ever owned, and would be perfect for their only acceptable entry into society – Sunday services. One of the ladies at the dry cleaner where Mama worked was fashioning a bonnet to match the dress. It would be ready for Easter on April 7th, so Mama made her wait two Sundays before she could wear it out of the house. But after school, while Mama was at work, she would put on the dress to admire how it looked and to explore how it felt as she moved about. She especially liked the way both the dress and her long blond hair responded in one accord, flaring out as she spun in circles, or bouncing up and down as she sashayed about.

Daddy had been out for two solid weeks, with both her and Mama having grown accustomed to the freedom his long absences offered. On Good Friday, April 5th, she donned the dress immediately after school, and was prancing about on the back steps. These were made of poured concrete, leading from the kitchen to the backyard. The sounds of traffic were common there, as main street was only a block over. She paid no attention to the noise. While completing another downward cycle on the stairs, his car must have pulled into the side driveway, stopping short of her view. Though she had not heard the engine, the clinking of the dog's chain immediately brought her attention to the shed, as Daddy was anchoring the animal in its usual spot.

Normally, the sight would have sent her bolting indoors… but there was something different this time. He was drunk – no doubt about it – but his behavior was especially peculiar. Much more so than on those times when she would spy on him from her bedroom window above. The dog also sensed a difference in its master, remaining silent though it had already spotted her on the back porch. With his back to her, Daddy seemed to be fretting about something with an air of desperation. He was wringing his hands while mumbling… which contrasted severely with his normal arrogant confidence. As he pivoted about, suddenly aware of her presence, she knew before the turn was completed that something horrid had happened. He was filthy. Nearly his entire front was covered in a dark stain. And he was angry drunk… which went much deeper than being just plain drunk. In her memory, it was like something evil had taken hold and driven all reason from him.

He crossed the yard before she could get the back door open. Taking hold of her neck with one hand, he wrapped his other arm around her waist, gripping both with a will to cause pain. To this day, she can not remember anything he might have said, only that there was rage in his voice. She nonetheless screamed her loudest as he hoisted her into the air and retraced his steps to the shed… but there was no one to hear her other than the dog. It just growled and lunged for a piece of her, relieved that its master had returned to form. Instead, it received a hard kick to the ribs for its loyalty.

She blocked out what happened next… partly by choice and partly from a scarred memory. She could only recall that her beautiful new dress was destroyed… and that her childhood had been ended.

Afterward, he bellowed at her for crying, shaking her in his fury until she ceased. She remembered him saying 'it's all your goddamn fault – you were to be a boy.' Then he slapped her over and over. She went semi-unconscious, knowing that he was there yet oblivious to what he was doing. It was pure evil, what he inflicted upon her for not being a son. But more got added on. Blurry eyed, she watched as he took a broomstick and smashed the overhead bulbs before turning to leave. She remembered seeing a gap of light shrinking to a sliver... and then total darkness as he padlocked the door behind him, leaving the dog to guard the shed. Surely, she thought, the neighbors could hear its nonstop barking... yet no one came.

Later, not knowing how long, she ventured off the cot to check the door, but it was firmly locked on the outside. As the windows had long ago been boarded over, she resorted to banging on the interior and calling for help. The dog was the only one to hear, and it matched her tone for tone. When it began to throw its body against the door, she fell silent and fled back to the cot, fearing that it... like Daddy... would find demon strength to enter into the shed.

Time passed. The space was hot, and reeked of urine, wood oils, alcohol and body odor. She repeatedly went in and out of consciousness... but at some point, she became aware of blood on her forehead and the taste of it in her mouth.

The thing she both hoped for and dreaded eventually happened. Mama's arrival was signaled first by the dog's bark... and then by the calling of her name. Though her throat was dry from crying, her voice raised to its loudest with a single word – 'Mama!'

Mama was yelling and she was pleading, but the dog remained between them.

"Hold tight, Camellia! I'll be right back!"

It suddenly became quiet except for low growls and flexed chain. Though Mama was only gone for minutes, it felt like hours until the dog once again announced her return.

"Camellia, Sweetie, put your hands over your ears! Real tight now! There's going to be a loud noise!"

A moment later, the sound of a shotgun blast filled the shed... and the barking ceased. Then Mama was at the door with a crowbar prying off the lock. It was fully dark inside, and dusk out, but she could still see every detail of the horror, grief and anger branded across Mama's face. Then Mama carried her out of the shed and into the house, her head firmly tucked into the crook of Mama's neck.

Many years later, she would find unpleasant irony in the recollection of how a journey into the shed in one parent's arms contrasted so starkly with the opposite trip in the other's.

Delirious with fatigue, pain and trauma, she was not fully aware of what was happening. Mama placed her in the tub intending on a hot bath, but contact with the water sent her thrashing about... right before she fainted in Mama's arms. Mama then put her to bed, though sleep was shallow and fitful. Time after time through the night, she awoke into instant screams... or sometimes with eyes wide open into a stillness that barred all speech. Each time, Mama was there to hold and kiss her, providing soothing words of comfort.

Near to dawn, yet while it was still dark, she awoke for the first time to find Mama gone. She would have gone into panic had not the bedroom door been wide open, with light streaming in from the hall.

"Mama? Are you there?"

Having gone hoarse, her voice simply would not carry through the darkness of her room and out into the light of the hall. Sitting up, she swung her legs over the edge of the bed. Though the motion was done smoothly enough, as in countless mornings before, she had not been prepared for the response her body gave back. She ached all over... especially in her head. Once when she was nine, Daddy had caught her hammering on a piece of wood – one he had labored over for hours to make smooth. He hit her in the side of the head with a fist, sending her crashing against the shed wall. The throbbing she felt now was far worse. Her hands were on the way to her head when her body intervened. As her legs were too shaky to bear weight, her arms were needed for steadying herself on the edge of the bed.

Eventually, she felt able to slide her feet all the way to the floor, hesitantly testing their ability to bear a burden. New aches coursed from thighs to midsection, surging and subsiding in waves of sharpness and dullness. Resting both hands on her knees, she noticed for the first time being dressed in one of Mama's nightgowns. Seeing it gave her strength. So she slowly shifted her full weight onto her legs and began taking cautious steps toward the light, convinced that Mama sat just around the corner, keeping guard... just in case.

Reaching the door frame and leaning on it, she called out again. Her voice was stronger now... so much so that she was certain it had carried down the stairs and into the parlor.

"Mama, are you there?"

Again, no answer.

Dread immediately arose within her, growing in severity the longer time expanded out from the last echo of her call. She turned to retrace steps to the bed, not quite sure if she intended to hide in it or beneath it. Neither occurred, as she suddenly became aware of a difference in the window hangings. The mind of a child is a magnificent thing – at one moment gripped with fear, and in the next captivated by a strange flickering of light. It pulsed sporadically, almost as if aided by a breeze blowing irregularly through the window. Yet the room's air was still and warm, proofs to her that the sash was closed tight. She moved more quickly to the window than she had to the door, powered by curiosity. There was no doubt that an odd light outside was responsible, and the nearer she got, the brighter it grew. It was not the steady, soothing purple of an eminent sunrise… that, she knew well… but an angry red, rising and falling in intensity.

Slowly at first, her hand slid aside the curtain, and she gained a full view of this strange light. It came from the shed, which was fully engulfed by fire. There Mama stood in the yard facing the shed's open door, itself wreathed in flame. She was tossing items from her arms into the shed. Each time, the opening sent back a small burst of light that seemed to say 'thank you' and 'more, more.' The sight was mesmerizing – the collaboration of Mama feeding and the shed consuming.

But then Mama unexpectedly turned back to the house, having depleted items to burn. So she reflexively withdrew her hand from the curtain and took a half step backward. She could hear Mama on the back steps, though the sound seemed to stop there. Returning cautiously, she hazarded another peek outside. Only the shed, the fire, and a shotgun lying across a tipped-over gas can. No Mama.

Her gaze then followed the flames, which had reached the level of her second story window. Flame gave way to spark… and spark, racing upward… gave way to darkness. Yet not the darkness of night. It was a thicker, blacker one resulting from smoke… which nonetheless intermittingly yielded back little reflections of the fire's light in a mocking reminder of the hope being consumed below. The sudden realization came upon her that Mama was burning Daddy's things. The fire was Mama and she was devouring all of him, sending out only a hazy and vapid reminder of his part in their lives – forever gone up into a darkness of both smoke and night.

Her eyes moved back to the yard as she became aware of Mama approaching the shed with another armload of items, many of which she must have previously moved to the back stoop in her systematic way of doing things. Knowing her, Mama would likely have preferred carrying the whole lot in a single trip if she could, burning away all of Daddy in one fell swoop. But Mama was a small woman… and there were plenty of things left in the house still bearing a remembrance of him.

As Mama crossed to her previous post before the door, an object fell from the load to the ground, but Mama did not stop to pick it up. It was clearly important not to delay, to keep feeding the fire. So she also ignored the fallen item and remained fixated upon Mama as she regained the rhythm… and the flame flashed in time. A coat… a boot… a bundle of odd clothing… then a piece of woodwork Daddy had made. It was the kitchen cutting board, given to Mama for Christmas a few years back. Beautifully made, it had deep grooves around its edges to catch drippings from carved meat. Then more men's clothes… a picture in its frame… a dress given to Mama… and a bundle of envelopes bound by a ribbon.

She continued to watch until Mama had emptied that load and turned back for the fallen item. It was the other boot to the one currently burning. In a smooth underhand motion, Mama flicked it into the shed to join its mate, the pair fated together for fire.

She, however, did not track Mama returning to the back porch for more of Daddy to burn. The boot had fallen from Mama's arms into an oddly darken spot on the ground about eight feet from the shed door. The fire's light showed that this spot was not a normal part of the yard's coloring. As she tried making out what was so odd about it, the thought occurred to her that the dog was nowhere to be seen. Spurs of darkness leading into the shed from that spot brought back memory of a flash of light and a loud boom. The dog was dead. Mama had most definitely dragged its carcass into the shed before starting the fire… and then just walked back and forth through that dark spot as if it were nothing. But she now knew it to be the dog's spilt blood.

Then another recollection came to her – of the front of Daddy as he lurched toward her on the back steps. He had not been discolored with something natural, as first imagined, but with blood. Whether his own, or some animal's, or someone else's, it had stained him from collar bone to trouser pockets. Then the smell of it came to her – blood mixed with whiskey and sweat.

Reflexively, she brought both hands to her mouth, covering it as any normal child would at such a discovery. Holding them there, staring out at that dark blotch, all thought – of Daddy and the dog, and of Mama and the shed in flame – was suddenly driven away by an unpleasant and unaccustomed lack of sensation. Her hands moved slowly and laterally, each to its own side of her face and upward. Then she screamed as if nothing else mattered. Just her hands, her head, and screams that would not stop, growing louder and more grotesque as she searched for that which could not be found.

She was later told that on reaching her room, Mama had found her by the window wrapped in a tight ball shrieking into the floor. Gently lifting her back into bed, Mama had desperately tried comforting her… but to no avail. For there, on a young head that had once been so beautifully adorned with locks of flowing blond hair, now lay only ragged shards and disfigured strands… Daddy's last remembrance left just for her, as he had taken a carpet knife and cut it all off.

CHAPTER 18

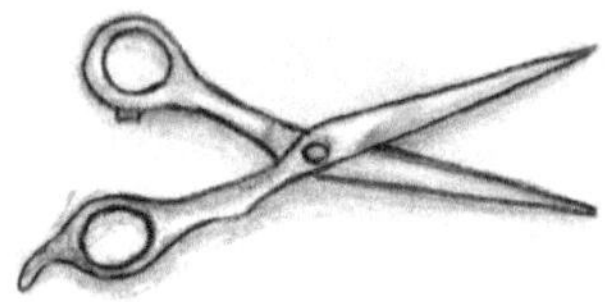

LIVING IN SHAME

Her existence had been torn apart. For days, she did not speak, did not hear, did not see… just breathed. The daylight hours were bearable only because Mama stayed home from work. Wrapped in a blanket that covered her from head to toe, she was Mama's shadow, moving together even into the bathroom. But at night, she was truly alone. Nightmares ripped open her mind, as image after image invaded her sleep, forcing her to relive the horror of that day. An armchair pulled up beside her bed allowed Mama to be there with words of comfort and reason. She was compelled to talk her way through every dream, and each account was made to end with Mama shooting the dog and busting into the shed. Although neither slept much for those weeks, eventually she came to realize that some of her dreams actually incorporated aspects of Mama coming to the rescue.

They were together, and together was the only path of healing for both. Despite the brokenness of that first week, there were certain memories she would retain… and even dwell on before bed as munitions against the dreams. For instance, the town sheriff was the first visitor… and Mama handled him expertly. His arrival on the day after the attack was initiated by a strong wrap on the front door.

"Camellia, this will only take a minute... but no matter what you hear or who's at that door, you stay put here at this table, you understand me?"

A nod of compliance was all she could return. Mama then took hold of her cheeks and stared holes through her eyes making certain that the nod was backed by a will to obey. Once convinced, Mama seemed to brace herself for unpleasantness, and then left the kitchen for the front door.

"Mae... it's my unpleasant duty to inform you that Buck has been arrested and charged with murder."

Those words have resonated in her mind ever since... probably would for a lifetime... but at that moment, they meant only shock intermingled with a strange sense of relief.

The sheriff continued. "The matter is, of course, under investigation, so I can't go into the details. This brings me to the purpose of my visit. There are questions I need to ask you and your daughter. May I come in?"

No effort had been made on the part of the sheriff to keep the conversation private, despite Mama's frequent interspersing of 'hush' and 'shush' throughout. However, upon the request to enter, Mama's voice rang out clear.

"Sherriff, you are not stepping foot in this house, and you are not seeing my Camellia!"

"Mae, it's my duty to..."

"I don't care a lick about your duty!"

There followed a stillness in which she could almost sense each adult marking their position, assessing their opponent, and developing new strategies. Mama had clearly won the initial advantage, as the sheriff yielded.

"Well then... what can you tell me about yesterday, did you see your husband... I mean... the suspect, at any part of the day?"

From her vantage point at the kitchen table, she could not see the front door, but imagined Mama making a face that could strip bark off a tree when the sheriff uttered the word 'husband.'

"No."

"May I ask your daughter if she did?"

"No, you may not!"

The sheriff now lowered his voice for the first time, though she could still make out the words.

"Mae… he's been talking freely… Well… mostly incoherently. But he's been saying some terrible things. Things no father should be saying. I need to know if there's any truth to those things." But Mama just remained impassive. "I know this isn't easy, but it's my… umm…" This time he silenced himself without a word from Mama. "At least let me send a doctor over for a visit – one who knows how to deal with these situations."

"My daughter is not a situation!"

Perhaps regretting the wording, he played a final stratagem.

"Neighbors reported a large blaze in the back of your premises last night. What can you tell me about that?"

"Shed caught fire."

There was another longer silence in which Mama seemed to be waiting him out again.

"We'll need to investigate that for evidence. We'll also need to search your house. I could get a warrant."

Mama was ready for this too.

"Won't do no good. Nothing of his left inside. I burnt it all up in the shed. All that remains is ash and twisted metal – go see for yourself."

She then heard the front door being closed and locked. Mama came through the kitchen and proceeded to the back door without acknowledging her. The back door bolt was thrown, and then Mama watched through a window as the sheriff scrutinized the remains of the shed.

She never heard anything regarding his investigation. In fact, she would not set foot out the back door or peer out a window for months… partly to avoid the memory, but mostly for fear of being seen.

There were other visitors to their home that week, and each time Mama was there to intercept. The sheriff did send a doctor and their preacher came by, both intent on providing healing in their own way. Mama was respectful, but would not allow either to enter. There were also visits from her teacher and principal, both of whom Mama met on the front porch. She did not get to hear any of those conversations, though later was told that arrangements had been made for her to be excused for the remainder of the school year. The head of the deaconess committee came bearing a cobbler. Mama accepted the dish, but would not allow the woman inside. As Mama's circle of friends had dried up nearly two years previous due to Daddy's drunkenness and drug dealing... and since she had no living relatives at the time... no additional visitors came.

On the third day, she saw herself for the first time since the attack. Still cloaked in a blanket, she was following Mama about the house. The parlor had a large mirror near the front door... (She clearly recalled that Mama had purposefully hung a towel over the one in the bathroom.) ...which in times past Mama had used to examine her appearance before admitting visitors. On passing this mirror, she inadvertently came face-to-face with her disfigured image. Staring back was a freakish mutilation of her former self – a badly bruised face displaying a spectrum of colors, with one eye and the lower lip still noticeably swollen. As if drawn by the macabre, she lowered the blanket to take in fully the shambles that was her hair. A few strands appeared unmarred, stretching to below her shoulders, but the rest had been shortened to unnatural lengths no greater than a few inches. There was even a sizable section up front cropped close to the scalp where the knife had also scored a gash in her head just above the hairline... which fortunately had already scabbed over.

The whole sight was too terrible to produce sound or tears – just utter disbelief at how dissimilar to a girl she appeared. But Mama was quickly there to steer her away.

"Sweetie, I'm sorry you had to see yourself just now. You know... I've been putting this off for a bit longer until you were more ready. Might as well get to it. Go to the kitchen table."

After sitting, Mama wrapped a table cloth about her neck, and asked her to keep her eyes closed so as not to see what was happening. With electric razor, scissors and comb, Mama then commenced cropping her damaged hair down to a uniform quarter inch length all around.

Sometime years later, she would read somewhere that the other senses of the blind frequently became more attuned in their tasks through greater dependency. As she closed her eyes, the sharp friction of scissor blades metallically rubbing across each other seemed to resonate more sharply in her ears, every one proclaiming as a bell toll the new wounds being inflicted upon her head. She felt more keenly the severed stubble falling across her face and upon her neck, each clump timed perfectly with the echo of a snip. The razor's high-frequency grinding travelled the full length of her body such that every strand of her vibrated with the humiliation. Despite that, she could sense Mama garnering support by leaning hard against the back of the chair, as whispers of sniffles betrayed the tears being fought against with great effort. But most of all, it was the sweet smell of wisteria in the air... in combination with a lingering taste of blood... that stood out so strangely in her mind. That flowering vine would never again bring enjoyment to her without memory of that terrible day.

When the job was completed, Mama went about sweeping up and disposing of the remains before giving her clearance to open her eyes. Without delay, she was back at the parlor mirror. If she had been a boy, the result would have been deemed acceptable by many Southern standards of grooming. Instead, she beheld the very outcome her drunken and enraged father vainly strove after – the cruel transformation of a daughter into a son.

Images of both the hacked and closely trimmed would not release her mind for over six years.

She received her first hoodie within two hours of that haircut. After checking, double checking, and triple checking that she felt comfortable being left alone, Mama departed the house for the first time since the attack with a stern command that she remain in her own bedroom.

"And don't you dare leave even if heaven and hell come banging on the front door all at once, you understand me?!"

The Carlton town center was only a ten minute walk from their house, affording Mama ample time to make purchases without being gone for long. She remembered that first one – it was bright yellow... a sign of hope according to Mama. It was all warm and fuzzy on the inside. Mama said wearing the hoodie as a covering would provide protection from gawkers until the hair grew back. More hoodies would follow of varying styles, colors and fabrics. Each was inducted into her life by a silent ritual that included a welcoming hug and preferential use for a week.

It sometimes happens that the wounded find themselves in a position to offer healing, and in so doing have their own hurts lessened to a degree. It was the morning of Mother's day, May 12th, when she was awoken by the sound of Mama crying. Such emotional displays were rare for her mother, and it scared her.

"Mama? Are you hurt?"

"Yes, Sweetie... terribly. But not for you to worry – I'll be fine. Come on in."

She entered the room to find Mama lying in bed with a tissue box balanced on her stomach and many spent wads scattered about.

"Happy Mother's Day, Mama."

In child-like expectation, she had chosen this moment to present a token for that day of recognition. It was merely a heart-shaped pattern cut from pink construction paper, then adorned with sparkles and the words: 'Thank you for being my mother – I love you.' This simple act was intended as an encouragement and a sign of appreciation... and in the end was so received... though the immediate response was more fitful sobs that openly confused and alarmed her. Mama, seeing the effect, rallied herself.

"Oh, I'm fine. It's just so lovely. Get yourself up here!"

She climbed into bed and into Mama's arms. They spent the entire day there still clothed in pajamas, passing the time by playing every board game they owned while Mama regaled her with stories about the craziest of their ancestors. It was just a start – she was feeling that maybe, with Mama, she could survive.

Yet the Summer of 1996 did not bring the rapid healing hoped for in the Spring. She experienced a significant loss of appetite, and frequently found herself inexplicably erupting into fits of anger or tears. She seldom left the house, and then only as far as the yard... but never without a hoodie on. The sight of men, even ones whom she knew well, sent her cowering, while the barking of neighborhood dogs brought instant panic attacks. The smell of varnish, cut wood, or tool oil caused her to vomit.

She began to bury herself within herself, staying all day in her room. Yet such inversions led naturally to prisons of self-imposed guilt. Guilt that she had caused Mama to miss so much work... that she had been wearing the dress against Mama's instructions... and that she had not made a better effort at being his son. It was at those times Mama would take her by the hand and lead her to the kitchen table. At that table, Mama said, she would always be safe. There, they could talk about anything. It became a sanctuary for them, a place to realize and a place to forget. There, they would be unfettered, bestowing upon each other sincere encouragement. The liberty of such openness between a damaged daughter and a disgraced mother helped both of them through the worst summer of their lives.

That summer also brought her the love of books, which began the slow process of subduing the worst demons of her mind. She devoured the written word with an appetite that grew the more she read, slowly supplanting the bitter food of remembrance. It was then that she discovered Camille. The name instantly became for her an existence that had not been beaten, raped or disfigured. The name meant hope and survival. She was proud to be Camille, and longed to thrive as Camille. It was her way out.

Also that summer, her father was tried by a jury of his peers and found guilty of first degree murder. Neither of them attended the trial, though both were subpoenaed. According to Mr. Ferguson, Daddy had killed a man during a dispute over money and territory in their mutual line of work. Testimony indicated that the attack was premeditated, as Daddy had shown up at the scene with blade drawn. The victim was not just stabbed once or twice – the coroner testified of sixteen separate knife wounds. The severity of the crime and the criminal disposition of the accused garnered a life sentence.

The facts of the murder and the rumors about what Daddy had done to her combined to both horrify and fascinate the small town of Carlton. The progression of the Larson family's fall from grace became a popular topic for discussion in diners, beauty parlors, barber shops and church yards. People would say it all started long before the sawmill closed with Daddy's compromise of siding with the owners. In four years, he went from an up-and-coming member of the Carlton working class to a man who had destroyed his family and his future. Daddy was labeled 'liar,' 'failure,' 'murderer,' 'scum,' and just plain wicked. The remnants of his family, the townsfolk could pity, but not get close to – the Larsons were cursed.

Human hair grows, on average, a half inch per month. As summer ended, the hair on the child that had been Camellia was not yet three inches in length. This newly named Camille that was her had strongly resembled a scrawny, undersized boy. It would take over a year before the look of a girl was fully regained, and nearly three before her hair returned to its original state. She once overheard Mama telling Mr. Ferguson that it did strange things to a girl, being forced to look like a boy for so long.

She reentered school in the fall bearing not just the hoodie, but also a defiant insistence that all refer to her only as 'Camille, the Warrior Queen.' In the first week of seventh grade, there was general sympathy for what she had been through, along with tolerance for her odd means of coping. The second week of seventh grade brought whispered concerns about what else might have gone on inside the Larson home to account for the murderer's daughter calling herself 'warrior.' Fresh tales began to spring up regarding the dog, the shed and the fire, each growing out of proportion such that anxious parents began phoning the school to voice concern. Entering the third week of seventh grade, classmates sensed that their teachers were becoming inconvenienced by the disruptions caused from her constant corrections of them regarding her name, as well as the determined emphasis placed on their use of her title. It was then that the teasing about her appearance and her 'experience' began. By the end of the first month of seventh grade, inconvenience had blossomed fully into annoyance such that teachers were openly challenging her use of a title, and insisting out of principle that she lower her hood in class.

She battled both student and teacher with a force of will that would not waiver. She was frequently sent to the principal's office, with Mama being summoned from wherever to account for her daughter's rebelliousness. The teasing intensified, moving from taunts of 'jail bird' to much worse. Many attempts were made by classmates to expose the 'boy's' head. She was a pitiful fighter, but still she fought. The first graffiti appeared on her locker in early October – an obscene cartoon image of a man with a little girl. Similar artwork found its way into her locker on a regular basis. By November, her constant insistence on the title 'Warrior Queen' had caused all authority at the middle school to write her off as hopelessly marred, starting her journey down a path of marginalization. The prankster and the tease were becoming leery of the freak, resulting in fewer targeted attacks. Her tenacious persistence was now bordering on spooky, and the belief in the Larson family curse had fully taken hold.

By the end of 1996, she, as the Warrior Queen, had fought her way through much adversity to reach the blissful state of being ignored by teacher and student alike. The hoodie now provided the distinct advantage of disappearing in plain sight. Internally, though, she was far from recovered. Sporadic nightmares revisited her sleep, weight lost from the summer had not returned, and she was still distrustful of all males. That is, until she met Old Joe while helping Mama at Fergie's Diner over Christmas break. She remembered him immediately hugging her and telling her how beautiful she was… and that she should hold her head up and show Carlton what a true Southern woman was like. He was the only person besides Mama who went out of their way to encourage her. From then on, because of him, she was content with simply being Camille.

The constancy of time moved the girl out of middle school, and the love of books followed. She read widely and deeply in every field of learning put before her, excelling beyond her classmates through the sheer joy of knowing. Though having led in grade point throughout high school, she deliberately allowed the metric to fall at the end in order to avoid being designated as valedictorian. Since the principal had prohibited her from wearing the hoodie during the graduation ceremony, she did not even bother attending. It mattered not. She was the hoodie and the name… for it was impossible to separate herself from either.

CHAPTER

19

CONTROL OF SELF

"The class roll has you down as Camellia J. Larson."

"Please call me Camille. That's the name I go by."

She had high hopes for this third study session with Mr. Reynolds, especially since the second had ended awkwardly due to the hoodie question… her having spent the weekend wondering whether to return. Fortunately, they had seen each other briefly on Monday when the first take-home essay was collected. The smiles they exchanged more than covered over any lingering discomfort from the previous parting. She was, once again, eager for a Thursday night.

As on the first occasion, she waited patiently for classmates to leave the session before approaching him. Once alone, she moved from the back, sliding a front row desk up to the edge of the table in order to sit across from him… vaguely aware that the experimental aspects of her interactions with him had lost their appeal. The class material had transitioned from the Greeks to the rise of the Roman Republic, and the subject fit surprisingly well with her request.

"Yeah… I like that as a nickname."

"Actually… it's not a nickname. I adopted it based on a character in a book."

"Seriously?! Which book?"

"Virgil's *The Aeneid*."

His face instantly lit up. "You're talking about Camilla, the warrior queen, aren't you?!"

"I… I didn't expect… but of course, you'd know. I just wasn't thinking that… you know, most people aren't even aware of that book."

"I've read *The Aeneid* – even wrote a term paper on it once. It's a beautiful piece of literature." A subtle smile then gradually developed on his face. "So tell me, warrior… with whom do you do battle?"

Slow in catching on to the familiarity being shown, she was still dwelling on his recognition of the name's origin. Her mind and heart had always been accustomed to inner turmoil, though not with respect to the opposite sex. On that subject, her teenage years had been spent in complete agreement – neither had any use for boys. Now, a conflict was brewing within regarding Mr. Reynolds, and she could not tell which part of her was on what side.

With whom do I do battle?

Growing up as she had, there were many mental and emotional breakdowns… from fits of anger to deep depression. The persona of the Warrior Queen had been adopted to help her subdue the past, which nonetheless had not ceased from tormenting her. Her efforts at redefining who she was all too often yielded to the hurricane version of Camille – reckless, destructive and beyond control.

Why can't I manage my feelings?

And why can't I make my mind focus where I want it to?

Though such frustrations continued to inundate her, her biggest struggle had always been in having little control over who she was. Though renamed, hers was still an existence defined by an act of cruelty rather than from the unique essence of a soul.

Mama had been desperate to find ways of helping her diminish the forces wearing away at her sanity. She once offered an illustration on how the mind, the heart and the will could work together. Mama's imagery had made a deep impression on her… though only in concept. They had been seated, as usual, at the kitchen table.

"Camellia, imagine two massive horses harnessed together in a common yoke attached to a cart. They're fighting each other, each struggling to take control of the cart and set the direction of motion. One of those horses is your mind. It *thinks* it should lead. The other is your heart. It *feels* it should lead. Which one's right, Sweetie?"

"I don't know, Mama. That's what I'm trying to figure out!"

"Why child, neither one's right! The mind and the heart are no good at steering the cart. What they need is someone with a strong hand at the reins to make them work together… not against each other and not against the cart."

Then Mama just sat there waiting for the obvious question.

"So… who's driving the cart?!"

"Now that's a good question. The team needs a driver, that's for sure. One they can trust. And this driver has to be good for the team and good for the cart. Won't do any good if the driver gets them under control and then takes the cart right off a cliff. Will it?"

"Of course not. But you're not telling me who would…"

"Child, life's full of drivers more'n ready to take control of your cart if you let them. Other people, for instance, but things too. Ambition, fame, money, smarts, looks, power, security, comfort – you name it and I guarantee you it's tried to drive a cart. Even the past can take control of the future direction. But only you should decide. Do you have a will that's strong enough to drive it all by yourself? And the wisdom to pick the right direction? If not, who're you going to trust to help you? And how much control are you willing to give up?"

"I trust you, Mama!"

"Ahh… that's sweet, Camellia… but a bad choice."

"But why?! You've always known how…"

"Won't do no good if I tell you – you have to learn for yourself. But just you think on this – the world… in fact all of history… is full of those two-horse teams. Every person alive and that did ever live. Look and see where their carts were driven. Look very carefully. Seek out in all those books you read who were the best drivers, and follow their examples. Choose those who guided their teams with wisdom and truth, mercy and kindness. Study them – then you'll know for sure."

All through high school, she had disliked this illustration of Mama's because she could not tolerate the notion of thoughts and feelings needing to be harnessed and controlled. Yet the facts could not be denied – she was personally unable to manage either. Her tongue was proof enough. It would, at one moment, be razor-sharp against her mother for no reason at all. Then in the next, when a single word of encouragement could make Mama's day, it would go mute. She knew she was smart, but intelligence mattered little in this battle. She felt weak…

and that weakness added shame to the burdens already laden upon her. And shame... in tier upon tier... covered her over, encapsulating her within the past. So she decided that the only safe course of action was to hide beneath the hoodie. It would hold it all in with an illusion of control. The hood would cover over the rage, the shame, and her intense fear of others. Most of all, it would prevent her from spilling out blame onto Mama.

But the horses... they would be set free, replaced by warriors who fought it out in an arena of her own imagination. As a teenager, she was convinced that two gladiators in battle better approximated the struggles of her mind and heart... with her will sitting in passive judgment over all.

This image of two warriors had become an addictive distraction... though it offered no more usefulness than that of the two horses. She so wanted to see her thoughts as burnished in hardened steel, polished to reflect the truth about everything. Yet the armor of her mind was woefully brittle and incomplete. There were far too many holes and blind spots. Her thoughts, hampered by vivid memory, were fertile soil for self-incrimination, willful misunderstanding, and poorly-conceived plans. At the same time, she wanted her heart arrayed in a golden light that dispelled all gloom... though at any moment, her emotions could burn up whatever was in the way... or be frigid as ice, locking all in a cold immovability.

In reality, she considered her existence to be nothing more than a small pilot light, ineffectual at giving off either brightness or warmth. Being in college had changed nothing... other than to convince her that Mama's illustration warranted more consideration. She knew it was time to grow up, and that meant putting aside her childish thoughts of warriors. Her dependence on Mama, she had to admit, must also lessen. Looking now at Mr. Reynolds, she acknowledged to herself that she liked this man, so she decided to answer him truthfully.

"I guess I'm most often at war with myself, trying to control what I think and how I feel."

They lingered in that classroom discussing the battles within, neither realizing how transparent they were being with the other. At 8:40, she did not have to ask him for an escort. They just rose together and headed for the door, continuing their conversation seamlessly from study hall to dorm walkway... with her doing most of the talking. She related to him the illustration of the two horses, the cart and the driver, concluding with an admission that it was her life's ambition to find a way to get her mind and heart working together in the right direction. Arriving at her dorm just before 9 PM, she was not really aware of their progression across campus… nor that a deeper connection had been established between them.

As before, he did not walk her to the door, stopping purposefully on the sidewalk. This time, though, she welcomed a change from previous walks with him. Deliberate or not, he positioned himself with his back to the dorm… not blocking her way up the walkway, but subtly indicating that he was not yet ready for them to be parted.

"You might like this talk that I heard at an education seminar last year…" She noted his quick downward glance before continuing. "I enjoy history… but the thing I really want to do most is teach it. I'm thinking maybe high school…"

Standing in the semi-darkness at the edge of the dorm's lighting, she could not fully make out his expression. But by shifting a step along the sidewalk, she was able to turn him slightly so that light fell upon his face.

"I can tell from how you talk about history that you'll make a fantastic teacher." She was pleased with the smile produced by these words.

"Thanks… So… this is going to sound weird… the speaker showed some videos on something called 'the marshmallow test.'" As Mr. Reynolds started explaining how this psychological assessment helped evaluate self-control in children, she was very much paying attention… but also very much distracted. "Here's how it goes – an adult comes into a room with a child and places a marshmallow on a plate before a hidden camera, then says: 'I'm going to leave the room now. You can have that marshmallow anytime you want, but if it's still here when I get back, you get a second marshmallow. If you've eaten it though, then you don't get the second one.' After the adult leaves, most of the children comically struggled with their desires… and most caved in. I remember this one boy who held out to the end, fighting through absolute misery as he pulled on his hair and banged his head on the table. He eventually got his two treats."

She was picturing this child in her mind, fleetingly admiring his warrior-like quality of battling through the temptation. At the same time, she was not missing a detail of the expressions on Mr. Reynolds' face.

"Personally, I was most struck by one child the speaker hardly mentioned. It was a small boy who turned away from the marshmallow and followed the adult's departure from the room. He avoided the battle altogether by keeping his eyes on the door, knowing that the adult had promised to come back. Then it hit me, the kids who struggled the most were those who kept their eyes on the marshmallow the whole time. They were never really free of its influence. That's why I like to think of self-control a little differently. It's all about turning thoughts and feelings away from the temptation lying within, and toward the door through which a promise will come."

'Avoid the battle altogether!?' How is that even possible?!

They eventually said their goodnights, and she headed up the dorm steps alone, just as on previous walks. This time though, on reaching the porch, she turned back to him… and there he was, standing where she had left him… watching her all the way to the door. She gave a small wave goodnight, which he promptly returned. As the door closed behind, and she moved through the lobby's usual curfew chaos, the image of his reciprocated wave occupied all thought and feeling. She did not recognize this for what it was – a sign of having fallen in love.

PART

2

"It's all about turning thoughts and feelings away from the temptation lying within, and toward the door through which a promise will come."

Robert

CHAPTER

20

A WALK ABOUT WALKS

She learned his first name by way of a wonderful happenstance. That evening, it being work-study, she was completing her shift by reshelving books on the library's fourth floor. On the last leg of her route, determined to empty her cart before 9 PM, she hurriedly veered into a narrow aisle between two stacks… and was brought up short by nearly colliding with someone sitting on a footstool. Such encounters with library patrons were commonplace, and she was trained not to distract. While backing out the cart, she came to recognize the person… who at that moment was perusing books on a bottom shelf completely unaware of her presence. The standard library etiquette moderated the excitement in her whisper.

"Hello, Mr. Reynolds."

He snapped up like some marionette tugged on by its strings.

"Camille! You startled me!" His eyes then took in the cart. "So you're a work-study here – that's great! I should have known that this… of all places… would suit you best."

"Yes. I love it here. But what're you looking for? Maybe I can help."

"I'm just hunting for some references on Asian migration across the Bering Strait. Prof. Simpson… that's my supervisor…" She had not forgotten. "…still wants something on native Americans, so I have

143

the idea of re-examining the initial inhabitants and their explorations within the context of the age of European Explorers. Kind of a twist on what the Asians might have encountered… you know, as seen through the eyes of a sixteenth century explorer. I'm preparing a brief for her on my ideas."

"That's fascinating! I'd love to hear more… but I really shouldn't be disturbing you."

She once more moved to back the cart out of the aisle.

"Hey. Do you… always work at this time?"

The question was nonchalantly offered, though framed in boyish awkwardness.

"Yes… every Tuesday… though I'm wrapping it up for the night. I have a few more books to shelve, and then I'm heading back to the dorm."

"You know, I've got all I need from here. Maybe I can… escort you?"

"I'd like that, Mr. Reynolds."

"Please call me Robert… seeing as we're not in the context of the History class. How about if I meet you at the check-out desk in…"

He waited for her to fill in the blank.

"Ten minutes?"

"Great. See you down there."

That night as she lay in bed reliving the chance encounter and the *very* slow walk to her dorm, she was deciding things. The next step in the friendship should be to somehow move it fully outside 'the context of the History class.' She told herself that this decision was simply the natural consequence of liking the name 'Robert' more than that of 'Mr. Reynolds.' Yet she refused to acknowledge that it was actually because of her pleasure in being with him. Their long conversation outside her dorm about people-group migration had opened up her imagination to an unexplored world of possibilities not fettered by the student-TA relationship. Unfortunately, she was sure any such opportunity would have to wait until after the semester ended. But by then, he might not have time for her. Her class next semester might have a different TA… and he would be out of her life. Having that heavy thought suddenly saddened her.

What she really needed was advice from someone who understood friendship. So she went through a brief mental checklist.

Not Mama. At least not yet.

Mrs. Riley?

She shuttered.

A dorm mother's hardly the type.

Not Amber either…

Her roommate's approach to boys was far too brazen.

So what about Cameron?

The senior likely knew a great deal about guys, but she sensed that her RA was more a woman of action.

Her advice would probably be something like… 'stop messing around and plant one on him!'

That was hardly helpful. Though unsure of what she was after, it was definitely not kissing. No… she needed the thoughts of someone more compatible with who she was – contemplative, systematic and cautious.

But who?

Then it hit her.

Ms. Kelley! Who better than the person that challenged me to learn in the first place?!

Without really knowing how to go about it, she fell asleep within an assurance that Ms. Kelley would know what she should do.

Seating herself in English, she was still considering how best to pose her request to Ms. Kelley, feeling more so the urgency of finding answers before tomorrow's History study session. The format of the English class had moved away from spontaneous essays to topics of Ms. Kelley's choosing. Today's literary concepts were epiphany – the sudden realization of a hidden truth – and dissuasion – the use of argument to change a previously held perspective. The assignment was to prepare a personal story illustrating how one or both of these concepts had played a significant role in some event in their life. This story, to be written in the journal, was due on Friday. She jotted all this down in her calendar, then returned to her annoyance over how the clock was barely dragging itself along. When class finally ended, she loitered about in order to be the last student out.

"How can I help you, Miss Larson?"

"I was wondering if I could get your advice on something not totally related to class. Are you free for a few minutes?"

"Of course. Walk with me."

They headed out as she, not paying attention to where they were going, busied herself with the request.

"I was wondering… remember that essay on love we did some time back? The one where I only wrote 'I do not know,' and you wrote back 'That is why we learn'?"

"Yes, I remember."

"Exactly how do you think I should go about learning on that subject? Should I start maybe by… reading something… or going to a lecture… or perhaps getting advice from an expert?"

This was not even close to how she had planned the request to go, but it was out… and Ms. Kelley responded without critique.

"Unfortunately, Miss Larson, I do not consider myself to be an expert on the subject of love."

This came as a total surprise. Surely someone of Ms. Kelley's understanding, knowledge and sensitivity would have ample experience. Suddenly, she was ashamed of herself for having not considered a different perspective on this woman before putting her in an uncomfortable situation. Perhaps the 'Ms.' part of 'Ms. Kelley' carried with it some sad story of lost love. After all, very few Southern women insisted on its use. Yet her instructor seemed not to have suffered from the request.

"You could do those things, Miss Larson, and probably learn something. But my advice would be that if you really want to understand what it means to love… and be loved… then you would need to make it real. You would need to get personally involved."

"What do you mean by 'involved'?"

"I mean you would have to make yourself vulnerable. There is little doubt you could learn about a thing by examining it up close. You could study its appearance, record its habits, and prod it to see how it responds, yet real knowledge only comes by experience. There is no way for me to say what that should look like for you. It's just not possible to tell someone else how to experience love… or friendship, for that matter. But I know this for certain – a person will never make progress in any area of life unless they invest something of themselves into it. Does that make sense?"

"Yes, ma'am." *And it's terrifying!*

"Oh… and just so we're clear – I'm not telling you to do something crazy like date random guys just for the experience. Without regard for the person, that's just an ill-conceived experiment with potentially painful consequences."

"No, ma'am. Don't worry about that. I can guarantee you I'm not that type."

Yet Ms. Kelley just remained looking at her without response. Becoming uncomfortable with the scrutiny, she glanced down to realize that they were standing in a parking lot beside a somewhat dated compact car.

Ms. Kelley said goodbye and drove off, leaving her to a slow walk back across campus. Though her schedule had her in the library working on English, her mind could not be pried away from that advice. Getting involved to the extent that led to dating was unimaginable – she was still trying to figure out friendship! Equally certain, she knew that a relationship with a freshman was not something on Mr. Reynolds' mind.

But you're not really interested in him… beyond friendship… are you?

She fought against the question, for to consider it deeply was to give in to it. Yet the notion, already banging around within her head like the clangor in a bell, was creating such a mental racket that no other thought seemed possible.

The dorm's wide lawn lay before her, so she departed from the walkway just to welcome a softer feel underfoot. Grass always had an inexplicably powerful way of calming her… something that concrete could never replicate. And calm was what she desperately needed in sorting through her thoughts and feelings on Mr. Reynolds. For some reason, she decided this issue must be settled before stepping back onto stone. The entire green expanse could be roamed freely, but to pass its borders without an answer to the question would be an inexcusable admission of defeat.

She did not go far before plopping down. There was only a meager level of activity at the time – two guys nearby tossing a football and a small group of students on the far side of the lawn – nothing to distract her from dissecting and analyzing the problem of Mr. Reynolds.

She started by combing the fingers of both hands through the blades of grass before her, fully expecting the action to bring clarity… though it did not. Her attention was then diverted toward tracing the spiraling football's arced path through the air. The two guys were playing some kind of a game where one would throw, and if the other caught, then the separation between them was widened by a few paces. She could see that the objective was reaching a distance that strained their ability to catch and throw. Watching their game brought back the strange memory of Daddy hurling her farther and farther into the Tombigbee waterway, forcing her to swim by stretching the distance needed for returning to safety. It was a terrible thing to do to a child.

She was no longer a child, but these walks with Mr. Reynolds were beginning to have the same feel. She was throwing herself deeper and deeper into a regard for him, trying each time to regain the shoreline of sensibility.

Just then the football fell short, and the two guys returned to a meager separation in order to resume their game of expansion.

Was love that easy? If you dropped the ball, then you just picked it up and started over? Or was it more painful, like learning to swim Daddy's way?

From Ms. Kelley's expression, she gathered that love was both perilous and costly.

Mama had nearly drowned.

After thirty minutes of watching the guys trying to reach some unreachable distance, she became weary of searching for meaning where no meaning could be found. Conceding defeat, she rose and headed for the walkway that led to Switson Hall, glancing back just in time to see the two conclude their game and head off together in the opposite direction. They departed in typical guy fashion, half-wrestling and half-hugging each other. Their game had been a success irrespective of whatever improvement had been attained in catching or throwing.

She found the dorm room empty. Crashing down on her bed, she stared up at the ceiling, searching its blankness for insight. Sounds of dorm mates echoed along the hall as girls came and went. She envied them for their places to go and things to do, craving the distraction that such urgency could provide.

Shifting focus to Amber's side, she scanned over her roommate's mess without criticism. Their relationship had improved considerably after she opened up about her feelings. They were growing in friendship, as shown by Amber's reciprocation. She had shared about having bailed out of college after the fall semester of her freshman year because of some poor decisions. What those were, she did not elaborate, only that she had left Garland with the plan of returning the next fall to give it another go.

So far, everything's working out for her. I'm so glad she's...

And then epiphany struck, and it was terrible and wonderful at the same time. Her mouth provided a release to the growing intensity within. A slow, very audible 'WOW' flowed out. The analogy of Daddy's way of teaching her to swim was completely wrong for love because it was just one person risking it all while the other was safe on shore. Sure, there were probably plenty of people unfortunate enough to experience love that way. Yet that was not how she and Amber were growing in their friendship. They were both being vulnerable, both sharing how they felt, and both trusting each other. One would throw and the other would catch, then the order would switch… just like the guys playing football. Neither quit simply because the ball got dropped or a bad throw was made. They were in it together.

She instantly knew what she needed to do… even what she wanted to do. Suddenly, being vulnerable with Robert took on a completely different perspective… just as it had with Amber. Tomorrow, at the History study session… even before the walk home… she would tell Robert exactly how she felt about him. She would risk losing 'Mr. Reynolds' in the hopes of gaining 'Robert.' Then it would be up to the both of them to decide how far the game went.

But exactly how do you feel about him?

Amber's portion of the room provided no new epiphanies. For a moment, she envisioned her roommate sitting there speaking on behalf of that side: 'Don't look over here. We've already done the hard part for you – you figure out the rest!'

She turned back to the ceiling, acknowledging to herself that focusing on Mr. Reynolds as a specimen had been because he differentiated himself from other males. He was kind and self-controlled, but also intelligent and insightful.

Well… that's something I could tell him.

Yet telling him about himself somehow fell short of the epiphany she received on considering Amber. When she had allowed herself to be vulnerable, it was not to tell Amber anything about Amber – it was to tell Amber something about herself. So there it was. She wanted Robert to know how he made her feel – that there was a guy out there who made her want to put the past aside so she could be his friend. No way could she see herself telling him anything about that past… but maybe it was enough that he knew how much she liked being with him. This, she could manage. It would be her first small toss of the ball.

CHAPTER

21

COMPETITION FOR MR. REYNOLDS

Progressing through Thursday classes, she grasped at anything capable of offering a distraction. She was trying not to dwell on the upcoming study session, though it was actually all she cared to think about.

In Calculus, the material had progressed from slopes and limits to derivatives. Rate of change was basic to translating a continuous function into its differential response – that being nothing more than the slope at each point on the function. This related back to the concept of infinitesimal change. In that moment, she was immensely thankful for Newton and Leibniz. Aside from being the geniuses who invented calculus, they were providing her with a much needed diversion from the fluctuating tendencies of her insides.

After Calculus, she ventured to the library, followed by a late lunch before Chemistry. The content of the lab had progressed slightly ahead of the lecture, which in her mind was not the best way to introduce scientific concepts. It should be the theory first, and then the student moved into the lab. An unpleasant thought suddenly crossed her mind – she had absolutely no theoretical basis for this friendship experiment with Robert.

Ugh! Back to molecules, girl!

As in Calculus, she was thankful for a scientific pioneer to distract during Chemistry.

Amedeo Avogadro was so amazing!

Almost 200 years ago, he observed a proportionality between the volume of a gas and its mass for a set pressure and temperature. Scientists of the 1800's expanded on this relationship to determine laws of gas dynamics still important today in many areas of physics, chemistry and engineering. About a hundred years after Avogadro, a French scientist named Perrin accurately determined the proportionality constant and named it after Avogadro. Her Chemistry professor said this constant was as important in all areas of chemistry as 'pi' was to geometry or 'e' was to calculus.

She had already learned this in the lab. They had performed a simple experiment to determine Avogadro's number using the surface area of an oil droplet as it spread out on a pan of water. There were some assumptions to be made… such as the density of the oil and that the film was only one molecular layer thick. Yet the results obtained by college freshmen were remarkably similar to Perrin's true proportionality named after Avogadro.

A small voice in the back of her mind then interrupted these thoughts of Chemistry.

Better to be in a lab on Robert than a lecture on Mr. Reynolds.

Leaving Chemistry for the library, her head was awash with thoughts of infinitesimal changes and universal proportionalities… and the decision to be acted on in a few hours. Now that the day's classes were over, she found it impossible to hold back thoughts of Robert. The nervousness was building beyond control… though she was well past changing her mind. There was a plan to be followed, and if that plan led her off a cliff… She only hoped that some proportionality between thought and feeling could be reached by an infinitesimally small change on her part… and that the Robert she had come to know would not be unkind.

Chicken pot pie! I absolutely detest chicken pot pie!

This, unfortunately, was the main dish served in the cafeteria that evening. With no appetite for supper, she used the offering for its only true purpose – to be stabbed, churned and mashed. Mama once said that her chicken pot pie recipe was well-known in Carlton church potluck circles. She had no memory of church potlucks.

Though dinner had been totally distasteful, she was reluctant to leave the safety of the cafeteria. At 6:50 PM, she deposited the mangled meal in the return-tray window and exited for Cunningham Hall, outwardly shaking from the tension within. It was October 17th, the day she would tell Robert how she felt about him. Concentrating hard on keeping herself moving forward, she reached the building and made her way to the classroom. With as much resolve as could be summoned, she placed her hand on the door knob and boldly entered.

"Oh hi, Camille! How're you tonight? Mr. Reynolds was just explaining to me how Roman roads were so advanced for their time. Made world conquest much easier. So very interesting, don't you think?"

The wind instantly fell out of her sails as the ship of her resolve slowed to a complete stop in the doldrums of Charity Perkins.

There the flirt was, seated at the front table so very close to Robert and not in one of the classroom desks where she belonged. From her vantage, the vixen might as well have been in his lap considering all the incidental contact in play. Somehow, Charity had managed to compress his chair into a corner of the table so that he could move no further. From where Charity had obtained a second chair was a mystery as the room only ever had one. It would not have surprised her to learn that Charity hauled one all the way across campus just for this occasion. As a result, a wide variety of descriptors were flowing through her mind, and 'so very interesting' was definitely not one of them.

The circumstances were clearly to Charity's liking, as she gave her chair an approvingly audible 'scootch' toward Robert... just for her benefit.

Sizing up her opponent, she decided to go on the offensive.

"Charity, I'm so glad you're finally taking advantage of Mr. Reynolds' knowledge. I've learned *so much* in the many hours I've spent with him discussing history."

Shot across the bow.

"Well bless your heart! And here I was not noticing you making any progress in class seeing as you never speak up."

Return fire!

"It doesn't show? I'm so disappointed. Maybe you should... leave... seeing as you think I'm the one who's in need of tutoring time with Mr. Reynolds."

Fire at will!

Such back-and-forth sniping was standard in Southern female conversations, especially amongst rivals. And though she had no past experience in such matters, the Southern gene was there... and her quick mind and tongue had acted in combination to access it.

She selected a front row desk and dragged it up close to Robert's corner of the table, placing him between herself and Charity... yet still maintaining a line-of-fire to her target. How he had gotten himself into this dilemma was academic, as her main concern was Charity.

If she only could have stepped outside herself at that moment, she would have seen that the one really uncomfortable with the situation was Robert... who nevertheless was rapidly transitioning in her mind back to Mr. Reynolds. As the two continued trading volleys, she noticed him fumbling with the pages of his book. Yet most of all, he was silent... not because he was enjoying himself – that much was clear from his downturned face – but because he recognized himself to be nothing more than a bit of battlefield that two freshman girls were fighting over. That should have made her sad... but she was still too worked-up over Charity's presence ruining her epiphany.

For in having passed before them, she had obtained a sweeping panorama of her rival. Charity wore an extremely soft-looking plum cashmere pullover that clung snugly to her upper body. Eye shadow of the same hue made a strong association in the observer's mind. With delicate liner and fine blush, Charity's skill with makeup was clearly evident. Then there was her rich dark hair, bound gently behind by a single strand of ribbon that constrained the waves to flow smoothly over her back... without obscuring a single detail of her front.

Once seated, she could see beneath the table to note that Charity's lower half was attired as sumptuous as that above. Chartreuse slacks conformed neatly to every curve of her slender hips... as those legs of hers were shifted in a blind search of thigh-to-thigh contact with him. But back up above the table top, she was most alarmed when Charity leaned forward to address her... for the girl came dangerously close to touching Robert. It was then that she observed a silver heart-shaped pendant swinging gracefully from Charity's neck, its surface reflecting brightly all light with the good fortune to fall upon it. On seeing that, she suddenly became aware of a delicately seductive scent that... like the charm... lent a hypnotic air to the room.

"You look unusually nice tonight, Camille. Wearing white after Labor day – so very bold! Now, as I'm not up on the fashion, would you say that hoodie's a standard part of your fall wardrobe?"

She was suddenly struck by Charity's greater intentions. The girl was there not only to make advances toward Mr. Reynolds, but also to flaunt her superiority with an intimidating impression: *'Camille, you can't possibly think yourself capable of having him!'* The contrast between them was far too stark. Faded blue jeans and a plain white hoodie with the hood up. No jewelry, no perfume, no makeup, and no hairstyle. She was hiding all of her femininity, whereas Charity was openly displaying hers. The comparison had its intended effect – a realization that she had such a long way to go toward becoming a woman. For now, she felt outnumbered, outgunned, and out a man.

But Robert's looking at me!

He had not even registered Charity's latest 'scootch.' His embarrassment seemed to be diminishing, being replaced by the pleasure of her own presence.

"Now Mr. Reynolds, please continue with what you were saying before we were interrupted."

Charity's hand came to rest upon his forearm, startling him back to the tactical complexity of his situation. Aware that he was being cornered both above and below 'see' level, Robert abruptly sprang up and backed into the whiteboard. His fingers came to rest on a marker, and he grasped it as a lifeline. Apropos, seeing as his ship was taking on water. But it was only then she belatedly came to realize that every salvo between her and Charity had actually struck him.

Clearly embarrassed at having responded so abruptly, he sheepishly turned to the board and began to slowly write the word 'Roman.' After completing the name of the empire that had ruled the world for over half a millennium, Robert leaned back to survey his work... then moved forward again to add 'conquest' more quickly... just before swinging about to face her alone. And then she knew. She really, really knew that epiphany was there for him too. *Infinite* change leading to recognized *proportionality*.

It was now only Charity's glower that oscillated between them, and there was venom in the expression. Maybe things would have turned out differently had an additional student shown up. Maybe there would not have been conflict, a climax, and this wonderful conclusion. But it was just the three of them.

Suddenly, she and Robert were startled back to the awkwardness of the setting by Charity's book slamming shut.

"What's up with you two?! Whatever it is, it's not right!"

The hypocrisy of the statement was not lost on her… though she had no desire to point it out, for to do so would only delay the departure of Charity… who quickly gathered her belongings and stomped out of the classroom. Silence transpired as the remaining occupants stared at the reverberating door, each hesitant to face the other. Finally, Robert turned to her.

"Sorry about that."

They remained placidly looking at each other for several seconds before both of them burst out laughing… continuing as loud and as long as they pleased… neither of them being concerned with whether Charity Perkins remained lurking just outside the door.

22

HOW TO SURVIVE AN ATTACK

Their laughter eventually subsided as they both regained composure. Before anything else could be said... before any other distraction could present itself... she looked directly into his eyes and gave in to the vulnerability of her heart, saying much more than was originally intended.

"Robert... I like you. I like you very much."

"I like you too, Camille. Very much."

The moment could not have been more perfect... except that he was still at the whiteboard with marker in hand. That distance unfortunately allowed reason and propriety to return to the relationship, for Mr. Reynolds was back.

"If it's alright with you... Miss Larson... I think it best that I should walk you home now. I have... things to think about."

He added the last slowly and purposefully... possibly only to himself... and she had the good sense not to inquire. So they gathered their possessions and headed out the door on their usual route to Switson Hall. She chose not to speak, being pleased for the moment to concentrate on the feelings already shared between them.

On rounding the corner that would take them across the main lobby and out the front doors, they discovered that the way was blocked. The night crew, getting a jump on the task of floor polishing, had begun early on the lobby. There was liquid wax being poured out by one man, while another was starting up a buffer. The one with the wax pointed to the warning placards already set up.

"Sorry, you can't come through here. You'll have to exit out the back."

Of course, she was silently pleased for the detour, hoping it would prolong the duration of their walk. With him in the lead, they backtracked, passing their classroom and continuing on through a series of hallways to a set of glass doors. Out this side of the building was an arboretum, with walking trails, benches, and displays of a wide variety of native trees and shrubbery, complete with little signs for the enthusiast. She had discovered this park before the semester began, but not yet made time to explore its expanse. It was quite dark out, but campus lighting and a nearly full moon provided sufficient means to see. Off in the distance... perhaps fifty yards or so across the park... she could clearly make out Fulton-Hamner Avenue, named after two of the university's founders. This marked the western boundary of campus, across which were a variety of businesses catering to students – a diner, a bookstore, a bank and an assortment of other nondescript establishments. Nearly all were closed now. The avenue was unusually quiet, with no pedestrian traffic on the sidewalks. She did detect some movement in an alley between the diner and the bank. It was just a dog, by the looks of it, foraging for food.

Robert, assessing the layout of the park, and perhaps sharing her desire to prolong the walk, suggested a route that would approach her dorm from the rear.

"Sounds wonderful."

"I occasionally come out here during lunch, just to escape the noise and activity of Cunningham Hall. It's very peaceful during the day, despite the traffic along the avenue. I've forgotten who founded this park, but some donor about sixty years ago noticed that the campus lacked a quiet place where students could contemplate nature. I've seen pictures of it from back then – this was a football field. There was nothing beyond Fulton-Hamner but scrub pines."

He had chosen a slightly meandering pathway angling through the heart of the park. Along this were many well-tended bushes, flower beds, and small groves in which she recognized witch hazel, alder, holly, azalea, and laurel.

They had just passed a beautiful, broad-branched magnolia tree, and were not more than ten feet from the avenue's sidewalk, when they both heard it. A deep snarling growl originating in the direction of the four lane. From a distance, the dog had appeared of no significant size or threat, but now… as it charged across the avenue toward them… she could see that it was big and mean.

Instinctively, she turned to flee, but Robert grabbed her arm and shifted her behind him.

"Don't run!"

No sooner did he say this than the dog was upon them, snarling and snapping at Robert. Fortunately, he had managed to shift his backpack out in front just in time.

"Stay behind! Grab my belt!"

Aware that she was shaking terribly, she nonetheless managed to steady herself with a hand on the small of his back while the other felt about for his belt. She could not see the dog, shielded as she was by his body, but she could hear it and sense it repeatedly making moves at him. Memories of Daddy's dog were forcing their way into her consciousness. Memories of her being lifted above its lunges, and of the endless hours of darkness filled with only its snarls and her screams. She was going back there now. She was there… and she could feel herself fainting.

Then Robert's voice burst through.

"NO! NO!"

He was addressing this dog, she knew… but the command somehow went out to the other also, pulling her back from the past.

"The tree… how far?!"

She quickly peered about to see that the magnolia's perimeter was a short distance away. The gardeners had pruned this tree so its lowest lying branches originated from only a few feet off the ground. Even the least coordinated person could find their way up into it.

"Not far!"

"Up the tree! Now! Trust me!"

She released his belt and sprang up into the branches, climbing six feet up before pivoting about to see what was happening below. From that vantage point, it now seemed as if Robert and the dog were engaged in a weirdly convulsive dance. The beast appeared to have gotten ahold of his left arm and was ripping at it… tearing it back and forth… twisting and turning… trying to knock him off his stance. She was on the verge of screaming like never before when his voice rang clear again.

"9-1-1, Camille!"

Remarkably, her backpack was still on her shoulder. Pulling it around, she retrieved her phone, dropping the rest to the ground below.

"9-1-1, what is your emergency?"

She could not reply, for it now looked as if Robert's arm had become detached from his body, with the dog focusing its full ferocity upon the severed limb. She started to scream for real this time… but once more abruptly stopped. A two-armed Robert was darting up into the tree with her. Looking down, it was actually Robert's backpack being torn to shreds.

"Hello? Hello? What is your emergency?"

She came back to the phone.

"My boyfriend and I – we're stuck in a tree and… and… this dog's attacking us! It just tore my boyfriend's arm off!"

A part of her knew that the things she was saying were not quite right, but that part was not speaking. Hysteria held the phone, and it did not believe the part of her that had clearly witnessed Robert use two arms in climbing this tree.

"Camille… I'm not hurt. Just hand me the phone."

She could not see how this was possible, but gladly yielded over the responsibility of the phone. Her eyes went back to the dog, which had abandoned the backpack in favor of trying to get up into the tree at them. At the same time, she could somehow hear Robert describing where they were before requesting animal control. When finished, she was thankful that he pocketed the phone rather than handing it back, telling her instead to hold on tight. That, she thought, required no special admonishment – her hands ached from gripping the branches. The dog was now circling about them, occasionally returning to its fruitless attempts to bring them down.

"Are you absolutely sure you're not hurt?"

"I'm pretty sure. I'll know better once we get out of this tree."

They did not happen to share the same branch. Being higher up, his afforded him a better view of the distant reaches of the avenue from where help might come. He was facing that direction, so she turned her head about to see far off flashing lights.

It was then, with the realization of rescue at hand, that her unbidden tears began to flow, shaking her from the force of the ordeal – both past and present. Suddenly, there was an arm about her shoulder... for Robert had shifted to her side.

"It's OK... you're safe. That dog can't get to you now."

But her crying only intensified, so he pulled her in close and held her hooded head against his shoulder. Her tears, though, were from relief, because in her heart she knew that he was right. It was not just this dog below that he was protecting her from, but the other also.

Shielded in his arms, she lost track of time... only becoming aware of the emergency vehicles when Robert pointed out that they were near. With a deep soothing breath, she smiled her thanks to him. In response, with his face mere inches from hers, he asked a simple question in an absurdly normal tone.

"So, Camille... let me see if I've got this straight... I'm your boyfriend?"

Looking dumbstruck at him, she tried to equate the monotone measure of his words with the seriousness of the situation.

"What?!"

He then smiled the obvious answer to both of their questions... just as the recollection came to her of the manner in which she had spoken to the 9-1-1 operator.

"Of course! Was there ever any doubt?!"

The words came out without reservation. So she gave a sniffled laugh while wiping away a tear with her free hand. But then the 'Mama' side to her arose.

"But my real question is... are you out of your mind?! Taking on a dog like that! That thing could have torn you to pieces! Just look at your backpack!" They both turned to see where the animal had ripped open a seam along one side, with the contents spread out in a large circle about the spot. "You clearly need a girlfriend to keep you from getting yourself killed! So how in the world did you avoid getting bit? It looked like the thing was tearing you apart."

"I put my arm through the straps and held the backpack out like a shield. I was kind of offering it to the dog as a place to start... and it took me up on the deal. That's when I decided to get up this tree."

Just then, police and paramedic vehicles came to a stop on the avenue opposite them. Quickly assessing the situation, they moved into action. An officer, donned in padding, waddled up and stuck a long stick into the dog's flank. There was a zap, a spark, and a yelp… then the dog was down.

"Stay up there until we secure the animal and remove it."

A burly policeman soon approached and said it was safe to come down. He moved to her first, arms extended in an offer to catch her. So she started to shift forward… but drew back in surprise. Robert had jumped down in an instant and… not too politely… nudged the policeman aside in order to offer himself instead. She was stunned… as was the officer… though Robert just stood there waiting patiently. Then the man started laughing, waved off the offense, and she jumped down into Robert's arms.

It was a long time before they were able to leave. The paramedics had to check over Robert, making him get into the back of their vehicle and remove most of his clothing, before being convinced that there was not a scratch on him. While that went on, she picked up his belongings… and then gave a statement to a different policeman.

"Your account is consistent with the numerous reports we've had tonight about that dog. Not a nice animal. Apparently, it's owner keeps it mean to better guard his gas station after hours. Somehow, it got loose and has been chasing folks about on this side of town. Killed someone's Siamese a few hours ago, but disappeared before we got there."

This policeman then entered the paramedic vehicle to interview Robert, who eventually emerged… returning her cell phone.

Finally, the burly one offered to drive them home. As they both departed the patrol car at her dorm, the cop spoke his goodbyes.

"Sleep well – you both earned it. You, my friends, are brave."

As he drove off, she amended his statement in her mind.

No! Robert's truly the brave one!

Extending a hand to grasp hers, he led her all the way to the dorm door… though she had no intention of going inside. Taking his other hand, she leaned upward and kissed him on the cheek. She made it soft and sweet, putting all of her deepest feelings into it.

Slowly and without speaking, he raised his hands out of hers and slid them within the hood, carefully pushing it back off her head in the process. Frozen in anticipation, she scarcely thought it possible… for she certainly felt his fingers moving into her hair. With great care, he gently set each strand free from the hoodie, allowing them all to fall unfettered upon her shoulders and back. With fingers still interlaced within her hair and upon her neck, he then gently drew her forward until their lips met. She could not breathe… could not move. She was certain that her heart had stopped. When he moved back, they were eye-to-eye… and it was just them.

"You… you saved me. Thank you, Robert."

This time, she kissed his lips… again and again… as they lingered together on that porch to relive the experience simply to remain in each other's presence. The lobby curfew had long since passed, with the rate of girls returning to the dorm having diminished to the point at which they had been alone on the porch for a long time. Still… they stayed there holding each other, gently kissing, and softly expressing their love.

Eventually, Robert made her open the door and say goodnight, with a promise of seeing her first thing in the morning. She entered, following the path of countless other young women before her who had departed the front porch of this dorm bearing the remnant of a precious kiss.

On passing through 'the door,' she suddenly realized that Robert must have thought only of the dog when she spoke of him saving her. She meant that, but so much more.

CHAPTER

23

I FOUND HIM

It was late. Much too late to be calling Mama… though this news absolutely could not wait until morning. She climbed the stairs two at a time, hurrying past her room to the end of the hall… to a lone chair located beneath a window. She sat before placing the call, then shifted to a more comfortable position as ring piled upon ring, knowing that it might be sometime before Mama could be roused. While waiting, she purposefully tried not to think about Robert, wishing to hold in all that wonder so it could burst forth to Mama over the phone. Instead, she ventured into a rather serendipitous consideration of the attributes to her surroundings… simply as a means of calming herself.

This spot on the hallway was well-acknowledged as having both excellent cell phone reception and respected privacy. Residents made calls from here when wishing not to disturb or to be disturbed. The height of the window sill here was ideal for resting one's elbow while holding a phone to an ear. Depending on the purpose of the call, a girl could lean the chair back against one wall, placing the soles of her shoes on the other, easily forming a human bridge that spanned the width of the hall. The paint bore countless scuff marks indicating that this was commonly done. From such a position, the caller could gaze out the window and lull the time away in conversation. Or… if the moment required… the chair could be shifted forward so a girl might place the crown of her head on the wall, relying on it for support. To be in such a position, the caller must be indifferent to the contact between her hair and this dirty wall. But in facing downward, that orientation should prove perfect for contemplating the floor… and other such base things in life. The chair, she also noted, was sturdy enough… and plenty wide… ideal for those times when the caller was all tied up inside. It provided ample space for legs to be pulled up under and arms to be wrapped about knees. The chair could easily accommodate that female ball of physical and emotional knots. She had once seen a girl sit in the corner on the floor and use the chair as a shield to insulate herself from others. That position nicely adapted its function from supporter to protector… which was ideal for the caller who felt the entire scrutiny of the world directed personally at her.

Over the years, hundreds of girls had used this spot… and identical ones on the floors above and below. This chair and these walls were a testament to woman's passion for seeking connection and resolution… for emptying herself of frustration… for mutual laughing or weeping… and maybe even for finding or forgetting love. There was nothing to know regarding trust and betrayal, hope and despair, peace and conflict, to which these walls and this chair were not already familiar. They had seen it all. Yet they offered no advice… no warnings… no reassurances borne from those countless years of experience. They could not share in celebration or commiserate in tragedy. All were indifferent. The caller was alone.

As Mama's phone continued to ring, she satisfied herself that this was an ideal spot for the conveying of either good or bad news. This would be good news – the very best she could offer.

The calls went to voicemail five times before Mama finally answered.

"Mama!"

"Camellia… is that you, Sweetie?! Are you OK?!"

It had not occurred to her until then that the ringing of a little black box might be answered in alarm. Children, though attaining adulthood, sometimes forget that parents respond to late night calls with panic.

"I'm really, really sorry to be calling so late… and everything's totally fine! I'm absolutely fine!"

"Are you sure, Child? Cause you sound very much out of breath."

"Mama, something's happened! Something wonderful! I can hardly believe it myself! Mama – I found him! I *actually* found him! Oh, I can barely breathe to talk!"

There followed a stillness in which she strove to calm herself… at the same time becoming worried that Mama had not comprehended her… or maybe was growing peeved for having been awoken.

"Are you still there?"

"Of course, Child. Tell me about him."

The voice was alert… though a bit weak.

"He's so wonderful! I just know you'll approve of him – I'm sure of it! I've known him since being here, but only recently have come to love him. Mama – he's kind and thoughtful… but also intelligent and… And you won't believe this – he saved my life! He actually saved my life!"

She launched into the entire story, starting with Ms. Kelley's admonition and going all the way to the kiss on the dorm porch. When she had finished, Mama's first question totally surprised her.

"And the hoodie, Camellia… tell me about the hoodie."

She hesitated to fully relive that wonderful moment before responding.

"He… he removed it from my head… then he… he straightened out my hair… right before kissing me. How… how did you know to ask that?"

And now Mama was laughing… and she was laughing. And they were both crying.

"A mama always knows."

Totally taken aback with the wonder of Mama, she turned the conversation to an embellishment on her feelings for Robert, as well as observations on his courage and character. It was only the thought of Mama's phone running out of minutes that compelled her to say goodnight.

She remained in that chair at the end of the hall for some time after the call, just to soak in a calm rarely experienced in the dorm… and to dwell once more on that kiss.

Amber was asleep, so she did not attempt to change out of her clothes into pajamas. She only removed the white hoodie and folded it neatly… almost reverently… before placing it in the middle of her desk. She would find a way tomorrow of memorializing this friend. Kicking off sneakers, she climbed into bed, not intending to seek or find sleep.

CHAPTER

24

EPIPHANY AND DISSUASION

Because sleep most definitely could not be found.

The whole evening got replayed over and over in her head… from the opening of the study room door to sweet goodnight kisses on the porch. There were moments, such as being gripped with fear or when Charity was making snake eyes, that her recollections offered only poorly congealed images of Robert. That really bothered her. Above all, she wanted to remember everything about him!

Isolating on those parts of the evening that were Robert… much as a film editor extracts clips from a video… she began reassembling them on the movie screen of her mind. She compared Robert spelling out 'R-o-m-a-n' on the whiteboard to Robert yelling '9-1-1.' Or Robert holding her hand in the backseat of the squad car to Robert moving alongside her in the tree. Or Robert saying 'I like you' compared to Robert saying 'I love you.' This, she did repeatedly with as many instances and comparisons as could be made. Sometimes those associations surprised, and hands covered mouth… or they warmed, and arms hugged… or they exhilarated, and a fist got thrust into the air with a silent shout of 'yes!'.

But after a while, either from familiarity or fatigue, she began to wonder whether a particular image actually occurred as pictured. Perhaps she had fabricated some small detail to smooth over a rough spot in memory. This uncertainty swelled into a general concern over whether more significant aspects of the evening had transpired the way she thought… which suddenly evolved into a dreadful possibility that the whole thing might have been made up. There was a part of her which took up the challenge of proving that Robert, indeed, loved her and she loved him. So she began viewing the evening from a distance. Was there historical evidence to support these suppositions? This question, she knew, somewhat relegated the beauty of her imagery into an academic effort, but a precedent must be established. It was foundational to the future.

The ultimate proof for how much he loved her was offered in exhibition most vile. Her mind summoned the dog's image from memory, and its display suddenly blotted out all that was Robert. The dog became more than an isolated moment – it was the definitive proof. Yet her mind did not stop there – it began opening childhood archives, searching for a similar image of that first dog. She could not – would not – allow that comparison to be made! Abruptly swinging legs out of bed, her body sprang up all by itself into a standing position.

What to do, what to do?! Find something to do!

Her eyes fell to the shadowy outline of her backpack, lying where she had deposited it on entering the room. It had similarly been dropped from the tree after retrieving her cell phone… and then not given a conscious thought until the burly policeman had handed it over. An unbidden image abruptly emerged… an echo of the mind's argument. The second dog had repeatedly traipsed over the backpack while circling the tree. That thought sickened her. *But it's only a thing,* the comparing part of her brain attempted to reassure. She was constantly touching things that had touched other things… which was an inescapable part of life.

Mercifully, her thoughts somehow jumped to the English assignment due tomorrow. She took up the backpack and removed the journal. Seating herself, she turned on her small reading light… then cast a hesitant glance toward the still sleeping Amber. All was well.

In starting out, she kept the folded hoodie on the desk where she had left it. She would work with the journal on top. Afterall, the hoodie was a central part of the story and surely had earned the privilege of being present. It would stay, supporting the journal and guiding her writing.

Though it was well past midnight, and now the 18th of October, she wanted the story dated on the 17th. This was more than history, she told herself, and not really a story as per the class assignment. This was life, and it had been lived out on the 17th.

She hesitated before placing pencil to paper, sensing that a distant part of her earnestly desired to take center stage in the writing. The innocence of this meek voice, emerging from the disturbed dust of her past, implored her to be heard in that moment. The warrior heeded the child. 'Camille' slipped off the armor, adorned her hair with flowers, and became 'Camellia' once more. On a blank page of the journal, she began to write.

Epiphany – the sudden realization of a hidden truth or concept.
Dissuasion – the use of argument to change a previously held perspective.

October 17, 2002
A Story of Epiphany and Dissuasion
By Camellia Jay Larson

When I was twelve years old, a thing took place that tore my family apart. This event left lasting scars on me and my mother. In its aftermath, we found a simple means of coping – we hid. It was a logical choice for us both. Hiding spared us from the additional pain of constantly revisiting our shame and humiliation before others. We each had our own way of doing this. I chose to always wear a hoodie. It provided a layer of protection against gossipers and maligners, but also formed for me a personal philosophy of defiance. I have ever since sought comfort in its covering, and believed in its power to shield me. My mother and I both thought that our isolation provided the only means of peace and our only pathway back to health.
But such things come at a cost. The hoodie held everything inside. My shame became my constant companion. I developed a perverse persuasion regarding life: security over transparency. I excluded beauty and enjoyment from my

In less than an hour, she had the assignment written, reread, corrected and finally deemed acceptable. She slid the journal into her backpack and returned to bed. Her last thoughts before falling asleep were on Robert… and an exciting idea for the following day.

CHAPTER
25

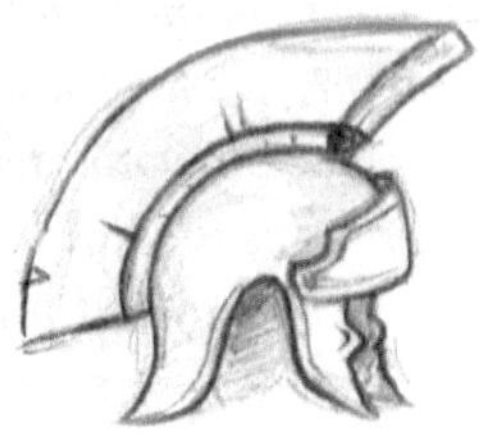

WARRIOR, DEFEND THYSELF!

Clothed completely in white, she was standing in a perfect whiteness that stretched out in all directions. In one hand, she held the only contrasting color – a black pen. She extended this to the whiteness and began drawing small boxes connected in a grid pattern. No sooner had each box been formed than it would detach itself and float off. She asked them politely to return and take on certain colors, but the boxes would not comply. She wanted one to be red, but it went blue… another to be yellow, and it turned green. The boxes then started revolving around her, teasing as they passed. Some flew in, tapped a shoulder, then fled away. Others came near her face, but darted off before she could snatch them up and put them back where they belonged. Then, they all unexpectedly began morphing achromatically with distortions of shape and size… each a blur in motion. She pleaded with them, though they only scoffed back. Little colored boxes laughing as they revolved about her. As one, they stopped laughing and began snarling. Their colors all went to black as they ripped at the cloak covering her head. So she screamed, and her tears began to flow. So many tears that the space between her and the boxes became filled with them. Tears swirled faster and faster, forming an epicenter about her. An 'eye' developed, and she stood in its very center. Above was clear blue sky… but all around, the

tears were doing battle with the boxes. Then the tears became rain…
and the rain washed away the blackness so that the boxes fell to the
ground. She bent down to pick one up… and her ears were suddenly
filled with terrible, horrible music! It was everywhere!

She came bolt upright in bed, abruptly awoken from the strange
dream. Amber had switched on her stereo to a pop music station… and
then let out a shriek as her roommate unexpectedly rose from under
the covers.

"Don't do that, Camille! You nearly scared me to death! Lordy me,
I thought you'd already left!"

Ignoring Amber, she instead concentrated on clearing the fog from
her mind in order to appraise herself. She was a complete mess. Her hair
was in a tangle and she felt all disheveled from having slept in yesterday's
clothes… observations that Amber took pleasure in pointing out. This
experienced late-nighter was clearly putting the pieces together…
building scenarios to explain her roommate's surprising deviation
from schedule.

Oh! Those were the boxes! My schedule!

"Well, look who got to bed late and slept in! Camille – congrats!
You're now officially a college freshman! You go, girl! Soooo… who
were you out with last night?"

She disregarded her roommate's superb logic, as well as the smug
question. In fact, she registered only two words.

Go, girl!

This just had to be the first time ever that she failed to set an alarm!
Leaning over to view the desk, she read the clock's evidence against her.
It was 8:15 AM… only forty five minutes to get ready for her first class
– History! That meant Robert, and that meant…

Get a move on!

Of all the mornings to sleep in!

This morning was to be special, maybe the most significant morning
of her life. The first morning in which she loved someone and they loved
her… and hours of it had already been wasted in sleep. This morning
was also important because she had a special gift just for Robert.

She rushed through the stages of morning preparation: a quick
shower, extra time spent on her hair using Amber's blow drier, and then
dressing in the best looking clothes she owned. On passing the folded

hoodie from the previous night, she patted it twice – once for a 'thank you' and once for luck. Throwing the bedding about in a mock effort to make it, she gathered up her backpack and rushed out the door, shouting goodbye to Amber… and only vaguely aware of Amber yelling something in return. Something about something she had forgotten. Really – she had no time to stop for nonsense! She was on a mission!

There was no way to get there on time without running. The mad dash across campus soon became a balancing act between speed and composure – to be on time in case Robert was there, but not risk arriving sweaty or wind-blown. As regulating the motion of arms and legs became the imperative, her thoughts were free to consider that dream.

What in the world was that all about? How could such a thing emerge from a mind in love?

Yet her subconscious self had chosen that very night to reveal this disturbing dream – a storm of tears arising from within. Cunningham was just ahead, so she pushed out all such thoughts in order to focus on the moment.

She had arrived several minutes late…yet a good fraction of the class was still milling about, as oddly there was no sign of Prof. Dunsmore or Robert. She, in catching her breath, casually made for her usual seat… pleased that so many eyes were tracking her. Some appeared stunned, but most were smiling, making thumbs-up gestures, or offering small waves of the hand. Still… a few maintained strange smirks… and Charity looked downright hostile.

Oh well… it's their problem!

Nothing could mar this perfect morning. For the first time in over six years, she had stepped out into public without a hoodie.

To the casual observer, this young woman was confident and poised. She was, beyond all doubt, beautiful… displaying a fair complexion, graceful cheek and jaw bones, and delicate eye brows and lashes. Her blond hair flowed down in tangled tresses, curling about itself in a way that looked both natural and painstakingly arranged. With ends distributed on shoulders, back and chest, each strand highlighted a different portion of her upper frame. A simple purple cotton blouse, sleeves rolled up partway, provided the perfect backdrop… as well as a modest illustration of the contours hidden beneath. For her, no jewelry was necessary, as her collar bone more elegantly adorned the neckline than any pendant could do. With hands folded gracefully before her, a radiance in her bearing conveyed the impression of a lifetime of happiness. Her lips then parted slightly as if to smile or speak, binding her audience with expectation. Yet it was her eyes… crystal clear blue as sapphires… that held fixed the viewer's gaze upon their liquid-like quality. Not as from tears, but as mountain streams tumbling over polished rock. Those eyes sparkled with wonder and energy… and just a touch of mischief.

She was as Virgil had penned two millennia afore in adoration of his grand Camilla.

> *Men, boys, and women, stupid with surprise,*
> *Where'er she passes, fix their wond'ring eyes:*
> *Longing they look, and, gaping at the sight,*
> *Devour her o'er and o'er with vast delight;*
> *Her purple habit sits with such a grace*
> *On her smooth shoulders, and so suits her face;*
> *Her head with ringlets of her hair is crown'd,*
> *And in a golden caul the curls are bound.*

Every male wanted to be with her.
Every female wanted to be her.
She was perfect.

The upper door opened and a cloud descended into the lecture hall. Prof. Dunsmore slowly made his way from above – Moses descending Mount Sinai with a message of wrath and doom. In each successive downward terraced step, the class sank into a more somber state. Many seemed to have anticipated this moment, as heads nodded in response to hushed voices. Others, such as herself, were perplexed… but nonetheless picked up unmistakable clues from the rest that something was amiss. Something significant was about to happen.

In quickly assessing her classmates, she discovered that many were looking back and forth between the descending professor… and her. Some displayed pity, while others shook their heads with 'tsk, tsk' expressions. A few, such as Charity, were clearly reveling in the moment. As Prof. Dunsmore passed by her, it afforded the entire class a single moment in which to compare the two of them… and package the whole situation into one doleful image. The professor, however, did not slow. Did not even glance about the class until he had assumed his position behind the lectern.

"Before we begin today's lecture, I must share some regrettable news. This morning, Mr. Reynolds was asked to resign his position as a TA to this class."

An unnatural pause ensued in which the professor allowed shock to permeate the room. The in-the-know portion of the class was smiling, shifting their collective attention from the professor to the corrupting influence. Those slow-on-the-uptake were rapidly being briefed of the situation, and their focus was also turning toward her.

"I am not at liberty to discuss the details at this time." Here he lingered again, but this time awkwardly while searching the class for a face. Exhibiting some difficulty in this task, he was aided by tracking the focus of his students, as all heads had turned in her direction. Even the room lighting seemed concentrated squarely upon her. "Suffice it to say, the chairman of the department has begun inquiries into inappropriate student-TA behavior. Let me remind you that here at…"

She could hear no more. Outwardly, she sat as rigid as was humanly possible, but inwardly she longed to run from the room… or hurl abuse at the accusers… or maybe race along the counter tops stomping on computers. Her mind soon became subsumed with such terrible thoughts. Robert's livelihood was at risk, his reputation was being called into question, and maybe even his position as a graduate student was being reevaluated. Right now, he might be seated in the department head's office being chewed out for his indiscretions. Maybe… he was even reconsidering his feelings for her.

Her will fought to control such thoughts bent on imagination without substance. It fought the part of her that wanted to open the floodgates of tears. The struggle was intense… though she was gradually coming through its shock and embarrassment. The pair of them, thoughts and feelings, were slowly being brought back into control by the image – the one her will was forcing them to see… to feel… and to comprehend. Compelling them to move towards this image while disregarding all else. The image of Robert looking into her eyes.

As her will gained control, her mind and heart became more compliant. Anger got appeased, humiliation turned to concern, and reason was restored.

What exactly has he done?!

At worst, from a departmental ethics perspective, he had kissed a student. Not great, but not horrific either.

Like that's never happened before!

For a moment, the memory of that kiss came back… and it was the final tool the will needed to drive away all the bright lights… and the smirks… and the fears of expulsion. Now, a reddened face was not due to embarrassment, but from remembrance.

"Let this be a reminder to all that this university and this department uphold the highest standards of ethical conduct. We, the faculty, expect you, the students, to live up to those standards. A new TA will soon assume Mr. Reynolds' responsibilities, and I will assure you…"

She shut him out again… and essentially shut herself down. She went dormant, until the class would end, the talking would stop, and she could leave to find Robert.

At the conclusion, she took her time collecting her possessions, allowing the class to file out ahead of her. She could see that many were gathered just outside the door, either to get her side of things or give her theirs. She doubted any were waiting to console or congratulate. Charity's crowd would be out for blood.

Too bad. They'll just have to live with disappointment.

Turning away from them, she faced upward and rapidly ascended the terraces to the doorway above, not knowing where it went, not caring what was left below. She only knew that Robert went that way, and he might still be up there.

Passing through the upper door well ahead of Prof. Dunsmore… who was still at the bottom fiddling with his briefcase… she entered onto a narrow hallway configured only with doors similar to the one just passed through. These evidently led into other classrooms through which she could escape if she so chose. Yet Robert was clearly not that way. To the left seemed to lead into the bowels of the building, so she set off in that direction, not noticing the 'exit' arrows along the way. Turning a corner, it then became evident she had chosen incorrectly. This direction led only to a fire escape. Chiding herself that the ability to track compass points had failed her, she retraced her footsteps… the timing of which coincided with meeting Prof. Dunsmore as he emerged from the classroom.

"Sir, can you please tell me where I might find Mr. Reynolds?"

She offered him no explanation for why the upper door had been used against his policy or... for that matter... her part in his TA's removal.

"I can't help you, Miss Laramie." *Laramie?!* "I met with him this morning before his dismissal. Presumably, he has left the department. Now if you will excuse me, I have more pressing matters to attend to."

In a previous life, she might have mentally maligned this man for his rudeness, but her mind at that moment was only on Robert. She watched as the professor proceeded down the other stretch of hallway and out of sight around a corner.

Where would Robert go? Would he try to find me? Would he call?

And then she remembered the cell phone stashed in the side pocket of her backpack. Unaccustomed to owning one, she had overlooked the possibility that Robert was simply a few buttons away. Flipping it open, a blinking light informed her of a message, though there was no cellular service available to retrieve it. Her room was filling with the next class, so she moved along checking doors until an empty lecture hall was found. Entering and descending its terraces, she swept the device through the air, attempting to gather in signal as she had seen other cell phone users do... having no idea if the technique actually worked. It was not working for her. Stepping into an unfamiliar hallway, she began searching for an exit. To the right was a sun-lit doorway onto a fully enclosed courtyard occupied by a few concrete benches. More importantly, the open space ended up providing her with two precious bars of reception.

A computerized voice informed her of three messages, which she played in succession.

"Good morning, Camille!" Robert's cheerful voice! "Can't stop thinking about you. Call me when you get this. I'm hoping to see you before class. I love you! Bye."

She was momentarily lost in the warmth of this message, but nonetheless saved it at the phone's prompting. There would be time to return and savor.

"Camille, please call me as soon as you can. We need to talk. Love you."

Saved. Finally, the last one.

"Camille, it's really important that you call me as soon as possible. If you can't reach me for some reason, please leave a message and let me know that you're OK. And Camille... DO NOT go to History class. I'll explain later. Love you. Gotta go. Bye."

The electronic voice gave time stamps of 7:13, 8:22 and 8:53 AM. She had been asleep for the first, in the shower for the second, and dashing across campus during the third. Robert had tried to prevent her from going to class... perhaps even attempted to intercept her. Maybe his presence there was why so many students seemed to know what was happening before she did. Regardless, she pushed a speed dial button set up by him and waited.

"Camille, is that you?"

"Oh Robert... I'm so sorry! So very sorry you got fired! It's all my fault! Can you ever forgive me?"

"Fired?! What're you talking about? Did you go to History class?"

"Yes..." She then related all that Dunsmore had said.

"That pompous ass! I did not get fired, and there is no departmental inquiry."

"Then you've not been kicked out?!"

"Of course not. It's only the TA position. I just felt that if you and I were going to be... you know... together, then I should resign so there wouldn't be any impropriety. I met with him and the department head at about eight this morning."

"Then you're OK?"

"Yes... I'm perfectly fine. But this really burns me up! I can't believe he'd put you through that. You know... I thought something like this might happen. Word was bound to get around to your classmates, so I went there to head you off. When you didn't show, I just assumed you'd gotten my messages. Sorry I didn't call again. Been meeting with Prof. Simpson. But right now... I'm so mad I could punch Dunsmore out!"

"No! It's OK! I'm OK! Please, Robert, promise me you won't do anything foolish!"

"Of course not... but where are you?"

"I'm not sure. Somewhere in the middle of Cunningham Hall... in a courtyard with stone benches and ivy growing up the walls."

"Stay there... I'll be right down."

"Hurry! I... miss you."

Closing the phone with much relief, she moved to a bench and sat, purposely choosing one in the corner of the courtyard being brightly lit by the morning sun... which had just peeked over the rooftop.

Neglecting to ask where he was, she nonetheless assumed him to be in the building… though perhaps not so near that he could have seen her from one of the courtyard windows.

Her gaze drifted upward. The enclosure had a cozy feel to it – not too big and not too small. There were three floors, with a multitude of windows facing into this space. Each pane of glass was set back slightly into the brickwork of Cunningham Hall and framed in white concrete. None appeared to have blinds, allowing her to easily make out computers, houseplants, and various personal effects within many.

Offices.

There was movement in several… and a man in one briefly considered her before turning back to his work.

Operating on instinct instilled through a six year habit, she reached up to adjust the hoodie… except it was gone. The sudden discovery of a bare head, not nearly so shocking as when she was twelve, nevertheless sent ripples of panic through her. She was seen. Each window now seemed an eye, and each eye assailed her with its scrutiny. The sun, moments before a warming influence, now illuminated her as a celestial spotlight. The courtyard slowly collapsed inward upon her, with every eye bulging forth.

Her first thought was to flee. Robert would not care if they met just inside the glass door, not fifteen feet away. Her hands went to the bench to push herself off… to lift herself into flight… but she nonetheless stayed. Fingertips slid beneath thighs in affirmation to the rest of her body that she would wait there, exposed as she was. Perhaps it was the cool touch of stone that somehow focused her. She knew she could choose to stare back at each eye, daring them all in concert to challenge her new-found freedom. She could fight each and every one if need be. She had done that before. Or… she could choose to lower her head to the courtyard's concrete floor, acknowledging the right of the eyes to question her resolve. She could find a way to hide even without a hoodie. She always had.

She chose neither. Her eyes moved toward the door, locking in on it. The windows were gradually pushed out of her thoughts and feelings, being replaced completely by the expectation of seeing him come through.

And soon, there he was. He took two steps into the courtyard and froze… not moving an inch. She had no idea what was happening – he just stood there gaping at her. If she had a small hammer, then she could have tapped him… and he would have shattered into a million pieces.

Almost as in a whisper, she nonetheless heard him clearly.

"You're… you're… so beautiful!"

In an instant, his words washed away years of vicious taunts and jeers… and so many hurtful remarks regarding her appearance. Those pains were completely replaced by the wonderment that this man would deem her so. That he would choose her! This moment would never be forgotten. It was as if they were meeting for the first time – her as her true self without the hoodie. Her gift to him.

She rose quickly and sprang across the courtyard, wrapping him in her embrace. Pressing herself against his chest, she could feel one of his arms wrap about her shoulders, but the other was unaccounted for. Opening her eyes, she found his hand hovering inches from her hair, hesitant to touch it. So she shifted to look up, offering a serene smile as permission… and he began to gently stroke the full length of it, sending chills of delight into her heart. Curling his fingers, he then lovingly caressed her cheek, just before lifting her chin from off his chest so they could kiss.

"Come on, let's get out of here. Can you be done with classes for the day?"

"If it means being with you." But then she recalled the story in her journal, it lying within her backpack on the bench. "Oops… I'm sorry. I just remembered that I have English… but that doesn't start until one… and after that, I'm totally free."

"Then shall I provide you with chauffeuring service… and see you again when you're class is done?"

She instantly felt the warmth of knowing that it was more of an assurance than a request.

"But of course, messier!"

She was all giggles.

"Then how's about an early lunch… just us two?"

He led the way through a series of hallways, out an exterior door and into a parking lot… all the while saying how excited he was to be with her. He held her hand, guiding her around barriers and parked cars to the passenger side of a small red sedan. He opened its door for her to get in first. As he made his way around, there was an eternity for her in which to recognize this strange feeling. She was happy. Something she had longed for through many years of loneliness.

He entered his side mouth first, jabbering on about every little thing, clearly beside himself at having her there. He was saying, for the fourth time, how beautiful she was… and then please excuse him for the carpet not being clean. Before starting the engine, he put considerable effort into making sure that her seat was positioned just right, explaining carefully how to make adjustments. He then began listing off restaurants in rapid fire succession, trying to guess from variations in her smile which she liked best.

"You know, I'm just going to take you out of this town!"

He then started recounting how the sunlight in the courtyard had glistened off her hair… and how he so loved her smile… and would BBQ be OK? She should let him know if the temperature needed adjusting… and he would try not to drive too fast… because she was so beautiful. He did not seem to be aware of the disjointed nature of his conversation, commenting on his car's gas mileage… and how her blouse brought out the blue in her eyes… and then that the drink holder was wide enough to handle a Big Gulp. As he continued to scrounge about for new triviality, she bathed in the pleasure of his attentions. His excitement was speech, and hers was listening in silence. It was not so much the words as the voice. A strong, loving, masculine voice, speaking just for her. One she could call her own.

CHAPTER

26

A FIRST DATE

The drive was spent reliving the night's adventures and the morning's mishaps. The former were beautiful to her, whereas the latter had turned comical now that she was with Robert. Yet one thing still gnawed at her – that she had overslept and not been there to support him as he resigned.

"It must have been humiliating for you to face all those professors and admit that you'd fallen for a student."

"Camille… you've got it all wrong. This is the best day of my life."

He had to pull the car over, for she had suddenly burst into tears.

"For me too!"

They stopped in the gravel parking lot of 'Honey's BBQ,' located some twenty miles west of Garland. He exited the car first, and she waited for him to come around… to fulfill his role as her gentleman. They moved together from the car holding hands, and he opened the restaurant door for her to enter first. The place was empty, as the lunch hour had not yet arrived. They ordered the same platter with sweet tea, all the while maintaining a gentle grip on each other's hand. But as he withdrew his to take out his wallet, the separation immediately brought her indecision.

Is this a date… or just lunch?

Should I pay for my own?

What if he wants to?

But shouldn't I offer?

Or would that be an insult?

But if I said nothing, wouldn't that be worse?

Countless such variations tumbled through her mind as she watched him search for bills. There was urgency, so she abruptly decided to pay for her own... but then realized that her backpack, along with her money, was in his car.

"Robert, can I please have your keys? I left my pocketbook in your car."

"I've got it... seeing as this is a date."

Against her better judgment, she hazarded a glance toward the cashier. The woman had been set to receive payment from Robert, but quickly retracted her hand, leaving his suspended there in midair holding two twenties.

Shoot! Now she's going to make this difficult.

"Umm... thanks... but you really don't have to. I'm thinking... I should probably pay for myself since..."

"Camille... are you my girlfriend?"

She looked to the cashier again. The woman was smiling directly at her... but with a quick flick of the head toward Robert, made it clear that she should answer him.

Just great – she's enjoying this.

"Yes... of course."

Without thinking anything else needed saying, he thrust the twenties forward to the cashier... who reluctantly took the money now that it seemed the show had ended... before it got real good. The lady dumped the change into Robert's hand and uttered an unenthusiastic 'order 47.' She left the counter following in behind him, wondering where the other forty six parties were.

That interaction had been terribly awkward... yet also funny, what with Robert's hand held out, the cashier's relish for the opportunity, and her wanting to dash out to the car. Only one day previous, she would have been mortified to be in such a situation, as it had always been her practice to avoid any setting in which vulnerability might develop into even a minor spectacle. Yet now, from a different perspective... an 'unhooded' one... it was all quite humorous.

They sat at a table to wait for their number. Robert then sprang up unexpectedly and dashed over to the tea stand, returning with two filled glasses, straws and lemons… just in case that was the way she liked it. They fiddled a bit with their drinks in silence before he spoke.

"I'm really sorry about that back there… I should have said something before we ordered. So… since we're a… a couple… it's my privilege to pay for things when we're together. I hope that's OK with you?"

He seemed to be bracing himself for resistance, as if leaning into a strong wind.

"Yep… Thanks."

"So you're not going to argue with me?"

"Nope. I won't interfere with something you feel strongly about. You see… I hope to spend as much time as possible with you. Putting up a fuss about who pays for what on dates won't be on my radar."

She took a long sip of her drink while he seemed to think it over.

"Thanks. So… what *is* on your radar?"

In that moment of considering his question, she realized the specimen study was over. Of course, there was still so much she wanted to learn… but learning was not the thing she now wanted most. She had originally embarked upon a silly, made-up 'class project'… but everything from here on would be different. She was in a relationship, so a much bigger transition was occurring in her life. Suddenly, she no longer felt like a girl. She was becoming a woman.

"Just being with you. You're incredible… and I know I've only begun to discover it." As she waited out his blushed smile before continuing, a hesitancy somehow tried to push its way back into her heart.

Yeah… you're in a relationship… but you're still just a kid in college.

"Robert… I've… never been in a serious relationship before. Actually… I've never been in any kind of a relationship at all. I've got loads to learn. I'm only eighteen, you know." This casual admission suddenly came to her as an instant shock. He surely could guess her age based on her position in school, but saying it out loud made her seem so much younger than what she wanted to be. So she was almost afraid to make eye contact while asking. "How… umm… old are you?"

"Actually… just about to turn twenty five. On the 20th."

For the moment, the proximity of his birthday displaced all other thought.

"That's the day after tomorrow! Wow! I'll have to think of something special for you."

"Camille... this is special. You're the best birthday present I've ever received."

Her eyes, filling with tears, flittered between him and the tip of her straw.

Why do I keep looking down?!

She so wanted to hold onto his eyes, but the intensity was too much. Yet her smile suddenly faded away as a genuinely uncomfortable thought took its place... one that she now admitted had been trying to pop out all morning.

"Does it... bother you... I mean... are you concerned about the... the differences in our age and... maturity?"

"No. Not really. I figure, if you're patient, I'll eventually catch up with you."

He just sat there smiling... and now she was the one blushing.

"Don't be silly, Robert." Though touched that he would suggest... even lightheartedly... that she was more mature – she knew it not to be the case. She so wanted him to think highly of her... but also needed him to understand what he was up against. "Seriously... I should warn you – I'm far from perfect!"

"Try me."

"Well... for starters... I'm an obsessive planner! I plan everything! I make plans about making plans!"

He put on a face that she was inclined, at first, to interpret as 'don't exaggerate'... at least until he followed it up with words.

"I know that. Remember, I've been grading your papers for the last six weeks."

"Oh. OK... So... I'm a planner and... well... you should be on your guard."

"From what?"

"From me planning, of course!"

Now he was laughing at her... and she was getting slightly annoyed.

He doesn't get it!

Just as she was beginning to wonder if he had the slightest clue what he had gotten himself into, he reached across the table and gently took hold of her hand.

"You want to plan the relationship? Well then... plan away. I asked you to trust me. What would it be like if I didn't trust you? I do trust you. I've trusted you from the first time I walked you to your dorm. I don't know why I agreed to do that, but sometimes a person just knows. I put myself in an awkward position… as a TA… but you didn't take advantage of that. It's another thing I really like about you. So… plan away… just… plan *with* me."

In her mind, that was about the best thing he could have said – 'with me.'

At that moment, order forty seven was called, and Robert rose. But instead of heading directly to the pick-up window, he leaned across the table and gently kissed her on the lips.

"But let's not start planning just yet. Let's enjoy this moment together first. We can start planning… tomorrow… OK?"

"OK… I guess I can hold off until then."

She leaned up to provide a playful kiss of her own.

By the time he returned with their food, she had the next part of their conversation planned out.

Oh well… I lasted all of fifteen seconds.

They busied themselves slathering BBQ sauce on the brisket, taking those first few bites, and exchanging assessments regarding the tastes, textures and smells of their lunch. Then she submitted her question.

"So, Robert… let's see how smart you are. When do you think I was first attracted to you?"

She was surprised that he did not hesitate in providing an answer.

"I'd say on the first day of class when you and I locked eyes on each other."

She had a fork full of brisket on the way to her mouth… but it never arrived. Suddenly, she was startled into considering… and ultimately admitting… that she had been attracted to him from day one… and he knew it too. For there he was, slyly smirking at her like Mama would say – 'as smug as a bug in a rug.' He even accentuated the look with a low-volume humming sound, making his message clear enough – 'got it right, didn't I?'

"That's not what I was thinking, but now that you mention it… I think that's right. It was at that moment. Still… I wouldn't say I was *romantically* attracted to you… though obviously I am now…" She felt herself reddening at her own admission. "It was more like… fascinated by you! Especially by the way you were looking at each person in the class. What were you doing?"

"That? It's no big deal… but it'll take some time explaining. Mind if

I tell you later… when a mouthful of potato salad can't get in the way?"

"Sure… Then tell me what you were thinking when we were looking at each other."

Instantly, he pulled his eyes away from her… though she knew it was only to more clearly recall the moment.

"I hadn't really noticed you in the class yet… so when we looked at each other… I nearly came unglued. Of course, I thought you were very pretty… though TAs aren't supposed to think such things." He turned back with that wonderful smile of his. "But I can say it now. You're amazingly pretty! Actually… you're beautiful. I hope you know that."

She wanted to forever dwell on those words… but also wanted more.

"Thanks. I think I'm starting to believe you. You've said it a dozen times so far this morning… though I don't think that's nearly enough. So don't stop!"

She gave him her most whimsical laugh… just as she imagined any girlfriend might do… though was not at all laughing on the inside.

I love it! Please don't ever stop!

"OK – you're beautiful, and I mean it. Now… what was I saying? Oh yeah… when I first saw you, I wouldn't call it 'love at first sight.' I don't know if that really exists. It was more like… 'know' at first sight. Not as in 'I know about you.' When I looked at you, I thought this was a person I could get to know… someone I really wanted to know… maybe even knew a little bit already. It's hard to explain. One thing for sure, I was attracted to you. And I thought I was doing OK… you know… managing it as a TA and all… until you started showing up at the help sessions."

There was a brief silence in which they both took small bites of food – not enough to delay them from talking for long.

"But you were thinking of a different time?"

The instance on her mind occurred weeks into the term. She suddenly felt a bit foolish. During those weeks… and especially throughout the time spent studying him as a specimen… she had actually been attracted to him in the very way she worked so hard to avoid.

"It was when I was watching you respond to those students after the first exam."

"You mean the one you got a 98 on?"

"Uhh... yes." She smiled back, but with lips barely parted, dipping her head slightly to conceal any embarrassment that might be showing. "Anyway... you do remember the situation, don't you?" He had just taken a bite, but nodded as his eyes rolled in a 'who could forget that' gesture. "When Prof. Dunsmore told the class one thing about the iron age and then did another..."

She noticed him swallow in a hurry, so she allowed him to get a word in.

"He just got it mixed up and tested everyone on the wrong thing. What a mess! Kind of surprised I got out of there in one piece. You know... I don't remember you being there..." As he paused, she could almost see him reconstructing the event in his mind. "Pretty sure you were the first one done and long gone by the time the class got going at me."

"That's true... but I was waiting outside the door for Charity." At that name, he gagged a bit on his drink, but she ignored it. "I would have left, but had an arrangement with her for afterward. I was sitting in the hall when the uproar started. Half the class was cursing Prof. Dunsmore, and the other half was cursing you."

"Pretty sure both halves were cursing us both."

"I saw you through the door. You had such a controlled expression on your face. It kind of reminded me of Mama... my mother. I'll tell you about her in a minute. Anyway... you didn't raise your voice or get defensive. You just dealt with the situation calmly and coolly. I'd never seen anyone do that before. That's why I started coming to your help sessions... to know you better. You're so... different from other guys. Patient, thoughtful and kind. And you're so super comfortable in your own skin!"

He just sat there for a while pondering those words more seriously than she would have expected.

"Umm... thanks. But you know... it's kind of sobering to think... what if I'd lost my cool? You'd probably never have come to my help session... and maybe never given me a second thought... and I'd have missed out on you. I can't tell you how much that would've hurt... but I sure am glad you did. So... tell me about your mother."

The character and dimensionality of Mama could not be adequately captured with any words she might conjure... though she tried. She told him about Mama's upbringing, about wisdom borne out in adages and analogies, about how hard she worked, and how she always dwelt on the positive even though they were very poor. Mama had not been educated beyond high school, but was as smart as a whip, and always knew the right thing to say and do. Yet all of her accounts circled around how the two of them had always been best friends.

At one point, she asked him about his family, and he gave a nondescript response before steering the conversation back to her. When she spoke about how Mama had raised her single-handedly, there was a natural opportunity for him to ask about her father, though he did not. She appreciated him all the more for the sensitivity. It would take some thinking to formulate a comfortable explanation for why that man was no longer a part of her life.

Their lunch conversation meandered over other subjects ranging in seriousness from the ingredients of their ideal BBQ sauce to the consequences of him no longer being a TA. On the latter topic, she continued to place blame on herself… until he reminded her that it was his choice, and he had chosen her.

He eventually pointed out the time, it being only forty minutes before her English class. They departed the restaurant for his car, lips colliding purposefully along the way. Her first date was a huge success… yet this was much more than just a date. She was in a relationship… and as crazy as it seemed, Robert Reynolds was her boyfriend.

CHAPTER

27

ROBERT'S STORY

In backing his car out, he craned his head over a shoulder while also nodding it in the direction of the restaurant.

"Mind if I return to something you asked me in there… about why I was staring at your classmates on the first day of history?"

"Not at all."

Yet he delayed in actually saying anything as he drove out onto the highway. Of course she waited for him to continue, though it now seemed he was more occupied with bringing his car up to speed. From the delay, she gathered that what he had to say was important… perhaps even difficult. Driving was something she had no experience with, having never had a license… or even spent much time as a passenger. Once, as a child, she saw a movie in the theater where actors depicted characters having a serious conversation while driving. The scene stuck in her memory because… for her… operating an automobile had always been mystical. So she wondered if it was a common understanding in America that this particular setting was ideal for certain subjects. The seriousness of managing a ton of steel and human cargo must moderate even the most challenging of discussions.

"Actually, I should start by apologizing for something first. You asked me during lunch about my family, and I sort of… blew you off. Sorry about that."

"It's OK."

"What I was doing… it had a lot to do with my family. So I suppose it'll make more sense if I tell you about them first."

After another quarter mile or so of quiet, he picked up again.

"I was born and raised in Atlanta… and had a pretty cushy childhood. You see… my family had always been well off… but I wouldn't have gone so far as to call us filthy rich… though maybe we were. Yet I *definitely* wasn't spoiled because my parents really appreciated the value of hard work… so they were careful not to lavish me with stuff. They actually made me earn things… I bought this car with money from working summers. Still… I never lacked for anything… Kind of embarrassing when I think about how you and your mother had to struggle in making ends meet."

More fluidly now, he went on to relate how his parents had been corporate lawyers when they met. They eventually married, then started their own practice, working around the clock in building their reputation as experts in law pertaining to taxes and investments. Theirs eventually became one of the prominent firms in the city. He was not sure if they had planned to have kids, as he was born when they were nearing their forties. As a child, he never sensed any resentment from them. In no way had his presence in their lives been communicated as an inconvenience… though neither were they what might be considered typical PTA parents.

"Mother would have been mortified to be referred to as a soccer mom… and I think Father thought little league was the arena in which personal injury law got practiced. Growing up, I was groomed to be a lawyer too… and they placed such high hopes on me one day taking over from them. But somewhere along in high school, they must have figured out that I didn't have an interest in the law."

The smile he sent her way was quite purposeful. This was no carefree account of his childhood. Something obviously was plaguing him. Yet that he would have the courage and security to spill out his past to her – a girlfriend of only one day – touched her immensely.

"Probably had something to do with me telling them every other day that I hated the idea. Anyway… they were pretty different from me… from my contemplative nature. I'm obviously not saying they weren't smart… or that I'm smarter than they ever were. It's just that I spent a lot of time by myself… and they were very outgoing. To them…

especially Father… knowledge was a tool for gaining influence. He never really understood my desire for knowing simply for the sake of knowing. Mother – she was all about relationships… you know… making connections. She was so good with people… but there was never enough of her to go around. I guess one major disappointment I had from my childhood was that I didn't get to see much of them… between their work and… other things."

Because of how his continued use of the past tense had grown foreboding, she was barely able to interject.

"What do you mean?"

"Nothing really… just that they were super active socially. You know… always with other people. It's like this – they believed in using knowledge and connections to grow their influence and wealth. I'm not faulting them… Well… I did at the time… but not now. The good they accomplished was incredible. Investing in the community, helping non-profits, raising funds for causes… things like that."

The pace of his words had picked up, but now he paused to breathe out deeply… perhaps to resume at a slower cadence. Her heart, though, was racing.

"Honestly, I couldn't keep track of their exploits. I was mostly insulated from them by nannies and such. But then… when I became a teenager… they started getting me involved in their activities. I can't tell you how difficult it was for me to be paraded in front of important people. But even worse – all those formal dinners! It was torture being abandoned night after night at a table full of strangers while they went off to work the room. Of course… you've probably already noticed that I'm really bad at small talk."

He smiled over at her, but rather weakly… so she returned hers with as much sympathy as a face could muster.

"Not at all. I think you're an excellent conversationalist."

"Well… regardless… I was mainly interested in reading… and exploring the past. At the time, I didn't see anything of value in what they were doing… and I definitely had no interest in building a future… with them."

There was another awkward silence covered over by him doing the blinker thing… and then making a turn onto some other highway. She had no idea where they were, and could not care less. Only Robert mattered.

"It's a major failing of historians… thinking that we can influence outcomes simply by being knowledgeable about what's already happened. It's like walking backward into the future… you know… facing only the past. My parents… they were always looking ahead at what could be accomplished. At least there was one thing we could agree on – we all loved art. There were paintings and sculptures throughout our house… and I always got to go along with them whenever there was a new piece they were interested in. I remember this one occasion when they took me to a museum. It was during some fund-raiser they were involved in. I was in middle school at the time… and had just read a book on the Renaissance. And then there I was, facing some of the very art that made history. It was incredible! They were so excited to discover something we had in common that they actually ditched the event and walked with me through the museum. Only time that ever happened…"

He checked over his shoulder before pulling around a semi.

"Sorry – I'm getting off on a tangent. Maybe we should talk about something else."

"No… it's OK. Please keep going. I really want to know."

"Alright… but I guess there's not that much more to it. So after high school, I went off to college… to Vanderbilt… and majored in history. I just wanted to get away from them… to see life from a different perspective. I was a pretty good student, and I think I made them proud. Graduated two years ago… and they drove up to see my ceremony. You know… I didn't actually think they were coming… but they did. Somehow… I think my father was hoping that me graduating was equivalent to getting the silliness of history out of my system… then I'd be ready for pursuing the law. He got so upset when I told him I wanted to teach. Anyway… they did come… and it was great having them there. We celebrated with a late dinner… and I thought they were staying the night… but they had some important function to attend in the morning… and needed to get back to Atlanta."

After another pause, his voice unexpectedly dropped and hardened.

"I don't know exactly where it happened. Somewhere on I-75 south of Chattanooga. To be honest… I don't ever want to know."

A silence transpired through which all available space in her heart got filled from the bottom up with heaviness. She could feel her eyes tearing over, but she kept them untended… fixed upon him. Available for only him. He, instead, angled his face away with a firmness coming into his voice as fortitude for finishing.

"The Georgia State Patrol concluded that Father had fallen asleep at the wheel. He was killed instantly... but Mother lingered for... I don't know... days. Frankly... it's all still a bit of a blur."

She noticed that they had entered Garland... and wished very much that he would pull over so she could hug him.

"I'm so sorry, Robert. That must have been unbelievably painful."

He nodded, but did not otherwise acknowledge her words.

"I'd been accepted into graduate school at the University of Chicago. That's a very prestigious program. Of course, I was anxious to get started... but I also wanted to spend some time with them... you know... to smooth things over. I had wasted so many years fighting with them over stupid stuff, so I planned on using some of that summer to rebuild our relationship... to show them how much I appreciated them. We talked about going off to Paris... for a week... just to see... art."

The final word came out as but a whisper.

They entered campus... and his car came to a stop in the exact spot on the same looped driveway where a taxi had dropped her off nearly two months prior. Only vaguely did she register that coincidence, for tears had been silently streaming down her cheeks for miles. As he turned about in his seat to face her, she had not at all considered their impact upon him.

"No, Camille... please don't cry."

He reached over to wipe her cheek... then gently stroked it. His touch was so sweet... so amazing... yet so sad.

"I'm incredible stupid... I can't believe I just dumped all that on you... and this our first date. Now you've got class in only a few minutes... I don't want to be the reason you're late. Hey – smile for me." He was trying to cheer her up, but she was on the verge of skipping class to do that same thing for him. "Tell you what – I'll be waiting right here when you get out. Then we can spend the rest of the day together... and I get to take you out to dinner too."

They kissed, she left the car, and he drove off. Turning toward English, her thoughts remained within Robert's story. She tried to envision what it must have been like to receive the news that a parent had died in a car crash, and that another was lying on the edge of death. It would have been unbearable.

But you know what... he's really hid that pain well.

She considered this conclusion while pushing through a hoard of students just like her, all rushing to get themselves places that really had nothing to do with anything important in this world.

No... he didn't hide it... and it didn't make him hard. It made him kind.

CHAPTER

28

MORE TODAY THAN YESTERDAY

How does one measure the depth of a relationship?

In pondering over this question, she searched back over the month in which they had been dating. She was seeking for some way of encapsulating how she felt… and at the same time how she always wanted to feel.

There was a word, she was sure of it, that best answered this question.

They were in love – that was certain. The power and purity of that word could take her off in a wonderful direction… yet 'love' was not the word she sought after. Not that it, in its essence, was in any way deficient at expressing her feelings for Robert. 'Love' just somehow lacked something of what she was struggling to describe.

They had spent a good part of each day together, from the night of their first kiss to this very one. They so enjoyed each other, and that enjoyment brought joy back into her life. Yet 'joy' was not an answer to the question.

A distinct personality of them as a couple was emerging, as they shared meals, conversed, studied, and simply hung out together. They were developing their own rituals, such as reading to each other on Sunday afternoons… or their nightly partings on the front porch of her dorm. There, they would kiss… just like that first one… and then say goodnight. Once inside, she would rush to one of the alcove windows and follow Robert's trek around the building to where he had parked, with one last wave goodbye as he passed. She longed for them to be together every moment of every day. 'Togetherness' had an aspect of the word – she could sense that – though it was not the one.

She did not exaggerate to herself in thinking each new kiss as special as the first. Each was its own moment in time with him. Though Romeo's with Juliet was fabled in the lover's mind, theirs was mere ink on paper to her, carrying no distinction and in no way comparable to even the most recent one they had shared.

Yet her first with Robert would always be the model for remembrance. The low light of the porch struck a fine balance of illumination – a soft glow that highlighted his every feature. The night breeze touching the back of her neck brought sudden and surprising vigor, heightening those precious seconds of anticipation between the unfettering of her hair and the start of the gradual draw toward him. The crickets in the hedge about the porch were constrained by that same cool air to provide a slow, soft symphony just for her, matching a desire for timelessness as her lips met his. Arms about him, her fingers explored the strength of his back – she had never really touched a man before. Yet most prominent in her memory was the softness of his hands cradling her cheeks and cushioning her with a sweet, soft firmness. Soft and sweet was their 'tenderness'… though that offered only a mere fragment of what she expected from the word.

The month of dating revealed that they had more in common than first realized. Both were only children, both loved books and history, both were introspective, and both were drawn to the other's way of thinking. And even though she had grown up as poor as he had grown up rich, the contrast was oddly a connection for them, as neither had a normal childhood. Their individual likes and dislikes were beginning to settle comfortably into themselves as a couple. There was 'harmony' and 'compatibility,' though those words did not go far enough toward being the thing she hunted for.

They had their first argument, as all couples do – theirs, a silly misunderstanding about plans she had crafted that he interpreted as suggestions. After making up, she recounted to him an illustration Mama had sometimes given whenever they quarreled.

"Child! You're spreading manure all wrong!"

"If I ever have any friends, Mama... never, ever tell them that! It's disgusting!"

Her mother felt that every relationship made its own share of manure. The good stuff of being with someone – the laughing and playing, the talking, the working and sharing – could not prevent manure from happening any more than eating and drinking could. There would always be the bad stuff to deal with – inconsideration, irresponsibility, misunderstanding, and neglect. Since two Southern females could never be confined in a small space without some incredible fights erupting, theirs often came down to one or both of them not understanding the other. Expert farmers, Mama would say, knew how to use manure properly to generate more of the good stuff. She could almost hear Mama saying it...

"The best way to deal with misunderstanding is to get understanding, and the best way to do that is with a sincere heart and simple questions."

So she was absolutely determined to grow in her relationship with Robert by building both 'trust' and 'understanding'... though neither of those felt like the word.

Because they came from different social strata, extra care was required to understand the other person's perspective... especially regarding time and money. Being poor, she was averse to spending on anything outside of 'bread and water,' as Robert would tease. In the way she had grown up, time was always in greater abundance than money. In contrast, she sometimes needled him about his 'throw money at the problem' way of doing things. He was raised in a family where challenges were seldom evaluated based on how many zeros were in the cost, but instead on whether the day possessed enough hours to take on one more thing.

On that first Saturday of November, he had driven her to Jackson for a day trip that included an afternoon walk through a large shopping mall where he attempted to buy things for her.

"This would look great on you."

"Don't you need one of these for your dorm room?"

"What would you say to me getting you a computer?"

They left with only a pair of suede boots purchased at a discount shoe store. Though not yet comfortable being the recipient of Robert's financial resources, she was beginning to see his perspective – that money was a tool just like any other tool. His apartment, car, clothing and lifestyle were all devoid of tendencies to elevate money in esteem above people. So… when he displayed an eagerness to spend on her, she came to realize it as simply his way of showing love. She was gaining new perspective – that having money and being owned by it were two very different things. 'Perspective' very much was unlocking new aspects of their relationship… but this was not a sufficient condition on which to base the word.

Robert was so eager to give her experiences she never had. The trip to Jackson included a visit to the Mississippi Museum of Art. There, they feasted their eyes on a touring National Gallery of Art exhibition of impressionistic paintings. In these, she was exposed to nature's beauty in wholly unexpected expressions of color and texture.

On Saturday the 9th, he took her to a home game, her first experience with football. That turned out to be a laughable misadventure as it rained the whole time, and the Warriors got trounced by the visiting team. Huddled together under a single umbrella, they passed the time telling stories from their youth… interspersed as those were with much lighthearted ridicule for the Garland cheerleading squad, whose boisterous chants were inconsistent with the scoreboard.

And then tonight's date was the absolute best! He had hinted at something special all week, then surprised her with dinner at a fancy restaurant, followed by a performance of *The Merchant of Venice* put on in period attire by the Garland Theatrical Department. Having read most of Shakespeare's works… including that play… she was familiar with them as literature, but not as drama lived out on stage. For over two hours, she sat in wonder, completely captivated by a third row view of the artistry, eloquence and wisdom of the Bard. It was the first occasion in her whole life where imagination was not needed in order to take her out of the South, and into another place and time. The 'wonder' of their experiences together was a continual delight… though that word did not scratch the surface of what she was experiencing.

Even though Robert had parted from her hours ago, she still did not want this night to end. Yet just like with the play's finale, she knew that morning would eventually be upon her. But equally, she was determined to linger in this alcove as long as it took in her search for that one word.

Her thoughts turned to the hoodie, unsure if what she sought lay somewhere in an association with it.

Dating Robert was synonymous with freedom from the hoodie.

Even on a superficial level, not wearing a covering allowed her to feel more a part of what was going on in the world around her. It was almost as if life had invited her back to be a regular attendee rather than an unwelcomed guest. Little things were such new expressions… like the wind blowing through her hair… or not having to pretend regarding seeing and hearing. She was also regaining that childhood delight of *wanting* to look good… as well as the distinctly different awareness of feeling good about how she looked. Setting aside pride, she had finally allowed Robert to pay for several blouses, slacks, shoes, and even a dress – a stunning floor-length satin gown in royal blue. She had never worn a more gorgeous thing in all her life! His continual admiration throughout this night at how she looked in this dress was more than worth her small personal compromise on spending!

But being free from the hoodie meant so much more than her appearance. It had always bottled up her feelings on the inside. Now, a more expressive side to her had emerged, having gained permission to speak… to shout for joy… to free-fall into tears of thankfulness. Sitting here in the dark of the alcove, she immediately recalled one very meaningful instance. This took place while she stood in a cashier line at the student union store. Songs routinely played over its audio system, though she rarely paid them much attention. While waiting her turn, a singer's joy at new-found love flowed into her heart. The voice expressed perfectly how she felt – that each day with Robert was better than the one before. As the song concluded, she found that she had drifted out of line and was standing beneath a speaker in the middle of the store's busiest aisle, students streaming by her. Somebody said she was in the way… and all she could do was laugh and cry out an apology at the same time.

Later that day, she told Robert about the experience.

"It was so beautiful… and I made such a fool of myself."

"No – you're making something special of yourself… and of me too. Never be ashamed of those expressions that flow from a true heart."

Yet 'freedom' and 'expression' were… at best… only vaguely connected with what she sought in the word.

Real change was taking place in her life now that the hoodie was gone. She was discovering that people were more comfortable around her. This was evident from the first time she walked into English without a hoodie to proudly hand over her epiphany/dissuasion story. Ms.

Kelley did a double-take… then provided her with the biggest smile a teacher had ever given her. The entire class seemed to finally relax now that this beautiful butterfly had emerged from her hooded cocoon. In the weeks to follow, she found that classmates were conversing more openly with her… and she was no longer an annoying distraction to girls in the dorm, as the 'spookiness' of her hooded presence was gone.

But it was Amber who showed her how far she had come from the hoodie. One night as she was preparing for bed, her roommate suddenly broke down into tears to reveal why she had left school her freshman year. It was on that day a year ago that she discovered she was pregnant. After weathering the initial shock and disbelief, she decided not to return to Garland for the Spring semester in order to see the pregnancy through… and then eventually put the child up for adoption.

"I'll never be whole again, Camille. Somewhere out there… there's a part of me that'll grow up not knowing who I am."

They cried and hugged their way through the night, falling asleep together in Amber's bed.

Her recollections of Amber's bravery was abruptly interrupted by a hushed commotion outside the dorm's main doors. As she watched unnoticed from her alcove, two girls entered with their boyfriends in tow. Being many hours past curfew, the four silently crept across the dorm lobby and then disappeared through 'the door.' Though clearly a breach of rules, she left them to their own devices without criticism.

Since shedding the hoodie, her attitude toward others had somehow softened. New sympathies had replaced her previous cynicisms. This even extended to the predators, whose interest in her had intensified since casting off the hoodie. It was now common for her to feel ogled while crossing campus or sitting in class… and the Racquetball boys were falling all over themselves to be in the same court with her. Still… she was most surprised to realize that a sort of kindness had arisen within her regarding those advances. Not that she desired or encouraged them – they still unnerved her – but through them she came to know a profoundly sad realization. The attraction many guys had to what she only recently has come to accept as beauty was fueled, in part, by their intense loneliness… and a deep longing to be special to someone special. A campus of fifteen thousand should be an ideal environment for building relationships, but for most students it was, in actuality, a place of isolation.

Life in learning may move fast, but finding true love takes more than just time... especially for those like me who've not yet... within this timelessness of youth... discovered the essence of their true selves.

Before coming to college, she had never really given other people's lives much consideration. It was alien to her way of thinking, being absorbed by her own shame and unaware that other people had also endured horrific events. Her thoughts on Amber had brought new awareness – a marvel at a person's courage to overcome the worst.

Robert had survived an equally harrowing ordeal. He said he had not shared the trauma associated in the death of his parents with anyone other than her. How watching his mother fade away in a hospital bed had caused him to lose all interest in life. How he wanted only to stay in their home all day and do nothing, living off of memories and regrets. History, for him, went back only as far as his recollections of them. He spent over a year in that state until a friend of the family encouraged him to give school another try by attending Garland. Its History department was not nearly as well respected as that of the University of Chicago, yet it was a calm and safe place to renew a love of study.

'Change,' 'awareness,' and 'empathy' were all bearing fruit in her life and in her relationship with Robert. Yet none of those could possibly be the special word that eluded her.

Having sat alone in the alcove well past midnight, she finally collected herself, departing for bed with two thoughts in mind. She was thankful and discontent at the same time. So very thankful for every aspect of him, for all that he had brought into her life, and above all, for the connection between them. Equally, she wanted more... much, much more of him.

The word she sought... though had not found during that time of reflection... was simple, yet so uniquely profound. It came as she rested her head upon her pillow.

Oneness!

CHAPTER

29

IN PURSUIT OF ONENESS

In the week prior to Thanksgiving, Robert led her into the arboretum behind Cunningham Hall for a break from studying. At the northern end was a small white house with a back porch facing the park. Known as Milton Hall, this house was once the residence of the university president, but now served as the campus affairs office. On the back porch of that house was an iconic swing – one built for two. Early on in their relationship, he had suggested that they make it a mission of theirs to put that swing to good use. As they sat side-by-side, holding hands and gently swaying, she recognized in him the distant look he often took on before starting a serious conversation.

"What's on your mind?"

"Camille… I'd like to get your thoughts on… the future."

"The future? As in space travel and robots and…"

"No. You know what I mean. Our future… together. I know we've only been dating for a short while…"

"One month."

"…and you're probably wondering why now…"

"Not really."

"…and I agree it's a bit early for… What'd you say?"

"I'm not really wondering why now. I'm a planner, remember?"

He shifted sideways in the swing to face her.

"So the subject's crossed your mind?"

She, however, did not move around in his direction, but instead allowed a soft smile to gradually develop on her face… simply because she knew he was looking at her. Having a conversation about their future together had caught her a bit by surprise… though not really. She, being that planner, had been trying to plan in some alone-time to start her own thinking on the subject. Inwardly, she wanted nothing more than to know his thoughts. She was convinced he was right for her… but 'getting to right can be done wrong,' as Mama would often say.

"Yes. It's passed through my thinking a time or two."

"Good! You know I love you… so I'll be direct. I've been thinking about us together nonstop from the moment you jumped down out of that tree into my arms."

She sensed him nod in the direction of the park, and allowed her eyes to venture that way too. From their vantage on the porch swing, she could just make out the top branches of their magnolia. Suddenly, she was reminded of how wonderful it had been to be caught… and how the policeman had laughed so.

"I'm not trying to put you on the spot by moving too fast. I was just thinking that we should be on the same page regarding where we see our relationship going."

"Well, Robert… where do you see us going?"

"I'm glad you asked. Now… it's just a starting point for discussion… so don't freak out… but what're your thoughts on… the concept of marriage."

"Ahh… you're not *actually* asking me now to marry you, are you?"

"No. Of course not. I mean… it's way too…"

"Because I'm only eighteen, you know. You might not think that's a big deal… and I'm not asking it to put *you* on the spot, but honestly… what makes you so sure that I'm even anywhere near mature enough to discuss this subject?"

"Seriously?! In many ways… most ways, actually… you're more mature than half the faculty in the History Department. Think about Dunsmore – he's arrogant, insensitive, and supremely insecure. You, on the other hand…" He lifted both fists up to start counting off her properties with his fingers. "…are honest, sensible, patient, caring, thoughtful, intelligent, imaginative, hardworking, perceptive and stable."

"I'm stable?! You've *got* to be kidding?! Maybe you don't know me so well after all!"

"Come on! Think about the students you know – the ones on your hall or in your classes. I can't tell you how much instability I've witnessed as a TA. Stability is dependability. How many eighteen year olds do you know who are as responsible as you are? How many could you really depend upon? By comparison, Camille, you're bedrock. I don't even view you as a teenager. Not in the least. What you've been through personally – it's made you mature beyond your years."

"I… never thought of it that way. Thanks."

She turned back toward the park to consider his words in silence, with only the squeaks of the swing straining back and forth to interpose upon her thoughts.

He's… not the type to exaggerate. It's really against his nature as a historian.

So maybe she was more mature than she felt, and able to at least discuss the responsibilities of a deeper relationship… not that she had the slightest idea what those were. Looking toward the magnolia tree, she remembered being hesitant at their first daylight visit there after the dog attack. The branch they sat on was not nearly as high off the ground as memory had constructed. That tree was a marker of where their relationship had started… a sort of 'stake in the ground' serving as the reference point for going forward.

But that tree was also a reminder of a dog, and then another dog… and a secret. She had not yet revealed to him enough about her past, having only told him that her father was a drunk who abandoned them… how she and Mama lived as outcasts in Carlton… and how they were very poor. Robert, to his credit, had not pressed for details. So he had no idea that her drug-dealing daddy was also a convicted murderer… or about the other terrible things he had done. Those things were too painful to relive in memory, let alone in conversation. Yet one day, she might owe Robert a deeper explanation about her past… and no way could she even think about doing that without Mama's advice.

She then realized that her hand might be gripping his too tightly… and consciously relaxed.

"I don't think I'm ready to talk about it just yet… not that I don't want to be. But think about it… you've not even met Mama. Robert… I really need her to like you… and approve of you. Then the three of us need to spend loads of time together. You should know – Mama's a *very* tricky lady! She has ways of hiding how she feels… and at the same time getting you to reveal more than you want to. I suppose a major factor would be your willingness to have her as part of your life. I'll need to see that you like her, just the way she is… and can even grow to love her. And I can't expect you to say anything about that until you've actually spent time together. I don't see how it could be fair to you or Mama otherwise."

Her response in no way seemed to diminish his eagerness.

"Excellent! That all makes perfect sense. So… a timetable on a discussion of… our future together… might start with me meeting your mother and not… say… you graduating from college first?"

"Yeah… I'd say that's pretty reasonable."

"So, how do you think your mother will feel about you… perhaps… marrying before you finished school?"

"Honestly? I have no idea. You'd have to ask her yourself. But you're not seriously thinking of bringing *that* up over Thanksgiving, are you?!"

"Of course not. At least not without your permission. I was just looking for some way of letting her know how much I love you and… what my long-term intentions are."

She smiled at how he had worded that.

"I seriously doubt you'll get out of Carlton without Mama finding out what you're intentions are… but it won't happen before Thanksgiving day, that's for sure. She'll want to size you up first… and give you time to get comfortable."

She reached both hands over to squeeze his, just so he would feel… as well as know… the magnitude of what was coming his way next week.

"And believe you me, *you'll* need the time! Like I keep telling you, Mama's a one-of-a-kind!"

"So… let's start planning other ways for the three of us to be together. Like I keep saying, I'm happy to drive us there any time you want… and I can spend as much of Christmas break there as you'll have me. Does that sound… reasonable?"

"Sounds like a blast to me! I'm sure Mama will love you, and equally sure she'll approve of you as husband material."

"Really?! And… what do *you* think of me as husband material?"

She gave him an exaggerated rolling of her head and eyes.

"Seriously, Robert! Stop fishing for compliments!"

30

HEART AND HOME

Mama and Robert – what more could she possibly want or need? Drawing closer to him meant drawing more upon her for advice. Over the last month, the minutes on their cell phones had to be replenished several times as a result of her frequent calls home. In fact, she had become a regular in the chair at the end of the hall. She had so many questions about how men think, why they acted the way they did, what was most important to them, and how she should behave in certain situations. She was building a foundation of understanding upon which the prime question could be posed – how to know for sure that he was the one. But before that could ever be considered, she needed guidance on how best to tell Robert about Daddy. Yet Mama had repeatedly refused to discuss *that* subject over the phone… which she suspected had something to do with their pact at the kitchen table.

All questions, though, were tangential to what she most desired… which was introducing Robert to Mama and seeing their relationship grow… because she had such grand plans for the three of them together. Mama, however, was being cagey about a visit. As each weekend in November approached, there was consistently some reason why the time was unsuitable for a visit.

"Sweetie, I so wish you would have told me before now. The clinic needs volunteers this weekend. There's flu running rampant in the streets. Best not bring him here to get him sick."

"No, Child, the weekend of the 9th won't work. Absolutely not! The ladies of the church are gearing up for the holiday charity season, and they've completely booked up those days."

"Sorry, Camellia. The Patterson girl's getting married on the 16th, and it's all hands on deck. Nearly the whole town's in on it."

Even short weekday trips were seemingly incompatible with Mama's busy schedule. This made no sense seeing as her mother had virtually no social life in Carlton. Now... Mama never told an outright lie... but was an absolute master at getting close. Through the month of November, a pattern emerged to the excuses. An event in Carlton would be stated, and then Mama's involvement was always implied. Yet worse than all those excuses, she gradually stopped giving out advice as the month wore on. She would listen ("Hmmm..."), acknowledge ("How nice."), and exclaim ("I declare!"), but the stream of analogies and quotes had completely dried up.

"You'll figure it out, Camellia. You always do."

Something was amiss, and she was determined to get to the bottom of it. Next week was Thanksgiving, the single most extravagant culinary experience of the year for any Southerner. It meant hours spent together rushing about the kitchen in preparation of the meal, then feasting on roasted turkey, candied sweet potatoes, corn bread stuffing, Parker House rolls, green bean casserole, cranberry sauce, and pecan pie. The three of them would cook together, eat together, cleanup together, and then collapse in the front parlor with no energy left for anything except laughing, reminiscing, and getting to know each other better. She had been anticipating that day ever since the very first phone call home about Robert.

Next week, we're coming to Carlton... whether Mama's ready or not!

On the Sunday four days before Thanksgiving and three days before leaving for Carlton, she experienced a most distressing phone conversation with Mama. Plans needed to be made for the visit: the timing, the activities, and whatever objectives Mama might have in mind. Yet she had been unable to elicit her mother's involvement on any of these subjects.

"Mama, did you hear me?! We need to plan!"

The chair creaked to match her own annoyance as she stood to commence pacing the hall.

"Oh… yes, Child. My mind wandered. I've been very distracted lately. Now, you were saying?"

"I was asking if you were interested in a day trip to the Gulf on Friday. We could walk along the beach a bit, just the three of us. What do you think? We could bring a basket of leftovers and have a picnic if the weather's fine. Then we could… Mama? Are you still there?"

"Yes… leftovers would be nice."

"Are you even paying attention?"

"Of course. But I've had so much on my mind. Sweetie… are you even sure you want all that… Thanksgiving bother? It seems like… such an effort for one meal. Wouldn't you rather stay up there and…"

"You can't be serious!?"

"Just a thought. Listen… I'm sorry, but I… really need to end this call. We'll… talk later."

"What's going on? Why are you being so…"

"I really need to go."

"OK. Fine! I'll call you tomorrow to discuss…

"No!"

This was the strongest response she had elicited, and it startled her. "Mama?"

"I'm sorry. I… won't be ready to speak with you again. Not just yet. I have some… errands… to run first. Let's… just not make plans to talk again… until you come… OK? You're so special to me, Camellia. I love you so much. Goodbye now."

"I love you too, Mama. Can't wait to see you on Wednesday."

The static of a severed connection left her wondering whether her final words had been registered. Frustrated out of her gourd, she could not believe this sudden lack of sincerity to Mama's *supposed* desire for her to visit. Maybe that was the heart of it – for a month now, Mama had been putting off meeting Robert. With this realization, doubt suddenly gained a strong hold on her heart, tampering with a confidence that Mama would find him acceptable.

Going against Mama's wishes, she still phoned home come Monday. That call went to voicemail… along with three more attempts that day, and a half dozen on the next – each entrusted to an electronic repository with no reply from Mama. The mental hopscotch game just kept beleaguering her with so many ridiculous imaginings… most of which could be sorted into two very distinct possibilities. Either there had been a dreadful accident, or Mama had done something really stupid… like dropping her cell phone in the toilet. No matter how Robert tried reassuring her, she could not find peace anywhere within the spectrum of possibilities bound by those extremes. Of course, they would have departed for Carlton immediately had it not been for History.

"What kind of a person reschedules an exam to the day before Thanksgiving?!"

She and the entire History class were fuming at Dunsmore. Professors, it would seem, were like captains of naval vessels. Within the confines of their ship, their will was absolute… and no mutiny was tolerated without reprisal. This captain moved the third exam of the semester from the previous Friday on a pretext of a 'scheduling issue.' Whereas afternoon classes on the Wednesday before Thanksgiving were cancelled by the University as a benefit to students travelling home, the morning classes remained in session at the discretion of the professor. Most cancelled those too… but not Dunsmore. The entire Honors History class was convinced that he was punishing them for the loss of his capable TA, who had been replaced with… in Charity Perkin's assessment… 'a moron.' The stand-in made a royal mess of the second take-home essay. Even she received a failing grade, as the new TA had not approved of how she used the passive voice in describing the barbarian invasions into Europe. The professor was forced to re-grade each essay, which put him in a foul mood coming into the third exam. Of course, the general sentiment of the class placed blame for both the lousy TA and the rescheduled exam squarely upon her. The hoodie would have offered no protection against the snide remarks hurled her way – she needed true warrior armor.

With the exam finally completed and Robert waiting outside Cunningham Hall, they were soon on the road. She spent the drive to Carlton in escalated fretfulness. The Southern countryside offered no remedy for this agitated state. Her only interest was in the number of miles yet to be traveled.

They eventually pulled into Carlton, and she directed Robert to her house. Having instructed him to park around back, she bolted out of the car before he could disentangle himself from his own seatbelt. Up the porch steps, she charged indoors already yelling.

"Mama?! We're here! Mama?!"

The house just echoed with her voice. Through the kitchen on a run, she went stock-still on entering the parlor. All of the furniture was gone. Her panic, mixed with confusion, lent new volume to her shouts, as she bounded up the stairs still calling out to Mama. Every room up there was empty. So she quickly retraced her steps to discover that that kitchen bore the only remnants of the house's previous occupancy – the table and chairs. She had ignored these on the way through. On the table was a handwritten note attached to another piece of paper. She grabbed both and darted out the back, nearly colliding there with Robert in the process.

"I was unloading the luggage when I heard…"

"Read – I can't talk."

She thrust the papers into his hands and fell back against the screen door, closing her eyes.

"Umm… this top one's a note from your mother. It just says 'Camellia, come soon. Mama.' The handwriting's very sketchy. But there's clearer writing below. It says: 'Camille, please stop by the diner before heading over to Pinecrest.' It's signed 'Mr. F'. Who's 'Mr. F'?"

It was too much to respond… or even open her eyes… so she merely pointed in the general direction of the notes, hoping that he would understand to keep reading.

"OK… this last one's a typewritten letter to you from that Pinecrest place. Hold it a sec… this is… this is from a hospice house… in Wyatt Crossing. Just… let me summarize… if you don't mind. It… umm… basically informs you that your mother has been… admitted… and that you can contact their office for details. Camille… what's going on?"

Unable to maintain herself standing, she slid down the screen door to the concrete porch.

"Something terrible… something horrible…"

A clear picture was forming in her head to account for the oddities of Mama's behavior over the previous months… especially her unwillingness for them to visit. The pieces somehow now all fit together to form an ominous picture… of two houses – an empty one and hospice care. Yet her heart vehemently contended against all of this… even though a void was already forming where previously had been the thrill of the three of them being together. The resulting implosion drew her tightly in upon herself... as her head went between her knees and her arms wrapped about... the whole of her suddenly rocking back and forth uncontrollably.

"Camille... let's go. We need to find this Mr. F, and then get to this Pinecrest place."

His muffled words could not reach her, for all she heard were the echoes of her own shouts within the house.

"Camille?"

Suddenly, she found herself being lifted into the air. She was in his arms... so she threw hers about his neck and buried her face there.

"I'm going to carry you to the car... and then we're going to find this Mr. F."

The next thing she knew, he was asking her to let go... for she was right back where she had been five minutes ago... though it felt like in a different lifetime. Somehow, being in the car woke her up, for she clearly sensed the vehicle rock while he threw their luggage back into the trunk. As he entered the driver's side, she noticed him look with concern toward the wide-open back door.

"Leave it. No one will bother."

She managed to provide simple directions to Fergie's Diner. The Gulf was delivering a thin layer of clouds over Carlton... insufficient for deterring townsfolk from going about their business on the day before Thanksgiving. As they passed slower moving vehicles plodding the streets, she wondered if their drivers were aware of the world crashing down around them. Pedestrians ambling about on their ill-defined purposes – did they not know to despair? Surely the dreadful news had spread throughout! To her, Robert's car was moving out of control at the speed of sound, with the resulting sonic boom deafening all of her senses. But sound in Carlton moved at the speed of the South... which was slower than the years. Nobody had heard and nobody cared.

Robert soon pulled into a parking place. She immediately leapt from the car like before, crossed the sidewalk, and entered Fergie's... once again aware that she had left Robert behind. Mr. Ferguson was just rounding the diner's counter as she moved through the entry area.

"Camille! I'm real glad you're here. I'm so sorry... forgive me... but it was your mother's wishes. You know how intensely stubborn she can..."

"Please just tell me what's going on."

But before responding, Mr. Ferguson registered Robert's presence and drew out of himself a slight smile… so inconsistent with the moment.

"Excuse me… but you the fella… the one Mae's been talkin' about? The one who's…" She noticed him glance toward her hoodless head. "…been helping Camille?"

Robert nodded, so Mr. Ferguson turned back to her with an explanation of how her mother, on being diagnosed with cancer in the late summer, had sworn him to secrecy. Mama was most concerned that her daughter be kept unaware of the condition for as long as possible, knowing that she would immediately abandon college if she knew. Of course, she had already reasoned all of this out. She knew Mama's way of thinking better than anyone. Everything that had been done was with the sole purpose of keeping her at Garland.

"Where is she, Mr. Ferguson?"

He turned to Robert with the directions… and then eventually back to her.

"I'm sorry… but you need to know… it's not good… not good at all. She insisted on staying in that house for as long as possible, so I've had a nurse looking in on her. Camille… she absolutely refused to be moved. We had her out on the prayer chain… and everyone's so… Wait, Camille – don't go yet! We need to discuss what's…"

But she would not wait. She was out the diner door with Robert at her heels. As he busied himself in following the route to Wyatt Crossing, she was left to struggle through the dreadful implication of cancer… both in reality and imagination. The progression of her thoughts was akin to water filling behind an earthen dam, one as yet untested by any storm. Fears flowed in, straining the limits of resiliency and slowly covering over all of her wonderful plans with a cold, dark realization. Acknowledging that Robert had come through something similar presented only a small comfort – as in knowing that there were structurally sound dams elsewhere in the world capable of holding back massive quantities of water. She was not one of those. She was facing the weight of this water alone, as it steadily rose at the base of her mind and heart. Looking up the valley above her dam… to the full extent of her foresight… she strained to comprehend the enormity of sorrow yet to gather upon her… so terrified that its weight could not be held back.

Hospice care, she knew, was for the terminally ill. It was a one-way trip – an 'in,' but no 'out.' Such thoughts, as rain-soaked rivulets feeding into her reservoir, spilt in dreadful awareness – of life alone without Mama. No Mama to come home to. No Mama to call upon for support, or to share with. No Mama at graduation, birthdays or holidays. No Mama to watch her marry… and no Mama to hold a grandchild. No dam could hold all that back.

Yet sadness was not the only force acting upon her being. Anger was growing in proportion, feeding into her reservoir from hidden founts beneath.

How could Mama not tell me?! How could she shut me out at a time when she so obviously needed me!? Doesn't she want me there?! Or am I that much of a burden?!

These seemingly incompatible emotions – dread and outrage – were, in fact, fully soluble within the terrible contemplation of Mama's cancer. All contributed equally to the pressure building upon her.

Looking over to Robert, whose eyes were only peripherally on the road, she spoke at last.

"I'm scared. She's dying… I just know it. Please believe me, Robert… I wasn't even aware of her being sick! That's gotta make me the absolute worst daughter ever! I've been so… absorbed with myself… that I couldn't see this coming." The burden of her thoughts shifted her eyes to the passenger side foot well, as she decided to be completely candid. "But I'm also really mad! How could she keep this to herself?! She should have told me!" They sat in silence for miles worth of fretting before she could continue. "Is it wrong for me to be angry? I left home mad at her for sending me to college, but she was right… if for no other reason than having met you. But now… what am I to think?! And what does it matter anyway?! She's dying, and I'm going to be left all alone without her!"

Her final statement was not provided as a way of invitation. He was here, and that was of great comfort to her… but also of concern. What was about to take place, was about to take place in front of him. Meeting him… knowing him… loving him… it all was the best thing that had ever happened to her.

But what if the sight of Mama brings back memories of his own mother?

What if he remembers that pain… and whatever darkness followed?

What if he can't handle it… and leaves me to face this alone?

"Camille… I hope you realize that we're in this together."

With his words, a small ray of light cut through, proving that the sun still shone above… though heavy rains continued to fall.

CHAPTER
31

PINECREST

Southern seasons smoothly blend, one into another, with little fanfare from Mother Nature. In the deep South, it seldom freezes and rarely snows, so it is not uncommon for an awareness of autumn to skip straight over winter and into spring. As for her, on exiting Robert's car in the visitor lot of Pinecrest Hospice House, she decided that winter had begun on November 27th – the day of an awful icy-cold awareness. Mama was leaving her forever.

Pinecrest was situated on a well-tended grassy incline set back from the state highway connecting Carlton with Wyatt Crossing. The wide grounds were adorned with many shrubs and beds, though the season was not affording any to flower. The establishment's name was likely derived from the stately pines distributed all about. They were the kind with tall, thick trunks and branches located only way up high. Those trees gave off a symbolic feel of life ascending into the heavens – an illusionary sensation of comfort for families facing the death of a loved one.

The complex itself was a single story building finished in red brick, typical of much Southern architecture. The main driveway subdivided into one part on the left, which led to a circular entry running up under a sheltered overhang at the facility's front... and to the right, a parking lot designated for visitors. It was evident that the main entrance was for drop-offs only. A narrow lane running around the back was presumably for employee parking, deliveries… and departures of former residents.

As they walked toward the visitor entrance, she grabbed Robert's arm and wrapped it about her shoulders, gripping his hand tightly on the other side. The action was not intended as affection, but as desperation. He squeezed her hand in reply.

Inside, a large, rather serious-looking woman stationed behind a counter in a small waiting room greeted them with a surprisingly soft and sympathetic 'hello.' After registering their names and relations, they were given visitor badges and gestured toward seating.

"A nurse will escort you in as soon as your mother's ready."

The sign on double metal doors requested that they be quiet and wait patiently.

Sitting there for nearly an hour, they did what anyone would do while waiting to visit the dying – they waited. Each held a hand of the other, with Robert maintaining an arm around her. Talk was sparse, and neither partook of the waiting room's magazines. Whenever she did dare to make eye contact with the woman behind the counter, she received back only a slight motion of the head… which unmistakably communicated 'not yet, dear.'

It was late afternoon when another woman, this one in nurse attire, opened one side of the double doors and called for 'Miss Camille' and 'Mr. Robert.' In moving through, they were no longer holding hands as the setting preempted all other sensory inputs. The nurse led them down a wide straight hall tiled in linoleum and covered by a standard drop-ceiling. This corridor attempted to give off the feel of a residence, but failed. Though the walls were adorned with artwork and sconces, they also bore occasional signs of damage from wheelchairs and gurneys. Doorways to either side were capped with numbered lights and accompanied by slanted bins for medical records. Almost all of these rooms were closed off from view. But more so than these things, it was the odor that revealed the true nature of the place – industrial sanitizer inadequately covering over other smells. The presence of nurses also made a strong impression on her – that the residents were not in control of their stay.

"Are there currently many… people here?"

"Yes, Mr. Robert, we're nearly at capacity."

The phrase did not sit well with her.

They had walked half the length of the building, and could now see a richly decorated lobby on their left connecting to the front entrance. Across the hall from this was a nurse's station. Their guide pointed to the lobby seating.

"Mr. Robert, since you're not a family member, can I ask you to sit here while Miss Camille visits her mother? If she's up for additional visitors, then Miss Camille can fetch you."

Robert fell from view as the nurse continued on to room twenty three. The lady, however, unexpectedly stopped before the door… with them both nearly colliding there in the process.

"Excuse me, Honey… but let me have a moment of your time first. You need to understand the seriousness of her condition. Your mama… she's real sick. The cancer's spread in the last few weeks."

She could feel her dam cracking. Quickly glancing back toward the mostly hidden lobby, she garnered a modicum of strength from the sight of Robert… for he had slid a chair a bit out into the hallway in order to maintain line-of-sight with her for as long as possible.

"Her nurses, her doctor and the specialist – we're all doing our best for her. Now it's your turn. I can't tell you how to feel – that's not my place – but it is my job to look after that woman. She's only been here a few days, but I can tell she's a special one. No screaming, no cursing, no whining and no crying. I'm told she had everything worked out before the ambulance rolled up to her front door. Honestly, she should have been admitted here a week ago."

The word 'ambulance' carried with it an unexpected reproach. The image of Mama riding alone in such a vehicle from Carlton to this place was both an indictment and an epitaph. Not of the mother's mortality, but of a daughter's exhibition of care.

"What I'm trying to tell you is that you can make things easier on her… and probably a bit easier on yourself too. I say this to all first time visitors – how you act in there is your last gift to her. Think about her first and yourself not at all. Now, you steady yourself… 'cause I'm sure the mama you knew isn't the mama you're about to see."

Swallowing hard, she nodded, managing only a feeble 'thank you' before entering.

She would not have been repulsed by the person she beheld, though the nurse's admonition did help summon courage to opened chambers of memory revealing the love she had for this dearest of persons. Mama, lying motionless in a hospital bed, was a wraith compared to the person she remembered seeing just two months previous. A tube of oxygen was being held under her nose by a strap that circumvented her head, with the tube itself looping around each ear before proceeding downward toward a respirator. This standard piece of hospital-ware somehow accentuated the apparent thinness of the skin about Mama's cheek bones, as well as the sunken nature of her eyes. About her face was a tint of yellowness… both unearthly and sickening at the same time. Yet it was the condition of Mama's head that nearly propelled her into tears. She was bald, a state inadequately concealed by a baby-blue beany. Some form of chemotherapy had been successful on the outside at removing hair… but not on the inside with respect to the cancer. No child should ever have to see their parent like this.

As she crept closer to bedside, Mama… eyes still closed… suddenly whispered.

"Is she gone? That nurse you was talking to… is she gone?"

The voice was weak, but the words were definitely Mama's. With this recognition, she felt an immense surge of relief. She took Mama's hand in both of hers before answering.

"Yes, Mama… she's gone."

Her eyes came open… and in their vacantness was also still a bit of Mama.

"Good. I don't have strength for being poked right now."

"Mama, how do you feel? Is there anything I can do for you?"

"Nothing, Sweetie. Unless you can roll back time to my better lookin' days."

"Aww, Mama… you look just fine."

"Nonsense, Child. And I don't have time for foolishness either. Thank the Lord you were always such a terrible liar."

"Can I… would it be alright if I… hugged you?"

"Of course. Just don't knock off this tube doohickey cause it'll send whistles blowing back at Fort Nurse, and they'll come riding in here looking for…"

But it seemed that that many words in succession had exhausted Mama. She quickly retrieved a cup with straw from a side table and brought it near for Mama to drink… then gently hugged her. The feel was not so fragile as she had expected. Instead… it seemed more as if bones was all that remained there to hug. Once again, she must fight off the tears.

"Thank you, Sweetie. Now let me look at you. Pretty as ever. So proud of you… rid of those hoodies… walking about free. Lord, what beautiful hair!" Another sip. "Tell me about school. Are they being nice to you… the others?"

"Yes, Mama… everything's fine."

"Grab that thingy… tilt me up… I won't break."

Mama lifted a thin arm in pointing over the edge of the bed. She found the remote… double checked which button did what based on the little images over each… and then gave the appropriate one a quick tap. Relieved when the bed responded as expected, she slowly tilted Mama up… then allowed the remote to dangle as before.

"Now you talk. Tell me everything."

She briefly described her progress in each class, her work-study position, and life with a roommate, before transitioning to the subject of Robert. At that name, Mama's eyes widened… which unfortunately emphasized their hollowness.

"Is he here?"

"He's waiting in the lobby."

"Should I… see him now?"

The question was almost child-like, making her unsure how best to respond… even unsure whether she wanted to share Mama at all.

"Soon, Mama. Soon."

The words, like an incantation, produced an unexpected surge of energy in Mama.

"Child, I know that look! I might be as sick as sin, but I still know you. You know I have to meet this young man who's made such a difference in you. You with no hoodie… holding your head high… and going to college."

She fell back the slight distance she had raised herself and became silent. Panic rose within at the thought she had just pushed Mama too far… but then Mama spoke again… though scarcely in a whisper.

"Let me rest for a bit… then you bring him in."

Irrespective of the willingness, it was apparent that Mama… having closed her eyes… was finished for the day. Retrieving the remote, she slowly lowered her back down, and then gently kissed her on the forehead.

"I'm never leaving you again. Never! I love you, Mama."

She could only process scattered moments from then onward. She was unaware of having left Mama's side… yet suddenly found herself crying in the ladies' room. Then somehow she had gotten herself into the lobby for a conference with Robert and a nurse… but also stood with Robert for some indeterminate time in the hall outside Mama's room watching through the window as she slept. But the order to all those events was confusing and the exchanges unclear. At some point, she overheard him ask some other nurse a question about tomorrow, and then… he was seat-belting her into his car. In a scatter of words, she picked up something from him about a plan… followed sometime later by 'reservations'… then 'a bite to eat'… and finally 'how's that sound?'

She knew of herself being walked into some place… a diner… then being seated… with him ordering something for her. A salad of some sort was placed before her… and she stared down into that lifeless lettuce while he ate. He kept talking about interconnecting rooms… and privacy… and Thanksgiving being just another normal day… and something about visiting seven days a week. Another 'how's that sound?'

As he led her out to his car, she sensed more keenly than anything else that moment in which she went from the light of the diner into the outside darkness… a presence so thick that it could be felt. That darkness seemed as a river… and his car a raft… as they moved along with the night's current… through and around rapids of blackness. All the while, she heard the steady rush of air moving past her, droning on with the consistency of a cascade.

She eventually became aware of the car moving under the bright light of a sheltered overhang… yet she had no idea where they were.

"I'll be right back."

She sat without registry of time, thinking only that they had planned to spend four days with Mama. Four days with nothing to do but enjoy each other.

All was gone.

He returned with two magnetic card keys, drove around the complex, and then ushered her into a motel room, opening an interconnecting door to another. She managed to follow his comings and goings between the car and the room… all without having the life needed for moving an inch from the spot where he had left her.

"Camille... please sit down. You don't look well."

"I'm not well. I'll never be well..."

Only one drop lacking to break the dam. She watched Robert draw back the sheets on the bed before sitting her down... making her lie down just as she was... then removing her shoes and pulling covers up over. Having no will of her own, she still managed to roll onto one side and draw knees up close to her chin. The lights went out, with only a faint glow from the adjoining room. She sensed the desk chair being pulled alongside the bed... then felt him holding her hand... just in time for the tears. Big, convulsive, breath-stealing sobs. Cries of utmost anguish resonating within the narrow confines of the room... each refocusing itself back upon her. Despair beyond comprehension. The dam shattered and the reservoir drained, its contents spilling downstream to the oceans of time and no one else's concern.

Yet there was Robert. She could feel his hands about hers... just as with Mama six years before. As the tears slackened to a trickle, she felt his grip on her relax... then fingers brushed her hair behind an ear... just as warm lips rested briefly upon her forehead.

"Good night, Camille. I love you. I'll be right here. I won't leave you."

The dam, though broken, would be rebuilt... ready for tomorrow... just in time for new rains and new floods. And then the whole misery of Mama dying would start all over again.

Mercifully, the world somehow closed itself off in sleep.

CHAPTER

32

MEETING MAMA

She awoke to the sound of a car door slamming shut just outside the motel room. An engine started… and then tires crunched across the parking lot, onto the smoother highway, and out of her hearing. White light eking around the perimeter of the room's heavily shrouded window asserted the time of day, though she did not bother searching for confirmation from the bedside clock. Her eyes went instead to the vacant chair… and then to the closed door connecting the adjoining room. Alarm immediately arose within her.

"Robert?! Robert, are you there?"

Noise from next door brought calm washing over her.

"You decent?"

Sitting up in bed, she inspected herself in the dim. Fully clothed from the previous day and a total wreck – the second time she had slept this way in little over a month.

"Ugh! I look absolutely atrocious! Does that qualify as decent?"

He stuck his head around the edge of the door frame and found her in the semi-darkness.

"Good morning, Sweetheart."

"You too. What time is it… and how long have you been up? Oh, did you happen to find out when visiting hours start?"

"Eight, two, and nine."

"What?"

"It's eight, I've been up for two hours, and visitation starts at nine."

"Oh."

She rose from bed and went directly to him.

"Thank you for being here. I don't know what I'd do without you. You're the only thing holding me together."

She gave him a quick kiss... but a much longer hug – the kind a child might give a parent who had just bandaged a scrape or fixed a broken toy. With arms tight about his midsection, she buried her face into his chest and breathed deeply. He smelled so fresh... like having just stepped from a shower. If only she could stay this way all day...

But she made herself release him, depositing another kiss before letting him know that she would be ready to go after a quick shower of her own.

Intending to make it brief, she nonetheless lingered beneath the stream for a long time. The hot water beating on the crown of her head and flowing off on all sides shielded her with a canopy of sorts... insulating her from the reality she must soon face. Somehow, the water also cleansed her of the previous day's sorrows, steeling her resolve to put Mama first. After all, it was Thanksgiving – their last one together.

As she was not interested in breakfast, they headed directly to Pinecrest. After hardly a wait, she was admitted to Mama's room... and was immensely relieved to find her mother in a better state. The nurse... a different one than yesterday... said this was a good sign. ("Your mama's still got some spunk left in her.") She spent several minutes adoring and being adored, before beckoning Robert into the room.

"Mama... this is Robert."

As subtly as could be done, she placed his hand into Mama's and then stepped back to observe. Mama smiled at him, and he smiled back.

"What a fine young man you are. I have so much to thank you for... and so much to say to you. Doesn't seem fair we can't sit together and chat for hours on end. I had hoped to hear about all those important people you know."

Robert gave her a sideways glance... as she had simply told her mother over the phone that he was a historian-in-the-making, learning about famous people.

"Yes, ma'am... I would enjoy that immensely. And I have much to thank you for – for raising such a wonderful daughter. I expect you'll be better soon… and then we can spend hours talking about whatever you'd like."

She was not surprised to see Mama appraise him briefly before responding.

"Another terrible liar… You two make a great pair."

With the clearing of the throat that was a message in itself, Mama addressed her directly.

"Sweetie, mind going to Fort Nurse for me and fetching… oh… what's her name? You know… the head honcho lady. I've such a terrible bone to pick with her."

She glanced toward Robert, being unsure about leaving him alone with Mama for even a short time.

"Go on, Child. I'm not going to steal your boyfriend."

Of course, she knew otherwise.

This is probably some ridiculously drawn-out diversion to get me out of the way so she can be alone with him!

She nonetheless complied. Yet before departing the room, she looked back once to take in the sight of the man she loved leaning over the mother she cherished. The image was not at all what she had hoped for from this Thanksgiving visit.

At the nurse's station, she discovered that Mama's errand was actually not a wild goose chase after all. They were expecting her.

"There's some paperwork for you to sign with our resident affairs manager. She's down the hall on the left by the doors you came through."

So she mechanically followed the nurse's directions, pondering instead on what Mama and Robert might be talking about. There was a brief moment of apprehension in which she wondered whether their conversation might stray near to the subject of Daddy… but then relaxed before knocking on a door labeled 'Administration.'

Mama would never do that without my permission.

"Can I help you?" It was the lady from behind the visitor counter, except now they were in the same room together.

"Yes, ma'am. It's… ahh… me again… the daughter of Mrs. Larson in room twenty three. I was told to come here regarding some paperwork."

She was ushered into an interior office labeled 'Resident Affairs,' and introduced to Mrs. Fawcett… a rather squat woman who nonetheless rose briskly from behind her desk to shake hands.

"Miss Larson, please have a seat. Allow me first extend my sincere sympathies to you. I know this is a very trying time."

She could not reply – just weakly grimace.

"As the facility's resident affairs specialist, it is my honor to assist you in whatever way possible… even on holidays. I'm sorry for the timing of this meeting… it being Thanksgiving and all. We do try to schedule these for when residents are admitted… but I understand in your case that you were unaware of your mother's condition."

Again, all she could do was tip her head in acknowledgement.

"I just want to assure you – this is a common occurrence. Many residents prefer to enter without informing their families."

While talking, Mrs. Fawcett opened a file on the desk before her. From the formal mannerism in which this was done, she gathered that she was about to be navigated through the final business matters of Mama's stay at Pinecrest.

"Your mother is unusual. Not only did she research this establishment two months previous, but she also put all of her affairs in order before admission. As you are aware, because she has not designated you as power of attorney, you won't be able to…"

At this, her head jolted upright with astonishment.

"Oh… my apology. I thought you had been informed." Mrs. Fawcett made a quick examination of the records before her. "A Mr. Ferguson has been designated as both her power of attorney and the executor of her estate. By chance, have you spoken with him yet?"

She nodded… but then remembered that she had ran out of his diner before discussing Mama's affairs.

"Miss Larson… there is no cause for you to be concerned. Your mother has attended to every detail. You have been completely freed from such burdens to focus fully on the time you have remaining with her. Now, where was I… oh yes. Your mother has made certain stipulations in her living and final wills. Regarding the former, she instructed Pinecrest not to initiate life-preserving measures in the event of heart failure. This, however, was not to go into effect until after you were able to visit."

She sat dumbstruck. To think that Mama was in such deliberate control of her own death… and to the exclusion of her only daughter.

How can this be?! Doesn't she trust me to honor her wishes?! Or does she think I'd just mess things up?!

She wanted Robert there, if only to provide some reassurance that she had not failed as a daughter.

"I would like your signature on this form verifying that Pinecrest has complied with your mother's wishes."

The woman rotated a page from on top of the open file and extended it to her along with a pen. Removing the sheet from the folder had revealed a photograph of Mama that was slid into a paper frame on the interior of the folder's left side. It could not have been taken when Mama checked in, for the image was clearly of her healthy self. Maybe, so typical of Mama, it was provided with foresight during her initial planning. Though this photo was inverted, the habit of playing with perspective suddenly betrayed her. It was really she who was upside down in this situation, while Mama was right-side up and in perfect control… even though she lay dying in a hospital bed.

Considering the sheet before her, she recognized it as a simple acknowledgement that one step in the paperwork of Mama's impending death had been accomplished. A wide blank line above her printed birth name awaited a signature. It was not true, but she suddenly felt as if she was about to sign Mama's death warrant. She haltingly wrote in her birth name, just as requested, handing back the form along with the pen.

"Keep the pen, dear. We have more to do."

She looked down at the implement in her hand. It was a token guilt offering… like thirty pieces of silver. Payment in the form of the very thing that had signed away Mama's life. So she gripped it tightly, willing it to break… but it would not.

"Your mother has instructed me to inform you that all financial matters regarding her stay here have been taken care of by Mr. Ferguson. Your mother has also made arrangements for her service and…" A kindly delay of proper length then followed. "… burial, but has asked to have you sign a waiver stipulating that you will not alter those arrangements once she has passed."

At this, she willed herself to speak for the first time.

"I don't understand."

"It's not uncommon for family members, once a resident departs, to attempt a change… or to disregard… their loved one's wishes. Without this signed waiver form, Pinecrest has no legal basis for contradicting those loved ones."

The words bore an acidic tinge, delivered as a firm reminder that Pinecrest was a business – one that took full advantage of all legal protections in its dealings with clients.

Again, she signed and handed back what was required of her. She now had no legal standing in any of her mother's affairs… on this side of life or the other. Since sending her away to college, Mama had withheld the news of cancer, deliberately deceived on multiple occasions, vacated the house, entered hospice care, and then made her daughter sign away all rights in death and burial.

What more could I be excluded from?!

Yet Mrs. Fawcett was already holding out to her a third piece of paper signifying that there was yet another form to be processed.

"This is the final matter, dear. As your mother's only living relative, we need your current contact information. This has nothing to do with your mother's will. Sometimes, residents leave behind jewelry, articles of clothing, or other items from their stay. We simply require an address in case something should be shipped to you."

The request was more than reasonable, yet it felt to her as if Pinecrest was asking where they could send Mama's junk after she was dead.

"I don't know where I'll be living… since I'm not going back to college. I'm… currently staying in a motel because… I… think my mother's sold our house."

Mrs. Fawcett then gestured toward a box of tissue positioned on a corner table, so she extracted a single sheet. After discretely wiping her eyes, she turned back to reply as calmly as could be managed.

"May I get back with you about this after speaking with my mother?"

"Of course, dear. I'll leave the form here, and you can ask any of the ladies at the visitor window to retrieve it."

"Can I know from you what Mama's plans are regarding her funeral?"

Mrs. Fawcett ran a finger down a checklist in the file until the appropriate entry was reached.

"No… I'm sorry, dear. She has not authorized us to speak on her behalf regarding that matter. Perhaps you should discuss it with the executor of her will… assuming you're uncomfortable asking her yourself. Well… that is all I need from you today. Thank you for giving Pinecrest the privilege of serving you and your mother in this time of need."

CHAPTER

33

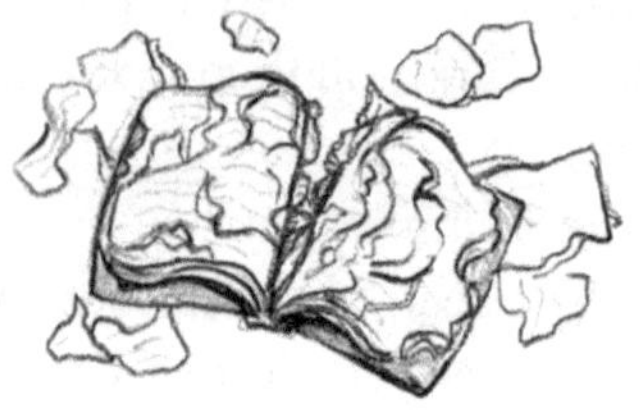

I DO, I DO

Mrs. Fawcett's final words echoed in her mind all the way down the hall. She had played no part in any of her mother's decisions during 'this time of need.' That phrase resonated in her head with self-condemnation… along with a subtle suggestion of insignificance.

Robert was not in the main lobby, which likely meant that he was still in Mama's room. Fighting against a twofold urge – to barge in and save the day, if necessary, and to not miss out on another second of them together – she nonetheless opened the door quietly. Mama was asleep… with Robert sitting in a chair on the bed's opposite side. So she mouthed 'Is everything OK?' and he nodded, giving her eyes free rein to flow over her mother's face, the frail shoulders, arms, and hands. One of those was partially concealed beneath a blanket, whereas she hoped the other had just been holding Robert's. She beckoned him to the door with a flick of her head.

"Question is, are you OK? You look like you've been… having a rough time."

She was sure he meant to say 'crying.'

"Oh, everything's just fine… except the part about my mother dying… and her having to make decisions all on her own… and me being absolutely the worst daughter on the planet! I don't blame her for not trusting me with…"

"That's not true. You know she did this for you. She researched this place on her own, and then arranged for a lawyer and a will. She told me all about it. Everything was sold off... including the house... and then she checked herself in when she couldn't go any further on her own. That was on Monday. It's the very reason why you couldn't reach her by phone. She did all this... to fulfill her dreams for you. She's a remarkable woman."

"Robert, this isn't helping! I should have been here... not off learning about stupid, useless..."

She stopped herself, took a deep breath, and tried to refocus on Mama. Finishing that sentence would serve no purpose other than to demean the sacrifice being made on her behalf.

They reached the lobby and chose seats facing a large Christmas tree situated in one corner. It was clearly fake. Though possessing an acceptable form, it offered only a meager connection to the Norse origins of the practice – a sign of hope in the worst of winter. No matter how cold and dark it became, the evergreen was ever green. Yet like the well-adorned substitute, she felt plastic. An imitation daughter.

She commenced staring into the tree's lighting... in no way for enjoyment... but because it was a convenient enough place from which to collect those few thoughts mercifully left unaffected by Mrs. Fawcett's pen. Bulbs blinked, ornaments sparkled, and tinsel glistened, all in the usual 'Season's Greetings' and 'God Rest Ye Merry Gentlemen' sort of ways. Yet the decorations offered nothing festive to her. A particularly long strand of multicolored lights looping several times around the circumference flashed out a mocking message with its two short pulses of light followed by a brief pause, then the two pulses again... over and over in an endless pattern. The blinking kept time with the word being repeated in her mind: *Ma-ma, Ma-ma, Ma-ma.*

She turned in her seat to face Robert.

"What'd you two talk about? Tell me everything! I want every word! Don't leave anything out!"

As he collected himself for responding, she silently marveled over how attached she had become to him in such a short time. In fact, she told herself... then and there... that she wanted to spend the rest of her life with him. It had nothing to do with Mama dying *per se*... or the prospect of her being left alone. The real reason both surprised her and made perfect sense. It was because she just realized that he had stayed in Mama's room rather than fleeing to this well-decorated lobby. He had stayed with Mama, in spite of whatever memories that might have been dragged up from his own mother's deathbed. That meant he would also stay with her through Mama's death… and beyond. So in that moment, she declared to herself that she would never leave him either.

But she had also come to know him well. His hesitation was not to recall details of the conversation – it was to decide what to and what not to tell her.

"Well… I started out by saying how beautiful the room was… and what a nice place this was… and how great it was to finally meet her. But then she cut me off with 'Child, do you not see me lying in this hospital bed?! I don't have time for such nonsense!'"

She could not help but smile at the instantaneously conjured memories of Mama's fiery bluntness. She wanted to get up and unplug the tree as a sign to herself… and to the tree… that the trait had been passed on from mother to daughter. Instead, she remained focused on Robert.

"I think she must have surprised herself because I felt a little squeeze from her hand. She then asked what it was that I liked most about you, and I said that you're the best friend I've ever had."

She had not been expecting either that question or his answer… and hearing them made her all teary-eyed. Though he was perceptive enough to offer a hug, she hastily wiped away the moisture and insisted that he continue uninterrupted.

"Well… after that… we just talked about… routine kinds of stuff."

What followed next was another poorly executed pause – one in which he fidgeted about a bit in his chair. That immediately confirmed her suspicion.

I just introduced my boyfriend to my dying mother, and already they've got secrets!

"Oh… I almost forgot about when the nurse came in to make adjustments on…"

"I don't care about the nurse. I want to know what you two talked about!"

"Sure… sorry. Umm… she wanted to know about that night in the park, so I told her how we outsmarted the dog… and then you called me boyfriend… and how we kissed on the front porch of your dorm. I guess that's about it."

"That's it?! Seriously?! There's nothing more?!"

"Oh yeah... she did ask me something odd. Said it was really important that she hear it from me. She wanted to know if I lowered your hood before kissing you. When I said I did, she got this... sort of... furtive look on her face. Something like a sigh... but with a little smile mixed in. From then on, it was all business. 'What're your plans?' 'How long do you have in school?' 'Any money in history?' 'Do you have family left?' I guess you must have told her about my parents. Umm... she... ahh... even asked what my intentions were regarding you."

She leaned back in total surprise.

"I'm not kidding – she was pretty direct."

Suddenly, a measure of joy began to bubble up within her, because she knew her mother's mind. He was a done deal.

"Robert... did you ask her if you could marry me?"

"Well... actually... I did."

She could see that he was initially proud of himself... but suddenly faltered on misreading her surprise.

"Hey... I'm sorry. I know you wanted us to spend time together first, but... under the circumstances... I thought it was the right thing to do. I only hope I asked properly... After all, every family has its own expectations regarding such things. Did you know that in some African cultures, prearranged marriages start out with..."

"WILL YOU STOP MESSING AROUND! WHAT'D SHE SAY?!"

"Yeah... sorry. Umm... let's see... after I told her that I loved you... and that I wanted to spend the rest of my life with you... I just... sort of... asked if I had her blessing to marry you one day. Right off, she said 'Of course, Child, you can marry my daughter. You should marry my daughter'. Frankly, I got the feeling that if a shotgun was standard hospital equipment, she'd have sent for a nurse to fetch one."

He fell silent and she waited, expecting much more than this. Instead... he slowly slid off his seat to one knee and presented her with a small black box. Not believing what she was seeing, she drew in too quick of a breath at the sight, straining to hold it as he slowly lifted the lid to reveal a diamond ring.

"Camille, I do love you... and all I want in life is to be with you. So I ask you... Camille, love of my life... will you marry me? Will you be my wife?"

She could not be hearing this correctly. It made no sense. The previous day had begun a long, cold winter of the soul... yet now... just one day later... on a day of thanks... how could a spring be blossoming within?

"Wife?"

"Yes – wife. From the moment you placed your hand on the small of my back and trusted me... from that moment on... I knew I wanted only you. You didn't run – you trusted me. I can't tell you what that meant to me. There was no way that dog was getting by me."

In being speechless, a part of her wanted to point back to plans made on a porch swing. Plans for taking things slow so the three of them could spend time growing close. Yet another part... a part that could still feel a pen of death signing away a life... that part reminded her that there was no time, that there would be no future, and it was only now.

"Yes, Robert! Yes! I want to be your wife more than anything!"

Broken hearts and broken minds are just normal people with gaps waiting to be filled. Many things claim to fill gaps. Some offer a temporary fix... a mere distraction... while others are a cheap imitation delivered with deceptive promise. And some stand the test of time. Hope is the friend that holds open the gap for love, fights to keep it from being filled with lesser things – anger, bitterness, resentment, regret, despair and resignation. Those things can occupy the gap but never quite fill it. Never really make the heart whole again. Hope holds the pieces together waiting for love's arrival. The broken heart filled with love becomes defined by love, and no longer by the gap. For her, a heart rent apart by a father who should have loved her, and by the imminent loss of a mother who did, was somehow now being made whole by the one who promised to love her forever.

Fresh water is to salt, and gentle rain to the gale, as was her new formed tears of joy to yesterday's sorrow. Robert slid over her finger the band that supported a spherically cut diamond. Her diamond! It was like nothing she had ever seen before. Though the band itself was slightly too big, she took it as a positive sign. *Room to grow.* As the Christmas lighting glittered off her jewel, the greater sparkle was in his eyes as she threw arms about him. They kissed and hugged, unaware that Pinecrest nurses had congregated behind them, smiling and wiping away tears of their own. Both of them got brought back by a round of applause.

Now as fiancée, Robert kissed her hand before taking in fully the ring on her finger.

"I can't believe how amazing it looks on you. That was my mother's. I confess – I brought it with me on a whim… and not at all because I thought any conversation with Mama might… you know… bend me in the direction of a proposal. This may sound silly… but having that ring with me gave me courage to meet Mama. Kind of like part of my own mother was here with me. It's the one thing of hers that makes me feel… close to her. I remember as a child always twirling it on her finger…"

He took that opportunity to do likewise with this ring now upon her finger… and the feel of it matched the tenderness in his eyes. Of course, *her eyes* were mostly on her diamond… though her ears were fully available to him. But when he did not continue, she looked up to see a frown.

"Camille… I don't want that memory to get in the way of us. So I just want you to know… if you don't feel comfortable with it, then we'll go pick out a different…"

Lickety-split, she jerked her hand away from him.

"You are not touching my ring! Got it?! This one's so much more precious to me now that I know it has double meaning for you."

With that matter settled, she immediately lunged at him with kisses and hugs… and a whole lot more tears of joy. Only for the pleasure of hearing him speak more about the proposal did she fall back into her seat.

"So… one of the last things we talked about before your mother… Mama… fell asleep was when I intended to propose. Obviously… I hadn't thought that far ahead… but before I could answer, she hit me with this weird adage about trying to pick today's fruit tomorrow."

She had heard that one many times before.

"In other words…"

"She meant that I should get right to it. Her only… umm… well… it's nothing really. Never mind. So… like I was saying… she was real happy to…"

"Excuse me?! Her only what?!"

"Oh, it's nothing. Don't give it a…"

"No, it's not – I can tell. What'd she say?"

"She only asked me to… do her a favor."

When he did not continue, she contorted her face into a most intense 'what-are-you-up-to' expression.

"Camille... I can't tell you just yet. She made me promise not to."

"That's ridiculous! I'm your fiancée... which means you have to tell me everything – right now!"

"Nope. That's not how it works. Talk to Mama."

Her repeated insistences were to no avail, so she instead compelled him to recount again his every interaction with Mama. Yet within minutes, she had taken over the talking, excitedly exploring every facet of the ring, of his proposal, and of one day being his wife. Of course, she ignored the fact that he was fighting off yawns, having spent much of the previous night uncomfortably camped at her bedside. That was his problem. But eventually, she decided to set him free ("Robert, take a nap."), and made a giddy beeline to the nurse's station where one woman was motioning for her to come over... all of them waiting expectantly for details on the proposal, along with a closer look at the ring.

Sometime later that morning while Robert still slept, a nurse came by to inform her that a facility doctor wished to speak with her. She was led to a gentleman standing by the nurse's station. He was in casual attire, maybe having just come from his family's preparations of the Thanksgiving meal. The nurse made the introduction.

"This is Dr. Marinaldo."

"Miss Larson, I'm pleased to meet you... but also saddened. Will you accompany me to a conference room where we can speak in private?"

They walked to the far end of Pinecrest... to a space set aside for family consultations. On passing room twenty three, she was tempted to peek in on Mama, but instead remained focused on the doctor, who was a step ahead. They entered the conference room, and Dr. Marinaldo began speaking only once they were seated.

"I was told that you've already spoken with a nurse about your mother's condition. The form of cancer that she has – pancreatic – has a low survival rate unless it's diagnosed early... and I'm sorry to say that your mother's wasn't. By the time it was discovered, it had already begun to spread. Now... your mother chose to delay the start of treatment for several weeks, though we really don't think it would have made much of a difference. Her doctor in Jackson tried some chemotherapy, but the cancer did not respond."

This was far worse than being with Mrs. Fawcett. Again, all she could do was nod in recognition.

"Miss Larson… I want to assure you that we'll be doing everything possible for your mother. In particular, we're aggressively managing her pain. For the most part… aside from being very tired… she should have her faculties about her up until the end… unless we need to increase her medications." The doctor then leaned in to lower his voice. "I'm terribly sorry, Miss Larson… we don't think she has much more than a week or two. I could go into detail as to how we know, but perhaps you'd prefer not to know."

"I don't want to know."

"I understand. A nurse also mentioned that you'll be staying nearby – is that correct?"

She nodded.

"What you're about to see over the next week or so will not be easy to forget. We have counseling and chaplaincy services available anytime you need them."

From that, she understood that he was giving her a chance to ask anything on her mind, but no words could convey the depths of her grief and fear. So he just smiled sadly and continued on.

"I'm glad we had a chance to meet. I'm sorry we can't talk longer right now – I need to get back home. But we'll have more time to speak this weekend. In the meantime… I want you to know that your mother is an extraordinary woman. She's facing her situation with the utmost courage and dignity. You should be very proud of her."

The doctor rose, thanked her again for being here, and excused himself.

She, on the other hand, remained in that room for some time contemplating the injustice that cancer was inflicting upon her mother. Like Old Joe, Mama had lacked the benefit of advanced notice.

Only the poor die young.

But then reason came forth to scold her for the insensitivity. Robert's parents were far from poor, and they had been tragically taken from him. As there was nothing more that she… or anyone else, for that matter… could say or do to lessen the pain, she headed back down the hall… this time stopping to look in on Mama. She was fast asleep.

As was Robert.

Reoccupying her previous seat, she began pondering two general lines of thought that were combating for prominence in her mind. She wanted to get married… right away… in Mama's room, and with Mama as her maid of honor. Somehow, from the moment Robert had lowered her hood, she just knew that he was the one for her. Silly, but true! She loved him, so the 'when' did not seem so important now that the 'if ' had been decided. But all that wishing made no difference, seeing as she knew that getting married in Mama's room was equally silly. They were far from ready… and had not even begun making plans. Then there was the issue of a marriage license. She had no idea how to go about getting one of those.

Yet it was the second contemplation that formed a dark cloud over her. She was sorely afraid of getting married. It was not about sharing the rest of her life with the same person… or dirty socks on the floor… or the toilet seat… or even having babies. And her apprehension, she marveled to herself, was not wholly on *a man being with a woman*. Sure… she was likely to be nervous… and even more so dreaded the possibility of freezing up at that special moment of them together. There was even the dread that her thoughts might go back to the shed. Yet a part of her repeatedly reassured herself that sex was something that literally billions of people had done. Apprehensions aside, she was so very anxious to be close to him, and believed that they would find a way to be fine together. It was getting there that truly frightened her, for there was one significant difference between her and most women. She bore a scarlet mark that Robert deserved to know about… and she was too terrified of telling him.

When she was sixteen, she had made the mistake of reading Thomas Hardy's *Tess of the d'Urbervilles*. She had been drawn to this 19th century novel because Hardy had called his main character 'a pure woman faithfully presented,' and she so wanted to be that pure woman.

What a crock!

She received a terrible shock shortly into the novel on discovering that Tess was raped by Alec d'Urberville. Wishing now she had put the book down then and there, she decided to stick with the story, anticipating that the heroine would rise above her shame. Tess eventually met and became engaged to the dashing and affluent Angel Clare, whose family owned the dairy where she worked. Surely they would get married and be happy together. But Hardy's novel was not about a happily-ever-after. Tess was rejected and abandoned by Angel on their wedding night after she confessed her secret. Her ultimate end, being hung for murdering Alec, was the cruelest and meanest conclusion to any book she had ever read. It stole from her every hope of redemption and healing.

She remembered Mama coming home from work to find her sobbing in bed and the room littered with the fragments of many torn up pages. To her credit, Mama did not make her pay for the library book. Instead, together, they built a small bonfire over the shed's concrete slab and burned it, torn cover and all. This time, she did not follow the flames and smoke upward. She kept her eyes fixed upon the embers, concentrating hard on obtaining the same feeling Mama must have had the last time a fire burned on that spot.

It took her months to recover from that novel, and she swore never to read another by Hardy as long as she lived. Yet the seed planted in despair had now fully grown into fear. Sitting in the lobby of Pinecrest watching Robert sleep, she dreaded the choice he might make. She could not see him choosing Angel's way, but also could not endure the thought that she, like Tess, might bear forever the name of the man who abused her.

All through life, she had been defined by others – by a father's neglect and brutality, by a town's ridicule, by a mother's strong presence, by the persona of a fictional character, and even by a garment. And now she was engaged to be married… with no clue how best to tell her fiancée of her deepest fear. So in a moment of resolve, she swore to herself that she would not make Tess's mistake. She would not wait until it was too late. Here was history in fiction that would not be repeated. Tonight, she would find a way to tell Robert.

A voice of doom then whispered to her. *He will abandon you just as Angel did.* But another shouted all the more loudly. *No! He will accept you. He will love you!*

She could not live otherwise.

Robert snapped out of his nap as if an electrical shock had been applied to his chair. He took in the surroundings with a 'where-am-I' sort of look… that is, until his eyes fell upon her, his fiancée. As he leaned over to kiss her, there was a smile on his face of more than recognition.

"I was wondering… would it be alright with you if I… left for a few hours? There're some… errands I need to run."

"On Thanksgiving day?! In the middle of nowhere?!"

"Well… yeah. We have cell phones, so I can rush back if you need me…"

He was now standing sheepishly before her, noticeably fiddling with things in his pockets. And though she was tempted to ask what was so important that she should be left alone, the ring on her finger reminded her that it was there for company.

"I'll be fine. Go do your 'errands'!"

He was gone all afternoon.

She spent the time moving from the lobby to Mama's room to the ladies' room, and then back again to the lobby – a migratory pattern encompassing many cycles. The duration at each site varied, with much more time than expected being spent crying in the ladies' room.

Her mother was awake after a few passes, affording her the first opportunity to proudly exhibit her ring in the time-honored and well-established method that all engaged females employed – arm out straight, wrist bent slightly downward, and fingers spread wide so the rock got prominently displayed. Mama took in the ring for the first time in its new home on her daughter's finger.

"Lovely."

To her surprise, Mama drew that hand to her lips… then her cheek… then her lips again.

"I'm so… excited for you. He's such a… fine young man. But, Sweetie… let's… talk more… after I've rested."

Being careful to withhold her full weight, she leaned over and covered Mama in a sheltered embrace, whispering her back into sleep with many an 'I love you' before finally departing for the ladies' room.

It was several more cycles about Pinecrest before she found Mama awake with sufficient energy for conversation.

"Camellia, I want to speak with you about Robert."

She braced herself. When Mama started a conversation with 'sweetie' or 'child' or some other affectation, it was no big deal. But when she started with 'Camellia,' it was equivalent to bringing a board meeting to order. Business was about to be discussed.

"Yes, Mama?"

"Straight off, just tell me from your own lips before I get going, do you love him enough to be married to him for life – the whole way?"

"Yes, Mama. I do."

"And do you believe he loves you the same way?"

"I do."

"Any other person, and I'd say they were crazier than a mulberried coon, what with how short a time you've known each other. But I trust you, Camellia… I trust you not to settle for… second best."

Mama now lay in silence, though not entirely as a result of her condition. She could still recognize the look – her mother had made it through the first step in a plan. The resolve to push on was present in the tone, despite the face lacking much resemblance to the one she had grown up being accustomed to.

"Good. Glad to hear it. Asked your young man the same things and he gave the same answers. 'I do. I do.' And you know me – death bed or not – if I didn't believe…"

Mama unexpectedly started wheezing, so she hastened with a straw to her lips.

"Thank you, Child. I'm better now. So… I take it he's left on his errands?"

She was instantly set on edge by the question… for it had brought back that unpleasant feeling very much part-and-parcel with the plight of a loner – that of being the last to know what was going on.

"What's he doing, Mama? I need to know. What'd you make him promise?"

"Sweetie, you're an adult and entitled to be treated as such… but right now… you're the one suffering and need the most help. And that's saying a lot since I'm the one who's dying."

"Don't say that, Mama! Please don't!"

"No sense denying the obvious, especially when it's right in front of you. I have some strength now, so let's not use it up arguing. That young man of yours has *resources*, and he's intending on using them. Just wanted my permission first. I made him promise… to take care of you."

That explanation was far from sufficient, though her thoughts and feelings were too tangled up to contradict. As Mama briefly rested once more from the burden of speaking, the many interwoven concerns vying for a place within her took over. She was immensely curious – even worried – about the promise… yet juxtaposed against this was the dreaded subject that she purposed to reveal. Fear of how Robert might respond set the tone for all other feelings… though an equally significant realization vied to displace it. There was so little time left with Mama, yet still so much she needed to say… and feel… and learn – especially about marriage. That desperation, however, was being suppressed by a general concern of taxing Mama. Her own feelings could not be allowed to sap her mother of strength. That particular fear was intimately connected to a suffocating grief – the finality of Mama's cancer. To this was somehow attached a poorly suppressed anger, as if somewhere on the inside, she was still livid with Mama for being kept in the dark. Those ill thoughts, paired with a disgust at how absorbed she had been with herself, nourished a blossoming guilt. Mama had killed herself to see her daughter firmly placed in college… but she had no interest whatsoever in returning. This spun off a final twinge of self-reproach – that she could so lightly abandon her mother's dreams.

Like Hercules fighting the many-headed Hydra, each voice was distinct, and each carried its own individual ferocity. Yet all attacked together as would a single beast. She could not choose one head, cutting it off from among the others, without all weighing in on her. And certain heads grew back stronger no matter how vehemently assailed.

Her chance to choose never came, as Mama took control once more, reminding her of yet another dreadful facet of concern.

"I need to speak with you about your father."

She immediately stiffened.

"What about him?"

"When I'm gone, there won't be anyone left who really understands that man. No one who can fully protect you from him."

"But you said he's in jail for life."

"These days, you can't trust nobody… leastwise the government… or the courts. Criminals end up on the streets all the…"

"Mama, I really don't want to talk about him."

"He could get out! You know it's true. That's why you need to tell your young man. Does he know?"

"Parts."

"What parts?"

"Seriously, Mama! I don't want to discuss this!"

"Sweetie… I know it's difficult, but you've got to. Maybe I could say something to…"

"STOP!"

She turned on her heels to leave the room… but a fit of coughing brought her dashing back to Mama's bedside. It was many tense minutes before either could speak again.

"I'm just concerned for you, Child. Let's… talk about something else. Where's that cup?"

After a long sip of water, Mama changed the subject.

"I expect that Fawcett woman's told you about my affairs?"

"Yes, ma'am."

"Sorry, Child – I cleared out the house. But the kitchen table and chairs… Mr. Ferguson's supposed to pick those up. I figure you might want to keep them as a memory of us together. He's also got… a few boxes of your things. You'll need to go see him. You should know I don't own the house anymore. Sold it to pay for this vacation I'm on. Don't worry – there'll be some money left over to help you with college. You know… I heard the new owner's going to do some remodeling… I expect you won't recognize the place next time you see it."

She nodded, but knew for certain that she would never go back there again.

"Mama… why didn't you tell me? I could've been here for you. I could've made things so much easier for you. It's… it's not right that I wasn't."

"I'm sorry, Child… it was the way it had to be. But I don't want to get into that now. There're more important things to discuss. I… I didn't sort out every detail before… before running out of myself. Never did figure out where you'll be living during breaks. I had Mr. Ferguson working on it… but I expect your young man's going to solve that problem for me."

"What's that supposed to mean?"

Mama just ignored the question. Instead, with great effort, she twisted her frame away in order to speak to the opposite wall.

"I don't know what I did to bring about this sickness… Whatever it was, I'm doubly ashamed of myself. I've let you down. I so wanted to make it through your first term… I can tell even without looking that you want to interrupt – so don't. Let me speak my peace. I know you want to stay here with me… and not go back to school. I'm not going to fight you. Too tired fighting this cancer to fight anything else. I only hope you can understand that… what I've done… it was done for you."

"Yes, Mama. It's hard… and I'm trying to understand."

More quickly than before, Mama turned back to her.

"You know I love you more than life."

"Yes, Mama… I know… and I love you too."

CHAPTER

34

TESS OF THE D'URBERVILLES

She felt as a spectator to the plans of her two true loves. One had arranged for everything regarding her own death... and she was powerless in influencing that outcome... whereas the other was forging a future... of which she feared her secret might just as likely destroy.

She was nothing more than a withered leaf taken along by the river's flow.

Although having preferred to stay beside a sleeping Mama... just as Robert had done... she was far too restless for sitting. Motion was certainly no remedy for this anxiousness, but it offered a temporary release. A few more migratory cycles, and she once again found Mama with strength for conversation.

"Please tell me what Robert's up to!"

"Not my place to say... but he's got *lawyers*, and he's intent on using them."

The way Mama said lawyers was akin to how one might speak about artillery... or gold reserves... or huge tracts of land. Mama had a lawyer too. Even small-town folk availed themselves of such legal services. But to Mama, 'lawyers' meant brigades of black-suited, briefcase-wielding, don't-mess-with-us power. In another setting, Mama would have been offended... and intimidated at the same time... by anyone with 'lawyers,' but with them on her future son-in-law's side, it was very different. She could easily see that Mama was relieved.

"Lawyers?! What're you talking about?"

"He's going to take care of you, Child – I just know it."

"Mama, seriously! Stop fretting about me. It's you who needs care."

"Ain't that the truth."

Mama was done for now, and needed to rest.

So she kissed her… and just wanted to keep on kissing her… but made herself break away. She left Mama's room to start anew the next migratory cycle through Pinecrest.

She had been told by a nurse to expect a high volume of visitors at the hospice house this day, seeing as it was Thanksgiving. Over the course of the afternoon, she was obliged to share the lobby, bathroom and hallway with a variety of other migratory fowl – family members come to face death. The diversity was as extensive as any hospice house ornithologist could desire… though there was no pleasure for her in this 'bird watching.' From the perspective of her wounded imagination, species were not distinguished by age, race, gender or socio-economic status, but by attitude. There were people who clearly had no desire at all to be here, either because death was so repulsive or because they never really liked the sufferer in the first place. These people, she could not help but notice, walked fast, were rude to the nurses, and displayed an air that it cost them more than the price being paid by the dying. Yet she could not bring herself to be hard on these folks for their lack of compassion.

No way I'd have shown up if it were Daddy lying in there!

Another species of Pinecrest visitor was the 'enthusiast.' These, from her perspective, spent far too much of their loved one's remaining time engaged in outward displays of service. She had been distracted on and off that afternoon by one such person who kept moving from her uncle's room to the nurse's station and back again in rapid succession.

"Excuse me… I pushed that button, but nobody came. Is it possible for him to get some more juice please… oh, and another pillow?"

"It's me again… He's complaining of a glare on the TV. I tried, but there's no way to dim the lights… and the curtains won't close properly."

"I thought you should know – that thing attached to his breathing tube beeps every so often. I'd like you to come check it… just in case it's not working right."

"Sorry – but this meal's gone cold... and he says it tastes funny. Can we order something different?"

"There's a terrible draft in his room. I'm really concerned he might catch cold."

She did not want to judge this woman for her persistence... though it was quite evident that her efforts on the part of her uncle were amounting to a major source of irritation to the staff. Of course, if there was something she could do to make Mama more comfortable, then she would certainly pester a nurse to get it done. Yet these enthusiasts... they simply could not stop long enough to consider the enormity of what was happening. Their loved one would soon be stepping into the eternity of the beyond... forever gone. Instead, they seemed to keep up a constant stream of activity so as not to focus on the person who was dying.

There's no patience... and no acceptance.

That's it! These folks are fighting against acceptance. If they bustle about enough, then they won't be confronted with what's happening.

She then wondered whether she had fully accepted what was happening to Mama. Maybe that was why she was spending so much time roaming the halls and sitting alone in the lobby while Mama slept.

No... she did it for a different reason. Though painful, she felt that this quiet self-reflection was actually critical toward making those brief moments with Mama count.

Another species of visitor was the 'fearful,' for they were clearly afraid of death. These seemed to display the most unease. She was sure they loved the sufferer very much, because they were exerting such effort to be here. These folks moved slowly from the visitor's entrance to their loved one's room, being careful not to touch anything along the way. Yet they did not stay long, moving rapidly out of the building once done. Nor did they engage in conversations with the nurses as perhaps this would prolong the time spent within these walls. Maybe some of these family members were simply afraid of catching something... though most seemed more afraid of having the mark of death left upon them. It was not the inconvenience or the guilt, but the fear of making sad memories that defined them.

She knew she bore a trace of the fearful side in her... yet she earnestly wanted to be a different breed – a fourth species of Pinecrest visitor. These people came because they deeply loved the sufferer. They were there to share in as much of this horrible experience as they could, not caring what imprint was being left upon themselves. They were willing to have the moments go as deep as possible, as a tribute of their love and affection.

Into the evening, she happened to share the lobby for some time with a thin black man who was of this species. He was waiting for his father to wake up… or so she gathered from overhearing his interaction with a nurse. He took up a seat in the lobby across from her and waited. From time to time, their eyes met… though no words were exchanged. None were needed. She recognized in him the feelings she herself was experiencing. In him was an outward air of calm reflection that… like for her… hid an inner tumult of memories – some good, some bad – washing over him from years of soul-to-soul contact with his father. She knew that this man did not have control of the moment, but he… like her… had chosen to be here. To allow the terrible and precious final moments of a dying parent make one last life-long imprint on his mind and heart. This man and her… they were kindred spirits on the same journey… one of death and life.

Robert did not return until just before 8 PM, giving them only minutes before visitation hours were over. As they walked back from the check-in lobby, he made a request to see Mama again – alone. A weariness, in combination with the strange sensation derived from a piece of beautifully fashioned carbon suspended on the ring finger of her left hand, somehow eased the sting of being left out once more. They entered the room to find Mama awake, though not particularly coherent. She right off kissed Mama on the forehead, resisting a powerful urge to keep on kissing… as if her lips could fancifully summon divine intervention in the fight against cancer.

"Mama? Robert's back… and he'd like to speak with you… alone."

The last word came out more sour than intended. The craving to be with Mama… to not share her with anyone… was suddenly stronger than anticipated. Seeing her only briefly was like a long fast terminated with a morsel rather than a feast. Yet that ill feeling evaporated instantly on beholding Mama's smile.

In turning from bedside, she whispered so only he could hear.

"Please don't keep her long… she seems terribly tired."

He nodded, and she left without looking back. She already held one memory of him leaning over Mama, and that was enough.

She had barely situated herself in the lobby when he returned bearing an air of determination… oddly covered over by a faint smile.

"Is she OK?"

"I think so… She fell right to sleep. We should go now."

But they had not made it much past the nurse's station when he suddenly stopped her in the corridor. Gently placing a hand on her shoulder and turning her about, he took hold of both her hands before speaking.

"You know I love you… and I know you love me too. So… I'm just going to say it – let's get married right here. In fact, in Mama's room. I want her to see it… and be part of it… and I want you to have her there. I think you want that too. I know this is really rushing things… and I'm taking a whole lot on myself to suggest it. But Mama… she asked me to promise that she'd see you married. Said it was her dying wish. I don't know what to do with that… Of course, I wanted to talk with you first… but she told me not to bother you with the question unless I was sure I could make it happen. I think I can."

Being totally taken aback, she allowed her eyes to drift down toward their interlaced hands… to the ring situated on her finger.

"Camille… you know my heart… and you know hers too… so it's up to you. We'll do whatever's on yours. Just don't say anything now. Don't say 'yes' or 'no.' Just… think about it… tonight. OK?"

"OK."

"But… ahh… there's this really awkward thing I need you to do first."

"What?"

"Follow me."

Pinecrest, being a hospice house, was also a fully-functioning clinic licensed by the state of Mississippi. Apparently he had spoken with some administrator… and perhaps with his lawyers involved. All she knew was that there was a form waiting to be signed… and a nurse with two needles. With noticeable excitement, this woman immediately began to explain the process.

"It's a requirement in the state of Mississippi that a blood test be performed in order for a marriage certificate to be issued. I need permission from both of you to continue."

Robert right off nodded… and then the nurse looked to her. She reluctantly did likewise, so the nurse immediately went into action.

Outwardly, she stood by calmly as this nurse drew blood first from Robert. Yet inwardly, her heart had been thrown into turmoil... split in three. One part riled against the insult of having been excluded from these plans... and at suddenly finding herself the unexpected object of Pinecrest's attention... whereas a second part desired a postponement of the procedure until a verdict could be reached on her worthiness. But a third part welcomed what was happening. Robert was preparing the way for something wonderful... something that both she and Mama had deemed as unattainable without decades of forgetfulness. So she gave into this third part and extended her arm to the nurse. As the vial filled with her blood, within her also arose a fount of courage from some source wholly different than that of this fluid of life... one that would enable her to tell him what she must.

Both containers were labeled and placed in a small box, which then was stowed in a refrigerator. The wounds to their arms were bandaged and immediately forgotten. They then signed the form. It was all accomplished so smoothly, as if this nurse had handled dozens of prospective newlyweds between her normal responsibilities of death.

Through it all, her eyes did not seek out Robert's, nor could she speak, as that third part of her – the part willing to yield blood – did not control all... especially the overpowering urgency of fear building within.

As they departed Pinecrest and drove to where she did not know, Robert excitedly began to reveal his plans. She, however, was unable to follow him. For once again, she had become nothing more than a quivering leaf riding a torrential current, aware only of the rapids all about... and of a spiraling free-fall ahead.

"I've extended your reservation at the motel, but have checked myself out. By the way, the bill's already taken care of. Here's the phone number of a local taxi service that will provide you with rides between the motel and Pinecrest." He handed over a card. "Just call, give your name, and they'll be there in fifteen minutes to pick you up. I've established a line of credit with them so you don't have to pay or tip."

The roaring of falling water was growing in intensity.

"I'm sorry I was gone for so long. I hope you were OK being alone... I really missed you."

He waited for her to respond... but she just casually turned toward the growing dark out her window, acting very much as if she had not noticed the delay.

"So... I, ahh... drove to Garland and tried to get into your dorm... to get your dorm mother to gather up some things for you. Of course, no one was there... but I did manage to track down Amber's home phone number and called her. Camille – she was fantastic! Wanted me to tell you she was thinking about you and praying for Mama. I think she really loves you. She's going to collect some of your clothes and school things for me to pick up on Sunday. I know you have no intention of returning to Garland this term, but I'd like you to at least distract yourself by looking over your class notes. I'm worried about you sitting in there all alone with just your thoughts."

Again, he noticeably paused for her to speak, yet she still had nothing to say... other than the one terrible thing that would not go away.

"I also drove to Jackson... to deal with some... details. And I need to get back to Garland tonight. There are... other things to be taken care of that can't wait."

A mist had enveloped the river. The brink too soon was upon her.

"I forgot to mention that there're some restrictions in the state of Mississippi for obtaining a marriage license when one or both parties are under the age of twenty one. I've been in contact with lawyers from my parent's old firm... and I think we've..."

The leaf began the plunge, inexorably pulled by the force of gravity and pushed on by the immense inertia of the river... directly over the edge.

"Robert, pull over! PULL OVER RIGHT NOW!"

He swung the car into an empty auto parts lot and slammed the gears into park. She could not consider what he might be thinking... just that the moment of dread was here. She was tumbling into darkness. Only after he shut off the engine did she undo her seat belt. Slouching down as low as possible, she lifted her feet to place the soles of her shoes on the dashboard – rude under normal circumstances, but necessary in this one. The combination of slumping and raised feet situated her knees close to her face. She used this posture to hide herself from him... as well as to limit what could be seen to only that which was straight ahead.

"We need to talk. There's... something you need to know. Something about me you should know... before it's too late."

Her mind was slipping back and forth between Robert and herself, and then Angel and Tess. She was losing herself into Tess, yet maintaining her own scars and shame added on top. She sensed Robert undo his seat belt… and then felt his hand upon her shoulder. Immediately, she recoiled against the passenger door.

"Don't! This is very difficult for me. I can't do this if you're touching me… or even looking at me. Please face forward, and please don't say anything until I'm completely finished. Promise me, Robert!"

"I promise."

She then searched the dashboard before her for a distinctive spot to focus on, hoping to speak toward it rather than Robert. She chose the glove compartment's keyhole, extracting an ounce of symbolism from its function to lock or unlock – to conceal or reveal.

"When I was twelve, something terrible happened to my family… to me. My father had been a good man… a hardworking man… and a decent husband. He never cared much for me… I knew that… but he wasn't overly cruel… more or less up until that point in my life. But it was no secret he would have preferred a son… wanted a son… maybe even needed a son. I don't know. All I do know is that he came to resent how much attention Mama paid me instead of him."

At the thought of what lay ahead in the story, she found herself fighting back a burning sensation rising in her throat… and had to swallow hard in spite of her dry mouth.

"He… umm… had an important job at the town sawmill… but lost it when the mill closed down. Lots of folks blamed him for the closure. It was all nonsense, but Daddy took it hard. He turned to drink. I don't know how or why, but he also turned to… doing illegal things. He'd be gone for weeks on end, showing up drunk and with a big wad of bills. Mama kicked him out of the house. Wouldn't have anything to do with him or his money. So he slept in the shed. I don't know if you noticed the concrete slab out back of the house – that's where the shed used to be. He built it himself. It wasn't part of the house when we moved in. Daddy really loved wood… probably more than he loved Mama. He had such grand plans for making things, but gave it all up when the drinking started. From then on, he basically lived in that shed… but we think he also kept drugs in there because he got himself a dog – a terribly mean and ugly dog. Robert… it was ten times worse than the one you fought off."

The moment was perfect for it… so she closed her eyes in order to build the resolve needed for seeing herself through… then returned to the keyhole and her story.

"Daddy would keep the dog chained up outside the shed. As a child, I used to think it was to keep trespassers away, but later I became convinced it was to keep Mama away. The thing I need to tell you… it happened on Good Friday. I know because of the new Easter dress I was wearing. He came home unexpected and really drunk… which wasn't so unusual. But I can still see it, Robert – he was covered in blood and angrier than the dog. He'd just murdered someone, and the deed somehow snapped something inside. He went pure evil. There would've been two murders if Mama had been home. As it were, I was the only one. I was on the back porch… in my new dress… and… and he… he took me… into there. And he… he…"

She absolutely could go no further. No amount of effort could complete that sentence. She was shaking so severely that surely he could feel it through the car.

"Did he do something to you in that shed?"

She could not understand how there was anything left in her, but once again the tears burst forth so violently that the keyhole could no longer be seen. All was black and wet. She only managed to answer his question with an equally forceful nodding of her head that would not stop.

And then he was on her side of the car in an attempt to hold her bobbing head still. Not to control it, but to care for it and to kiss it. He was kissing her eyes, not trying to block the tears, but instead to take them away as fast as they came. But they kept on coming… and she was not alone because he was crying with her. He then pulled her to his side of the car and cushioned her from her own trembling. There he held her tightly for what seemed like hours. She would sob, gasp for breath, calm herself, and then start crying all over again.

Eventually she relaxed, more from exhaustion than relief. He was then able to speak, clearing her tears with his fingertips.

"Darling… I'm so sorry. So very, very sorry, but… also really angry. Angry that any father would do something like that… to you. But you… you must know that this changes nothing between us? You must know that I still love you… love you more than ever before. You do believe me… don't you?"

She still could not speak owing to all the shaking and the crying that had begun anew. So she nodded her head as before… though it was totally different this time. Relief inexplicable was dawning, for he had not rejected her. And as proof to her heart, he once again began kissing her face… but soon went back to simply holding her and waiting.

"I… I think I tore a hole in your seat cover with my fit."

"Who cares about seat covers."

"Robert… I can't tell you how difficult it's been living with this shame. After he… after… He just beat me… and then left me in that shed. He locked the door on the outside and left the dog chained there. I don't know where he went or how long I was in there. Must have been hours. I just lay in darkness, terrified that the dog would somehow get inside. Mama eventually came home and found me. She shot the dog and rescued me. But the memory of that dog… I'm afraid it'll never go away."

She shifted in his lap in order to better see his face.

"That night in the park… I went back there. Back to that dog and that dreadful time. It was only your voice that brought me back or the second dog would have completed what the first left undone. That's what I really meant when I said you saved my life."

Though she wished very much to stop here, she knew the story was not done.

"There's… one other thing you need to understand. Daddy did one other thing…" The horrible memory of that terrible discovery instantly came back to her, but somehow Robert's acceptance had compacted it… made it infinitely smaller and immeasurably easier to speak about. "His last insult – it was almost as bad as what he'd already done. He cut off all my hair. All of it, Robert! Right down to my scalp! It was a bit blonder than it is now… longer and finer too. Sometimes I think he was… I don't know… removing in his mind the proof of what he had just done to me… and maybe turning me into the boy he never had. I also think he was destroying the daughter who Mama loved more than him. Or maybe he just hated me, I really don't know. It really doesn't matter why – for it marked me, Robert. It marked me so much more than… than that other thing he did to me. It took years to grow back… A scar upon me and Mama. A constant reminder to everyone in town of what had happened. That's how I got started with hoodies… which answers that question you asked me on one of our walks. Mama bought them to cover my head until my hair grew back. But even then, I… still needed them as a different sort of covering. Of my humiliation. That's also why I changed my name from Camellia to Camille… because of what he did to me. Becoming someone else… if just in my imagination… that was the only way I could survive."

Due to a sudden tightness to his body, she lifted her face from off his chest… and flinched at the sight. A significant change had come over him since the last time she made eye contact. His face had gone rigid… and when he spoke, it was with a rock-hard determination.

"Camille, where is he now? What's happened to him? I need to know. You need me to know!"

"I've no idea… and I don't want to know. He's in jail somewhere on a life sentence. I remember Mama saying for me not to worry because they'd locked him up and thrown away the key. But I'll tell you this – if the sheriff hadn't found him first, I'm afraid Mama would have killed him. That's how angry she was."

"But even people like that don't stay locked up forever."

She did not want to delve any further into that part of the story, and was relieved to have him drop the subject… though his jaw remained clinched.

"Thank you for loving me… for not rejecting me. I wouldn't have blamed you, you know, if you were… disappointed to discover what I am."

"What do you mean?"

"That I'm… not the sort of woman a man would be proud of… and that you're stuck with…"

He immediately interrupted by forcefully turning her body in his arms so as to hold her face directly in front of his. He was so close – there was absolutely nowhere else for her to look… even if she had wanted to. The dimness to the lighting in the vacant lot could not conceal the intensity in his eyes.

"Let's get something perfectly clear – right here, right now! You are the most amazing woman I've ever met, and I'm honored to think you'd want me. I mean it when I say 'I love you.' I'm not stuck with you – I want you! I want you more than anything I've ever wanted. Knowing what you've been through… what you've overcome… that makes me want you even more. You're mine! Don't you understand?! I wouldn't trade you for anything!"

Though he had ceased to speak, he continued to hold her face so that their eyes could not possibly avoid each other. At first, she thought he was searching hers… to see if she believed… but then it became abundantly clear that he was offering his eyes to her… imploring her to search them and be fully convinced of how much he desired her.

So she believed.

Then, launching herself at him, she began exchanging his previous kisses of mercy with hers of immense gratitude.

CHAPTER

35

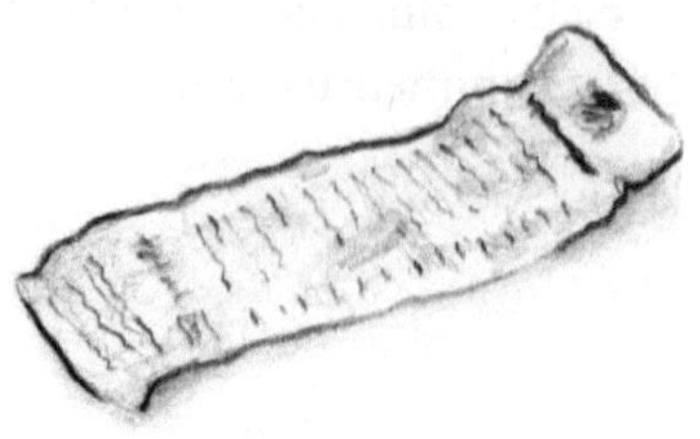

BORN LAST NIGHT

After sitting for hours in Robert's parked car, much of which was spent in crying, she found herself to be both physically and emotionally drained. Cataclysmic events that included discovering her mother dying of cancer, becoming engaged to be married, dwelling in a combined state of dread and sorrow, revealing the darkest secret of her life to her new fiancée, him fully embracing and accepting her, and the growing awareness that she would soon be married, all combined together to completely sap her of strength. As she had hardly eaten since leaving Garland on Wednesday morning… and with an immense burden finally removed… she reverted to base necessities. She was suddenly very hungry.

"Let's go eat somewhere, anywhere! I'm starving! And I just want to be with you as long as possible before you have to leave."

"In case you might have forgotten, it's Thanksgiving night and we're in Wyatt Crossing, Mississippi – not exactly a city that never sleeps. We'll be lucky to find a convenience store that's open."

"Then let's drive to Jackson. There'll be something there."

"Camille… that's two hours away. It's after nine… so there wouldn't even be anything open on a normal night by the time we got there."

He nonetheless started the car and drove out of the auto parts lot in a direction he thought offered the best prospects of finding a store. They were rewarded by a fully lit and open-for-business minimart.

"Sky's the limit, Camille! Let's buy the place out – whatever you want!"

For the next twenty minutes, the two of them moved up and down the store's five small aisles, joking about what they perused as if scrutinizing the menu of a four-star restaurant. All the while, she clung to him as if life itself. The contact was sustenance beyond awareness for her. As they went about the odd task of constructing a Thanksgiving Day meal out of convenience store junk food, a freedom gradually and inexplicably came over her – one that could only come from a cleansed past. The shades of change were subtle though unmistakable, much like night developing into a clear crisp spring morning simply through the steady action of a sunrise. By the time they left the store, all four arms toting bags loaded down from a whimsical shopping spree, she was in love like she never thought possible. It was an overwhelming state of both warmth and confidence, unshakeable by anything. There was absolutely no doubt in either her mind or heart that becoming Mrs. Reynolds in Mama's presence would be the culmination of every wish and every dream she ever had.

They drove back to the motel, and together laid out a twenty four course meal over clean bath towels on the floor of her room. Sitting cross-legged opposite each other, they shared chips, nuts, granola bars, beef jerky, sunflower seeds, and a cornucopia of other highly unconventional Thanksgiving dishes. For dessert, there were pastries, licorice sticks, candy bars and ice cream, with bottled water and chocolate milk to wash it all down. Like two grade school children given free rein to construct their ideal meal without adult supervision, they ate, laughed and played in the purest state of delight.

At one point, Robert made her catch peanuts in her mouth, and she barked like a seal with each success. He then had to match her, catch for catch, complete with the aquatic mammal sounds. This led to an assortment of other catching games that progressively grew more messy. But it was her who first started throwing 'at' rather than 'to.' Within seconds, a full-scale food fight had erupted between them... interspersed as it were with much wrestling and tickling... eventually culminating with her smashing a Twinkie into his face and him pouring a bag of gummi bears down her back.

Then, as if by magic, they came face-to-face in a perfect stillness. The children were adults, and the adults were in love. It did not matter that they, like the motel room, were a mess. She was immediately in his arms in an instant, intertwining herself with him upon the floor… and the pull of passion was so nearly overwhelming.

Without warning, he abruptly rose… reached down a hand… and lifted her into a standing position in his arms. There, he held her in silence… and she wished it never to cease. But after a while, he moved her to arm's length, and with palms remaining on her shoulders, spoke low and sweet.

"I know it's horribly difficult… but I think we can wait. And it'll only be for a short while. Maybe it's good that I won't be staying here… I've got to be in Garland tomorrow anyway… you know, for an early morning phone meeting with the lawyers. They have to sort out which county seat should issue the license. Then I need to pick up the rings at… Oops – that was supposed to be a surprise."

She immediately perked up at that.

Oh my – I'll be wearing a wedding band! I can't believe it!

"I've got other running around to do too… and of course, pick up the license once it's ready. We'll both have to sign it… and then I think we can fax it in. But I've got to work that out also. Unfortunately… the University's closed, so sometime next week I'll be talking with your professors about…"

"Seriously, Robert… don't even bother. Compared to Mama… and you… all that's completely unimportant."

"I'm still going to see what can be done anyway. I know this is going to be a really pathetic honeymoon… what with being stuck in a motel room together while we wait for…"

She could not have heard correctly, so her question just popped out in disbelief.

"Wait – you're going to be here with me?!"

"Ahh… of course. What were you thinking – that I'd marry you, then go back to Garland and leave you here alone?! There's no way I'll be parted from you. I'll be here… maybe making occasional trips to… What?!"

The more he spoke, the more her heart warmed to the realization that he would be here in this motel room with her… as husband and wife… facing together Mama's end. That made all the difference in the world. Relief flowed in, and she could not keep from excitedly bobbing up and down in place… despite still being held at arm's length by him. But as her bouncing continued to intensify, he finally gave up the effort… allowing her to collapse back into his arms.

"I can't believe it – we're going to be married!"

As he kissed her a long slow embrace, she imagined herself being there… but he too soon broke away.

"Call me when you get up, OK?"

"Definitely! And please drive safe!"

Just as he was about to close the door on the way out, he stuck his head back in.

"Oh… and Camille?"

"Yes, Robert?"

"Do something about the mess in this room – it's revolting!"

He was gone out the door before she could retrieve the nearest item and hurl it at him.

It was going to be a wretched thing, being separated from him this night. Sitting down on the edge of the motel bed, she listened to his car start up and leave the lot, its departure slowly muting into silence. In that silence, she was able to think… and in thinking, to prepare herself for being alone. A plan formed, and resolve was called upon to implement it. She stood, walked to the motel door, threw the deadbolt, and slipped the security chain in place, then turned to survey the room. It *was* a wreck, though she did not want to change a thing. Before her was evidence of the happiest moment in her life, and she wanted it preserved – forever – as a memorial to how much they loved each other.

But that was not how the motel maid would see it in the morning. Resigned to have the memory retained only as memory, she set herself to cleaning the room before going to bed. Down on hands and knees, she began picking up the packaging and food fragments from their feast. She had never been the type of girl who hoarded mementos, but wished now that there was something in this mess that she could have as a keepsake of the night Robert heard the worst and loved the most. But all of the packaging was torn and sticky. Nothing was worth saving.

As she moved about picking up, her hands became filled with so much trash – she really needed something to collect it in. The plastic bags that everything came in would do nicely… and she spotted them shoved into a corner.

Then, suddenly dropping everything, she sprang across the motel room on all-fours, hoping it to be so. And there, in the third bag she checked, was the record of their purchases. Every item was listed with its price. There was the store's name and location too, along with the purchase time and date – 9:52 PM on November 28th, 2002.

She held this slip of paper as if it were a sacred text… a written release from bondage… a much anticipated letter of declared love. Cradling the precious document, she rose and moved to her backpack. Retrieving the English journal, she opened it to the 'that is why we learn' page, and carefully laid the paper over those words. The crinkles were smoothed out and the corners were unbent before she lovingly closed the cover. This was the receipt proving to her that the debt of sorrow and shame had been paid in full. Sliding down against the dresser to the floor with the journal clutched to her chest, she welcomed the coming tears. It was an overwhelming release… a sense of being unlike anything she had ever known. She was free at last.

Thank you! Oh, thank you so much! I can never thank you enough!

It was well after midnight when she finished cleaning the room. Her thoughts turned to Robert, who was still likely on the road to Garland. He would be as sticky as she was… and more so tired.

It was only after a brief shower that she was reminded by the empty towel rack that they had used all of the bathroom linen for their feast. There was absolutely nothing with which to dry herself. So… she decided to have the sheets do the job for her. But once in bed, weariness took hold, and she just managed to set an alarm before falling off into the sweetest of sleeps.

At 9 AM, the buzzer pulled her from that dreamless state. Reaching across the side table to silence it, her hand came down on the sticky overturned lid of an ice cream container unnoticed in her cleaning.

Ick!

Rolling out of bed and heading to the bathroom, she stepped on another relic of the feast – a cap from one of the plastic water bottles.

This is no way to be reminded of last night!

Returning to extract clothes from her suitcase, she opened the English journal and scanned the receipt's list of items while dressing… taking time to remember how each was purchased, spread out, opened, consumed and played with. By the time she was fully clothed, the richness of the Thanksgiving meal with Robert had returned, generating a calm to sustain her through another day at Pinecrest.

She called a taxi, and more because she wanted the journal with her than had designs on studying, slung the backpack over her shoulder before leaving the room. Walking to the motel lobby, she admired for the hundredth time since yesterday how beautiful the ring looked on her finger.

The management supplied complimentary donuts and coffee, so she partook in both while waiting for the cab. Having given the driver her destination, she opened her phone and called Robert.

"Good morning, Sweetheart. How'd you sleep?"

"Great. And you?"

"Not bad, especially considering I didn't get to Garland until after two."

They continued to chat in the way normal couples do in normal settings, sharing experiences and discussing plans. Yet the presence of the driver not three feet away kept her from speaking the way she actually felt. They both offered their love to the other before ending the call.

She got dropped off at the visitor entrance, and after a short delay, was ushered to Mama's room by a nurse... who maintained all the way down the hall the oddest expression on her face – a wobbly sort of grin clumsily maintained amidst watery eyes. On entering Mama's room, she instantly understood the nurse's behavior. The place had been transformed from its previous meager state into a floral paradise. Every surface and much of the floor bore vases containing lilies, irises, roses, carnations, tulips and, remarkably, camellias. There were also many bundles of Mylar balloons bearing messages of love.

"Mama! Where in the world did all this come from?!"

"Your charming young man! They showed up first thing this morning...and they're all for me! That boy's such a peach."

She made her way about the room describing each arrangement to Mama, bringing them up close for her mother's enjoyment. In the process, a long ago childhood experience came to her. She was both in the present, and as a small girl, reciting to her mother the names of flowers she had been taught to recognize. It was both spring and winter – a youthful mother and a dying one. The smell, color and texture of each bloom reinforced the association across time. Eventually, the circuit and the memory ended with her standing beside her mother's bed. The smile she beheld was as genuine as any from the past. So she reached out a hand to take her mother's.

"How are you feeling?"

"Finer'n whiskers on a melon and spry as can be… considering the circumstances. So… I heard your young man's been running around with his lawyers. I understand we're going to be having us a wedding."

Mother and daughter, one lying in a bed and one standing beside it, exchanged smiles that neither needed to explain.

"I'm so proud of you. It's beyond my reckoning to explain it. I've packed a lifetime of hoping into the last six years… and to think I'm going to see you married. I don't deserve it. But you, Camellia… you deserve a big church wedding… with a stunning white dress! We could've had so much fun picking that out!"

"Yes, Mama… that would've been special. If only…"

"Don't! There's no sense dwelling on the 'ain't-gonna-be' if you miss out on the 'is-gonna-be'… like I always say. We're all born to die. Still… don't seem right… him an orphan and you on your way to being one. But we do have loads to be grateful for, don't we? I'm thankful… morning, noon and night."

Mama paused here, though not to count blessings. Even for a spry morning, that many words was tiring for her.

"Mama, you need your strength! I'm worried about what all this is taking out of you."

"Nonsense, Child. I'm more ready for this wedding than you are."

She just smiled back, knowing that could not possibly be so. Yesterday had been the fulfillment of hopes not even considered as possible… and Mama deserved to know.

"I want to tell you something before you rest again. Last night… after leaving here… I told Robert about Daddy. I told him everything."

"Everything?!"

"Yes, Mama – everything."

"And?"

Her eyes strayed to the nearest flower – a camellia.

"I can't fully describe how he set me free from that terrible day… and all the terrible ones that followed. In some ways, he actually took my shame upon himself… like it had happened to him too. I know that doesn't make any sense, but that's how it felt. He was beyond understanding – he was pure love!"

She had not noticed the effect her words were having until Mama's emotions could no longer be kept silent, bursting forth in much scratchy-throated crying. She instantly brought a drink and some tissues to her, calming her out of the fit.

"Are you OK now?"

"Yes, Child… more than OK. Sweetie… your young man… he's set us both free. Finally free."

Slowly, her mother lifted one hand, straining the limit of its strength. But she knew to let that hand move unaided. It came to rest against her cheek for just a second before falling back to the bed.

"You're my dream come true, Camellia."

A lone tear then slowly slid down the cheek just touched. In that droplet, she expressed what could not be done with words – all the joy and all the sorrow dissolved together within its singularity, it running a course from eye to jaw… destined to silently evaporate there.

She sat holding Mama's hand, caressing her all the way into sleep.

CHAPTER

36

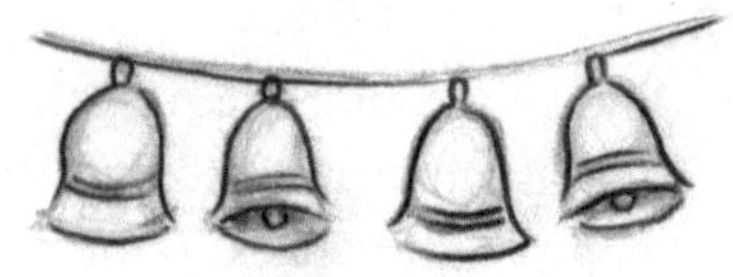

DEATH AND LIFE

Evalyn Mae Larson, formerly Evalyn Mae Campbell, died in the early morning hours of December 7th, 2002, succumbing to a two month battle with pancreatic cancer. Mrs. Larson's remains were cremated in accordance with her will, and then scattered along a portion of the Tombigbee waterway... also in accordance with her will. There was no memorial service and only one newspaper account of her passing, prepared beforehand and delivered through the executor of her will to *The Carlton Courier*. The only surviving family member was a daughter, listed as Camellia Jay Larson, 18, of Carlton, Mississippi. There was no mention of any other detail that comprised a life of forty nine years. The world continued to spin, the sun continued to shine, and all the institutions of human endeavor persisted in their seemingly important tasks. Babies were born, more deaths were recorded, and newly married couples began their lives together.

Camille Jay Larson, formerly Camellia Jay Larson, married Robert Nelson Reynolds on Saturday, November 30th, 2002, in the hospice room of Evalyn Mae Larson... who served as both the bride's maid of honor and the groom's best woman. The wedding ceremony was conducted by the chaplain of Pinecrest Hospice House, and witnessed by a dozen nurses and staff. The groom's lawyers had pushed through the appropriate legal channels all the necessary paperwork required for obtaining a certificate of marriage dated that day. Simple gold bands were received by eager fingers, and 'I dos' gave way to their first kiss as a married couple. The two became one. There was no official announcement and no registry from which to purchase wedding gifts… though Pinecrest nurses did pool together to surprise the couple with a small wedding cake, complete with bride and groom figurine, as well as a signature book to memorialize the occasion. Someone even strung a line of paper wedding bells about the room. But the thing that sent the bride into grateful tears was the laced veil that one nurse placed on her head, it running down about her to the floor. The bridal bouquet, composed from the room's abundant floral supply, was tossed amidst a scramble of nurses, while others flashed cell phone cameras to record the event. The newlyweds spent their wedding night in the honeymoon suite of Jackson's finest hotel, returning on December 1ˢᵗ to their exceedingly modest motel room in Wyatt Crossing. They remained there until December 7ᵗʰ. On the 8ᵗʰ, they took up residence in a small apartment in Garland.

For the next few weeks, she would lead a geminate existence. She was the newly married Mrs. Robert Reynolds and the bereaved daughter of Evalyn Mae Larson. All thought and emotion were in turmoil from the combined highs of getting married and lows of seeing her mother die. Time – that was what she needed most. Time to sit and remember, time to mourn a life lost, and time to rejoice over a new one found. Being alone in their apartment while Robert went about his business at the university was all she cared to do. There were no reserves for anything else. All contemplation was bent toward reconciling these contrary, yet coincident, conditions in her life. She knew that lasting memories were being made, although few could be recognized as such. However, the single most significant sensation she would take into the future was the feeling of utmost security derived from a new harmony between night and day – of being gently held by Robert into sleep each evening, and waking up each morning the same way. That, and making love.

Of course, she was in no state of mind for taking final exams, occurring the week after Mama's death. She had already missed the skills test in Racquetball. At some point, she remembered doing a calculation in her mind based on grades received up to the Thanksgiving break. There might have been enough for a C in English and a C in Racquetball. Chem Lab had finished, so that was a sure A. Still… there was little doubt she had failed all of her other courses, as the finals were weighted too heavily. She would be removed from the Honors program and lose her scholarship with its financial guarantees. Those outcomes were tolerable to her… though not to Robert, who kept reminding her that Mama would not have wanted her daughter to give up. Though her response to his encouragements were mostly the same ("I don't care."), she also had no will to contend against him as he took matters into his own hands.

"I've made an appointment for you with the dean of student affairs… and we're going over there together. Everything's taken care of. He's arranged for your professors to reschedule your exams. He just needs your signature to get things rolling. After that, we're heading over to clear out the remaining things from your dorm room. Amber's promised to hang around and help."

Together, they walked from their apartment to Milton Hall, passing through the arboretum and around to the front of the building. In a brief glance, she caught sight of the swing hanging tranquil on the back porch. It seemed like eons ago that they had sat there discussing the 'concept of marriage.'

That girl had led a completely different life… with both a mother and a boyfriend.

Entering Milton Hall by way of its columned front veranda, they were greeted in the foyer by an admin who led them into an ornately decorated room that likely had once functioned as a parlor.

"Please wait here. The dean will see you soon."

She seated herself on a floral patterned love seat beside Robert, and had just begun to take in the room's wainscoting when an adjoining door opened into the office of Dr. Tucker, the dean of student affairs. He greeted them, expressing condolences and congratulations as only a Southern gentleman could – with sincerity, succinctness, and respect. He then motioned them to high-back leather chairs, picking up a manila folder as he rounded his desk.

"Mr. Reynolds… thank you for sending over a copy of the death certificate."

Her eyes immediately shot to the folder, then to Robert, and then back to the folder, hoping that the dean would not open its contents to her. She sat stiff while he examined what was inside, then relaxed as the folder was closed off on his desktop.

"Miss Larson, we just need your…"

"Mrs. Reynolds."

She surprised herself with the promptness of her correction… though the dean showed no offense.

"My apology – Mrs. Reynolds, of course. We just need your signature granting my office the privilege of advocating on your behalf with regard to the University's student bereavement policy…" She signed the form placed before her as he paused. "…and then we'll have your exams rescheduled for next week. Someone from each department should be in contact with you soon."

They thanked the dean and rose to leave, but were surprised when the man stopped Robert midway out the office.

"Pardon me. You wouldn't happen to be related to Nathan Reynolds, would you?"

"He was my father."

"I thought so. There's such a strong resemblance. He was a good man, and a good friend." Dr. Tucker reached out to shake Robert's hand once more… this time with real feeling… before glancing toward her with a bit of a blush. "His father and I were in school together some forty years ago. We were such hellions back then…" In that brief moment of pause, she felt an unexpected admiration… and loss… for a father-in-law she would never know. "Mr. and Mrs. Reynolds… on behalf of the University… allow me to express my deepest gratitude to you both for the continued support of the Reynolds Foundation. It's making such a huge difference in so many lives."

As they left, she waited only as far as the entry area before asking.

"What was that all about?"

"My father graduated from Garland. I guess that's why I ended up here."

"What did he mean by the Reynolds Foundation?"

"Oh… that's where the majority of their estate went… after they died. I haven't been involved with it much… though I know the people who are."

Under normal circumstances, she would have inquired further, but having her own grief so near gave her some insight into what he might be feeling at that moment. She took his hand as they walked from the park to Switson Hall, just as had been done so many times before, though this time in silence. She did not consider until days later that this particular route across campus would likely never be tread by them again.

As finals ended that day, all but those few unfortunate enough to have an exam scheduled in the last time slot had already departed for Christmas break. As per their plan, Robert would wait in the lobby with the small remnant of parents lingering there to pick up their daughters. After depositing him on a couch, she made her way through 'the door'… it being propped wide open for the convenience of girls hauling things home. The stillness in the dorm was such a relief, as it meant that anyone who might inquire into the rumors of her marriage had already left. She stopped for a moment to listen at Cameron's door. Nothing but silence. Only Amber remained of all those who had endured that semester on the hall. As she entered, there was her former roommate facing the door, waiting for her just as she had done months before. Except this time, they were immediately into each other's arms, crying and consoling. Only after a good long while did Amber ask to see the rings.

"They're so beautiful! What an amazing diamond! I'm so jealous."

As Amber remained staring at the rings, a slight frown came to her face… from which it was evident that she had more to say.

"Umm… Camille… are you… sure about this? If you are, than I am too. It's only… everything seems to have happened so fast! I'm not saying anything bad about him… or you… please know that. It's just… what with your mother… you know… dying and all… Oh, Camille! I just want you to be happy! I can't bear the thought of you being hurt."

"Amber… I've never been more sure of anything in my life." And she meant it.

From there, they hugged and cried some more… then finally set about gathering up her possessions in the seclusion of the empty hall. An occasional echo to their voices mingled with the task, lending an odd sort of emphasis to each person's remembrances of their semester together. At such times, sadness, seasoned as it were by mutual affection, can be a more lasting witness to imprint in memory what once was so tangible. That feeling is not wholly unfamiliar to the camper packing up at vacation's end… or the last fans leaving the arena… or the host facing a remarkable party's inevitable cleanup. So it was for her. In that bittersweet solitude, their shared goodbyes sealed into her heart not only an awareness of her love for Amber – her friend – but also a realization that childhood, with all of its pains and wonders, was truly over. Adulthood was upon her.

As Dean Tucker had promised, she was able to take her final exams in the following week. Though Robert offered to escort her to each, she felt this was something Mama would have her do on her own. In most cases the experience was quick and strangely diverting – not at all the ordeal she had been expecting. All those exam questions yielded in her a surprising release... as if the recording of memorized facts, equations and concepts somehow washed through those parts of her most affected by the past two weeks. The only unpleasant experience was with Prof. Dunsmore, who insisted that she work facing him across his office desk. He provided her only with the exam and a straight-backed chair in which to accomplish the task. She had to use her lap as a desktop.

Remarkably, she performed very well on each exam, receiving A's in all of her courses except Racquetball... which she had not bothered to complete. In her way of thinking, the C she received was more than acceptable if it meant never having to set foot in a locker room again. By far, the best exam was in English. Her task was to share all of her experiences from the semester... leaving nothing out... over coffee at Ms. Kelley's apartment. It was the longest and most delightful exam she would ever take... and the only one in which she would either laugh or cry.

As Mr. and Mrs. Reynolds, they honeymooned in Paris from Christmas to New Year's Day... and beyond.

PART

3

"I am."
Camille

CHAPTER
37

TOWARD A DOOR

Love – what does that mean to me?
I do not know.
Camille, that is why we learn.

My first semester of English is over, but the need to record my thoughts is greater than ever. I start this new journal with the words that brought about so much change in my life.

The idea had come to her while on their honeymoon. Once back, she purchased a new journal – much prettier and far less academic-looking than the Ms. Kelley version. In its pages, she recorded her thoughts on the special moments of life… but also the things she was learning about herself, both as a wife and a person.

After all I've told him about Mama's kitchen table, Robert was taken aback when I decided to give it away. Though it hurts so much – like saying goodbye to her all over again – I know it's the right thing to do. I am not claiming to know who I am yet, as marriage is still so very new, but that table is a part of a painful past. A past that I am determined to leave behind.

277

• • •

Robert surprised me today with a new kitchen table – a wedding present. It's beautiful – oak, lightly stained, just like Mama's. He was worried that it might not measure up, but I told him this new table was more special to me. It would take us into the future.

• • •

The spring semester has finally started, and everyone in the Honors Program was all over me for the story. I simply smiled and showed off my rings. Most were excited, but I could tell that some were shrouding their congratulations in unspoken criticisms of me for having gotten married as a freshman. I know I've married young. I know I've hardly had a chance to experience life on my own. I know these things! But being married to Robert is, in every way, so very wonderful. And honestly, since I never wanted to be here in the first place, I barely got acclimated before meeting him. Now, after only being married for five weeks, this somehow feels like the way college was meant to be.

• • •

Amber became our first dinner guest as a married couple. We had the most delightful time together. Watching her and Robert interact was such a treat… that is, until they started comparing notes on the sounds I make in the middle of the night. They soon had each other howling in laughter. (For the record – I <u>do not</u> purr in my sleep!)

• • •

This past week was our two month anniversary. We didn't have much time to celebrate, what with the first wave of exams coming up, but Robert took me kite flying on Saturday. Of all the things to do! We had a splendid picnic, then put the kites together. After much running about like idiots, we finally got the things to stay up, and then settled down on a blanket together, allowing the wind to do all the work while we relaxed.

I think the biggest surprise since getting married is that Robert's become much more than a husband to me – he's the playmate I never had. I very much loved being with Mama, but she was never any good at 'fun.'

I've been pondering on perspective all week. In childhood, I remember imagining what the place where I happened to be standing might looked like from a distance. Then as a teenager, I started seeing myself as others might. But now, I'm wrestling with seeing things from being inside another's perspective. This is such difficult work. There are so many times when my emotions get all tangled up inside in imagining that Robert's thinking things he really isn't.

I was so conflicted in making him my first 'specimen' in the study of friendship, though now I tease him about it. ('I'm watching you – always watching you.') In truth, he's still my foremost study in life. For our marriage to be successful, I need to put myself into his heart and mind, not just his footwear. I know he feels the same way. Maybe that's what's meant by 'the two shall become one.'

I take up this new charge – to understand his perspective – because I love him. It will be my lifelong wedding present to him.

• • •

Got my driver's license today. I was so scared of failing, but Robert was there to encourage me… and then lavish praise afterward. I'm so excited to be out on my own.
Terrible picture!

• • •

I can't believe it! Not a week with a license and I've already been pulled over for speeding. Enough said.

• • •

Today's my birthday. I'm nineteen, a freshman majoring in history, and married to the most wonderful man in the world! Mama's note in the calendar is even more special than ever. I miss her so.

• • •

I seduced my husband last night. Actually, it was more trickery, but I'm in love, so I'll call it what I like.
He had a huge stack of exams to grade before morning, but I was in a bad way and needed him so. After giving him the impression that I had gone to bed, I quickly changed out of pajamas, and into lace boyshorts and a silk blouse that I

know drives him crazy. Then I lit scads of candles all about the bedroom. I was so jumpy – surprised I didn't burn the place down.

He was still working at the kitchen table with his back to me. I quietly sprayed several mists of perfume into the air outside our bedroom and waited for the fragrance to waft his way. Through a crack in the door, I saw his head jerk up to sniff the air, and then I dashed to the bed, sprawling there in my most seductive pose. As he pushed open the door, I just said 'April fool's day, Robert.'

So sweet was our time together that we lingered for what seemed like hours, yet in a magical rush, all of that tension just dissolved away from my body. He then tried to put on an act of being inconvenienced by my 'trick,' though the smile on his face betrayed his share of the pleasure. Called me his 'little warrior,' and then kissed my eyes into sleep.

Marriage is so much fun!

• • •

We started a Mother's Day tradition today – skipped church and slept in. We then lounged around all day in our pajamas playing board games and swapping stories about our mothers. Sometime after lunch, I just fell apart crying right in the middle of Parcheesi. I miss Mama so much. I know Robert misses his mother too. So thankful for him. His arms have comforted away my worst tears.

• • •

Yesterday was doubly difficult. The History department had a Fourth-of-July picnic for faculty and staff. Aside from the angst of providing a covered dish (Mama's recipe for shoepeg corn salad turned out perfect), it was our first social appearance as a couple. I was so wound up beforehand that we both arrived at the park in a huff, then I pathetically clung at Robert's elbow throughout the whole thing. Everyone there was so much older than me, and smarter than me... and more mature. I felt like such a child, especially compared to Robert, who is so at ease in the adult world.

I was terribly sullen as we left, anticipating the criticism that I believed was coming my way. But Robert couldn't stop thanking me and saying how proud he was of me, especially when I was discussing the French revolution with Prof. O'Brien. I just sat dumbfounded in the passenger seat. Then, with a big smile, he added: 'Besides, I have the best-looking woman in the department. In fact, in the entire university. No, wait – in the whole...' He was so sweet, expanding the geography of his admiration for me.

I am constantly fighting against the feeling that I bring so little to this marriage. I get moody and withdrawn, and then just as bossy when something needs being done. Somehow, he still loves me. When I made it my wedding gift to see from his perspective, I had no idea it would mean trying to see his bride just the way he does.

• • •

What do you get for the man who says he has everything? Robert turned 26 today, so I surprised him with an orange birthday: butternut squash soup, grilled pacific salmon, sweet potato soufflé, and a carrot cake with candles. Then we carved pumpkins. How can a guy be so pathetic with a knife?! His jack-o-lantern came out somewhere between existentialism and cubistic art. ('Camille, stop laughing! I've never done this before!')

• • •

I had a horrible flashback this morning while waiting in the hall for Sociology to begin. Charity and Tara started offering me congratulations on my upcoming anniversary, except doing it cruelly. Those two really enjoy making people feel bad about themselves. They were saying how thankful I must be that my marriage had survived its first year, what with all the temptations male TAs face from their female students. Standing there taking their abuse, it all suddenly came back to me – the teasing and the taunts I had experienced between classes in high school. I could feel myself shrinking back into the woodwork... when here comes Robert down the hall. Without a word, he takes me in his arms and plants a most passionate kiss on me. I was so startled that I didn't even close my eyes to enjoy it. Over his shoulder, I saw them – they were so disgusted by the display that they moved on down

281

the hall. When he broke away, it was to ask if they were gone. I nodded, and he just said, 'Good. See you at lunch.' Then he swatted me on the rear and continued on his way.

Thank you, Robert, for showing me that we're more together than just you plus me. You are my knight in shining armor.

. . .

I don't know what to write. I know I should write something. We just had our first Thanksgiving as a married couple and then our first anniversary. I should be able to generate volumes on the celebration we planned together, but I can't. There's no Mama to share it with. I just want to cry.

. . .

December 7th, Pearl Harbor Day. A date that will live in infamy. The day Mama died.

. . .

Robert's been acting somber all week, in spite of having successfully defended his thesis. I'm sure he's remembering his last graduation and the death of his parents. When I asked him about it, he said it was no big deal since he would still be in school getting his master's in education. But he said it in just the way a man does when he actually means it's a big deal. I can tell what he wants for a celebration – a quiet dinner at home.

. . .

I've given plenty of thought to what I want to do after graduation, though nothing's come of the effort. Robert says he's known what he wanted to do with himself since middle school. I spent middle school trying to survive.

I wish that becoming something special was as simple as a seed falling into the soil. Everything's already inside for it to become the thing it was meant to be – it just has to grow. It doesn't even have to know itself.

I don't know what's hidden in me, but I don't feel much like a seed. More like an ordinary pebble off the street. I so want to be the kind with hidden colors and intricate grains, though I know revealing those requires going through a tumbler first. It takes so much out of me being ground up by my thoughts and feelings – all just to reveal a tiny facet of something new.

• • •

I had a scare this week. My period was super late, and I became convinced that I was pregnant. Fortunately, I'm not. So... if I'm relieved, then why am I also disappointed? I know we're not ready yet – I'm not ready yet – I still have a year of school left. I shouldn't be thinking about babies, but now I can't seem to get the thought out of my mind.

• • •

Robert left day-before-yesterday for a job interview in Nashville. It's the first time we've been apart in three years of marriage. I'm pathetic, I know, but I swear – this apartment has never seemed more spooky. Everything's creaking, windows are rattling, water's trickling in every pipe, and even the refrigerator moans!
He gets back this evening – I'm so relieved.

• • •

Well... I've graduated. And I had it all wrong in my head. I went into the day with a 'whoop-de-doo' attitude, but wearing a cap and gown, walking with the other graduates, and being introduced on stage as 'egregia cum laude' – the highest level attainable for an undergraduate – it all sent chills up and down my spine.
I admit it. And I don't just admit it – I'm excited to write it. I'm proud of myself for having graduated from college, and thankful that Mama made me go.

• • •

I'm writing this in the car – I couldn't wait another minute to get this down on paper. Though we were packed up and ready to head out of Garland, Robert suggested one last visit to the magnolia. As we drew near, I recognized the change at once and dashed to the tree. Beneath was a new bench with a plaque: 'In memory of Evalyn Mae Larson. From Robert and Camille Reynolds.' After making several revolutions about it, I just collapsed there in tears. Robert then told me that the Reynolds Foundation had established a scholarship in her name.
I kept thanking him over and over... then just blurted out that one day I wanted to work for the Foundation and help

girls like me. His response blew me away. 'Someday, when you feel ready, you won't just be working for it – you'll be leading it.'

How is such a thing possible? I didn't argue with him, but I just can't see myself as being useful for much, outside of ordinary work – degree or not.

• • •

I have finally decided – the thing in life I want more than anything else is to become a mother – just like Mama. I want children, and loads of them. We are in agreement – we'll get settled in first and then start a family.

• • •

It's early evening, and I'm sitting on the back porch of our new home in Tupelo. The sun is minutes from setting, and then the day sounds must surrender to the night. Soon, mosquitoes emerge to wield their hunter's rights over us warm bloods, and I will retreat indoors. But for now, I claim sight, sound, and smell over the pines, oaks, and poplars bordering this beautiful yard. The lawn needs a bit of work, but I love how it ambles down to the fringe of the forest. Robert says there's houses some hundred yards off, though I can't see them. There's much out there to explore.

One day soon, I hope a child will be playing here. Until then, there are squirrels chasing each other about, wisps of tree fuzz floating by, woodpeckers heard but not seen, and the occasional curious dragonfly. Though the warmth of this summer day will slowly trickle away, I remain taken in by the beauty of all that God has made dear to me.

I am at peace.

• • •

Today's Robert's first day as a high school history teacher, and I just know he'll do well. He's so patient and kind.

• • •

I'm pregnant! I'm so excited and scared, all at the same time. When the test came back positive, Robert hugged me and said I'll be the best mother ever. I didn't tell him that I ran it two more times just to be sure.

I still can't get over it – I'm not even 24 and I'm going to be a mother! It's beyond my thoughts to put in writing what that means. I'll never be as good as Mama, but I know that having a child will make me appreciate her more. And miss her even more.

I still can't get over it – I'm not even 24 and I'm going to be a mother! It's beyond my thoughts to put in writing what that means. I'll never be as good as Mama, but I know that having a child will make me appreciate her more. And miss her even more.

CHAPTER

38

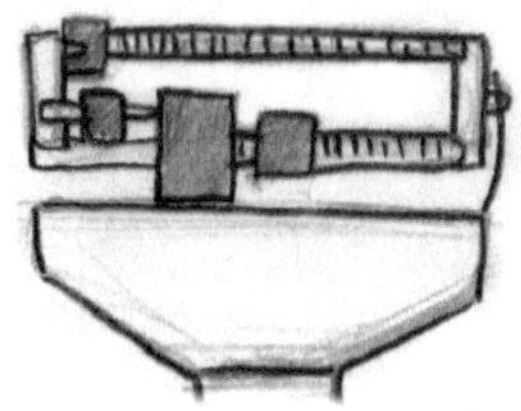

WARMTH IN THE COLD

She twisted the knob especially hard, wishing to break its mechanical workings so as to deny her access. But on recognizing the absurdity, she relaxed her grip and pushed through into the waiting room. Furtively scanning the current occupants, she took note of the young couple leaning together in one corner and two women sitting apart. All four briefly raised their eyes at her entry. Feigning indifference, she moved casually to the check-in window. There, she gave her name... though not without some apprehension... feeling certain that it would be registered as noteworthy. She had, after all, chatted there freely about so many different things on previous appointments. To her considerable relief, the receptionist made only a cursory reference to her arrival.

Turning about briskly, she headed directly for the seat she had already selected on entering – one near to the couple and away from the two women. She was counting on the husband and wife being too busy with themselves to engage a new arrival, something she suspected that either of the solitary women might attempt to do. Her assumption proved true, as the couple continued their back-and-forth whispering irrespective of her proximity.

This waiting room, she knew, was a place where patients frequently sought connection through the sharing of mutual experiences. Those

286

were often mingled in tones of both apprehension and excitement. She felt one keenly, but not the other.

Having anticipated an awkwardness to this part of the doctor visit, she brought along a distraction. In the weeks prior, she had been engrossed in the life story of Eleanor Roosevelt... though the account no longer captivated her imagination. She had no real interest in picking up where she had left off. The book was for show – a superficial deception that nonetheless inwardly embarrassed her. Reaching into her handbag without looking, she pulled out her journal by mistake... thrust it back in... and then retrieved the biography. Drawing in a slow, silent breath, she opened to the bookmark and adopted the appearance of someone deeply engaged. Though her eyes were fixed upon a page, her concentration was fully dedicated toward holding all thought and feeling in a combined state of emptiness.

The couple was making that difficult. By necessity, she ignored the wife as best as she could, allowing the husband to be the distraction. Though he repeatedly affirmed his eagerness to be there for his wife, all of his wiggling and hand wringing suggested otherwise. That kind of behavior was precisely the reason why she had forbidden Robert from accompanying her. Though he had repeatedly offered, she remained firm in wanting to be alone.

She reminded herself not to dwell on him... or anything else, for that matter. Still, her thoughts uncomfortably went back to how she had yelled at him last night. Sure... she eventually calmed down enough to make up before bed... and though she was still ashamed with herself for having lost control... her opinion was unchanged.

He can't possibly understand what I'm going through.

She was suddenly interrupted by a faint vibration coming from within her purse. Drawing the handbag up against her waistline, she attempted to muffle the sound... while at the same time maintaining her portrayal of a person immersed in a book. It was likely just Robert... or a friend... calling to offer a word of encouragement. A time might come when such support would be welcomed, but it was not now.

Only after the phone had ceased vibrating did she realize how tightly she had been clutching the purse against her stomach. Quickly checking that each person in the room was unaware, she gradually relaxed her hold. Coughing back the emotions threatening to bubble up from within, she made an elaborate show out of rummaging about in the handbag for a breath mint… sticking her face in close until the feeling could be contained. She had already cried… in fact, cried like never before… but was now determined to cry no more. She returned to the book, rereading the same sentence over and over until its familiarity was reduced to nothingness… and then mercifully, the English language finally got rendered into an endless propagation of irrationally sorted syllables.

"Mrs. Reynolds?"

She looked up to discover an unfamiliar scene in the waiting room. The young couple was gone, as were the two women, with different seats now taken up by new arrivals. She put the book away, and made for the inner door from which she had been summoned… being greeted there by a nurse she had not seen before in all her time of coming to Dr. Tixlier's office.

"So, how're we feeling?"

She offered only a shrug of the shoulders.

"Let's first get your weight and height."

She robotically dropped the purse to the floor and kicked off her sandals. Stepping up, she felt the scale wobble beneath her feet… gently oscillate for a few seconds… and then settle into equilibrium. She had not expected to be weighed… even though it was common practice at appointments with Dr. Tixlier. So she closed her eyes and hoped that the nurse would have the decency not to comment on the measurement. A metal bar was then lowered lightly upon her head… and its feel was crushing.

She was led to an examination room… one she had been in several times before. The nurse busied herself with temperature, blood pressure and heart rate readings, all the while chattering on about nonsensical stuff like the weather. It seemed forever before the woman ceased from touching her and moved off to a computer workstation. Now she waited in dread for that awkward moment in which routine gave way to the real reason for her visit.

"Do you still reside at Hamilton Court?"

Before she could respond, the nurse excitedly jabbed a finger at the screen and turned her way.

"Hey… isn't today your birthday?! Happy…" She waited as the woman took a moment to do the math. "…28th. Congratulations."

She smiled weakly before replying with thanks. There followed

some trivial talk about what normal people did on normal birthdays…
and then, without prelude, the nurse took on a somber tone.

"I'm terribly sorry for your loss. When did it occur?"

She looked away first, allowing the answer to come out stale.

"Saturday… a week ago."

"Can you describe…"

"I woke up to blood."

Out of the corner of her eye, she sensed that the woman's fingers were hovering over the keyboard, expecting more details. Even in providing the minimum, she still had difficulty suppressing the associated feelings – the panic, the screams, and that dreadfully long wait in fear, hoping not to be told what she already knew to be true.

"My husband… he drove me to the ER. They told me there… what had happened."

"How far along were you?"

"Thirteen weeks." She swallowed hard and repeated the answer just to break up the nauseous sensation building within. "Dr. Tixlier said it was nearly thirteen weeks."

"This the second?"

Again, she could sense the nurse running a finger down the screen. With all her will, she argued against the need for answering such a question… for it compelled her to relive that first ordeal, barely four years ago. Countless reassurances had been offered back then… by friends, medical professionals, and everything she had read… that a significant percentage of first-time pregnancies ended in miscarriage. So much hope had been wasted. There would be no reassuring statistics this time. But above all, she must fight to maintain control, for this nurse was surely glancing over by now.

"No… my third."

"I'm terribly sorry. I see that in your file now."

It was not her imagination – for just a second, the nurse had grimaced before adopting a more clinical air.

"Any appreciable bleeding since leaving the hospital?"

"A little. None since that Monday."

"Are you currently experiencing any pain or discomfort?"

Still facing away, she purposefully lifted her head toward the ceiling in a false portrayal of someone casually coming into tune with their nervous system.

"No. I'm fine." The words felt ridiculously unnatural flowing through her lips.

"We're a bit backed up today, but Dr. Tixlier will be in as soon as possible. Take your time changing."

The nurse handed her the standard gown – thin, light blue, and completely disposable. Instructions were politely provided, though unnecessarily. She knew to strip down to nothing and leave the back straps untied. She still waited for the woman to leave before sliding off the examination table. A suspended curtain hung on runners in a corner offered patients an arc of additional privacy. On previous visits, she had always pulled this curtain closed about her before undressing, but not this time. Slowly, she removed each item of clothing, leaving them draped across a chair rather than hung up on a wall hook. She slipped her arms into the gown and pulled it up over each shoulder, then climbed back onto the examination table. The paper covering, now in disarray from where her jeans had crumpled it, cut sharply into her exposed rear and thighs. She halfheartedly tucked the edges of the gown under, but the crinkles could still be felt. She might have, in the past, toughened out the mild discomfort… or at least asked the cosmos why nothing softer could be designed for the bottom of a pregnant woman. Now, all such effort had no real purpose. She pivoted to the right and to the left, pulling the worst of the creases out from underneath… then settled in to wait.

The room was cold. A vent somewhere in the ceiling behind was gently blowing air across her shoulders. Though it might have been slightly better had she leaned back on her elbows, she instead slumped forward, hunching over the edge of the examination table in order to stare down past her dangling feet. In short time, those bare feet began to feel as if suspended over ice. Goose bumps formed along both arms and legs. At first, she attempted to rub away the waves of shivers, but gave up the effort as cold air crept under her gown with each movement. Her clothing lay only feet away, yet she had no will for retrieving any of it. Of course, in happier times, she would have mitigated the cold's effect by creating some wild reverie… then later playfully describe the whole experience to Robert with a 'I-nearly-froze-to-death' hyperbole. Not this time.

She sat in stillness, having no desire to search about for a distraction. The room's medical equipment and cabinetry had been well-scrutinized on previous visits. Nothing there was of interest now. She also ignored the posters of happy women with hands caressing their progressing pregnancies… and she definitely did not turn about to study the chart she knew to be behind her – the one depicting the various stages of fetal growth. Her eyes saw only the floor.

She sat in silence, not tearing up or raging. She had already done so much of those things… to no avail. She had been angry with a mother who had left her, and cursed a father whose cruelty had destroyed her childhood. In her heart, she blamed him most of all for the previous two miscarriages, but now faced this failing as her own. She knew it to be true, even as the chill of this room slowly crystallized the verdict within her.

In desperation, she turned her thoughts to Robert. Since Saturday, she had insisted that he sleep on the couch, feeling… without blatantly expressing it… that his presence did nothing more than confirm the defect within her. Now… she begrudgingly accepted the fact that she had been selfish… completely consumed with her own grief. He also had lost a child… but held that burden in silence while tending to a brokenhearted wife.

Would it not have been better for us both had we never met?

No. That was foolishness. She had too many wonderful memories of life with a loving husband. The warrior, after all, had prevailed, and the storm had been stilled… at least for a time.

She was brought back by voices just outside her examination room. It was several seconds before she was able to make out the sweet Southern sound of Dr. Tixlier speaking with one of her nurses. The handle on the door rattled… then rotated downward… so she quickly ran through her rehearsed questions. In truth, she had already been through these following the second miscarriage. The possible causes, risks and preventative measures had all been explored. For that reason, she knew that her doctor would have reached a medical recommendation well before coming through that door as to whether it would be safe to try again. So her readying of the questions was really to dull the anticipated blow.

The door, however, did not open. Instead, the handle sprang up… and the voices faded to silence. She slumped back down to her previous posture, accepting that it was not yet her turn.

She nonetheless remained facing the door, allowing her eyes to fix on a placard mounted there. She had read this posting several times before, as it warned of the dangers of alcohol and tobacco. Picking out one of the sentences in bolder print, she began repeating it to herself, trying to achieve the same nothingness of her waiting room trick. Instead, a bizarre memory came to mind of Old Joe sweating over a cook top chanting out in a sing-song manner 'I don't smoke and I don't chew, and I don't go with women who do.' The humor was weak and fleeting.

She turned back to the floor, trying to recall a time in childhood when she had been this cold. There was that January in 9th grade when an artic front pushed its way through to touch the heart of the South. Their small house had never been equipped with heating.

Every faucet was set to drip so the pipes wouldn't burst… and Mama had to keep the oven running all day.

The reminiscence was real, yet hollow. Mama was gone, as were the plans to grow up just like her. The thought could no longer be warded off… so she gave into it, allowing the memories of her father's abuse to come wash over her. A despair so harsh as to lack even cold's false warmth.

"I can't do this anymore. I can't keep trying. I don't know why… but I'm broken."

The words went out to no one, as the declaration needed not to be heard – just spoken. Once more, her tears began to flow… this time accompanied by cruel shivers returning to provide proof and demand acceptance. Both told her so very plainly that she sat naked in the cold.

Always, she had been both the beloved and abused child. The outcast hiding beneath her wild imagination. Discovered, married, orphaned, and transformed into every character she had ever fantasized about from literature. Yet Mama and Robert… and the identities she derived from them… they were the only things she had ever believed to be real. And now… to never become mother would be an existence too horrible to bear. Yet all those things were not really her. In this terrible moment, something different inside her was vying for a voice.

Then who am I?

Her eyes darted up to the door, knowing that an answer to the question would not come through there. Without another thought, she sprang from the examination table, not feeling the floor beneath her or the cool air flowing about her gown. She seized the journal from her purse and hurried back to the previous spot, having already opened it before climbing up. There was a wild moment of frantic struggle with the pen cap before she breathed out to calm herself.

March 20, 2012: The 'whys' matter… they'll always matter… but maybe they're not as important as something else. Things in life happen, for good or for ill, but those things aren't me. They bring about pain or joy…, but that's not me either. Even my crazy heart and mind – my horses – they're not really me. There is a true 'me' on the inside… and only that 'me' can get them to work together just right. I really, really want to know that 'me'. So… I am

The examination room door suddenly swung open before she could finish writing the last sentence.

CHAPTER

39

WHEN HE RETURNS

There is no stage in life in which the soul is made more or less complete – it is a whole that can not be added to or subtracted from. Souls, some say, can be won or lost... saved or damned... but not increased or diminished... not bolstered through self-improvement or lessened by indulgence. A soul's worth is wholly unrelated to the container in which it dwells.

The value of the container of a soul can be gauged by a myriad of metrics that include size, shape, color, gender, age, lineage and condition. A container can even be assessed down to the base cost of its atomic construction materials – a few dollars... no more than an hour of labor at minimum wage. Yet certain containers are insured for tens of millions of those same dollars. But it is the soul that generates outcomes of great significance – art, music, prose, poetry, eloquence, humor, creativity, cleverness, ingenuity, industry, feats of athleticism and acts of valor. At the same time, other souls simply take and take... and are never satisfied.

Containers may be bought and sold on the open market, created almost at will and destroyed as easily. Some get damaged and are repaired, built back up when torn apart. Though in the end, Nature and entropy always win out – no container lasts. For a time, at their prime, some get displayed prominently for admiration and inspiration...

examples to other containers of beauty, wit, strength, intelligence, endurance and capacity. Or... when their usefulness has been exceeded and their risk to others has been established... containers can be locked away and forgotten... to be managed with the lowest esteem possible – nothing.

But all souls are the same. They have beginnings with no endings. They are eternal.

To her, the soul is a quantum of God's image, the smallest recognizable representation of himself. And each is of infinite worth to him.

Leigh Evalyn Reynolds was born to her in the predawn moments of December 28ᵗʰ, 2013. Named after their mothers, Leigh was all things beautiful to her. *Little fingers and toes*, she would write in her journal later that day. *They're just like peas – I want to nibble them up!*

Leigh's so serene in the way she looks at me with such trust.
Each time she gurgles a smile, I'd do anything to have the
moment back again. When she grips my pinky, I feel strong,
as if I could lift the entire world with it. I love this child.
Robert makes me laugh though – such a butterfly flittering
about the flower that's Leigh and me.

The struggles of being a mother were not insignificant to her. Through sleepless nights, ear infections, endless piles of laundry, and a constant battle to keep her house clean, she came to find that the ups and downs of growing together as a family were not actually the outcomes by which she appraised herself. Her existence was the value, and there was enjoyment in simply being. They were happy.

She, herself, had attained recognized status in the roles of 'wife' and 'mother', but also 'graduate', 'friend', 'neighbor' and 'engaged citizen'... all of which were valid outward descriptions of herself. She had been 'employee' off and on throughout much of her life, but now was 'teacher'... be it only in a one-child schoolhouse. And the label of 'student' would never be dropped, even though no institution currently listed her on its enrollment. Other titles might yet find their way onto her life's resumé: 'employer', 'mentor', 'leader', 'mother-in-law' and 'grandmother'. Yet she did not consider herself to be defined by or found lacking with regard to any of those things. She thought and felt... planned and imagined...

labored and loved. In all her ways, she endeavored to be thankful, being free of the past despite a lingered longing for a part of herself that had been dropped from thinking... never to be picked up again except in distant memory or human record – that of being 'daughter.'

But she was mistaken... having completely forgotten about Vernon J. Larson... aka Buck Larson.

———

Thinking back over the years, he now considered the highlight of his time in jail to be those occasions when he got shuttled about between a half dozen institutions at the state's convenience. That allowed him to meet more men like himself... some worse, most better... at least based on the punishment scale decreed by the state. But finally, he had beaten the system. There had been other unanswered charges levied against him in the distant past... though Mississippi, in its wisdom or laziness, had settled on a single count of murder. He knew that the parole board had no doubts that other laws had been broken for which he would never be held accountable... in this life, at least. But in the state's opinion, the time for judgment was over. Leniency had been earned by him through a suitable display of reform. And with the added motivations of a name removed from the records of the Mississippi State penal system and an empty cell for the next miscreant, he got his release with a promise of an outwardly clean slate and a small chance to regain some status in society. Mississippi had no further plans for him outside of weekly phone conversations and monthly visits with his new 'friend' on the outside – a parole officer by the name of Wilkes.

Of course, there would be other restrictions placed upon him: no association with felons, no possession of firearms, no further run-ins with the law, and a loss of voting rights. All that was OK with him – he did not need any of that stuff to get want he wanted most. So... the State, believing it had covered all the bases, processed the paperwork that gave him a new set of civilian clothes, lists of current work opportunities and halfway houses in the area, and a crisp $100 bill. He also received words of wisdom spanning a range from 'Give 'em hell, Buck!' (from other inmates) to 'If you end up back in, it better not be here.' (from the guards).

He stepped from the Mercer County Correctional Facility on January 19th, 2016 as a free man, having only served twenty years of his life sentence for committing first degree murder. From that moment on, there would only be one thing on his mind. Sure… he would pass the days doing odd jobs, connecting up with old acquaintances, visiting familiar spots, and learning how times had changed… all in being extra careful not to break parole. But he would not lose focus of his one objective – finding his daughter… for he had unfinished business with her.

Using a Mercer City library computer, he began his search not one day after obtaining his freedom. While jailhouses had computers too, available to inmates on a limited basis, he knew that using one of those always left a record for others to see. So starting with the state's largest newspapers, he combed through the on-line archives for certain names: his own, his daughter's, and his ex-wife's, who he learned via the prison grapevine had passed away from cancer. He found articles pertaining to his arrest, detention, trial and conviction, but his existence dropped from public record in 1996. He also uncovered a list of Carlton High School's 2002 graduates in *The Carlton Courier*. Camellia had finished second in her class, though there were no other references to her. He only found a single listing on Mae's death, that being in *The Courier*, but it just gave a small paragraph describing her passing at Pinecrest Hospice House. He made note of this on a pad of paper used to summarize his research. The blurb also made mention of Camellia, but there was nothing on the deceased having ever had an ex-husband. He was not surprised. She had divorced him faster than it took his jury to reach a verdict.

Later that day, he called the hospice house, asking for details on the deceased's family. The receptionist was hesitant at first to provide information, but gave in when he put on an impassioned front, saying how broken-up he was to have just learned of Mae's passing. Unfortunately, the form providing his daughter's contact information at that time was incomplete.

Now he had hit a road block. Random web searches on her name were useless. If she was still alive, Camellia might be married with a new last name. Then there would be a husband to deal with. This did not bother him. He had encountered many a murderer and thief. He could handle a son-in-law. He reminded himself then not to get caught up in imagination. First things first. Find her and learn as much as possible about her, then decide how best to carry out his plan… nearly twenty years in the crafting.

He left Mercer City after six weeks with no luck. He roamed about a bit making inquiries, while at the same time doing work as a laborer at any place that would accept his kind. No one knew anything about his daughter, though he was careful of whom he asked. He would only revisit his old hometown as a last resort out of fear that some busybody with a long memory might alert Camellia. He wanted her ignorant of him until he found her first.

At some point in his travels, he remembered a librarian saying that everyone left a 'digital fingerprint' on the web. He had left fingerprints too… on that knife he had used to kill that asshole… as well as the one he had used on his daughter. Well… now he would be the one doing the detective work. So the next step, he was sure, involved a search through the archives of higher education. He had discarded his daughter when she was only twelve, but clearly remembered her as having an inquisitive nature. The fact she had graduated at the top of her class meant that the intelligence needed for college was there. And because Mae had died of cancer, he was sure she would have had time to plan out Camellia's future. People died of cancer in prison too. He had seen the worst sort turn soft overnight, them getting serious all of a sudden about making plans for their families on the outside. So when it came time, he was sure that Mae would have wanted her daughter to be in college.

As for him, he had not graduated from high school. Actually… never attended. His education came in the context of the Mississippi State penal system, from which he learned to type, improved his reading and writing skills, and somewhat rid himself of the edgier side of his mountain accent. He also picked up on other things – connections. The fate of a hard time convict depended on those… as well as the crime committed, the cleverness of the inmate, and a whole lot of luck. He had been in a few prison fights. Even got stabbed once… though not too badly. Got stolen from, but also did his share of the stealing. That was the way of prison. Like any long-termer, he went through the stages: survive like an animal, consider committing suicide, rebel, reform, and profit. Those were not in any particular order, jumping from one to another at random. One thing he was real glad about – there had never been a record… public or by word-of-mouth… regarding what he had done to his daughter. Inmates with that kind of reputation never survived long in prison. So… he had been lucky.

In starting this new approach, he was sure of two things. One –

money would have been real tight… and two – Camellia would not have wanted to stray far from her mother. But after Mae's death, she might have gone anywhere and done anything. Sure… but he should not allow himself to get distracted by such 'might haves'. There was one thing that biding his time in prison had taught him well – stick to the plan and only re-evaluate later.

After but a few days on university web pages, he figured out that their alumni associations were mostly a scam thought up to keep the sappy tied to their past so they would cough-up more money for their school. Searching those websites turned out to be useless. In some cases, there was little information, but in others… the labyrinth of links was far too confusing. It reminded him of when he was a boy growing up in the mountains and how he had foolishly tried to explore a cave on his own. Nearly never found his way out.

Despite the plan, he soon grew irritated with this computer approach. Though the internet was supposed to be some great achievement of mankind, he was coming to see it as a rat's nest. So much trash out there… he was shocked to discover that anyone could post on the web. People should at least be licensed. The swarms of scammers were thicker than summer flies.

Then it hit him – he had been going about it all wrong. Why not get others to do the searching for him?! There were plenty of gullible people out there willing to do his dirty work. On this web thing, he could take on an identity, make inquiries, and then wait to see what came back. But he needed to be systematic. He had known plenty of con artists in prison… learned from them on both sides of the con. One thing they all said – inconsistency led to failure. So on a new notepad, he got started perfecting a secret identity for himself before reentering the labyrinth.

The time was good. He was staying in a Jackson men's shelter not too far from a public library. That gave him easy access to a computer. So he signed up for one of those free email services, then joined the alumni associations of as many institutions as he could, all under a single name. He chose this alias to be female with a common nickname. Settling on 'Bel,' for he had known many before his time in prison, he began building her background. He would make her married so his targets would not think much of an unfamiliar last name… and with kids too. Lots of crap to write about when it came to kids. He would have her graduated from college in 2006… about the same year that Camellia might have. Now… where she came from was not so important. He would pick some populated place if needed… but posters on the web could keep that detail to themselves without anyone thinking it odd.

With a new persona in place, he ventured onto the chat boards of various alumni associations to lay a foundation. Most of his initial postings were simple. He just had to condition his readers before getting to the con. Ultimately, it was important to establish a connection with someone who knew his daughter, so the tricky part would be how to bring up Camellia.

After three weeks of daily chatting about all sorts of nonsense, he was finally ready to set the hook – to con a college friend of Camellia's into providing information about her. He would take a chance on a direct reference to 'Camellia Larson' and see how it went. But then just in time, he became aware of a significant problem. His alias had a nickname… so what if Camellia's friends knew her by one too? He clearly recalled her liking the name Mae had given her… but kids do grow out of things. This could easily ruin the con.

After much thinking, he finally came up with a suitable solution.

Hey, y'all! So excited to hear from so many of my old friends. Y'all have meant so much to me. Has anyone heard from that Larson girl? I forgot her first name. Begins with a 'C' I think. Bye for now, Bel Robinson ☺

The smiley face was something he had seen used plenty of times before. More than that, he liked that Bel was asking for help. People were always in a hurry to help. It was the fuel of the con. He then cut-&-pasted this message into the alumni chat boards of the University of Mississippi, Mississippi State University, University of Southern Miss, Jackson State University, Garland State University, Alcorn State University, and so on… until he had made over a dozen postings for each school. Then he waited. If nothing promising occurred within a week or two, then he would reword the message and try again.

Yet success came to him much sooner than he had expected. In less than a week, he was on his way to Tupelo.

CHAPTER

40

AT THE MERCY OF THE QUEEN

On a bright Sunday afternoon, not too many days after an enormous Fourth-of-July block party that culminated with a do-it-yourself fireworks show, she and Robert were interrupted from their weekly planning effort by the ringing of the front doorbell. After nearly fourteen years of marriage, one child out and another on the way, they were careful to guard this time. Today, they were set to discuss room preparations for their second child, due in three months. She had made a crumb cake as a snack... there was always a snack... and they were just about to dive into both the treat and the planning when interrupted. As their neighborhood in Tupelo was fairly close-knit, it was not uncommon to have visitors, particularly on weekends. Robert got up to answer the door, expecting it to be someone wanting to borrow a garden tool or such.

Because of where she was seated in the parlor, she had a direct view of Robert in the entryway, but not of the visitor standing out on the porch. As he greeted this person, she could not make out any of their words... only that the strangest of expressions had developed on Robert's face. With mouth open and head leaning back, he seemed utterly astonished... with a good bit of confusion mixed in. Then he looked her way... and his face had gone totally white! Before she could ask what was happening, he turned back to close the door… yet only to an extent that might allow his face to fit through. He said something out to the visitor… and then he did the oddest of things. He shut the door and threw the deadbolt. After, he just stood there leaning with his head against the door.

"Robert… what's going on? Who was that?"

Without answering, he came to her and drew a chair in close… then gently took hold of her hands. Right away, she knew it had to be terrible news.

"Camille… there's an elderly man at the door. He… umm… claims to be Buck Larson… your father."

All ability to think and feel was suddenly sucked out of her being. It could not be so. That person was gone. That person was out of her life forever. That person would never dare to seek her out… to find her… to be at her door. So she looked intently into his eyes, trying to reinterpret his strange message.

He… he would never joke about such a thing. Never! But how can this be?!

Her eyes went next to the door, to make sure that he had, in fact, thrown the deadbolt… and then down to where Leigh sat playing at her feet… just to reassure herself that *her daughter* was safe from *that man.*

"He says he tracked you down through a classmate at Garland. Says he doesn't want to come in… and doesn't want to disturb you at all. He says he only wants to talk with you briefly… and then promises to leave you alone… forever."

She sat motionless, waiting for Robert to admit that this was all some crazy misunderstanding. There was really no one at the door… so she could stop holding her breath. Yet visions from the past were already rampaging through her mind. Distant memories of darkness, pain and tears… so many tears. Without really knowing what she was doing, she withdrew a hand from his. Slowly… almost imperceptibly… she brought that hand up to her hair… to prove to herself that she was not back there at the bedroom window, discovering again what that man had done to her life. Her struggle for control was intense – to not burst out screaming… or hide… or run to the front door with a butcher's knife. She only knew that she had somehow begun speaking… if but in a whisper.

"I… I knew it… I just somehow knew it. One day, he would find me. It… it's almost as if he had just closed the shed door after promising to come back through if I but wait. I've never really wanted to accept it… but I've been looking at the inside of that shed door all my life… expecting him to return."

She could even see it in her mind – that narrow crack of light about that shed door as he closed it on her… except this time, the crack was slowly getting wider and wider as the door opened toward her.

"What would you like me to do? Should I ask him to go away?"

"Yes! Ask him to go away and never come back! No wait! Don't ask him – tell him! Tell him from me!" And then she instinctively looked down to her child again. "I don't want him anywhere near Leigh! Ever!"

Yet Robert did not move. He just sat there in silence. Even Leigh had gone quiet.

"Camille… Sweetheart… I certainly would never allow that to happen. I hope you know that. And I fully understand why you'd not want to see him… but you should know… I really don't think he's dangerous. He has that… wounded look about him."

She knew immediately what he meant by 'that look'. They had reminisced plenty about that time their eyes met on her first day of class as a freshman. She knew that his eyes had not been studying the class – they were searching… looking for something not evident to her at the time. In all their years of marriage, she had finally come to understand what that was. Many who had experienced extreme trauma emerge scarred with guilt, regret, bitterness and pain. Yet there were people like Robert who could clearly recognize in others the effects of those experiences. Somehow, he had known about her suffering simply by looking into her eyes. She was striving to be more like that too… but this was totally different! It did not matter how much Buck Larson had suffered, he could never have suffered enough!

Robert rose and turned toward the door.

"Wait! I'll tell him myself… through the door. Don't worry – I won't open it for him! But please hold onto Leigh, *tight!*"

Only after Robert had picked up their daughter did she move to the entry way. Standing there, for reasons she could not explain to herself, the front door now seemed more of an interference than a protection. Without further thought… and with such decisiveness as to surprise even herself… she came to her full height, and in one fluid motion, unbolted the lock and swung open the door.

Before her on the porch stood an old man – a very old looking man. He could not be that much beyond sixty, though by appearances seemed nearer to eighty. She had been prepared to behold a childhood version of him – big and strong, only with gray hair. Her mental image was not even close to reality. This old man before her wore a laborer's attire – poorly fitting coveralls with a thin white cotton tee-shirt… both very clean. His hair was indeed gray, but considerably thinned so that his scalp showed through in many pasty blotches. Her eyes momentarily went down to his hands, which were in front of him nervously wringing a faded ball cap just removed from his head. The skin on those hands was weathered too… and dotted with age spots. And though his posture was stooped… almost in deference… it was his very thin frame that most affected her. He was not healthy… not at all.

If she was surprised by him, it was nothing compared to his response at seeing her. The relief and the pleasure could not be held back. They poked through for just a moment… then rapidly receded inward as a contrite nature reclaimed its place over his demeanor.

She, nonetheless, opened her mouth to unleash upon him all of her hurt and fury… when something within caused her to pause. It was not from hesitancy or a need for preparation. No… she would grant him one small chance… one brief moment to express whatever pathetic offering he might have to give… though nothing he could say might stand in exchange for what he deserved.

Yet within that simple pause… so inconsistent with how she had felt mere seconds before… suddenly sprang forth a lifetime's worth of understanding. No longer the storm or the hoodie… nor even the flower or the warrior… she found herself instantly unbound from this man and what he had made of her life. She was even free from Mama and those parts of her labeled as mother and wife. At this door, facing this man, she was Camille and only Camille… fully in control of who she was to be.

And in that pause was also hope for him. He had waited twenty years for what this moment might hold, and would not fill the opportunity with compliments, platitudes, or worthless greetings. He got right to the point.

"Camellia… I'm sorry. I am so, so very sorry."

She could see the tears trickling down his withered cheeks, though he restrained himself from attending to them. For it seemed as if any motion other than speech would serve to delay what he owed… and perhaps what he ultimately hoped to gain.

"I stole life from you and your mama… and I did it with no care for either of you. I got what I deserved… but not enough for what I did to you. I can't… I can't ever repay…"

He was now weeping uncontrollably. For Robert had come to the door bearing Leigh, and the sight of her family seemed to overwhelm him. Here was a father, holding his daughter close, united beside his wife – the precise image of everything he had possessed… yet never embraced. He had thrown it all away in exchange for his pride, his anger, and the satisfaction of returning hurt upon others. Yet something within told her that it was the sight of this granddaughter that drove him to his knees on this front porch. In that moment, she remembered… and knew.

> *The quality of mercy is not strain'd,*
> *It droppeth as the gentle rain from heaven*
> *Upon the place beneath: it is twice blest;*
> *It blesseth him that gives and him that takes:*
> *'Tis mightiest in the mightiest: it becomes*
> *The throned monarch better than his crown;*
> *His sceptre shows the force of temporal power,*
> *The attribute to awe and majesty,*
> *Wherein doth sit the dread and fear of kings;*
> *But mercy is above this sceptred sway;*
> *It is enthroned in the hearts of kings,*
> *It is an attribute to God himself;*
> *And earthly power doth then show likest God's*
> *When mercy seasons justice.*

Without really realizing it, she was on her knees beside the old man, weeping with him – for him – and no longer for herself, because she was finally whole. Shakespeare's pen, delivered through Portia's lips, swayed the heart of the Queen – mercy seasoned double over the justice already served.

She then did what moments before would have been inconceivable to her. She lifted the old man to his feet, and led him into her home… and into her heart. There was more crying, and more sorrow, and much more emptying of regrets. But eventually... after many periods of silence and speech... there were also smiles... and shared crumb cake... and new beginnings.

Then another unimaginable took place. She, with measured care, placed Leigh in Buck's lap and sat back to watch. One was amused by an old man's coverall straps, and the other was overcome by treasure immeasurable. A gift he did not deserve. A soul he had not known to exist.

There came a time when she sensed that Buck was spent, so Robert offered to drive him to wherever he was staying. She saw him to the door, promising to have it open for him again soon. There, they exchanged no hugs or any sign of parting affection... only a sincere look between Buck and her... between a father and a daughter... with expressions that had never existed before. A connection of understanding and forgiveness.

Only once Robert had led him out could she begin to cry... yet without a sound. Mercy, given the chance, had rewarded her with blessing – a lost parent reclaimed from long ago. She now wondered, at that moment of first seeing him, who it was that had been bearing the promise of a return at the door – him to her in her worst fears, or her to him in his wildest hopes. Had he, all those years, been fighting back guilt, shame and unworthiness, waiting – hoping – that she would one day come through a door to him?

Her two year old, oblivious to the emotions flowing over her, was struggling against the arms holding tight. So she lowered this precious life to the freedom and safety of the carpeted floor.

"Wub yuh, Mama."

"I love you too, Sweetie."

The front door rattled, and then opened just wide enough for Robert to venture his head through.

"I have your father in the car, but just wanted to make sure..." His eyes flickered down to their daughter and then back up to her. "Are you..."

"I am."

THE END.

ACKNOWLEDGEMENTS

I am indebted to my wife Pam for her patience, encouragement and love, but also for her many insights and improvements to this novel. *Camille* would not exist without her. I am also thankful for the encouragement and suggestions of family members (Bryce, Bond, Britt, Mark, Ed, and Ann), friends (Henry, Sarah, Noelle, Leni, John, and Stephanie), and friends of friends (Julie), as well as a critical appraisal by the Mateao book club.

MATERIALS USED IN PREPARATION OF THIS NOVEL INCLUDE:
- William Shakespeare's *Merchant of Venice*
- Thomas Hardy's *Tess of the d'Urbervilles*
- John Dryden's 1697 translation of Virgil's *The Aeneid* (available through Project Gutenberg)
- Several online and hardcopy resources on rape recovery, particularly L.C. Chanler's insightful (and painful) book: *Rape Recovery: A Personal Experience* (2012, iBooks, https://itun.es/us/I4GIH.l).

Wikipedia, where would I be without you?

AUTHOR'S CONTEMPLATIONS

(Spoiler alert)

In preparing *Camille*, my initial target for self-control was more-or-less in the definitions of Mama and Robert – that self-control is rooted in the mind and heart. While writing, I came to realize something of a deeper concept. This is expressed in what I believe is the key line of the book (ch. 19): "Though renamed, hers was still an existence defined by an act of cruelty rather than from the unique essence of a soul." Perhaps this is a bit existential in nature, but if one rephrases self-control to control-of-self, then the core principle becomes knowing one's self and having that knowledge define one's existence. Though outward behaviors often stem from inward battles of thought and emotion, at the center has to be an awareness of that unique soul.

So why is self-control a fruit of the Spirit? How can it reflect the truest nature of the Godhead if it were merely a quality that enabled one to resist a nasty habit? As the story goes, when Moses inquired of the one speaking from the burning bush as to whom he should say was sending him forth, the divine reply was 'I am.' Not a particularly descriptive response to someone embarking upon a life-altering mission. Yet in the purest sense, the answer was the only answer. The One who existed before time… before the substance and sorrow of this universe… knew better of himself than all his vast creativity could describe. Nothing else could add definition or clarity to 'I am.' For from before time existed, God was perfect within this understanding of self.

Though coming into being within the context of time, each soul is still the same way. To know one's self becomes the essence of self-control… or better yet, living perfectly controlled within self. Unfortunately, there are too many terrible events in life that act to corrupt one's unique awareness of self… such as what was done to Camille by Buck. Similarly, the roles we take on by necessity in living can easily be constructed into an identity of self. Then there is the damage inflicted by giving in to temptations… both large and small. For Camille, regaining and keeping her self-awareness amidst all of the pain in her life amounted to the height of self-control. In this sense, her statement of 'I am' reflects the ultimate achievement – her control of 'true self.'

As to Camille's final decision to receive back her father, it is my belief that no person is capable of expressing true mercy or true justice without self-control. Both mercy and justice must be able to look beyond the moment… and that requires pause. Perhaps only through self-control's 'pause of perspective' can mercy or justice overcome this world's natural inclinations for resignation or retribution. Of course, the choice of mercy over justice is personal… though one might argue, as Shakespeare has done, that the potential good to come from one far exceeds that of the other. Irrespective… Camille ultimately chose mercy because she recognized the 'I am' that she is.

Self-control… against such things there is no law.